MOTHERS HURLING BRICKS

A NOVEL

BILL NEMMERS

Minneapolis

Minneapolis

SECOND EDITION DECEMBER 2022
Mothers Hurling Bricks. Copyright © 2016 by Bill Nemmers.

All rights reserved. No parts of this book may be used or reproduced by any means, graphic, electronic, or mechanical, including photocopying, recording, taping or by any information storage retrieval system, without the written permission of the publisher except in the case of brief quotations embodied in critical articles and reviews.

This is a work of fiction. All of the characters, names, incidents, organizations, and dialogue are either the products of the author's imagination or are used fictitiously.

10 9 8 7 6 5 4 3 2

ISBN: 978-1-960250-37-7

Book and cover design by Gary Lindberg

"The truth? You can't handle the truth."

Jack Nicholson's character to Tom Cruise's character in
A Few Good Men

Also by Bill Nemmers

Crude

MOTHERS HURLING BRICKS

A NOVEL

BILL NEMMERS

List of Stories

01 The Iowa to Vietnam Story 1
02 The New Jersey to Canada Story. 15
03 The Camp Wood Golf Course Story. 24
04 The Frankfurt am Main Story 32
05 The 1st Heidelberg Story 39
06 The Neckargamünd Story 52
07 The 2nd Heidelberg Story 59
08 The Brussels Story 69
09 The Fulda Story 80
10 The 3rd Heidelberg Story 90
11 The 1st Zurich Story 94
12 The Neckarsteinach Story 101
13 The 360 on the Autobahn Story. 109
14 The University of Heidelberg Story 114
15 The 4th Heidelberg Story. 123
16 The 1st LaNapoule Story 133
17 The 2nd Zurich Story. 137
18 The Orange Story. 142
19 The Hockenheimer Ring Story 147
20 The Fork in the Critical Path Story 153
21 The 1st Berlin Story 159
22 The Paris Story 184
23 The 1st Prague Story. 192
24 The 2nd Prague Story. 200
25 The Concert at the Castle Story. 204
26 The Richard M. Nixon Story. 210
27 The Köln Story 216
28 The 2nd LaNapoule Story 234
29 The Last Berlin Story 249
30 The Zug Story. 257
31 The Last Heidelberg Story 268
32 The Vietnam to Iowa Story 272

01 THE IOWA TO VIETNAM STORY

It's dark as sin out there, and it's cold! Five pitiful degrees! I check the thermometer tacked to the jamb outside the front window. Seems normal for 5:45 a.m. on a February morning in the tundra. I notice it's also snowing. Dark, cold, and snow; seems apt accompaniment for the last day of my life—at least any life I'll remember having. So, this is the way it is. There's nothing left to do. I do the deed.

I give Mom one last hug. I shake Dad's hand then pat his shoulder. I lift my nine-year-old sister up to my level and plant a sloppy kiss on her forehead. I unlock the front door, pull it open, and without looking back step out into the frozen Iowa nightscape. I hear the door latch behind me. I hear Dad work the deadbolt. I take the three steps down to the driveway then shuffle through the new snow to the walk. It's half a block south. I turn right onto First Street and find myself pushing a stiff westerly wind as I aim for the Plymouth County courthouse. It's but four blocks down the hill.

It's only four blocks. And all of it downhill. But it's hard, hard work, and I'm pushing more than just the wind. I'm pushing this mountain of anxiety. I'm pushing all my dreams back two years into the future, that is assuming that there will even be a future! And I'm pushing back some tears also, though I'm guessing they result from the stinging wind. At the bottom of the hill is the courthouse parking lot. I'll wallow for a while in the sump pit of despair the army's assembled for us there. Then supposedly, the army bus will swallow me up and take me to Texas. I'm not expecting anything to exist beyond that.

I'd argued with my mom and my dad, more Dad than Mom, about both my walking and my walking *by myself*. They wanted to drive me down to the courthouse. They wanted to stand in the cold with other moms and dads and react to the base degradation of us twenty or so young men and watch as that olive drab bus swallowed us whole. I don't understand that. I doubt my folks wanted the last image they might ever have of their eldest son to be the one where he's swallowed by a dirty green bus in a snowstorm. I doubt they want their tears frozen to their cheeks. But mostly, I doubt they want to see their eldest son crying.

I told them to trust me. I didn't want them to be embarrassed if I made a scene. I might, against all my resolve, chicken out, turn away, perhaps even run. Or, could be my climbing into that bus might require some additional persuasive force. "Please," I told them, "let's cry our tears in the comfort of our own living room. You'll get a more satisfying hug from me in a warm house than in the dark in the disgusting, vapid snowstorm." Made perfect sense to me, and even to them, at least to my mom, and maybe to my sister.

Them staying warm in their house also allows me to continue my shadow fantasy—that any time before that bus leaves I still have the option of turning myself back up the hill and walking the mile to my friend Gary Rhuland's farm where I'd stashed my car in case I decide to chicken out. It's my Canadian option, and it's open for me until I take that first step up into that bus. At any time before I get into that bus, I can refuse the army's invitation and escape myself north to Winnipeg. Mom and Dad both know I have that choice, yet they trusted me when I told them I was going to get on that bus. That promise is the only way they'd let me take this walk by myself. We all know I didn't *specifically* promise them anything. I was careful about that. But I did tell them it was my *intention* to board the bus.

So, more than likely, I will be onboard when it pulls out. It looks like the army's gonna win this round.

Up till now I've won a few rounds, but they've been preliminary ones. I've been skirmishing with various army departments for the past year and a half. That's when they notified me I'd been drafted, and they didn't care if I was still in grad school. They told me they'd given me plenty of time to graduate and accused me of stalling just to avoid doing my duty. I'd successfully been fighting them off by arguing semantics—it was *their* duty rather than *my* duty that was the thing being avoided. Nevertheless, they were ready with the shackles as soon as I graduated last month with my master of architecture degree.

The army and I have an ongoing basic disagreement as to the value of that degree. More importantly, we disagree as to the value of my newly degreed life. I think the twenty years of education I've undergone has prepared me for a role in planning the growth of the world, and that means the country has some profound value in me being protected or at least well utilized. The army's thinking short term. To them I have no worth, except as a warm body available now to be shoved out of a helicopter door. In their eyes my worth equals that of the other high school dropouts and social losers who'll be traveling with me on this bus.

I told the army I'd obey their inane rules but only if they treat me with the respect I'd earned. We all know I didn't specifically promise them anything. I was careful about that, but I did tell them that was my intention. So, more than likely, I'll be on their dirty green bus, though I told them there would be conditions. I'm not sure the army understands that yet. I intend to talk with them some more about my demands. I'll see where this goes.

The dozen guys waiting for the bus all have mothers and fathers standing in the snow and crying with them. It's a pitiful sight. I'm glad my parents understood. They may not agree with everything I do, but they appreciate that I'm a responsible guy, and they allow me my distance. I stand a distance away. I lean against a naked elm tree and try to separate myself from the emotional swamp. All of us here know that most of us are getting on the bus now only so we can die in the jungle later. That thought makes me think again of my car. It's in Gary's garage, and its gas tank is full.

Thank God the bus shows up on time. It triggers wailing, hugging, and mothers sobbing. Mom and Dad will be glad they missed this miserable spectacle. I manage to slip onto the bus first so I don't have to listen to the wailing mothers and the boot-stomping fathers. A soldier in a spiffy uniform points me to the back. They're loading the thing quite orderly, back to front. I don't make a fuss. I secure a window seat which gives me opportunity to, at least, dream of freedom. Soon another guy, some pimply teenager, takes the seat next to me. I've been away at school for seven years, so I recognize none of these guys, and I'm not in a cheery mood so I don't make small talk, or really any talk.

This pimply guy's a piece of work; he has no idea what he's stepped into. Seems numb as a rock. He tells me he knows who I am because his mom, a friend of my mom, pointed me out while I was leaning on that elm tree a while ago. Davie's his name, and thinking he's gonna impress me, he tells me he volunteered and wants to be a paratrooper.

So I blast him, "Have you no heart? Think of the grief you're causing your mother." I'm absolutely stunned at his lack of respect. "You think she raised you so you can jump out of airplanes into jungles? Don't you realize you're gonna die in Vietnam? You'd best start composing that final letter to your mom now, while you're on this bus, so it'll be ready when you need it."

Davie looks at me, absolute terror in his eyes.

"Did you have the courage to tell your mom that you're gonna splatter your body parts all over the jungle floor? And that the desire to do so is greater than your desire to give her another hug? You are one cruel, insensitive son!"

Davie starts to cry.

I understand some of that's my fault. I was fairly rough on him, but I did it for his own good. He takes the easy way out. He quickly gets up and moves to another seat. I don't think I'll have much impact on his decision. He's one of those guys who's gonna jump out of a 'copter no matter what I yell at him. I don't feel sorry for him. It's his poor mother... I feel sorry for her.

★★★

The bus stops in Sioux City and again in Council Bluffs to take on more of us poor slobs and then, since it's almost full, takes off for Fort Bliss in Texas. One of the army guys traveling with us tells us that the trip's nonstop; twenty-two hours into Fort Bliss. There's a bathroom onboard, and later they'll have sandwiches, chips, and Cokes. I'm thinking I'm not eating Mom's meatloaf ever again. The army guy tells us it'll be a long boring trip, and we should try to get some sleep. I think that's good advice.

This whole damn trip could have been avoided if they would've let me file conscientious objector status. The conscientious objector board didn't buy my argument that I should be able to file as a conscientious objector specifically because I had no ties to any religion. My powerful rational argument, based on unadulterated science, was that it was actually God who supported the killing of folks in a war. Since religious crusaders have been slaughtering people in the name of God for eons, I insisted conscientious objectors cannot get any non-violent notions from any religion. The vapid board was not moved. Unless I believed in God, I couldn't even file for an exemption. I argued the first amendment, that I have standing to think for myself; that I even have several philosophers, including Kant, on my side. My intention is to keep the pressure on, argue my case with the muckety-mucks at Fort Bliss. Who knows? That might work.

The ride south is uneventful. The bus is as quiet as a rolling tomb. Perhaps these guys are already dead. It's hard to tell, except we do stop a couple times to stretch our legs and buy some burgers, and most of these guys still seem alive. At about 0900 the next morning we enter Fort Bliss, Texas. I step down off the bus and figure this is probably my last chance to bolt before some formal induction ritual. However, there are several guys hanging around with what look like weapons of some sort, so perhaps the odds for escape right here are slim. We're all lined up, short guys in the front and tall guys at the back. I'm in the middle someplace. Some guy walks us through the metal gate. I pull an invisible shield down over my head. I may not be invisible to them, but at least those automatons are all invisible to me now.

★★★

It wasn't me! My drill sergeant started it. We're standing in fairly straight rows, and he just blurts out the words: "You grunts have any questions before we start turning you into soldiers?"

Since I always have questions ready for occasions like this, I pull a reasonable one out. "I'd like to put in a request to speak with my commanding officer. I think it best that I establish the ground rules with him right away."

"What?" That's all he says. I think I surprised him.

"I'm not afraid of dying in Vietnam," I say. "I am, however, afraid the army will not operate in a logical manner, so as to use my talents to their best advantage. I want to talk to your general to make sure the army maximizes my value."

"That's not a question," says the drill sergeant. "It's a whole book!" He laughs. "And I don't read books. And so even technically if it *was* a question, the answer's no. Now, let's get started. Look sharp! I'm gonna get you guys ready for Vi-et-nam!"

★★★

Eight weeks later, and my drill sergeant is still pushing. He, in his own dopey way, is congratulating us for completing our basic training. He's certainly frightening us and probably mocking us. I'm standing at attention with my duffel hanging on my shoulder, and I'm getting tired of listening to this jerk enjoy himself by frightening us. We all, the rest of my company and I, are standing in straight line formation on the dirt parade field in front of our barracks. On the good side, it's the last day of basic training, so it's the last time I'll have to stand on this dirt parade field and the last time I'll breathe this arid west-Texas dust.

"You've just completed your first step on your way to Vi-et-nam. This morning, y'all will take your second step. Gotta look sharp! Forrr-warrrd, march!"

It's 1030 hours on this last Friday in April 1967. All five hundred of us basic training class graduates now take that second step as one unit. We march from our barracks for about a mile to the southern edge of the base where a formidable fence separates us from the rest of that bleak desert landscape. On the other side of that steel fence is a gravel parking lot with a collection of olive drab-colored buses.

I hear those bus engines idling. The noise suggests to me that I'd best prepare myself for the inevitable. I'm not sure I know how to do that. My drill sergeant marches us into a temporary-looking wood-frame barn. The words **"FINAL ASSEMBLY BUILDING"** are painted in large block letters above the double doors. That word **"FINAL"** gives me a jolt. All we find inside are rows and rows of olive drab-colored folding chairs. We're ordered to fill those chair rows, starting at the back and working toward the front.

I sit in my chair with my duffel on the floor in front of me, and my mind's focused on those buses. In a couple hours those buses will be carrying us grunts closer to Vietnam. I watch as each newly minted pre-soldier is called by name and then reports to the front podium. Each guy's given a piece of paper informing him of his personal travel plans. Each takes his orders and his duffel to an assembly area along the south wall where other men with the same abhorrent destination on their paper stand and wait.

When a certain number of guys have convened at a particular staging area, they're called to attention and marched out the door to an idling bus. One bus might be headed toward Fort Leonard Wood for infantry training, another to Fort Huachuca for artillery, another to paratrooper school. These are but temporary destinations, only the second step of the journey. In a couple more months, after schooling us in effective people-killing, a third bus will deliver most of us to some army airfield. From there it's "Hello, Vi-et-nam!"

At 1330 hours the last group leaves this room for their bus. They're headed to paratrooper school. I can't believe they signed up for an extra year just so the army can teach 'em to jump from airplanes. I recognize one of them—that Davie guy who rode down from Iowa with me on the bus. He's got no future and nothing to lose. He volunteered! Told me he actually *wants* to go to 'Nam. That kind of guy thinks war's a great adventure. He'll never get out of that swamp alive. I'll bet they've already got his box waiting, his name stenciled on it; there'll be room for him and his pretty green parachute. I wonder if he's told his mother that he's going to be jumping out of airplanes. How'll she react to that?

★★★

It's been over an hour since Davie and his gung-ho pals marched out that door to their olive drab bus. I've had adequate time to assess my situation. I've never much thought about being alone. I quite enjoy being alone. As a five-year-old, I walked by myself in the pitch darkness through the huge, concrete storm drainpipes that took the runoff from the normally dry Goose Creek, sent it under the Wilson Park ball field, then dumped it a quarter mile away behind the Sinclair station. I never told my mother I walked that pipe alone! I do not fear sitting alone in this room. That's not the point.

MOTHERS HURLING BRICKS

I *am* afraid of being left alone in Vietnam. Now *that* scares me! It's going west that scares me. Seems it's possible I've talked myself into being afraid, though I doubt I've ever been afraid before either. I do remember, as a nine-year-old, climbing the box elder tree in my front yard and, like a squirrel, getting into the higher branches and leaping across to the box elder on the opposite side of the street. My plan was to eventually return to earth. Despite the fact that this eventual return to ground turned into a sudden return, and I ended up crumbled on the gravel road below, I afterward told my mother I was never afraid. She contended my problem wasn't fear, but stupidity. She made me promise to never do anything that stupid again.

I, probably naively, assumed my past history would ensure I'd be one of the few not destined for the land of exploding helicopters. It's my contention that any halfway intelligent army guy would ship me east to DC instead of wasting my talents by shipping me west. I should be behind a desk in the Pentagon where I can plan things. Mom would probably think me stupid for buying into such dreams. But my talent's designing stuff or advising army guys on strategic stuff. The army must need guys like me to do things like that. Nevertheless, I'm sitting here alone, and now afraid, I start to think I'm being stupid. *No!* I argue. *It's jerks like Davie, jumping from helicopters—they're the ones bein' stupid.*

Thank goodness I've made alternate plans, or at least a rough outline of one plan. If my calculated dream of going east to Washington, DC rather than west to Vietnam blows up, I plan to run north. My Canadian option is still active. I've secured, in my billfold, the phone number I'll use when I reach the border. But there's a catch. I can't use that number until I get to said northern border. I'll have to take a smaller transitional step. I first must get home to Iowa.

I believe there's a reasonable chance my mom'll agree with my fleeing to Canada. But Dad's a harder sell. He knows I'll do what I want without consulting him, not because I disrespect his position or his experience or his authority, but because he knows that I do not require parental input. I must analyze data for myself. I think he's proud of my independent mind. But this episode did expose a problem—because I've never consulted him on stuff, I don't know what he actually thinks about stuff.

But it's too late now, and I being a planner have to plan for the possibility I'll be forced to go north. If I do that, I'll send them a card from Toronto or Winnipeg, telling them I'm safe, and they needn't worry. Mom might even be relieved, and Dad, well, Dad might, in time, come to accept it.

★★★

As it turns out, I've reasoned correctly. I will not need my Canadian option. At least not yet. I must give those guys credit. The army made a smart decision, and they're sending me east. Not into the Pentagon, but to New Jersey! They first put me on a Greyhound back to Iowa, where I pack everything I think I might need into my white Triumph TR-4. Then I drive to New Jersey for what my orders tell me is continuing education.

Continuing education?

I'm thinking those words might mean education concerning machine gun maintenance or battlefield toilet design. I make a couple calls but am unable to discern what either of those two words mean in army-speak; except, perhaps, that what they mean in New Jersey probably does not concern education I will need for combat. I sense I can now stow both Canada and Vietnam in a secure canister at the bottom of my duffel. Canada'll be well concealed there, but I know exactly where I've stored it.

★★★

I'm wandering through coastal New Jersey trying to find the specific facility the army wants me to report to. They've either hidden it or given me bad directions. But I'm not lost. I never get lost. When I was six, I followed a cornfield drainage stream out beyond my house. I followed it under several county roads, through the aluminum culverts under the highway and the railroad tracks, until several miles away it dumped itself into the Floyd River. Though it was dark by the time I solved that puzzle, I'd no trouble finding my way home. I may've taken a while, but I never considered myself lost. And neither did my mom. She knew I couldn't get lost. That's why she saved my meatloaf and scalloped corn in the oven.

I've no idea where I am now, but wherever it is, I'm exactly where I'm supposed to be. It's the building I'm ordered to report to that's missing. Considering my short acquaintance with army things, I realize the army's inclined to be non-specific. My orders say I'm to report to the post engineer's office at Camp Charles Wood in Fort Monmouth, New Jersey. It seems Fort Monmouth might be an army thing, but it could also be a town, or just an area. I've seen no signs displaying words like Fort Monmouth Army Base or Camp Charles Wood. I notice a tall steel fence with an angled top fashioned of barbed wire, and it's hidden behind thick unruly hedging like it might be an army thing, though I see neither signage nor entry gates to confirm that.

I recognize that small strip mall. I've passed here once, maybe ten minutes ago. There's a coffee shop in there. Folks in coffee shops know stuff. A heavyset girl with plenty of blond hair sees me approach the bar. She wanders over.

"What can I git fer ya?"

"I need directions," I say. "Where's the entry gate for Fort Monmouth? Or maybe Camp Wood?"

"Don't think Fort Monmouth has any gate," the girl says. "It's just here." She swings her arms about to suggest a wide, all-inclusive area.

I get a bit frustrated. "Since everything's 'just here' do you know where a specific place called the post engineer's office might be?"

"Engineers?" She repeats the word like she's never heard it before. "They do secret stuff over at Camp Charlie. Do they need engineers for that?"

"I've no idea. Is that part of Fort Monmouth?"

"Oh, I think it is. But it's a secret place, so nobody's supposed to know it's there. However, we deliver coffee to the MPs at the gate all the time. You can see their fence from here if you know where to look." She points out the window. "It's over there, beyond those trees, on the far side of the highway. Ya take a right at the stop sign." She points again. "You'll hit Highway 14. Take another right on 14, and the entry is maybe a quarter mile, also on the right. The drive isn't marked because, like I told you, it's secret. I've missed it a few times, and I even know where it is."

"Thanks. If I find it, I'll come back some time and buy you a beer."

"I don't drink beer," she says.

"Too bad," I say. "I'll drink it myself. Have a nice day!"

★★★

I find the unmarked turnoff, drive through some woods, and stop at a heavily defended entry kiosk. Some very small, black, italic letters on the white sign tell me I'm entering Camp Charles Wood. The stern-faced MP with the high-polished brass looks at me hard, as if driving my casual sports car through his serious gateway is illegal. I'm knocking on the door of his formal, top-secret facility wearing shorts and a T-shirt. His look is telling me he doesn't think I belong, so he's not going to let me spoil his doorstep.

Before I get a word out, the guard asks, "What kind a party's goin' on at the golf course today?"

"I don't know the answer to your secret-code question, sir. All I know is, I'm supposed to be at the post engineer's office at Camp Charles Wood by one o'clock. Can you tell me how to do that?"

"First, you're interrupting our cribbage game, and that makes me grumpy, and second, I'm not an officer," the impudent, and apparently non-officer MP guy corrects me.

I think maybe I should've brought him a cup of coffee as an introductory lever, but I behave myself and respond quite repentantly, "Sorry to interrupt your secret work, sir, but could you *please* tell me where the post engineer's office is?" I thought that sounded more respectful.

The MP shakes his head and says something I don't catch to another guy in the booth. "Ya turn right back onto the main road, then left at the first cross street, and after a half a mile you'll come to the golf course. The PO's office is on the second floor above the clubhouse, but you gotta use the door on the backside. Parking's on the backside too. Don't park in the main lot, you'll get towed."

"What do you army guys have against signs?" I'm frustrated with such incompetence. "What you gotta do is stick a sign with an arrow on the highway sayin' *Golf Course and Engineer's Office,* and another at your drive." I point back down his entry road toward the highway. "*Charlie's Woods - Top Secret.* If you do that, then guys like me wouldn't keep interrupting your secret cribbage games with 'How do I get there?' questions."

The guard guy unprofessionally gives me the finger.

I try to stay honorable, not let him drag me down into his swamp. I do a quick u-turn in front of him, taking care not to spray gravel in his face, and head out the drive. A wind gust throws me a smell of what I think is salt water. That means the Atlantic's nearby. Seems I'll be checking into an army golf course on the big water. That's about as far from playing army with helicopters in Vietnamese jungles as I can imagine.

I turn left where I told the jerk to put the sign and head toward the ocean. Maybe if the army stuck a couple signs pointing toward the ocean in Vietnam, guys could find their way outta the jungle and head toward the Pacific. Could be that's all it'd take to get our guys home.

I'm headed for the Atlantic. I don't need a sign to tell me that, and I'm thinking my mom is gonna be pleased I'm smelling the Atlantic and not that other ocean.

"Goodbye, Vietnam!"

02 The New Jersey – Canada Story

Part #1 - The New Jersey to Vermont Part

When first I'd read the words "New Jersey" on my orders, I prepared for the dark side. I'd read about Newark's urban squalor and Atlantic City's gambling. But following the MP's directions, I'm soon driving through an English countryside with white fencing and grazing horses. I see no hint of urban squalor. I park my TR-4 between a red Corvette convertible with Indiana plates and a red Bel Air convertible with South Carolina plates. I leave my gear in case a quick getaway's required. I go through a white gate and down a brick walk to a door, above which someone's tacked "Post Engineer's Office" in dainty scroll-font letters. Seems awful cute for army stuff. I open the door.

A middle-aged lady in a flowery print dress smiles at me. I cross the creaking wood floor toward her desk. As I approach she says, "Honey, I'm guessing you're Walter Kneubel."

"So, this is it, huh? The post engineer?"

"Right chu are. I'm Lynnette. David Hanson's the post engineer. He's in a meeting, but'll be back shortly to talk with you boys. And Percy Bradley's out today. He's usually gone when the weather's nice."

She extends her hand and snaps her fingers. "I gotta see your orders… make sure you're who you're supposed to be."

I fish the envelope from my back pocket and hand it over.

"Thank you," she says, then points to the stairs. "Mr. Hanson said you're to wait upstairs. The others are already there."

"The others?"

"Yeah, and you're all now here, and I get to relax."

"I've got a question, ma'am."

"What's your problem?"

I point toward the huge French-door-type windows, on the other side of which several square miles of manicured greenery sparkle in the midday sunlight. "What am I doing on a golf course?"

"Doesn't it look nice? We keep it well-manicured."

"Ya got me drivin' a lawn mower?"

She laughs. "Oh no, Mr. Kneubel. Mr. Hanson will tell you about your job when he gets here." She looks at her watch. "He said one o'clock. He's usually quite punctual."

I climb the dark stairway and open the door at the top. I'm thinking about wormholes and time travel but calm down when I see a pine-paneled room with a cathedral ceiling. Cute dormer windows march along both sides, and there's a smattering of lounge furniture. I walk into the space, look about, and notice the door to a deck is open. There's movement on the other side, then three men my age come into the room through that door. One wears an army dress uniform, one's in shorts and a T-shirt, and the last guy's in jeans and a sport jacket.

"Hi guys," I say. "I'm thinkin' I'm lost. This here the army?"

"Lynette said it is. So it could be. Who the hell knows?"

"My name's Wall Kneuble. You guys any idea what's goin' on?"

"Not a clue, Wall. Not even close. I'm James Fisk. Just drove up from Charleston."

"The Bel Air, right?"

Fisk gives me a thumbs up.

"Scott Laughters, Indianapolis."

"Nice 'Vette, Scott."

"I'm Jay Stoltzman, Wall. I flew out here from California under the mistaken opinion I'm in the army. Left my Jeep in Ojai with my surfboards. I think I screwed up."

Scott pulls aside a window curtain. "You the Triumph?"

"Ya suppose it means anything," I ask, "we all drivin' ragtops? That's why we're all standing here lookin' stupid?"

"We're architects and planners," says James. "You?"

"Yeah, me too, from the U of Illinois."

"There's *Twilight Zone* stuff here, Wall," says Jay. "Rod Serling's gonna step into this room about now."

But the guy who opens the door and walks in ain't Rod Serling, but a standard issue golfer—fiftyish, plaid pants, Titleist hat, and very tanned. It's not yet May, but this guy's already burnt to a crisp.

"Afternoon, gentlemen. I'm David Hanson, the post engineer for Fort Monmouth." He looks at his watch. "I'm nine minutes late. Sorry. The foursome ahead of us wasn't in business mode." He smiles. His teeth flash little sparkles like he's electrified them.

"I'm on a tight time budget, so I'll cut right to it. First off, I expected you guys here Monday." He looks at his watch, like maybe a nifty dial might explain his time-warp problem. "I'm frustrated and angry, so I'm initiating innovative procedures.

"Second, my time budget insists we leave for my house in Vermont immediately, so I'll answer questions, if it's possible, while we're on the road. It's a five-hour trip.

"Third, you guys bring up the stuff from your cars and stash it over there. It'll be safe. The door'll be locked. And your cars'll be safe too. That gate's locked all weekend.

"Fourth, you'll find four backpacks on that couch. Each of you fill one with clothes and a sweatshirt, as it still gets cold in the mountains, and some work clothes if you want to help me around the farm. I'd appreciate that, and if you want to work, I'll pay you for your labor. And I'll pay well. Better than the army. They don't pay squat.

"Fifth, since you're army guys, I'm assuming you have army questions. Don't expect those questions to be answered till after you're back on the golf course first thing Tuesday morning. I'm no army guy. I don't answer army questions.

"Sixth, be downstairs next to that white gate in..." he looks at his watch, again, "thirteen minutes. We all set, now? Good!" He abruptly turns and hurries out the door. We hear him bounce down the stairs before the door closes.

"We all set, now?" Scott mocks him. "How the hell we answer that? It's absurd."

"And what's he mean?" James asks, "after we're back Tuesday. What's he got planned for four days?"

"I've not yet hit a golf ball," I say, "and he's putting us to pasture in Vermont. Something seems very wrong."

"He claims he's not an army guy," James says. "I'm no army guy either, but I sense a high percentage of military blood flowing through his veins."

"I'm thinkin' he's not even a human guy," says Jay. "He doesn't say the word 'hello,' yet he invites us to Vermont like we're longtime buddies. We're interchangeable disposable guys. We'd best watch him vigilantly. I'm thinking we're heading for an instant bonding exercise."

"You mean like at summer camp? Four terrified guys, singing camp songs and huddling together so's the coyotes can't get an easy bite?"

"Or maybe it's a test," Scott says. "Last guy uneaten wins."

"You ever heard anyone say to be somewhere in thirteen minutes? Can we trust any guy who says that?"

"Could be Hanson's not on our team," I say. "I suppose we should verify he's not on some other team."

"Some other team? What the hell's that mean?"

"Could be he's CIA," I say, "or a Russian spy! I gotta see his ID, make sure he's legit before we abandon this real world and head for the Canadian border with him."

"You're making a big leap, Wall, if you're thinkin' this here golf course mirage is part of the real world."

Part #2 - The Vermont to Canada Part

Our first task Saturday morning is confirming we're actually in Vermont. I look out the window and see pine trees. That looks right. No barbed wire or rice paddies. The second task? Hanson leads us on a half hour run through those trees. It looks and smells like Vermont, or at least a very good ruse. He feeds us breakfast and puts us to work. He morphs into his affable, backwoods, bed and breakfast owner guy and works alongside us with no apparent boss-drone or officer-enlisted guy bias; no shouting of military orders.

His small rehab project has obviously overwhelmed him. He is way behind schedule and doesn't know diddly about construction, and it is obvious that he needs some major league help. So we help him with the fourteen room inn his father started fitting into the barn and silo before he died suddenly a couple years ago. At least, that's his story. Jay shows him a redesign that will save him time and money while I tear up and rebuild a stone-walled planting bed so it drains well. James and Scott rebuild the unsafe scaffolding he's erected to rehab the silo exterior. We take half an hour for lunch, half an hour for a nap, then go back to work. We scrape and paint, build rock walls and fences, and stud a few walls. Then, in late afternoon, and while Hanson cooks our meal, we pull on our sweatshirts, open our beer, sit around the picnic table, and wait for food.

"Okay guys," says James Fisk. "So far life in the far north's been uneventful. Strange, certainly, but uneventful. We've no assurance our lives aren't going to explode tonight, tomorrow, or next week. However, we've got to find control."

"Exactly," says Jay. "We know Hanson's isolated us from the rest of the Great Olive Drab Machine and hidden us in the Vermont mountains. That doesn't sound like something the army should normally do, so our job's to discern why they did it."

"I'm thinking any reason we're in Vermont has to do with proximity to Canada," says Scott. "And, except for Lynette, not one person knows we've checked into a secret golf course on the Jersey shore and then checked out for Vermont."

"The secret's in us," says James. "We must discern who we each are before our future path can be discerned."

"You a Buddhist, James?" asks Jay. "Somethin' like that?"

"No. But we must find out why the army selected us four design professionals for this experiment. And before that, we must find the common element, inherent in us, that specifically required our selection."

"And," I say, "it's got to be something that Scott, our engineer and city planner guy, has in common with us three architect guys."

"You're the Buddhist now, huh?" James asks.

"I'm thinking Scott should talk first," I say. "He's the engineer. Our architect stories can then be compared to his odd engineering story. You know what I'm saying, Scott?"

"I agree, Wall."

He takes a sip of beer, then starts.

"My story begins when I was eight. My dad and his older brother, Paco, died in a traffic accident when Dad was home on leave from the army. Mom went to nursing school so she could support my little sister and me. We lived in east Indianapolis in an apartment with my aunt, my uncle Paco's widow, and my two cousins. That worked out well except for a few things. My aunt thought God would somehow bring Uncle Paco back. My mom continually cursed that same God for taking Dad away. My life revolved around Mom. Purdue was as far as I ever strayed, even then. I came home most weekends. I worked summers after graduating Purdue doing

Critical Path Analysis for the engineering firm clearing the path for the new interstate through downtown Indianapolis. As you might guess, I'm missing my mom something terrible. I'm all she's got. She's afraid I'm gonna be sent to 'Nam and won't come back. Same vision sneakin' through my head too."

James goes next. "I've also spent my life in one place... Charleston. Dad's a civil rights lawyer and associate pastor at the AME church. Grandfather's also a pastor. The whole family's active in Reverend King's human rights coalition. One of my sisters works with him. Everyone in the movement's argued in our living room and eaten in our dining room. Dad wasn't happy when I transferred to M.I.T. and chose architecture instead of law or the ministry. There's important work needs doin' in Charleston guys, and I can't be wastin' my time playin' army."

Jay takes his turn. "I'm an only child, the last in a long line of Jewish musicians. Mom's a violinist, and I play piano like my dad, my grandfather, and my great-grandfather. My parents entertained musicians, artists, and scientists at our house in Ojai. But, like James, architecture's what fascinates me. My dad was disappointed, but since I stayed in the fine arts, and my degree's an MFA, he thinks he's kept me in the fold. I miss playing music with Mom and Dad. I miss it something fierce."

"I see no common threads yet," I say. "I'm from a northwest Iowa farming town. My life centered on the Catholic school and especially the church, whose steeple and influence could be seen from, and felt in, every house in the community. Dad's a civil engineer and runs a construction company with his brother. Mom, however, is a city girl from Chicago. She introduced me to her extensive library when I was three or four, and I've not stopped reading since. Dad believes I've joined the forces of evil because I chose architecture and not engineering."

"What's with the *Wall* thing? Why not just 'Walt' like everyone else?"

"Wal-ter is a two-syllable word. As is customary, I use the first syllable for my nickname. Consider Ben for Benjamin, or Phil for Philip. Walt's plain wrong. It includes a letter from the second syllable. I think such frivolity's illegal."

"Anybody ever told you that's weird?"

"Not and lived to tell about it."

★★★

The burgers, beer, and conversation mellow us. I watch the sun slip behind a small mountain leaving a cloudless, darkening, gray-blue sky.

"Don't move!" David says. "Slowly turn and look into that birch grove left of the silo. A doe with two fawns!"

"Any other wildlife we should be watching for?" asks Jay. "Like maybe army commandos crawling through the woods with machine guns?"

"Settle down, Jay. Once in a great while, a bear. Though at this time of year they've normally moved higher up the mountain. Foxes are around and other nighttime critters like raccoons, skunks, voles, and snakes."

"Never heard of voles," says James.

"Me either," says Jay. "What the hell's a vole?"

"They're soft furry rodents, like possums, with long snouts and tawny fur. It's impossible to see 'em unless the watcher is much more patient than any of you guys."

"You think we're not patient? You're wrong David," says Jay. "We're confused and anxious. And need to know stuff. Like, what the hell we doing out here talking 'bout voles?"

"A fair question. I'll be as honest as I can. When you work for the army you do what they tell you to do. I'm a private citizen working for the army as the post engineer. My task is running the base maintenance, especially the golf course. Sometimes I'm given tasks to perform unconnected to anything about being post engineer. One of those tasks is to house soldiers, mostly architects and engineers, for short stays, though four at one time's not happened before. Also, I've no idea why you are being detained or stored at my facility, instead of at a normal base like other army guys. The army doesn't tell me that."

"Come on," says Scott, "tell us something!"

"I can't. I don't know anything. My guess is the army wants you to perform a specific task but needs to complete security investigations or wait for slots to open."

"That's awful vague, David."

"It's all I got, guys. I'm only in Monmouth Tuesday through Friday. Guys usually show up early in the week so I can settle them in before I leave for Vermont. Since you guys came in on Friday afternoon, and with me needing to get up here and miss the evening New York rush, I really had no choice but to take you with me."

"So," I say, "you're telling us you don't know why we're here, or how long we're staying?"

"Sorry, guys. I can't help. How about another beer?"

Scott's not distracted by beer. "I'm thinking of my mom, David. What am I supposed to tell her? How do I keep her from worrying about me? I'm also rethinkin' about Canada. And I want to know? How far's the border from here?"

03 The Camp Wood Golf Course Story

Part #1 - The Sandy Hook Part

David brought us back from Vermont late last night and told us to be at breakfast by 0930. That almost sounds like an army guy giving us an army order. That's why we four soldier guys are sitting on this patio on this perfect spring morning. We're overlooking the first tee and drinking our morning coffee.

"This is almost like bein' in the army," I say. "Up at the crack of dawn, hard exercise on the putting green, and eatin' breakfast on the battlefield. Man, do I hate bein' in the army."

"Know what you mean," says James. "The air perfumed with lilac, the salty aroma from the tide slipping into the estuary south of the eighteenth fairway. One could almost get used to this, huh?"

Despite this flippant attitude, the hint of army in the air seems ready to ambush us. That hint of army's now approaching our table expertly balancing a platter piled with our breakfasts. David Hanson's our post engineer, our golf course manager, and at this early part of the season he's also our breakfast chef.

"Oh my God!" says Jay. "What a feast!"

David distributes the plates, piled with sausage, hash browns, scrambled eggs, and toast. He tops off our coffee, then sits himself down on a fifth chair he swipes from an adjacent table. He looks at his watch intently to make sure he's in the right time zone, or month, or something.

"Okay, guys, I'm back to my army job. I'm now technically your superior, though as you can see, not your 'superior officer.'" He removes his white golf hat and looks at it for a few seconds as if that look imbues it with any special powers he thinks he needs. He returns the thing to his head. "I can tell you the official army things I've been told to tell you."

"Should this exotic orchestration you're throwing at us poor slobs be frightening us? Should we look under our seats for ordnance?"

Hanson laughs and drinks some coffee. "Don't go there, Wall. The situation appears odd... I'll admit that. But I don't think you need worry about Vietnam, not for a while at least."

"You're not getting me to relax yet," says Scott. "Words like 'for a while' and 'at least' won't do it."

"We expect comforting type words," Jay says, "like 'never' and 'guarantee.'"

"I've got my army hat on guys." He points to his golf hat. "You know I can't do assurances. More eggs? Sausage?"

"Don't change the topic," I tell him. "You know damn well you're not wearing an army hat. What're we doing here? Sitting under the lilacs, eating perfectly scrambled eggs, enjoyin' the sunshine? Could be we're feelin' the calm before the storm?"

"The army dumped you here on short notice. I wasn't prepared with real work for you. But I've been racking my brain, and I think I've found something."

Hanson searches in his jacket pocket, and then, with some ceremony, puts the object that search produces on the table next to the coffee decanter. It's a rather normal brass key, though elevated in stature by being attached, via eight inches of linked brass chain, to a three-inch by six-inch brass plate with finely etched detail around the edges. A blue plastic rectangle carrying the words "Lighthouse Gate" is glued to the top.

"Thing looks fairly impressive, David," James says. "Seems kind of a dinky key, though, for such a stunning hunk of brass."

Scott stands up and does a horizon search. "Don't see no lighthouse from the office here. What lighthouse is that thing a key to?"

"This golf course is one of several interesting properties in the kingdom I patrol as Fort Monmouth's post engineer. Besides the two golf courses, there's the Electronic Surveillance Research Facility hiding behind its hedges west of here at Camp Charles Wood, there's the Fort Monmouth Signal Corps School across the estuary beyond the ninth fairway, there's the crumbled ruins at Fort Hanson, no relation to me, built by the Dutch on Sandy Hook, which has now mostly eroded into dust, there's a marvelous beach, some crumbling cannon bunkers, and finally, the Coast Guard station at the northern tip of Sandy Hook which contains the Sandy Hook lighthouse. This key," he picks the thing up and wiggles it, "fits the padlock on the gate that allows access to Sandy Hook."

"You keep saying Sandy *Hook*. Why?" I ask.

"That's a weird question, Wall," says Scott.

"No, it isn't," David says. "It means there's interesting history involved. When you look at the map of this thin, curving, hook-like peninsula you shouldn't think about fish hooks. You're supposed to think of the Dutch word meaning an ocean caused sandbar which they called a *hoek*. English speakers find it easier to say hook."

"Enough with history, David. What's with the key?"

"The entire peninsula of Sandy Hook is abandoned, except for the automated lighthouse, which juts into New York Harbor. Guys from Brooklyn Navy Yard come over by boat to change the batteries and oil the gears. Eventually the hook, which the navy's used for decades as a firing range, will be transferred to the National Park Service for a public beach. But before that happens, the army must do historic and environmental surveys and remove dangerous material. The army has no money for that survey work now. But I, as post engineer, have the requirements for that survey in my file, and I'm thinking you guys could do that survey work for me on the cheap. You're engineers, right? Can you do this? What do ya think?"

"I'm the only engineer," says Scott. "These other clowns are architects. But I think we can handle it."

I grab the brass plate. Having it in my hand reinforces my assumption that I now control this conversation. "If you want us to act like professionals, I think we must be treated as professionals and paid as professionals. I suggest we four incorporate ourselves as a private planning and design firm. We'll contract directly with your office. That way you'll have a signed contract with a legitimate firm that will save you time and trouble at the next stage, when—"

James, in a deft move, grabs the key from me. "Don't pay attention to Wall. He's crazy! We'll look at your project." He ceremoniously puts the key in his pocket, which he thinks will seal the deal. "You're sayin' this work has the potential to guarantee our staying here for two years. Like, goodbye Vietnam?"

"And you think *I'm* crazy," I scold him. "You just threw away our big buck potential. You owe us all beer."

"You guys are both dreaming," says Jay. "Stupid army'll never abandon us here for two years."

Part #2 - The Fort Dix Part

We're halfway through August, and the four of us pseudo-soldiers have wasted three months playing golf, running mock surveys on Sandy Hook, and working at our private sector jobs. I've just returned from my day job, doing structural design for a local architect in Redbank. Scott's put in eight hours tuning suspension systems at a local garage, a speed shop that prepares stock cars for the next weekend's races at local tracks. Jay and James are building a boat from materials found on Sandy Hook. The thing should be testable in another month.

It's only 1630, and there's time left to play. The temperature's in the nineties with no ocean breeze for relief. We four are fairly inert under an umbrella on the stone patio and watching action on the eighteenth green. We bet pennies on the putts. We sip piña coladas. We play bridge and eventually, as it usually does, the topic comes around to what the hell we're doing here. Are we any farther away from Vietnam?

"We gotta start thinking about long term," I say. "Summer's only gonna last another month. What beach ya think we could get ourselves shipped to for the winter? I'm not going near Texas, but the army has stuff in Puerto Rico, right? Maybe Hanson can find us work down there."

"You're weird, Wall. Pay attention. I dealt and passed. It's your bid."

"I'll open with a spade." I look up and see Lynnette walking toward us. I note the sour look on her usually sunny face. "Oh-oh, guys. I'm thinking we're not going to be able to finish the bidding."

James immediately says, "Pass."

"Pass," says Jay.

"Pass here too," Scott says. "See, Wall! You're wrong. We finished the bidding. You got it for a spade." He looks at the approaching Lynnette, now only ten feet away. "You're right. Something's in the wind. I've fifteen cents says we won't be able to play out the hand we've just so artfully bid."

"Afternoon, boys," says Lynnette. "Sorry to interrupt, but I'm afraid your afternoon fun is over."

"What's the problem, Lynnette? What're you doing here in this stifling heat?"

"David needs to talk with Wall and Scott. He received a package from a messenger, and immediately he tells me to find you two and bring you to his office." She frowns, looking like she's gonna cry.

"What?" says James.

"That can only mean your orders arrived. Means you'll be leaving soon. I'm gonna miss you guys."

"Do we take the chance, Wall? Can we be sure we've not won the Vietnam lottery? Do we go see Hanson? Or do we hop in my 'Vette right now and head for Quebec?"

"We talk to Hanson first. Could be I was right before, and they're sending us to winter in Puerto Rico, especially since we've aced our 'continuing education' here at Beach Bum University."

"You're weird, Wall. Anybody ever tell you that?"

★★★

"Afternoon, Wall, Scott," says Hanson. "Sit down. These came sealed, so I, not being your superior officer, can't open 'em. You've gotta do that."

"I don't suppose," I ask him, "we can open them with Jay, James, and our piña coladas?"

"Sounds good, but that's not the way it's done." He stares at us. "Open the damn envelopes."

We open our envelopes, pull out our papers, and scan our words.

"Doesn't tell me shit!" says Scott.

"I got till 0600 on the eighteenth," I say. "What's today? I've no clue!"

"Today's the fourteenth."

"I report to Fort Dix. Oh God! Isn't Fort Dix where grunt soldiers get their pre-Vietnam training? Stuff like bayonets, machine guns, land mines?"

"Mine says the same thing, and you're right about infantry training at Dix. Damn, Wall! We've got three days to get ourselves to Canada."

"I've been planning for this. We'll take my Triumph. It's on its last legs. We ditch it in the Vermont woods and walk across to Quebec. Simple!"

"Not so fast, guys," says Hanson. "Let me take a look."

I hand the single page of my life sentence to him. Hanson spends a minute reading the small print.

"Relax guys, this ain't so bad. Maybe even it's good." He lays the paper on the desk, upside down so Scott and I can read it right side up. He points to some gibberish with his gold-plated pen.

"Look at this. Thing's written in army code. It's all in the initials. The most important initials are up here at the top. The authority issuing these orders is USAEUR."

"United States... Asian... enemy... unit... recon?" Scott's balancing himself on the knife edge. His mind's halfway to Stowe already.

"Calm down, Scott. The initials mean US Army in EURope. You're not headed to Vietnam. And these letters, USNETHF, mean you're flying into the Northern European Transportation Hub, Frankfurt. You're headed to Germany."

"So what's this Fort Dix thing? That's not Germany!"

"True. But again, understand the code. You report to Fort Dix USAATC. That's the Army Atlantic Transportation Command. In addition to teaching Vietnam 101, Fort Dix has the army's longest runway in the Northeast. One of their big jets is gonna fly you to Europe."

"So, what's your code say we'll be doing in Frankfurt?"

"I'm fairly certain you'll be doin' design stuff. That's what you're doing here, right? German guys are very secretive, though I can tell you it won't be England, or south of the Alps. Soldiers headed there fly into London or Rome."

"Thanks, David."

"No problem. And a couple other things. I'll transport you to Fort Dix, so don't worry about that. And second, we'll discuss the disposition of your two cars. I'll take any steps with regards to them and other things you want shipped someplace. We've plenty of time to settle that. Then, tomorrow night, dinner at the officers' club's on me. The four of you. Six-thirty. Civilian clothes. Okay? Now, go back to your buddies. Scoot!"

"Germany's not bad," says James. "They've great orchestras in Germany."

"All I care about," Scott says, "is no one's gonna push me out the door of a flaming helicopter."

A waitress comes over with another round of piña coladas. "Compliments of Mr. Hanson."

"Whose deal is it?" I ask.

"I'm thinking it's east's deal. It's a good direction to start, huh?" says Scott.

"I don't mind ending up there, as it's nowhere close to 'Nam. However, I can't get the idea of a Puerto Rican beach out of my head. Wouldn't that be sweet?"

"Like I've told you before, Wall, you're plain weird."

04 THE FRANKFURT AM MAIN STORY

I'm a design professional with seven years of study on the art of fabricating sensory perceptions. So I understand the reasons this army paints its world olive drab and marks its stuff using ugly font types. But they are inane reasons, and certainly there are subtler ways to establish sensorial control. These guys desperately need design help. I'll give you one example. The army subcontractor who owns, or maybe only operates, the airplane now flying me to Germany stenciled its name, **FEDERATED AIR SERVICE**, in clumsy block letters onto its bright silver fuselage. This plane, lounging on the tarmac with sleeker-fonted brethren, screams 'I'm a stupid US Army plane bringing more invaders into your country.' That doesn't seem productive to me. Perhaps my new job's upgrading their graphics. I could do that.

Eventually we land, exit this self-identified military airplane, and are herded into a building also burdened with clumsy graphics. Makes me sick. Gray's doing the shouting in here; monotonous, monochromatic, antiseptic gray. Gray covers the floor and the walls, the doors and chairs, the light fixtures and air ducts, and I'm guessing even the air molecules sucked inside from the gray day hanging around outside. I smell things and see things that smell and look similar to the naked room in the final assembly building these guys tortured me in at Fort Bliss. The entire planeload of olive drab soldiers who entered this dungeon with me have been marched out and shipped off to their new drab, or maybe gray, stations.

Except that Scott Laughters and I remain glued to our gray chairs. We sit side by side in the second to last row of an orderly array of five hundred, now empty gray chairs. We listen to sounds of our breathing bounce off the gray metal walls. We believe we're in Frankfurt because that's where David Hanson's code told us we'd be going. Scott and I see no confirmation, as there are no windows in this gray room to confirm the location of the gray exterior. I know we're not in Vietnam—we weren't airborne long enough to fly there. I counted only twelve hours airborne from Jersey; could mean we're in Alaska though.

"I don't think we're in Alaska, Scott. Though I read somewhere that Alaska's gray like this here gray."

"It's hard to know, just another dead waiting room, just like at basic."

"The situation's similar," I say. "But this room's imbued with a higher serendipity quotient. Or one of impending motion, or of longing for stability."

"Don't use those slick architecture words on me, Wall. It's another ugly, drab room. Damn depressing! I'm for calling their bluff. We check into a Holiday Inn, soak up the air conditioning, watch TV, and send for burgers."

"Though I badly need food and sleep, I'm nixing the hotel. I'm gonna behave myself, at least for another hour."

Our windowless dungeon's an undecorated and only slightly refurbished former aircraft hangar, with an arching metal ceiling. Gas heaters and other equipment hang like moss from the overhead beams. Sliding doors, big enough to let a bomber slip inside, are probably welded into place. Powerful floodlights, hidden in gray metal tubs, throw huge amounts of raw light onto the arch of the metal ceiling. Even so, the light's not bright enough to encourage me to read.

It's been an hour since the last army guy left us alone in this gray space. Another jet screams past on an adjacent runway. The exhaust noise reverberates around this gray room. Miscellaneous equipment rattles and vibrates. Some sympathetic vibrations bang around inside my skull.

"By my count, that's twenty-three," I say. "A busy day in the aerodrome."

"I'll give 'em two more takeoffs," says Scott, "an even twenty-five."

A distant door slams, and a pump motor chugs periodically. Having nothing but time, I time it.

"Pump's working twenty-seven-second chugging periods separated by two-minute, nineteen-second intermissions."

"Good to know that, Wall." Scott's trying to be respectful. "Seems well within the required guidelines."

A motorcycle or small tractor passes outside. A sudden thunder boom results in raindrops tentatively hammering on the metal roof.

"This room's designed for machines, not people."

Scott leans over. "You're forgetting we're in the army. Means we *are* machines. But cheer up. This room's not infused with black ideas like 'getting pushed out of helicopters.'"

"Then why'm I so anxious and tense, Scott? Why's my head threatening to explode? Why'm I sitting in this metal room after everyone else is gone? Why'm I still worrying about jungles?"

"Relax, Wall. I'm confident the specter of Vietnam is gone from our immediate future. Sadly, I've no idea what's replacing it. What's this army doin' in Germany?"

"Private Laughters?" While we weren't paying attention, a guy materializes at the podium at the front of the room, and his words, enriched by pre-World War II era electronics, echo around with some blunt force.

"Here, sir," yells Scott. He waves his hand like to a driver with a sign behind a rope at an airport.

"Would you approach this podium, please?"

Scottie rises and takes a couple steps.

"Bring your duffel bag with you, private."

"Oh! Okay," Scott says. He turns back to grab the strap on his duffel.

"It's 'yes, sir!' to you, private. And you're moving much too slowly. Don't make me wait."

"This isn't going well," Scott whispers as he bends over his bag. "I'm thinking Norway."

"That jerk's in no hurry," I whisper back. "He's got nothin' but time. Nothin' to do 'cept messin' with us. Try havin' some fun with him."

"Don't think I'll take the chance. Downside—"

"On the double, soldier! Get up here now!"

Scottie scurries up and stands before the podium. Two big guys enter and stand, one on each side of him. A short discussion ensues, then all three do a rather uncoordinated turning maneuver and march through a door set into a breach in the block wall behind the podium. The ominous word **AUSFAHRT** is stenciled in big, black, block letters over that opening. The officer guy whose voice just bounced off the ceiling follows the three of them out that door.

"Private Kneubel?"

My eyes are sealed, and I've almost left the premises. But I'm no dummy. I remember the hard time the guy gave Scott. So I jump to my feet even as my sleepy eyes are in the process of opening. "Here, sir!" I say. And without even being told, I grab my duffel and stumble toward the front.

The same two MP thugs come in and stand close, a brace to my shoulders. They're bigger than me—six foot six, 250 pounds, defensive linemen types. They don't scare me. I'm a five-eight,

210-pound running back with great acceleration and blazing speed. They'd better behave themselves, or I'm gone. Touchdown city! The guy behind the podium stares a hole through me. I smile at him. Reminds me of arm wrestling. First guy to blink loses. I don't play his silly game. I roll my eyes to study the equipment dangling from the ceiling. I wait for something positive to happen.

"Are you forgetting something, private?"

I try to jerk around to see what I'd left on my chair. The thug on my right grabs my arm, preventing me from making any movement.

I shrug. "I'm guessing the right answer must be no! I've not forgotten—"

"The thing you forgot, private, is that I'm an officer, and military procedure requires that you, acting respectfully, must stand at attention as the soldiers on both sides of you are doing, then offer me a salute."

"Okay! I forgot that. Sorry." I quickly perform the required deed. I think about returning a pithy comment.

"Okay, what?"

"Aaaaaa?" I wonder what this guy's getting at. Then I remember, something bouncing around my head from basic.

"Okay, sir! Right?"

"Thank you, private!" the now-acknowledged superior being says, and he smiles. Although it could be a sneer, since it's obvious he's smarting from my insult.

The superior being gives the thug on my right an envelope and says something I don't understand; mostly numbers, letters, and maybe an address? The thug on my right gently pokes me. I look hard and notice he's saluting the superior being, so I mimic him. Then we three turn sharply and walk under that "**AUSFARHT**" and into the cavern that swallowed Scott. We walk—thug-Wall-thug—down some stairs and into a long gray corridor made longer and grayer because it lacks details like doors and windows. A bare-bulb fluorescent strip glares at me every fifteen meters. I'm thinking I'm in a tunnel, or a gulag, or maybe a science experiment—thug-Wall-thug.

"Where're we going?"

They've sealed their ears. "I get the message," I say. "Not talking's part of the torture regimen." Their sense of humor's gone too. Down some stairs, through some doors, turn, up some stairs. Lots of German signs— "**RAUCHEN VERBOTEN**," "**RICHTER**," "**EINGANG**." I know I'm in Germany, but I deserve English signage, don't I?

Up some stairs, through another door—"**AUSFARHT**." We break into an airport-type garage. Daylight's barely visible at the far end of long rows of parked cars. We march to a van parked against a wall under large blue letters: "**STATION-R**." That tells me nothing. The van's black, with black glass, and unmarked except for the number "**427**" painted in grey above the front wheel well. They're fooling nobody. The thing screams army.

One thug takes my duffel to the back. The other opens the side door, helps me in, then gives the driver the envelope. "The sun's returned, Private Kneubel," he says. "Nice day for a drive."

"Where'm I going?" I have to ask. But the door slams shut, the engine fires up, and the van moves. A Ford logo glows in the steering wheel hub, but no other words alert me to any affiliation with any business entity. The driver wears a powder blue jacket with a universal symbol for whatever is on his sleeve. It's possible he's delivering plumbing supplies. I've an awful thought. I'm being kidnapped and taken to the gulag. I respectfully address the uniformed driver. "Can ya tell me where we're going, sir?"

"Nein!"

"Sprichst du Englisch, bitte?"

"I'm not supposed to talk to you." He says this in English but with a pronounced drawl.

Those few words are enough for me. "Hey, I recognize your drawl!" I'm excited by this unexpected bubble of pleasure. "I spent six years in Champaign-Urbana. You're southern Illinois, right? What're you doing delivering plumbing supplies in Frankfurt? And can you tell me where I'm going?"

"I'm pleased you recognize my drawl, but I cannot converse with passengers."

"Can you confirm you're not a Russian spy?"

"Can't do that." He laughs. "Please, no talking."

"Danke," I say. I think that's right. I know a few German words, as my grandparents are Germanish speaking Luxembourgers.

The van makes several stops and picks up courier pouches—nondescript canvas bags that might contain plumbing supplies. Eventually we hit the Autobahn.

I assess my situation. I'm sitting alone in the back of an unmarked Ford van, being driven by a silent driver born in southern Illinois through the drearier suburbs of Frankfurt. And right now that's all I know about the rest of my entire life. I'm not frightened, though it's possible I'm lost. However, if I don't know where I'm going or where I'm supposed to be, I can't possibly be lost, can I?

I've been sitting continuously for thirty-six hours, half of that strapped in a seat. It started at Fort Dix at 0600 yesterday, and I sat for nine hours before I got airborne. The pilot told us we stopped in Thule, Greenland to suck up some fuel and waste some time. Then we hopped to an obscure air force base in northwest England so we could stare at fog for hours. My Federated Air Service escort service finally dropped me in Frankfurt around 0800 local time of day number two.

I've spent a half day sitting in an aircraft hangar and hours driving on the Autobahn. I've eaten little, slept sporadically, and seen no evidence my trip's close to over. Finally, my body gives up. I float away into a lush, terrifying dreamland.

05 The 1st Heidelberg Story

The Federated Air Service helicopter swoops low over the swamp. There's an explosion, everything shakes, the cabin fills with smoke, but I see no flames. The 'copter's deck is spinning wildly. My man Marley holds me upright in his chains as other guys are thrown to the floor, thrown against the walls. I see Davie Groetken silhouetted in the open door. He grins at me strangely, waves with a bloody hand, then jumps backward out the open doorway. Immediately, an explosion sets the rest of us screaming, pushing, shoving to escape. There's sporadic machine gun fire. I don't see Marley! Don't even hear his chains. My body's shoved through that open door. I plunge some distance, smashing into the mushy swamp. I look for Davie. Other guys land atop me. My vision fades.

"On your feet, Kneuble! No sleeping on the job!"

I struggle to raise myself, but I can't move.

"Will you sit still! First I undo your seatbelt, then you jump out."

I jerk awake. The exploding helicopter and the soggy ground disappear. That blue jacketed plumbing supply guy is reaching over me.

"Relax! Kneuble," he says. "Quit fighting! Let's undo your belt. Welcome back from the dead."

"I wasn't dead. I never die in that dream. It just stops, unresolved. What time is it?"

"About 1600 hours."

I'm on my feet now. I look around. I see several stone buildings, lots of trees, nice grass, and flowers. Place looks like a college campus from a movie set—no army stuff. "Where are we?"

"We're in Heidelberg," he says.

"Heidelberg? Like *The Student Prince*? What's this college got to do with army?"

He points. I turn around and am blasted by a monumentally oversized sign, made of several sheets of plywood. Blackish letters hand painted on an olive drab background. It's a very strange ugly sign! "**HEADQUARTERS-UNITED STATES ARMY IN EUROPE.**" It's like a highway billboard. It's so large it obscures the massive stone office building—I'm assuming it's the headquarters building—lurking a bit insecurely behind it. The courier hands me an envelope with my typed name, then retrieves my duffel. I hardly notice. That bizarre sign with hand lettered words is warning me something's askew.

"Follow me," my chauffeur says. "You'll check in with Heidi. I'm bringing her mail." We start up the three or four hundred steps aiming toward the front doors. I don't bother to count 'em, though I think about it.

"Germans do ceremonial steps well," I say. "The more important you are, the more steps you get. It's a bit medieval—maybe older, Egyptians or Persians?"

The courier pays me no attention. "We visitors must climb the mountain. It allows the watchers to watch us." He nods toward the armed MPs flanking the front door. "Normal people use the back entry. This may be the last time you'll climb this mountain. I do it every other day."

"I'm sorry."

"Other perks make it worthwhile." He winks at me.

★★★

We enter through ornate doors opened by an armed MP and approach a reception counter like one might confront in a high-end hotel. Several young women scurry about doing reception type things. Being alert, I notice one girl; big smile, eyes intently watching us, little lights flashing. She walks toward us.

"Hello, Heidi." The courier gives it away. Seems Heidi's his perk. "This gentleman is Private Kneubel. Brought him down from Frankfurt. Mr. Kneubel, say hello to Heidi. She'll take care of you."

"Guten Tag, Valter Kneubel. Ve've been expecting you." She holds her hand out, snaps her fingers, and I instinctively give this beer-garden-waitress-looking person the precious envelope I've only just been given. The thing contains, I am assuming, my orders, but since I've never peeked inside, I cannot verify that. I should have torn the damn thing open and looked at it when I had a chance.

She looks at my name on the envelope. "Kneubel? That's a German name, right?"

"Many generations ago, ma'am, mid-nineteenth century."

"Vhere you from, Valter Kneubel?"

"Iowa, the northwestern part."

"Ahhh. I have cousins. Live near Pipestone, in Minnesota. Not so far away, no?"

"Probably an hour-and-a-half north. Not so far."

"Put your bag on that couch, Valter." She points to a mammoth piece of ornate furniture set against the far wall, centered under an equally mammoth, eighteenth century battlefield painting—snorting horses, smoke and fire in the sky, bearded guys in shiny armor, bloody and gored bodies littering the landscape. "You can retrieve it later."

While I am busy positioning my duffel so blood from the battleground doesn't drip on it, Heidi and the plumbing parts courier have a private conversation that doesn't seem to me to have much to do with army stuff. That interlude completed, she walks back and returns her attention to me.

"First, ve'll valk down and see if General Clappsaddle's available. He'll vant to know you've arrived."

She puts her arm through mine. Then together we exit the area and, like two lovers strolling through the park, start the hike down this long hall. It's more a slender gallery than a hallway, with more of those great battle scenes illuminated by glitzy chandeliers.

I think I may have lost something important. I've no reason to believe I'll ever see my orders again and have no idea where I'm supposed to be. I might never find out if I've been delivered to the right place.

"Vhat took you so long, Valter?" she asks casually. "You vere supposed to be here a veek ago. You been doing partying? Some foolin' around?"

"No, ma'am, Heidi. My orders arrived only four days ago, and I hustled over here just as fast as the army could do it. I'm right on schedule."

"Oh, vell, it'll verk out. You cut it close though. Jerry's going back tomorrow, so you'll use his office."

That seems weird. "I've my own office?"

Heidi doesn't answer. We hike in silence. We encounter no people in this massive ceremonial hallway. All this pomp and painting, yet the place seems abandoned. I'm getting flashing messages from my sensors.

Heidi tries General Clappsaddle's door, but it's locked. I give her a questioning look. She doesn't care.

"It's Friday, Valter. And a beautiful afternoon. Everyone's probably on the golf course."

A pang of déjà vu! Same as Monmouth, I'm checking in while my new boss is playing golf; another goofy situation. She grabs my arm, and we climb some stairs, then walk three miles of hallway. Eventually we stop at an impressive looking door, though it's a normal looking door for this building. Hundreds of similar impressive doors line the hallways of this grand ceremonial structure. The portal we now confront consists of two oak doors, each three meters tall by one meter wide and each containing a frosted glass panel. On the right-hand panel, a calligrapher has lettered the title of the activity being conducted on the other side of this door in black, bold, italics of a Baskerville type font. Seems the work being done behind this door demands serifs. The words lettered on the frosted glass stop me dumb—**CRITICAL PATH ANALYSIS.** And below these words, smaller letters indicate the spirit watching over the mayhem being committed in the room beyond as **"Lieutenant General Alvin W. Bekker, Director."**

I don't remember being shot, though something similar must've happened. My clothes are immediately wet with sweat. Bits of information regarding Critical Path Networks collide inside my head. Back in Jersey, Scott said he'd analyzed Critical Path Networks for the Interstate; Jay studied Critical Path at Col Poly; I'd done Critical Path work on Illinois' radio telescope; James attended MIT where, I seem to remember, they developed Critical Paths!

Heidi holds the door open. I point to the words.

"Critical Path Analysis? What's that mean?"

"I don't know. I do know people verk here. They're a veird bunch."

That doesn't sound encouraging. I cross the threshold and quickly restart my sensors. Mustard beige ceilings, mustard beige walls, mustard beige concrete floors, though with colorful runner-rugs marking travel paths. So, first we have olive drab, then moldy gray, and now mustardy beige. I'm not sure it's a positive progression. I'm not encouraged. We walk through an archway into a short passage. She yells "Jerrrrrryyyyy!" That echoes down this hall at high volume but doesn't impact the ambient noise level emitting from back there.

"No verk being accomplished here," she says.

I notice huge windows with a panoramic view like a National Geographic foldout. I point to it and look a question at her.

"It's the best view of our castle in the city," Heidi says. She whistles, like to a beer vender at the ballpark, prompting several people to detach themselves from their conversations. "Ahh, zo, here he comes."

"Jerry, may I present your replacement—Valter Kneubel."

Jerry grabs me suddenly. He hugs me like a prodigal son returned from the desert. "I'll go home now," he says. "I've been waiting sixteen months, Valter." He also emphasizes the 'V.'

"Hi, Jerry." I stay focused. "I've no idea why this Heidi person keeps saying Valter. You'd best call me Wall with an American 'W,' or I'll punch you silly."

"Ya' gotta understand," Jerry says. "Heidi's a native. She can't prevent those 'V' things from escaping her luscious lips." Jerry blows her a kiss, then points to a cooler on a nearby layout table. "Beer will cure your pronunciation disease, dearest Heidi." He emits several more air kisses, making faces like a fish.

"Sorry, Wall." He turns to me. "We're a bit wonky. We're getting in shape for my party. My initial job with you, and frankly, my last responsibility to this stupid job, is to formally invite you to my party. Change outta that silly green uniform though! Be ready to jump onto my party bus—1700 sharp." He looks at his watch. "My God, people! We've only a half-hour. So little time, so much to drink!"

Jerry yells, "Hey! Listen up. My replacement's finally arrived. Wants us to call him Wall. Welcome, Wall." He raises his beer bottle. "I'm outta here. Wahoo!"

Several people, armed with liquid refreshment, gather around to introduce themselves. They seem in advanced party mode.

"I'm the Cartoonist, Wall. Can I get you a beer?"

"I'll have a Guinness." I sound like a pro, but I'm clueless. I'm from Iowa. It's the only European beer I ever heard of.

"Velcome to Germany, Vall. I'm Boris. I'm computer guy. I'm only person in dis building who knows vhat computer is. I vill teach you. And I first teach you—no Guinness! Never in Deutschland! You drink Heidelberger Pilsner. It's bottled there." He points vaguely toward the hovering castle.

"Welcome, Wall! I'm John Brezglyski. Welcome to my team."

Fuzzy black hair, big droopy mustache. My first thought is Frank Zappa, or maybe Einstein as a youth. And those eyes! Like they'd been fabricated in a physics lab.

"Tonight you stick with me. I'll answer questions, introduce you to people. And the first introduction, my wife, Marieka. She doesn't hang out here unless there's a party. She works across the river... watching Max Planck's little electrons dance."

"Hello, Marieka," I say. I'm pretty much dumbstruck. Almost snow-white blond hair, long white dress, sparkly blue eyes. I look for the pointy hat, the wand, and the several dwarfs she should've brought with her. "Who or what is Max Planck?" I ask. "And do little electrons polka or minuet?"

"You must not ask her those questions, Wall." These words, spoken in a soft voice, slip through the blond Fu Manchu mustache of a tall thin guy with long blond hair secured with a thin headband, from which dangles a medieval zodiac symbol centered on his forehead. This strange-looking specimen wears an army uniform. It's the only uniform, other than mine, in the room. But his uniform's a costume job. It looks like silk, and it's a custom fit set of beige desert fatigues. And he's pinned a flower to his chest where the medal array normally grows. "If you find out what she does, she'll have to kill you. Everything over at MPI is NATO top secret—"

"This weird wizard," John interrupts him, "is Lynx Girrard, our resident numbers geek."

"Wizard? Geek?" I'm confused, much too tired, and not yet drunk enough for this crew. "What's geek mean?"

The Wizard speaks. "Geek's of nineteenth century Germanic origin, related to the Dutch 'gek' meaning mad or silly. That describes me."

The Frank Zappa guy tells me, "Wizard's working on his doctorate at the university. He's a math guy. He bends numbers for us. A beautiful thing to observe."

"I'm observing stuff here," I say. "But nothing looks beautiful yet. Bizarre comes to mind. Or maybe *Twilight Zone*. Is Rod Serling gonna float through the door?"

★★★

By 1650 I've retrieved my duffel from beneath the bloody battle painting and changed into my party clothes. I wait on the humongous front steps with several dozen suitably primed partygoers. I'm told tonight's destination is a tent-covered rooftop deck overlooking the Neckar River.

"That *Alte Brücke Gasthaus* is a standard army venue," someone explains. "It's adjacent to the *Alte Brücke*, the Old Bridge, and close to the university and the *Marktplatz*. A nice fit for our boisterous group."

"Lieutenant General Alvin W. Bekker hired our bus. Isn't he the greatest?"

"Thank you Lieutenant General Bekker, wherever you are," says another celebrant.

"Shhh!" says her friend. "That could be him standing right there." She points a beer bottle at me. "I don't recognize you," she says. "My name's Claire. Would you be our new General Bekker?"

I stare at her. "I think I'm too young to be generalized. Don't you know the head of your office?"

"Oh, we know who Bekker is," she says. "We just don't know *if* he is."

"It's possible Bekker's an illusion," her friend says. "The Wizard and the Driver use his desk, make his calls, sign his paperwork. Seems Bekker does a lot of work."

"I've never seen him either," says another, "though he's one very productive dude."

"Let's hear it for our new General Bekker. Hip, hip!"

Everyone yells, "hooray!"

I need information quickly. I look around for John. He's hard to miss, like he's just walked off a magazine cover—six foot two, slender and athletic, with a thick mop of tightly curled black hair and, except for the mustache, clean shaven, but with the promise he could grow a full beard in a few days if he needed one. He could be the front man for a rock band. "Hey, John!"

He looks at me with eyes equipped with those new laser devices that bore holes through steel. I feel the heat inside my head. "What ja need, Wall?"

"Folks here tell me you and other guys take turns playing General Bekker."

"That's not true! Bekker's definitely not a general. He's only a lieutenant general. Clappsaddle's our real general, but he's seldom around, so he relies on his Lieutenant General Bekker to make daily decisions. And the second untruth, Lieutenant General Bekker doesn't consider what he does as 'playing.' Being Lieutenant General Bekker is damn hard work."

"My first reaction, John, is that you're full of crap. I remember some jerk in basic training telling me the US Army's the most powerful entity in the free world. You telling me the army here's an illusion?"

The Wizard puts a hand on my shoulder. "I think your skepticism's well founded, Wall. But listen to the Driver." He pats John on his shoulder, though avoids mussing his curls. "Such skepticism allows our Lieutenant General Bekker to better represent the US Army in Europe during these turbulent political times."

"You're full of crap too. I don't want to continue this conversation, Mr. Wizard. At least not before I've had another beer."

"Consider this teaching moment number one," Wizard says. "There be mirrors in the world, and you be noticing but half of them. Open your eyes, hold your tongue, drink your beer, and enjoy your free bus. Lieutenant General Bekker's watching over us. Don't be troubled. Lieutenant General Bekker's your best buddy."

"I'm gonna get another pilsner," I say. "Thanks for the insight, Lieutenant General Bekker."

"No! We thank *you*, Lieutenant General Bekker," says John. "And welcome to your new post. I'll get that beer for you. Free beer for you, Lieutenant General."

"Didn't you just say it's my beer? If I bought it, how is it free?"

"Whatever!" John says.

★★★

I've still not seen my orders, so I cannot be sure I'm not recently commissioned a lieutenant general. If so, I'm thinking someone should have told me that kind of news in person. Maybe that's the big secret this party's celebrating. I wait for a bus I've arranged. I drink beer I've supplied. I make small talk with my new teammates, several of whom, it appears, are also part of Lt. General Bekker. This teaching moment grabs me. Since I may be in charge, I probably shouldn't get too drunk tonight. I think I've been dropped into an opera, or maybe a painting like one of those things in that hallway I walked down earlier. It begs the questions: Who's the moron who dropped me into this scene? Who designed my Critical Path? I watch my party bus enter the drive.

"This should be fun," I say to the Wizard. I drain my pilsner, then toss the bottle into a bin. "A blind leading the blind sort of thing."

"I'm not blind," he says. He takes my arm and, pretending like I am, assists me onto the bus.

I remember nothing about the ride to the beer hall. My head's full of questions, dumped on a messy pile. Who's performing the Critical Path Analysis on my life? Might I discern if the word Vietnam appears anyplace in it? Has someone actually plotted out my next year's schedule? Can I find that guy, smash him good, then take the necessary actions to take back my own life?

"Hey, Wall! Welcome to the anti-Vietnam! Name's Patrick O'Sullivan. Everyone calls me Sully."

"Anti-Vietnam?" That makes me jump. I try to be serious. "What the hell does that mean, Sully? What role do I play?"

"I'm an outside consultant. I'm called when I'm needed. Me day job is to manage me wife's hotel. Her family's hotel, actually, a few klicks up the river in Neckargamünd. Me doing that frees her up to work 'ere in this zoo. 'Ere she comes, now. Say hello to Wall, Rhoda. 'E's just arrived. 'E be drivin' the Critical Path office bus after Jerry slips stateside."

Rhoda, five inches taller than her husband, has straight, short, black hair as opposed to Sully's curly, ash-blond mop, and she's gracefully constructed in contrast to Sully's dumptruck physique. She gives Sully a proprietary hug, then hands me a bottle. "Here, Wall, you need a beer. The strange characters on this deck call me the Eye."

"The Eye? What's that story?"

"I analyze aerial photographs. I see things nobody else sees." She wiggles her fingers at me like she might do over a crystal ball. "And so I do, or at least pretend to do, then I pretend to show the results to you. We're a team. I'm your private private eye." She gives me a quick hug and laughs at her little joke.

Everybody else laughs too, except for this tall, slender, middle-aged woman with short, smooth, glistening, white hair, wearing a very short, white dress, who glides smoothly through our conversation. "Many things here are private, many things are secret, many things unknown…" She uses phrases and words like a poet. Then she swiftly changes the topic. "We all, at least many of us, live at Rhoda and Sully's hotel." She says this in a monotone without emphasis. "You too must live—"

"Let's have a departure toast for Jerry," Boris interrupts. "Hip Hip!"

Again, everyone yells, "Hooray!"

"Jerry, why's a German like Boris yelling you a British toast?"

"He's learned that from Rita," says Jerry. "That's his wife, the wraith in white. She's the Brit."

I take a gulp of beer. I badly need fuel.

"Word of warning on our Rita, Wall. Some think she's CIA, maybe MI5. Mostly that's because of the way she glides rather than walks, she always wears white, her feet seldom touch the ground, and she never laughs."

"Boris is clever enough for both of us," says Rita. "I'm busy being a wraith. Can't be jolly too."

During the next few hours I meet several more non-costumed but well-rehearsed Critical Path Analysis actors. It seems neither Gen. Clappsaddle, the highest-ranking officer in the US Army in Europe, nor Lt. General Alvin W. Bekker, the seemingly imaginary titular head of the Critical Path Analysis team, has the knowledge, training, time, or even interest to make any decision concerning any Critical Path Analysis. I ask around, yet appear to be the only one on this deck, other than the outgoing Jerry Black, and perhaps the German computer guy, Boris, who knows what Critical Path Diagrams are diagrams of. It's possible that makes me the boss here. Since I may be one of the personages included in the joint construct of Lt. General Alvin W. Bekker, it may be that, by default, I actually am the new acting director of this Critical Path Analysis office.

I take a long draw on the beer. "John, don't ya think someone, like an officer or somebody, should have pulled me aside, told me that it's my job to pretend I'm a lieutenant general, and that I am in charge of NATO's Critical Path office?"

"It's not NATO's office. Your job is with US Army's Critical Paths."

"How can this silliness have anything to do with the US Army?"

"I'm sorry, guys," the Cartoonist interrupts us. "This discussion cannot continue."

"What? Why not?"

"Hear those bells? From the Heiliggeistkirche?" He cups his hand around his right ear, although the church bell chiming is plenty loud enough to be heard over the party noise. I can see the church tower. It's only a couple blocks away.

"Holy Ghost's tellin' us it's six o'clock. That's way past five o'clock. Means we're officially on weekend. Lieutenant General Bekker doesn't allow army talk between 1700 Friday and 0900 Monday. *Verstehn?*"

06 The Neckargamünd Story

I'm a stranger in a strange land. I've never been to Europe, so everything I'm seeing is new and weird. I know little of army protocols, a fact abruptly obvious on this rooftop fantasyland. I'm hungry, tired, and confused, and I think it's possible I'm lost. Even considering I'm lost, this party's a strange inside-out masquerade where the exterior wrappings are not the make-believe part. It's the people beneath the costumes who constitute the masked part.

Possibly a hundred and fifty people show up to pay their respects to the outgoing Jerry Black, to welcome his replacement, or to congratulate me on being commissioned general. Yet I've seen only one military uniform… that mockery the Wizard's wearing. I might divide the attendees into two groups, those who want to look like Americans and those who don't. Few of the second group give their true facade away by their choice of language, posture, shoes, clothes, or especially haircuts.

I thank my personal Critical Path designer for scheduling several months of downtime in New Jersey. That time allowed my basic training haircut to grow out, my face to weather on the beach, and my attitude not to be infected by those nasty army mannerisms which quickly ruin the pretense of those so afflicted. I display few signs to alert experienced people watchers as to my country of origin or army of occupation.

Perhaps this is the reason for alternative personalities and nicknames. Any guy named the Cartoonist or the Driver can easily manage to project that faux image in place of his actual facade and thus obscure the militarily constructed facade of a private first class or even of a lieutenant general. All this fabricated strangeness is assembled on this roof lounge on this late afternoon, and I now compel myself to study it, even though I'm an amateur and unfamiliar with personality investigation work.

Once I activate my sensors, however, I recognize the group of non-costumed folks in the far corner. I'm told those guys are Defense Department employees, civilians who work on our, now my, wing of headquarters building. Obviously, those quasi-military folks are here to drink the free beer. They don't attempt to participate in the frivolity.

"See that?" asks Lynx. "They're exposing their discomfort with, and even disdain toward us undisciplined, casually dressed, non-officer riffraff running Lieutenant General Bekker's Critical Path operation in the midst of their otherwise conservative army headquarters operation."

My sensors also recognize that people in this room know how to drink. Seems they have advanced training in the art. They assume the several attributes of sobriety while consuming large amounts of alcohol. I detect many different languages and realize English is not one spoken as often as I would have expected, this being an American Army party with a large contingent of American guests. And I hear much strange music blasting from the sound system.

Unlike the conversation, most all music lyrics I hear at this German venue are sung in English. I recognize Frank Zappa, The Velvet Underground, and other counterculture American music. I hear avant-garde European groups singing in English. And because this is Jerry's party, his favorite, Wilson Picket's "Mustang Sally," plays every five or six songs, imposing a rigid rock and roll tempo onto the eclectic playlist.

I find myself discussing this strange music with two furtive Czech nationals, music students at the university. My new friends seem uncomfortable, like continuously alert for that guy with a knife. They give me only code names—the Bassist and the Crawler. The Bassist's the talkative one. He introduces me to the strange sound blasting from the speakers. Tells me I must understand about the music.

"The Plastic People of the Universe," he explains, "are an underground classical rock ensemble from Prague, fronted by my friend, the poet-bassist Milan Hlavsa. I acquired this bootleg of a performance by TPPU two months ago in Prague. TPPU's created new music for a free Czechoslovakia. You'd best concentrate!"

"Soon you'll be hearing nothing else," says his companion. "In a few months, The Plastic People will push the Beatles off the top of the charts."

"The Plastic People will crush the Iron Curtain with sound waves. Just you listen. You arrived in time to witness the crumbling of the Soviet's hold over Czechoslovakia. Mark my words, The Plastic People of the Universe will bring that *steel blanket* crashing down."

★★★

I later talk to Sully. "Your friend, the Bassist, seems a bit overpowered by his music. Thinks Czech cellos can crush Russian tanks with sound alone. You worried he's slippin' off the edge a bit?"

"Maybe," Sully says. "But he's quite the promoter. He managed to get his music played on our sound system. Everyone in Heidelberg's livin' on some edge. No surprise if a few lose their handhold and slip off. Music's something to hold onto. 'Bout all many Czechs can grab."

It seems to me it'll be difficult to shut this party down when the 2300 curfew sounds. But partying here's a much-practiced affair, so festivities stop on a dime when the music stops, the lights dim, and the bus honks its horn downstairs in the *Steingasse*.

Lynx tells me, "It's a US Army mandated curfew. No party venues in West Germany are allowed open after 2300. Except, of course, for the officers' club, which, like an embassy, is technically considered US and not German soil. Wink, wink!"

Jerry and John walk across the deck toward me. "After our party here closes down," John tells me, "General Bekker's bus stops at Sully's hotel before it returns to the office. So, if you want to, and we're strongly suggesting that you do indeed want to, you should stay at Sully's hotel tonight. There's plenty of room. You should also make plans to live there, since Jerry's going stateside tomorrow. His apartment's available. I've put your name on it."

"I'm fairly certain I've not checked in with anyone, and all my stuff's back at the office—"

"Not to worry, Wall. Sully runs a complete hotel. He's got anything you need. I doubt anyone knows you're in Europe yet, so you shouldn't have to worry about checking in with the real army."

As a measure of how tired I am, or how drunk I am, I've not until this moment even thought about the real army.

"The real army? I'm not sure what that means."

Heidi said the real army expected me a week ago. I don't know where the real army is. And the thought hits me that not only do I not have a place to sleep, I don't have my duffel, and I don't have my papers that tell me who I am and where I'm supposed to be. But I'm super tired and super ready for a bed.

"All that official stuff's gonna have to wait till tomorrow. But should I be concerned, John, that nobody cares where I am?"

"Lieutenant General Bekker cares."

"Your Bekker's a mirage. I'm thinking this whole army's a mirage. And this here mirage is more bizarre than the one in New Jersey. At least in Jersey I was isolated, with no contact with any real army stuff. The entire thing was fantasy. Here, on the other hand, seems the fantasy branch is the real branch. Seems I'll need a lot more beer to do my job here."

"I know nothing of New Jersey, Wall. But I know Heidelberg, and I know that under Lieutenant General Bekker's guidance things are being run in an efficient, if perhaps a bit unorthodox, manner. Welcome to the old world, Wall. Though it's run by us new world soldiers. We, all of us on this roof deck, are truly the plastic people of the universe."

I look at the Driver as the pope might look at Frank Zappa. "What the hell's that mean?"

"Come on, Wall," says the Accountant. "You need sleep. It'll work out. Let's get to our bus."

I wonder if the unknown mechanic who's constructed my private Critical Path has planned my stay at Sully's Hotel Neckargamünd. Apparently the army doesn't care that their valuable soldier, Walter Kneuble, whom they were so anxious to separate from his education, has left the reservation. Should I be worried that the army, after flying me to Frankfurt and chauffeuring me down here to Heidelberg, seems to have quickly cut my tether and set me adrift?

★★★

I'm bouncing and shaking. It could be an earthquake.

"Time to rise and shine, sleepyhead!"

I'm unsure I recognize the voice.

I tell the shaker, "My body's tellin' me I cannot allow morning to happen yet. Gimme two or three days to restore—"

"We ran into the city this morning," says a second voice, another familiar one but with a French accent. "We brought back your duffel."

"It's a beautiful day, Wall!" I remember that guy's voice now, but I can't assign it a name.

"We can't let you waste it. Get up, get up, it's past noon."

It takes some willpower, but I force myself to wake. I open my eyes. I cannot make any connection between the room I see surrounding me and any room I remember ever being in before. The words I'm hearing make little sense. And my head's pounding.

I turn over. I see two vaguely familiar people. "I remember you guys! That party last night, right?"

John and Marieka laugh at me.

"Where am I?"

"You seem unaware of this, but you've just spent the first night in your new home. Welcome to Hotel Neckargamünd. Time to take a shower," Marieka says. "Then jump into your tourist clothes."

"We'll give you the A-one scenic tour," John says. "But first, we'll start with breakfast at the patio next door. You've fifteen minutes to get yourself downstairs."

★★★

Neckargamünd's a cozy village several kilometers upriver from Heidelberg. It's a pedestrian town, meaning it was built before cars, maybe even before they invented horses. There's little separation of pedestrians from automobiles. My new friends, Frank Zappa, Snow White, and Fu Manchu, walk me from my new home, the Hotel Neckargamünd, to the Pasticceria Yvette next door. I see villagers discussing heavy issues while standing in the middle of the plaza and no cars buzzing to interrupt their conversations. Several bicycles and a baby stroller lean against a low wall. We walk across a stone patio to a garden set above the dark brown Neckar River and settle in for our brunch.

The vine-covered side wall of my new home, Sully and Rhoda's hotel, abuts this garden, and the sun is slamming full blast onto it. I see now that the building's a medieval structure, four and five stories high and embellished with dark wood inserts, turrets, dormers, archways, and other medieval stuff. It's built right on the river so the stone base of the stair tower forms the side of the quay where several small boats are moored.

"It's a great breakfast spread, John. But then, I haven't eaten in about two years, so I'd probably say the same thing eating cardboard."

After the plates are cleared and we're sipping coffee, Lynx asks, "You ready for the official tour?"

"I'm not sure I've enough control over my schedule to answer that," I say. "I've no information with respect to anything I need to do, either this afternoon or for the rest of my life. I'll do whatever you tell me I must do. That will probably get tiresome soon, but I'm nowhere near there yet. I'm prepared to go wherever you point me."

07 The 2nd Heidelberg Story

I understand Heidelberg's a very old city, but oldness is relative. My oldness meter only records a hundred years or so. Heidelberg's meter is much older, seriously older. An Iron Age settlement on this site predated the Romans. Many buildings are over a thousand years old, and most new buildings are older than any structure I've seen before.

Heidelberg is strategically placed in west-central Germany and enjoys easy access to major highways and railroads. The gentle Neckar turns west and bisects the town, then intersects the Rhine a couple dozen kilometers to the northwest at Ludwigshafen-Mannheim, two manufacturing cities shouting at each other across the Rhine. Heidelberg residents understand their city is the intellectual capital and historical center of their country, and also perhaps of Europe. During WWII the old city was off limits to Allied bombers and suffered limited damage. The Heiliggeistkirche, old central city, the ancient residences, and the university escaped being rubbleized.

The university, certainly one of the oldest in Europe, was formally established in the eleventh or twelfth century, and the oldest of the current buildings date from the thirteenth and fourteenth. University scholars and the city's residents were heavily involved in the great discussions in the fourteenth and fifteenth centuries between Catholics and future Protestants. Back then, the town served as the unofficial headquarters for foreign intellectual refugees fleeing their hometown prince or bishop. This town and this university still welcome confused truth-seeking intellectuals from both sides of the Iron Curtain.

Heidelberg, a prime example of antique Germany, has the official crumbling castle hovering over the town and the placid Neckar flowing through it. A walking path, carved through the forest halfway up the hill on the north side of the Neckar, known since medieval times as the *Philosophenweg* or Philosophers Way, is one of the more stunning walks on the continent not located on a mountain. Supposedly, Goethe did his best thinking while walking up there.

It's important for me, as the new guy in this strange environment, to understand the context of my new life before I'm shocked by the reality of my mission. That's what John told me. So John and Lynx give me a thorough tour. We walk the full length of the Philosophers Way and ride the geared funicular up to the castle where we crawl through the ruins. We jump aboard the street trolley on the touristy Hauptstrasse to the main railroad station. We wander through the old university, and we survey a reasonable number of pubs and *gasthauses*. During this tour neither of them mention the words US Army, nor do they allow me to observe anything cloaked in olive drab or written using harsh fonts.

The joyous part is we three nerds find we've a common interest—a beautiful bonding and equalizing mechanism, which we much discuss on our Philosophers Way walk and over beer at the several *gasthaus* sessions. We all, in very different ways, have been captivated by the exotic beauty and power of the so-called Cosmic Big Bang. Lynx's doctoral thesis concerns the mathematics of the Big Bang's blast cloud propagation. John's focus at the University of Chicago was on the physics of element formation in the first seconds of the Big Bang. My graduate studio in radio astronomy at the University of Illinois built a half-mile-diameter radio telescope designed to verify the existence of background radiation produced by the Big Bang. This obscure common interest will, I'm thinking, help me overpower the sadness, stupidity, and incompetence I'm sure to encounter during my military stay in Heidelberg.

★★★

John and Lynx introduce me to the city of the past. They prevent me seeing the city of the present. That present city is home to a strange, gentle, or maybe inert, occupation army consisting of one hundred thousand US civilian Defense Department workers, fifty thousand army troops, and probably one hundred thousand wives, children, and hangers-on. Another one hundred thousand civilians and three hundred thousand troops are stationed elsewhere in Germany, and thousands more are spread from Turkey to Norway. The lives of all these hundreds of thousands of Americans are overseen, and perhaps loosely governed, by the crew in the headquarters building where I'll be working. John says most all these hundreds of thousands of US citizens hang around with little purpose except to be seen by the West Germans. The total military and civilian population must be understood as a calming force, a guarantee against further hostilities between ancient native tribes with several centuries of historical antagonistic relationships.

"This massive US presence," John says, "is punishment for their shameful conduct during the Big War. And the Soviets, loitering in a similar status in East Germany on the other side of the Iron Curtain, remind the East Germans of the same thing. Every soldier doing the watching on both sides understands the one big truth—or perhaps it's a big lie—inherent in this stagnant standoff: that there's no chance in hell any war is breaking out over this chimerical *steel wall*. We ain't gonna shoot your watchers, and you ain't gonna shoot ours!"

"And," says Lynx, "we all know this situation is deadlocked because such deadlock is guaranteed by the several, or several hundred, or several thousand nuclear warheads the US has lined up along its side of the Iron Curtain."

And every decision concerning the management, governance, and defense of this huge assembly of foreign occupiers—more US citizens occupy Germany than live in several of the smaller states like Vermont or Wyoming—is supposed to be made inside the stone walls of the USAEUR Headquarters Building by General Clappsaddle, who is considered the military governor of this US State of USAEUR, and his team.

"At least that's how the thing's set up," John tells me. "But that's not the way it's operating. You cannot believe as true any number I've mentioned in the previous several sentences. I'm guessing nobody knows how much crud is flowing down our pretty Neckar."

★★★

The next Monday morning, John takes me into Heidelberg for my first day of work. He must first drop his wife off at her job. So we cross over the *Alte Brücke*, run west along the north bank of the Neckar through the intense security apparatus, then to the dark stone *porte cochère* where he guns the engine to allow his deep melodious exhaust-pipe music to reverberate off the stonework, and skids to a stop in the gravel foreyard of the Max Planck Institute. Two bearded gentlemen in white lab coats rush to open Marieka's door. A third addresses John.

"As usual, John, thanks for bringing us Marieka." The three of them carry her bag, her umbrella, and the box of pastries she brings every day for them. I watch the four of them, operating as one organism, enter the glass doors of the Max Planck Institute for Nuclear Technology.

John's wife Marieka is one stunning woman. She is five foot four with curly, long, blond hair and looks to be about sixteen. She was born in Poland in 1939, and almost immediately her parents emigrated to southern France. She speaks four languages, was educated at the Sorbonne in Paris, and is now working on her doctorate in nuclear physics. Her high-powered brain is attached to a nuclear research group at Max Planck, and she is not, even remotely, the porcelain doll she looks to be. As Lynx told me the night of the party, Marieka "fiddles with electrons for Max Planck." I've no idea what that means, and something tells me I am not going to find out anytime soon.

John leaves Max Planck's campus, spins his VW through the *porte cochère*, east along the Neckar, then back across the *Alte Brücke*. Completely out of the blue, he says, "Wall, you have to know that Marieka's Uncle Jacob, who lives in Zurich, is, like both Marieka and I, isolated from family who are still back in Warsaw and still being pounded by oppressive foreign regimes. Nazis burned churches and synagogues and confiscated artwork and bank accounts. And, as a final obscenity, Jacob's wife, a Catholic medical school student, was assassinated—he points left toward a stone archway—in the university commons by her own uncle, a Nazi colleague of Jacob's at the medical school, who was afraid some Jewish vapor might sneak in and destroy the bloodlines of both the family and the medical school.

"Jacob knows that many Jewish and Catholic religious artifacts were buried for safekeeping in eastern Europe. And you should know this also."

"Why do I have to know that, John? It sounds like I may not want to know that."

"Jacob's in charge of the effort to repatriate that lost Polish religious art stashed by Catholic and Jewish families in anticipation of the Nazi invasion. His organization then reconciles those articles with their lawful owners living in the west or maintains them safely until time is right to return them."

"So, why do I have to know this?"

"You need to know this, Wall, because eventually you also will come to think of Jacob as your uncle."

I can think of no follow-up question to ask. I'm too confused, or maybe too frightened, to say anything, though I do believe I've just stepped on some sort of a mine.

John circles through the Marktplatz, then hurries down a narrow street with the beautiful sound of his exhausts echoing off the six-hundred-year-old stone facades. I'm oblivious to the scenery buzzing past my window. I wonder: *I've been here but a few days and already I'm in over my head. I think I'm lost. Perhaps I should be afraid!*

One thing I understand is that I've entered a space-time bubble equally as weird as the Sandy Hook beach bubble I exited several days ago. But this bubble isn't so soft and fuzzy as the old one. This bubble has a radioactive aspect to it and a Soviet-Army-pointing-tanks-at-me aspect to it, along with a living-in-a-medieval-hotel-on-the-river aspect to it. Curiously, I don't see any aspect of a real world in this bubble. And I don't see me in this bubble either!

The gatekeeper sees and hears John's red Beetle, and he raises the crossbar so John needn't slow down to enter the parking lot. John waves at him, flashes into the lot, then executes a ninety-degree skid into one of the parking spaces close to the back door of the USAEUR headquarters building. His space is next to the empty one with the "Gen. Clappsaddle" sign, and is marked by a sign indicating it is Lt. Gen. A. Bekker's space.

I hear the Heiliggeistkirche bells mark 0900 as John and I enter the headquarters building. We all climb stairs and head down hallways along with the rush hour crowd.

"Things don't quite feel right in here," I say.

John looks at me. "Seems a normal Monday morning. Folks goin' to work. What's wrong?"

"This is an army building," I say. "The headquarters of the US occupation in Europe at the height of the Cold War. Where are the suits and uniforms? Way too many sundresses and jeans on this college campus."

"Just because we're a military dictatorship, doesn't mean we must advertise it."

A cork-faced bulletin board's attached to the wall adjacent to many doors. A pink, eight and a half by eleven paper is tacked to each corkboard. I read the paper pinned to the Critical Path Analysis corkboard. It's a mimeographed note from General Clappsaddle with spaces allowed for changing information, spaces which are filled in with Magic Marker and underlined: "Congradulations, **Critical Path Office** on your **96%** precipitation in Friday's alert. A terriffic response!"

Underneath someone magic markered: "Especially for a weekend! Thanks!!!!"

"What's 'Friday's alert' mean?" I ask the Cartoonist.

"It's supposed to mean someone brings us free donuts." He turns to John and with mock anger asks, "Weren't we supposed to get the donuts today, Driver?"

"That answer doesn't begin to satisfy me."

"The Cartoonist is a cynic," John says. "The real answer is that Heidi, maybe suffering the consequences of Friday's party, copied last month's congratulatory note and put our name on it, but didn't correct last month's spelling mistakes or change our percentage. I'm hoping she still delivered our donuts."

"I ask you guys about alerts, but you answer me about donuts? What's going on?"

"You figured it out yourself. You're no dummy."

"What?"

"Time for teaching moment number two, Wall."

"Before I've had coffee or donuts? All right. Let me have it."

"Clappsaddle runs a bizarre place. And it doesn't get much more bizarre than this pink message. Every month Clappsaddle pretends the Soviets invade. Pretend tanks break through the Iron Curtain and pretend to rumble over the farm fields. The alert covers all Europe. It's theater-wide, coordinated with all NATO installations. Been having them for many years even though the Soviets would no more attack us than New Zealand. We know that, and the Soviets know that. And they certainly wouldn't attack with tanks and boots."

"Not when you've got airplanes and rockets," I say. "Stomping through mud with swords seems fairly stupid."

"There's nothin' fair or stupid here. This here's serious lying. Officers know exactly what to do and don't need practice so they always score one hundred percent compliance. Enlisted grunts can't remember diddly so the alerts are for them. However, few enlisted folks pay attention… mainly because there are no officers watching them, but also because alarm bells sound only inside the barracks.

"And, as you know after only a few days, few enlisted men here actually live inside the barracks. Many don't even know where the barracks are. We geniuses working at USAEUR headquarters are sophisticated folk with graduate degrees and fine cars. So, although most of us are privates, we gotta live in off-base apartments. The army has rules against this, of course, but Lieutenant General Bekker tells us those rules do not concern us Critical Path guys."

"I'm gonna need a beer with this donut."

"Pay attention, Wall. The USAEUR Headquarters Command is supposed to set a good example, so Clappsaddle can't be dishonored by having his own office have a measly five percent response rate. Therefore, Clappsaddle's underlings conspire to misinform him so he can officially report to himself that his headquarters achieved the single best response rating of any command in Germany. No wonder he gives us donuts."

"What's supposed to happen at an alert?"

"The Critical Path office and the Administration office should alternate the ninety-eight percent rating monthly, since that evens out the donut distribution."

"I don't mean what happens with donuts. I mean what happens at the alert?"

"Nobody knows that! Supposedly every soldier is supposed to jump outta' bed, don his armor, grab his sword, and line up on the parade field. He'll be loaded into a wagon and whisked to an emergency post. But very few soldiers come to the parade ground, and no swords are unlocked in the armory, so few drivers bring their wagons. The few, gung-ho soldiers who make it to the parade field hang in their jammies and smoke cigarettes till they're certain no Russians are running through the quadrangle. Then everyone returns to bed."

"Didn't realize the army still uses swords and wagons."

"It's called metaphor, goofball. But rifles may as well be swords since nobody's seen them around here either. Rules are so arcane nobody obeys them, nobody asks questions, and nobody cares. But lawns get mowed, hedges trimmed, and fences painted. And someone pays us our wages. And it all works like clockwork, thanks to Lieutenant General Bekker."

"Excuse me if I say I don't believe your fairy tale."

"You don't have to take my word for it. Hey, Accountant!"

A pudgy guy dribbling crumbs and sprinkles from his celebratory donut on his artistically tie-dyed private's shirt, walks over. "Whatcha need, Driver?"

"Missed you at the party Friday, Brian. Jeesh, you're still hung over. Say hello to Wall. He's just arrived to take Jerry's slot. Since you're the master, could you give him the one-minute explanation?"

"Sure, I love telling newbies 'the story.' This building's the grand headquarters for the most powerful military force in the world. Only the sharpest, smartest, best looking soldiers in the army can work here. Guys like the three of us for instance. Every private in this building has a master's degree or greater, loads of personal magnetism, and we drive neat cars. Right, John?"

"My Rosie's neater than your rattletrap, Mr. Accountant. We're the ideal type, progressive, smart guys any general would want as drones running his headquarters."

"There's a huge sad part though. Many officers are recovering from the diseases and injuries of Vietnam, and they're useless for normal tasks. It's us drones must do their work. We've masters, doctorates, real world business experience, and clear minds uncontaminated by jungle fever and painkillers."

John interrupts him. "Alcohol's a big problem with us college kids, but not jungle fever."

"Consider, I'm Princeton and Wharton School for my MBA. I was working numbers for an investment bank in Memphis, so I know how stuff's supposed to work. When I first got here last year, Clappsaddle showed me the hand-written ledgers, noted how neat and beautiful they look, and said he hopes I can keep them up the same way. I'm pretty quick on my feet, and I say, 'No prob-lemo!' However, after looking at them for about ten seconds, I realize the entire body of records is gibberish. The numbers make no sense. The information is entered into the ledgers by hand! They'd not yet heard about computers here! My predecessor told me he experimented on how screwy he could get and not get caught. And his ledgers did look beautiful."

John takes over. "Clappsaddle's headquarters is running on autopilot, Wall. What happened last month will happen the same today. Except maybe next month *you'll* get the donuts. Everything here's driven by a great fantasy machine and will continue infinitely with minimal help from us. Our job's to not rock the boat. We oil the gears once a month and look like we know what we're doing. Then we turn this zoo over to the next guy and just like Jerry did Friday, get drunk and fly away. You leave the place no worse off than when you came in."

"That's bizarre! Clappsaddle must know what's happening."

"Clappsaddle's doin' his job. Everything's running smoothly. He's playing golf. General Bekker watches his army. Welcome to Lieutenant General Bekker's team, Wall. Welcome to Heidelberg."

08 The Brussels Story

The Driver's invited me to this seminar held at *Der Philosophenweg*, a *gasthaus* shamelessly named to lure tourists and perhaps philosophers. It's never worked for tourists, but it's a reasonable grad student hangout. A waiter, whose appearance and manner evokes Charlie Chaplin, delivers three glasses of Heidelberger Pilsner to our table.

I watch him teeter around. I grab my glass and laugh.

"Please concentrate," says the Driver. "This is a serious technical orientation seminar. The Cartoonist will now explain European atmospheric phenomena."

"This is secret NATO stuff. European weather conditions are overseen by NATO's Critical Path office. Cloud cover is designed and implemented according to the dictates of their Atmospheric Effects Scheduling Department. On days when I fly to Brussels for USAEUR-NATO briefings, the AESD provides proper clouds and heavy rain."

"Thank God I've got beer," I say. "That'd make no sense with coffee."

"Pay attention. Those AESD guys understand the occurrence of sunlight and cloud cover over certain portions of Germany are unnaturally consistent, and they take advantage of that knowledge when scheduling briefings."

"I'm no expert on atmospheric phenomena," I say, "but I know you guys are full of crap."

"The program's top-secret," says the Driver. "You've yet to receive a security clearance, so you cannot officially be told anything about such things. Nevertheless, Lieutenant General Bekker knows you're the only guy who knows anything about many other things we can't tell you anything about yet, so we're exposing you to a few of the more peculiar aspects of the monthly NATO briefing ritual. The ritual itself isn't secret, only the SSBD."

"Okay, I'll bite. What's SSBD?"

"It's army talk for 'secret stuff being discussed.' That's the work you'll be expected to do once I'm allowed to tell you what it is you have to do when you get to Brussels."

"That's fairly abstract," I say. "Perhaps with enough beer I'll understand it."

"Here's the deal." The Cartoonist places a typed memo on the table. "Clappsaddle's van picks us up 0700 tomorrow at the east entry, then zips us out to the army airstrip a few clicks west of the city. We take one of Clappsaddle's executive propjets. After the short hop to Brussels, a van takes us into the NATO campus. We'll have plenty of time to get organized for the 1000 briefing."

"Wow," I say. "I've not flown in a small jet. I can't wait. I'll get a good view of the landscape, see how the countryside is laid out. It'll be better than reading a map."

"Will you pay attention! Didn't I just tell you about AESD's clouds? You'll never glimpse the ground."

"Like I said before, you're full of crap."

"The Cartoonist speaks the truth, Wall," says John. "I've taken that flight. You could end up in London, Paris, or Stuttgart. How could you know?"

"Do you suppose," I ask, "that your AESD do their work for agricultural purposes, so any alignment with our schedule is but coincidental?"

"You can mock us if you want, Wall, but it's clear someone's tinkering with Mother Nature."

Our strange discussion of tomorrow's schedule is interrupted by two guys with heavy beards, dressed in priest or monk outfits. They enter the room and approach our table. John stands up, so the Cartoonist stands too, and finally I stand; a gesture of respect for the clergy, I suspect. John introduces one of them to us as Father Lev, a theology professor at Heidelberg University.

After a short conversation in what I assume is Polish, John says, "Something's come up. I've got business with these guys." He stares at us.

The Cartoonist and I understand. We chug our beer, then exit.

As we hit the sidewalk, I say, "Two priests walk into a bar, but they don't order beer. The temperature drops about twenty degrees. Everyone not wearing a cassock rushes to the exit. I can't imagine any punch line to this joke, can you?"

"You are one observant guy, Wall. Two priests walk into a bar, the temperature drops. What else you wanna know?"

"I think you should tell me the punch line. It's another atmospheric phenomena joke, huh?"

"Don't think they're laughing, Wall. Probably a serious conversation gonna happen."

★★★

Next morning at 0715 I'm strapped in my seat and looking out the window of Clappsaddle's propjet. We're alone on this ten-passenger bus as it zips down the wet runway and, as the Cartoonist predicted, rams straight away into serious cloud cover. Within a few minutes we pop out, and I see nothing but fluffy cloud tops. I know what I gotta do. I take a nap.

The Cartoonist wakes me as the plane is diving through heavy clouds. We land on a black runway, and it's screaming rain so hard I see no grass. I may actually be in Brussels. But we may, as John suggested yesterday, be somewhere else. I hope I'm in Brussels. I'm not ready for the shock of finding myself in Stuttgart. A USAEUR van waits for us at the bottom of the fold-down stairs. It's a white vehicle and unmarked, except for the number above the front wheel. Heavily tinted windows make the dismal day outside seem somber and melancholic.

"Ahh," says the Cartoonist. "It's good to be back in Brussels."

"Or wherever," I say. "I don't feel good here. I'd be happier knowing exactly where I am."

"That ain't gonna happen. Remember, you're in the army!"

"Jury's still out on that," I say. "I'm in something though, and fairly deep into it. I'm afraid it's something other than a normal army. Maybe some imaginary voodoo army."

The van speeds us through the pelting rain. It drives down a ramp, enters a tunnel, and stops at a glass-doored entryway guarded by guys in strange uniforms holding machine guns.

"I take that back. I do believe I'm in some army. Although I must question whose army those machine gunner guys belong to."

"They're NATO," the Cartoonist explains. "City guys. They can't wear green, leafy-looking camouflage 'cause they don't work in the jungle. They blend into concrete, thus the urban uniforms with straight-line, right-angle camouflage."

One guard leads us down a hallway, up four flights of exit-type stairs, and through a door labeled "Projection B."

I slap myself back to reality. "This projection room's an exact copy of the room you showed me yesterday in our Heidelberg building."

"Good eye, Wall. But then you're the architect and trained to notice such things. This control booth's the only room we non-officer jerks are permitted to enter. It's an exact copy down to the location of electrical outlets."

"Makes some sense. Still, it's bizarre."

"I'll give you bizarre. This briefing's scheduled for exactly two hours. Doesn't matter if the big news this month is huge, like Russians bombing London, or insignificant, like East Germans crushing Latvia in a chess tourney. It's always a two-hour briefing."

"That's bizarre," I say, "but well organized. Do they actually discuss chess?"

The Cartoonist slaps the back of my head. "I only operate the projector and change the slides when Clappsaddle, or his aide, clicks his little button. Your job," he hands me some headphones, "is to listen intently, take notes, and answer all questions you hear from the joint USAEUR-NATO audience regarding the complex information contained on the slides my machine is projecting, detailing the status of the massive military constructions along the Iron Curtain. And Clappsaddle may ask you to answer other questions on topics like the bombing of London or chess results."

"I've just arrived in Germany. I've no security clearance. I've seen no slides. You tell me I'm responsible for building lotsa stuff somewhere, but I'm not allowed into the secret vault to review the project files. You expect me to use my psychic powers to tell me stuff I need to know about these massive construction projects, like perhaps where they're located?"

"They're over by the Iron Curtain. Everybody knows that."

"There actually is an Iron Curtain? I've heard those words but assumed it's only metaphor. Has anyone in that room actually seen it to confirm it's really there?"

"I doubt the Clappsaddle's seen it. Probably none of the guys down there've seen it. And so, just like you, none of those generals have seen any of the construction sites you're monitoring."

"I'm not yet monitoring stuff. I don't know stuff."

"Welcome to our Cold War, Wall. You're gonna have fun!"

It's time to zip open my banana. It's all I've got to eat, but I need something!

"You gotta understand," says the Cartoonist, his eyes never leaving his comic book, "I'm only the projectionist. I'll throw neat charts up for the generals to see. But I've limited ideas what's going on. The generals and their aides believe that you, Wall, will tell them when their unknown thousands of super bombs will be secure in their new bunkers. You alone know if they're operational or what button a button-pusher must push. You're the guy extracts reality from fiction. Or vice versa. The top generals in NATO wait for *you* to tell *them* what's happening out there."

"Wow! I think I need beer."

"Your job here is to assure the NATO brass that the construction and the implementation of the new missiles is on schedule so Clappsaddle can know when he'll be able to push the button. You are helping to make World War III a more efficient conflagration. You should be proud of that."

"I wonder how much more efficient we can get. I should think the several thousand existing warheads should cause pretty much absolute carnage Turkey to Finland. What's the advantage of having newer bombs?"

"Newer bombs are always better bombs. Ya get a new car every few years, right? We need new bombs too."

"I think I just gave myself my teaching moment number three, all by myself. I frightened myself."

The Cartoonist gives me a funny look, the experienced veteran to the raw plebe. He turns back to his comic book.

★★★

Since Scott Laughters flew into Frankfurt with me a couple weeks ago, I'm thinking he might work with the NATO version of the Critical Path office in Brussels, or with those AESD cloud schedule guys. He might be at this briefing, sitting on the other side of that wall in another projection booth. But if Scott is there, he'll be as clueless as I am. And sadly, seems neither of us will ever find that out.

And I learn one other odd thing. The Cartoonist tells me many of the USAEUR officers who participate in the Brussels nonsense will return to Heidelberg on Clappsaddle's jet, head immediately to the officers' club, get drunk, and forget everything they heard in Brussels. "Then it's Lieutenant General Bekker's responsibility to provide a safe trip home for these officers. The army wastes too many of them in Vietnam. No need of 'em running into German trees on the way home. Our Lieutenant General Bekker's one responsible guy!"

★★★

By mid-afternoon we're back in Heidelberg at the Critical Path Analysis office. I've stuff to discuss with our ghost general. "Hey, Driver, I've got questions." I pull a stool over next to his desk.

"Fire away, Wall. Have a good trip to the big city?"

"Interesting you choose to use the generic 'big city' and not a specific big city, like Brussels."

"What?"

"Makes me think I could've been anywhere. Everything's obscured in clouds and rain... dark windows in the van... secret underground entrances. Very spooky!"

"You need a beer."

"Okay, I'll settle down, though it'd be good if I knew what I'm doing. Do I really have to answer the questions those clueless NATO officers asked of the Clappsaddle while, I am assuming, we were in Brussels?"

"Indeed you do," says John. "By tomorrow night General Bekker wants a typed script put on his desk. It should include answers to all those questions. Eventually someone, perhaps Lieutenant General Bekker himself, will see to it that the information gets delivered to the questioner or put into some other relevant but secure place for future reference."

"But you realize, don't you, that I don't know the names of any questioners. They were only voices in my headphones."

"Don't worry! General Bekker will take care of that. After tonight's ritual at the officers' club, nobody will remember what questions they asked anyway. Understand?"

"No! It's complete nonsense. Could I ask... hmmmm, how am I going to phrase this so your answer doesn't have to be a lie? How about this? There's an outside chance any possible answer may rely on secret information which I'm not cleared to know. Thus, I'm forced to insert a disclaimer as to the security level being utilized. Can I then offer, as an answer, a best guess kind of statement, which I cannot be held responsible for if it turns out I was way off base? Is that vague enough?"

"Sounds like the right approach," Driver says. "Your predecessor, a less sophisticated and less wordy gentleman than you, condensed his lengthy responses into a few pithy code words. Took him only five minutes to answer every question on the list."

"I'm going out on a limb here, John, and assuming no questioner in recent history ever received a substantial answer to any question he's asked at any NATO briefing. Might that be true?"

"You got me. Remember, everything's compartmentalized. I don't know what Lieutenant General Bekker does with the answers after they're put on his desk. He's a ghost. Ghosts have their own ways of disseminating information. Perhaps some is passed along to appropriate personnel at NATO. I just don't know."

"I've seen the document incinerator in this building. It must get quite a workout after these briefings, huh, John?"

"Like I said before, I think you need a beer. Let's grab Lynx and hike over to Der Blaue Schwein for draughts and sausages."

★★★

Lynx carries three, cast-metal steins over to our table and distributes them. "Greta's gonna bring us sausages and bread. Think that'll be satisfactory?"

"Thanks, Lynx," I say. "This seems a real neat place."

"This woodwork's been here since the fifteenth century and heard many sophisticated philosophical discussions. Greta told me Martin Luther, Goethe, and Spinoza discussed heavy philosophy in this room, maybe at this very table."

"Wow," I say. "Wouldn't have thought she's old enough to remember that." Lynx throws an olive pit at me. "So I'm supposed to think that any convoluted or sophisticated discussion we might be having today is, what, small potatoes compared to the canons that historically bounced off these walls?"

"Something like that, Wall. Ears in these walls've heard things stranger than anything Lieutenant General Bekker might utter."

"I doubt that," I say. "I'm thinking your ghost general guy is aware that we're purposely not telling the truth. Certainly some general above him must also be aware he's lying. That guy knows our lies suit his purposes, though I cannot imagine what purposes those might be. Who could've designed this crazy subterfuge? Seems as medieval as this room, huh?"

"You gotta understand," John says, "USAEUR's a huge corporation, full of officer drones pretending to run the world. Our Lieutenant General Bekker's the only officer in our building who is not pretending. He's actually doing his job."

"He may not be pretending," I say, "but there're a couple people in this room who are pretending he's not pretending. Or something like that." I take a satisfying gulp of beer. I throw the olive pit back at Lynx.

"We gotta make our own rules," says Lynx. "General Bekker runs the army here. I've been here a long time. That illusion is the reality. That's why I wear my fatigues, so I remind myself that guys like me are the real army. Me, and probably our ghost general."

"You're not *in* the army," I say. "You're a civilian, Bekker's an illusion, and you, Driver, though not an illusion, are something, ahh—"

"The word you're looking for," Lynx says, "is simulacrum."

"What?"

"John is a simulacrum! An image or representation or a substitute for a real live—"

"Stop it! That's a medieval word. You're feeding me five-hundred-year old words in a five-hundred-year-old room while eating five-hundred-year-old sausages. I think everything's beginning to make sense now."

"It's not the sausage that's the medieval thing here, Wall! Only the recipe. I'm guessing the sausage was made last spring. And you realize, don't you, that making sausage is one disgusting job, such that those who watch it being made can't bring themselves to eat it."

"I've heard that, John, and I'm guessing you're going to make that messy revolting process relevant to our discussion, right?"

"Could be," he says and passes me the plate. "Have another sausage."

While I'm offloading a few disgusting links to my plate, he continues with my lesson.

"I have to tell you that many officers and lifer enlisted guys have been sent here not to fight the Cold War, but to cope with Vietnam-related physical and emotional problems. So the Defense Department finds it can best govern this isolated state of half a million transient employees living on an island in the middle of western Europe by not using them. However, some war related things have to be controlled by real army guys. And since they can't use their broken officer corps, and they can't use civilians, they gotta use us. We're highly educated, professionally degreed, drafted guys. We're academics, worthless as shooters and bombers, but smart enough to run the more technical programs required by the huge occupying military force plunked into the middle of a foreign continent without any real mission, other than to be visible."

"That means," Lynx says, "real army officers are freed from duties and thus able to rest, rehabilitate, and heal their Vietnam wounds. They've only to believe, imagine, or maybe dream, that they're still in charge.

"And of course we intelligent privates understand we're freed from simple army tasks demanded of normal low ranking enlisted men. That means we super soldiers can, essentially, give ourselves our own orders.

"Most of those professional army guys don't easily accept this complete breakdown of normal army discipline. But it doesn't matter since their primary function is plodding through each day without letting the specters and ghosts that followed them back from Vietnam overpower them. Many never stray from their bedrooms, the base hospital, or the officer and enlisted clubs.

"And though he's equally as absent as his colleagues are," Lynx continues, "one might make the argument that our ghost general is the most productive officer in our headquarters building."

"So, you're telling me I gotta listen to my ghost general. Though it doesn't appear he knows anything more than we three guys do, we're supposed to be satisfied not knowing what we're doing either? Could that possibly be right?"

"Sounds like a reasonable attitude," says John.

"So enough about the army. I can't listen to any more of this nonsense. How about we talk about Lynx's blast cloud propagation theory? And I—"

"We don't have the time to discuss cosmology now, Wall. Ya hear the bells? The Heiliggeistkirche's telling us our workday's over. It's been a long and eventful day. Time I return you to Neckargemünd."

09 THE FULDA STORY

I find out about Fulda a few days after I return from Brussels. I'm nowhere near sure it's a real place. It's a place well known to John, Lynx, and Brian Olsen because I'm hearing it mentioned often during this meeting we're having with the Bassist and the Poet at the *Alte Brücke Gasthaus*. The conversation's in Czech, so I understand nothing but the word 'Prague.' And the words 'und Fulda' are often attached to the word 'Prague' so I'm thinking the two cities are somehow linked. Fulda might be, in one sense, a real place, but it also could be a mythical place, a place our ghost general may have visited, though I doubt Clappsaddle's been there. It's not until later that I find out it's both.

I understand the word 'Prague' and know its subtext and context. The Czechs were terrified, so the word meant: Help! The Mongols are coming!

"By this time next year," the Poet cried, "if you do nothing, those Mongols will be dancing amidst the rubble in downtown Prague. You cannot let that happen. You have thousands of bombs. We only need you to use one. Push one button."

"You Americans must save Prague!"

The Bassist is desperate. He knows the Mongols are coming, and they'll trash Prague as Mongols have done in previous centuries. Precious things like money, heirlooms, ideas, people, and the primary topic of this meeting, new Czech music, must be removed from the path of that certain destruction.

The Poet insists, "National and personal treasures must be preserved until those fiends give us our country back. That is, if they give our country back. The west must protect our heritage."

The Bassist and the Poet take turns lecturing us. Pipelines, tunnels, and storage facilities must be constructed immediately. "You gotta build tunnels under that *steel curtain* now, Driver, before those damn Mongols attack."

The Bassist rises from the table and gathers his notes and papers. "Once those Mongol tanks rumble into our country—and they will come… we all know that—communication with the west will be lost. Our music will be lost! Can you not understand the magnitude of such destruction?"

Having spent vast quantities of passion, the Czechs leave frustrated. They're not happy campers.

"I know Prague," I say, "but what's this fulda word?"

"Fulda's what happens after Prague and Warsaw turn ashen gray," says John. "That's if Lieutenant General Bekker does nothing to stop it."

"It's your metaphor for basic human tragedy on a monumental scale," Lynx says. "We can't let that happen, even though the Bassist demands it. Nobody, not even our ghost general, can make fulda happen."

"Certainly not till we replenish our beer." I signal to Angela for another round. "Maybe more beer is the key to understanding what you're talking about."

Angela delivers the beer and offers us sausage and cheese. She wants to see us happy. That's not gonna happen. It's gonna take more than food to satisfy soldiers like us. Our project's simple—all we gotta do is save western civilization.

"But we're human," says Brian. "We have to do something, don't we? We can't allow the Soviets to smash our Czech and Polish friends. We have to do something!"

"Understand this, Wall," John says. "Drives us crazy! So, of course, we're gonna try. But our army's mired in Vietnam, and we've no resources. Except, of course, those thousands of nuclear bombs."

"What about four hundred thousand of us American soldiers?" I ask. "Plus the NATO troops. We send 'em through that *steel curtain* and circle Prague. The Soviets wouldn't dare attack a human curtain. Lieutenant General Bekker could do it for next month's alert exercise."

"Great idea, Farm Boy! We should be able to make that work!"

"First, Mr. Driver, who's this farm boy? Second, who you mean, we? And, third, no way you're getting this soldier to grab a rifle and scoot toward Prague."

"We can't do guns, Farm Boy," the Driver says, "but maybe we try something else. I've scheduled an inspection trip to Schwäbisch Gmünd next week. You come with me. We'll run past Fulda, see if we can find a good location to build the Bassist his tunnel under the *metal fence*."

"I don't think I can do that, John. I don't have a top-secret security clearance. I can't even look at your enigmatic Critical Path Diagrams yet. What makes you think I can look at the real dirt and concrete construction projects?"

"Oh, don't worry, Wall. We'll never find any real construction. Real missile sites are *really* secret. I think other secret army guys do those secret inspections."

"What? How can you inspect stuff if you can't find stuff? Oh, I get it now! Ghost general has ghost projects, huh?"

"It's our job to keep the army honest," John says. "Technically, we can't tell real lies unless we know the real truth, can we? I believe our ghost general wants us to know the true nature of the duplicitous Missile Preparation Construction Project. To know if his rockets are real or not real."

"You guys might need to know that I'm an experienced rocket guy," I said, "so I may be able to tell which of them are real. I'll bet

I've personally launched more rockets than any guy in Heidelberg!" My high school buddy, Gary, and I built a concrete launch pad in his uncle's cornfield, and we built and launched hundreds of rockets before one parachute failed to open, and the thing plunged full-speed through the roof of his uncle's dairy barn and missed Daisy or Clara by a couple feet. My mom and I quickly negotiated a missile test ban.

"I hope Clappsaddle's guys are as experienced with rockets as you are. You gotta understand, Farm Boy, it'll be impossible for you to do your job at NATO for our ghost general if you don't see what's actually being, or maybe not being, constructed in Schwäbisch Gmünd and Fulda. That's because your job is to design and monitor, not the construction, but the scam our ghost general is responsible for constructing."

"Ouch! My brain's not supposed to wrap around such contorted constructs."

"Well, yes, it is, Wall. It is specifically why you were chosen."

"What the hell does that mean. Chosen by whom?"

"Who knows. But believe me, someone's designed your private Critical Path Diagram, and you're exactly where your last green node says you are."

"I'm not concerned about my last node, but I'm frightened about my next one. Heaven forbid there's a red node lurking in my network."

"All you gotta remember is your Critical Path Networks require accurate, first-hand information that you can't get sitting on your kiester in Heidelberg. The silos, bunkers, runways, and other things are getting built, and approximately on time too. It's only the Critical Path Diagram aspect that's in question."

"And how do you know that's true, Mr. Driver?"

"Because our ghost general tells me it's true. Theoretically, every month the actual construction progress is scrutinized in the field. Then you, Farm Boy, appropriately manipulate the Critical

Path Diagram, which assures the message is properly palliated for Clappsaddle and his team—"

"Palliated? For God's sake, John! Whatever that means, it's pathetic."

"—to predict any new time adjustments so as to ensure things get done in the proper order so everything is completed by the due date. But most all the equipment and the rockets themselves are manufactured in the USA so many of the scheduling-node dates are set by aerospace contractors in Seattle or Florida. And it's possible a Berlin based firm owned by an oil field contractor from Houston is overseeing the actual construction. And the parts from the USA must perfectly mesh with the concrete construction parts built in Fulda, and Schwäbisch Gmünd, or perhaps in far off Norway and Greece."

"Oh, I see the problem," I say. "I've got to visit Greece, huh? And pretty quick? The architect in me needs to study stuff there."

"Maybe later, Mr. Architect. First we concentrate on local projects. I don't think Turkish or Greek bombs fit into Pershing nosecones. I believe they use bombers."

"What? Deliver the bloody things to Moscow by hand, like we did in WWI? What're the chances of our bombers making it to Moscow? I'm not messin' with nuclear bombs," I say. "I'll convert to a religion that doesn't enjoy nuclear conflagration. I'll hide in a Greek monastery and study ancient Greek architecture. Let the army forget me."

"I don't think that'll work."

"Seems to work for our ghost general. He's doin' a good job, and he's not here. So why must I be here? If the army doesn't know I'm here, maybe I'm not here. Why can't I be 'not here' in a Greek monastery rather than 'not here' here?"

"Because," says Brian. "The ghost general needs you here. Without you contorting it, a traditional Critical Path Analysis will not work in this atmosphere. The information stream from the field is extremely unreliable and in many cases unavailable. We don't even know which of the projects are real. However, the idea that there's a massive information problem must not reach the top USA and NATO officials. They must have monthly assurance that the construction is moving along nicely."

"Why do they even care?"

"Because they're NATO generals. And you must assure them. That assurance will be hidden in the wonderfully abstruse documents you will be creating for their meetings over the next year. As long as the Critical Path Diagrams look cleverly complicated and have the correct names and dates in the correct places, the brass can believe they show actual construction progress. See, it's not a necessity to use actual information. Anyway, actual information is impossible to get, and it's out of date way before we get it, so we pretend we are inspecting, and pretend we are scheduling, and pretend we are predicting, and we estimate lots of stuff, and that makes everybody happy. The whole system kind of runs itself. Mr. Kneuble, you are now the Farm Boy and in charge of fabricating the truth. That is your job."

"And," adds John, "in order to get accurate information, once every month we inspect each one of the sixty-two, or forty-seven, or 134, or it could be only eighteen, military construction sites so that we can accurately put the information on the monthly Critical Path Diagram and show it to the NATO brass."

"Bing, bing, bing," I say. "My truth sensor's going bonkers. Somebody must know how many sites there are."

"That information is hidden in the bureaucracy. The Eye helps us to monitor the large-scale event nodes, but we cannot even start to collect and analyze all these complex actions on our own. Therefore, we have to make a lot of stuff up."

"So, I've got a question. If you are making everything up, why do we even have to go out into the boonies to pretend to inspect the perhaps non-existent construction projects?"

"A very good question, Farm Boy. And the answer to it is a bit obfuscated."

"Imagine that!" I say. "Since nothing else is real, why do the lies have to be real? You guys ever read Kafka?"

"Now that you understand that, I suppose now is as good a time as any to introduce you to our ghost general's tertiary agenda."

"Tertiary agenda? I think I'll need more beer to get into that." I send a hand signal to my new friend, Angela. She smiles at me and nods. I've done my job.

"Let's say that you, Farm Boy, working as an agent for our ghost general's secondary agenda, find that you can make good use of the time you spent in close proximity to the *steel fence* to collect information, and sometimes other stuff, regarding the welfare of our brethren trapped to the east of said fence."

"So you're telling me this tertiary agenda is a spying operation?"

"Let's not use that word 'spy,' Farm Boy. First, I don't know enough about the definition of that word to be able to use it with any degree of conviction—"

"Jesus Christ, John! Did I actually hear you say that? And quit with the farm boy thing. You know who I am."

Since I'm responsible for quality control, I monitor Angela as she places new brews in front of us. She does a great job, then does one of those cross-the-feet-and-curtsy maneuvers.

"Ahh, danke, Angela," John says. But he stays on task and jumps right in where he left off. "And second, spy is an all-inclusive word with a bad reputation. The truth's more convoluted or perhaps subtler than that word suggests. In one sense we provide basic humanitarian services—mail and package delivery, banking, some equipment distribution, a variety of necessary legal document procurement services, and other non-spy type services."

"So you're claiming this third-level operation, like the stuff you guys were discussing with the Czech gentlemen this afternoon, can use the concept of intelligent guys poking around the base of the Iron Curtain for useful information to obscure our real task of bringing hidden, stolen, or lost valuables back to their rightful owners now escaped or hiding in the West?"

"Wow! You've made some very serious assumptions there, completely on your own, Farm Boy," says the Accountant. "We've never told you any such things."

"Okay, you guys," I say. "I thought this all was about the Russians preparing their stomp into Prague. But I've walked through another door, into another fantasyland overseen by our fuzzy Critical Path office, huh?"

"That's mostly correct," says the Wizard. "Though technically those stomping troops aren't Russian. They're Soviet or Warsaw Pact soldiers."

"Or maybe Mongols," says the Accountant. "You ready for teaching moment number four?"

"Oh God! You think you gotta give me stuff in little servings so I don't get so sick I throw up?"

"Something like that. You may've heard that it's against army regulations to station European-born US soldiers in Europe."

"No, that's not among the several pieces of info that've entered my brain yet. But it does make sense. And just for your records, I think we're on teaching moment number six or maybe number seven. And that doesn't include our previous strange discussion of secondary and tertiary agendas."

John pays me no attention. "The Soviets and East Germans have been known to compromise GIs born in, or with strong family ties to, areas east of the *steel curtain*. The possibility of pressuring a source to release information or secrets in exchange for keeping relatives safe is quite high, so the army doesn't allow it."

"Another conversation going east before it heads west?" I ask. "What's the deal?"

"Brian was born in Prague, Lynx is a Netherlander, and there are several Germans in our office. Then there's Sully who was born in

Boston, though both his parents are Irish IRA now living in Prague. I was born here, in Heidelberg, in 1939, while my mother was a doctoral student at Max Plank. My folks are Polish Catholics. Hitler had special plans for Polish Catholics, so my folks were forced to flee Hitler's Germany before the SS arrested, imprisoned, or shot them. My parents left overnight, abandoning everything they owned and cherished. They'd no chance of leaving Germany with anything but a hand-carried stash of books and papers.

"Even worse, Wall, three thousand Polish Catholic clergy were killed, many hundreds of churches and monasteries were looted, confiscated, closed, or destroyed. Priceless works of religious art and sacred objects were lost forever. Jews were targeted too. Hundreds of Jewish and Catholic clergy were eliminated as part of Hitler's effort to destroy Polish culture. Our people hid or buried much religious artwork to keep it out of Hitler's, and later Stalin's hands."

"And this means something to me, because?"

"It means two things, Wall. First, we," he motions to Brian and himself, "are here quasi-illegally, or at least contrary to army regulations. And second, much of the physical evidence of our past has been hidden by our families who still live in Warsaw or Prague. Our task is to find ways to move our Polish family treasures, both synagogue and church treasures, to new safe homes on the west side of the Iron Curtain."

"I don't think I want to know more, do I?"

"You don't need to know more. Just remember, we two, and several others at the Critical Path office, are stationed here in Heidelberg in a position from which we can actually move things west through that curtain. Can you guess what that means?"

"Someone in some high place loves you, huh?"

"There's a lot of love working here, Wall. Just remember that."

"I gotta ask if other guys like you, elsewhere in Europe, work on this so called tertiary agenda? And do they also use US-born, non-European guys, like me, in their operations?"

"I don't know the answer," Brian says. "I don't know any names. Everyone has codenames, so no one's exposed. That answer your question?"

"I haven't the slightest idea."

"Good," John says. Then he does the u-turn. "I think you'd best buy yourself a backpack, pack it, and keep it in the office. Sometimes we're required to do inspection trips, like instantly. Gotta be prepared."

"I already have mine, John. It's the one thing the army decided I needed while I was playing beach bum in New Jersey. My backpack's always ready to go, just in case I gotta run to Canada."

"What ya think about that, Mr. Accountant?" asks the Driver. "Farm Boy's well prepared."

10 THE 3RD HEIDELBERG STORY

Constructing Critical Path Diagram fantasies for NATO generals is not exhaustive work and consumes little time. The talented bunch in our office, therefore, must keep their minds occupied, civilian talents honed, and mental states in the sane range. The Wizard's got his doctoral thesis, a massive piece of theoretical mathematics, which attempts to uncover the shape of the expanding blast cloud resulting from the cosmic Big Bang. Or, he might be vacantly doodling. Who could know?

One guy's giving golf lessons to shellshocked Vietnam veterans in need of therapy. A History MA is writing a book aligning various famous chessboard strategies to success or failure in actual historical military campaigns. The Cartoonist, as his name suggests, cartoons. He provides content for a Los Angeles based, monthly anti-war magazine, while also preparing a crude and virulent anti-Vietnam War graphic novel. Joseph Brunelli, the Painter, built himself a studio in a storage room, where he copies eighteenth century religious paintings from color photographs. He told me that before the Big War, the originals of these paintings hung on the walls of Polish and possibly Czech churches. He keeps to himself. As an artist, he cannot fraternize with guys like me—guys planning unmitigated nuclear disaster on a continental scale.

I've a problem similar to these guys. It's called 'career-interruptus.' I must keep my mind sharp and my architectural skills honed for my future architectural career, so I've entered the Prix de Roma, a design competition for recently graduated architects. Like my friend, Joseph, I cannot risk the specter of nuclear conflagration seeping in to infect my creative effort. Therefore, when the weather permits, I'll take my drawing board into the garden south of the headquarters building, or up to the castle gardens, and work sitting on the grass braced against a tree.

Even our house general, the Clappsaddle, is working hard at leisure. He's moved a few walls and floors downstairs to build an indoor driving range and spends days ruined by inclement weather driving golf balls into netting. Not everyone is goofing off. Our Critical Path office has several dozen civilians laboring forty hours a week phoning people and analyzing stuff, some of which may have critical value. These civilians work for the army, the Defense Department, the CIA, or other unknown entities. Many are former US military who remain in their technical fields but are now paid civilian consultants to the army, the Defense Department, the CIA, or other entities. None of these non-soldiers wear soldier-style uniforms, and few wear suits or other civilian-type office uniforms.

Few of us enlisted men care diddlybunk about uniforms either. We don't worry about keeping the various parts clean, ironed, or polished. Polishing shoes, buttoning jackets, wearing ties or hats, even the long-standing army custom of saluting officers, are things not much done in the headquarters building. It's difficult to enforce a dress code when enlisted draftees are running the place. And overseeing this casual dress code nonsense is Lt. General Bekker, who may or may not be dressed appropriately. It's hard to know, because he's difficult to see.

Many members of the Critical Path office wear filthy, tattered army uniforms as a positive statement of protesting the army's conduct in Vietnam. Many of us keep a clothes change at our desk so we can change from protest mode into work mode of shorts and T-shirt in the summer and sweaters or sweatshirts in the winter. And most guys wear tennis shoes with their uncleaned and unrepaired uniforms. One's not expected to spit-shine tennis shoes. One exception to the nonchalant attitude toward uniforms is the Wizard, who used to be an army guy but is now a civilian consultant. In protest of the Vietnam War, he wears faux army fatigues constructed by his multi-talented seamstress wife.

The few officers wandering around don't usually wear uniforms either. That way they can patrol the halls without continuously arguing with enlisted guys who don't engage in saluting. Clappsaddle wears golfing duds. Some guys slap him on the back, yell fore at him in the hall, or offer him donuts, but few actually salute him. We all think this casual comradery stuff's better than saluting. Makes the workplace more relaxed. Such nonchalance, however, does cause a problem when we Critical Path guys must interface with Corps of Engineer officers working the construction projects near Fulda or Schwäbisch Gmünd. Those professional officers expect privates to be wearing uniforms and saluting them.

Our ghost general is concerned for the efficiency, safety, and comfort of his young Critical Path monitors. He knows we must spend time in the mud fields confronting brash young Corps of Engineer lieutenants who are ignorant of modern computerized construction planning procedures, or with scheduling issues and construction concerns. Occasionally we must criticize sassy young officers, and we can't get sidetracked worrying about who's supposed to be saluting whom.

So, we don't wear army uniforms, and we don't drive army jeeps. Also, Lt. General Bekker knows if we act like army guys we'll be unable to maintain our cover in the dirty *gasthauses* we find ourselves drinking beer in while inspecting various other things out there along the *steel fence*.

Such dresscode noncompliance has a serious secondary aspect. Most Americans, without even trying, or even after some effort at trying, stick out like sore thumbs here in Heidelberg because it's

1967. It's a time when no self-respecting college student bathes frequently. Even at mild US campuses in 1967, any military guy, even in civilian clothes, will be instantly recognized as an interloper. And the main giveaway is hair.

No matter if an American soldier or civilian employee slouches or sloppily dresses himself in an effort to blend in with this sloppily dressed college crowd, his military haircut will give him away. Therefore, for the furtive business we undertake for the ghost general, it's absolutely essential we not stand out as foreign substances on the fabric of the German countryside. We must not broadcast our military affiliation. We must blend in with forlorn looking French, Polish, and Czech students living in Heidelberg, and so we hang in the central city dressed as vagabonds. Many members of the American military establishment do not often recognize us Critical Path Analysis guys, even in the hallway of the headquarters building.

We Critical Path Analysis guys are often stopped and questioned at the army PX, or the army gas station, or the army officers' club. Technically, we're not even allowed into the officers' club, but Lt. General Bekker thinks that since his guys are pretending to be general staff officers, and since they're acting as some manner of undercover diplomats to the Eastern Block refugee population in Heidelberg, their ability to use the officers' club as a protected venue in their pseudo-ambassadorial work should be honored by the officer corps. We therefore carry passes issued by Lt. General Bekker which allow us, and our guests, access *into* the officers' club. This is a big deal since, to my knowledge, the officers' club, being on US and not German soil, has the only bar in Heidelberg that can legally serve both Old Speckled Hen and Guinness, perky beers that John and I, respectively, have taken a liking to.

11 The 1st Zurich Story

On this beautiful day in mid-September, the standard issue clouds are on vacation, so John, Lynx, and I decide to play hooky also. We hike to the castle, sit on a stone bench near a gurgling fountain, eat our fruit and Bundt cake, and discuss elements of Lynx's thesis concerning mathematical inconsistencies in the Big Bang Theory. Many other visitors frolic on the lawns, stroll through the massive flower gardens, admire the statuary, and enjoy various waterworks bubbling and geysering. Turning maples and birch trees add to the dramatics.

Eventually we break from cosmology and break out the Frisbee. We find space on the lawn and arrange ourselves in a rough triangular formation about thirty meters apart, and we toss the yellow disc one to the other such as to require the recipient to do a bit of strategic running to meet the disk when it finally floats down to catchable altitude. John gets too much air under his toss. The Frisbee arcs up, gets caught in the breeze, then starts a long curving descent, such that both Lynx and I immediately recognize the thing's going to drop into the no-man's-land between us. We both sprint toward the spot where we sense it'll land. I get there first, but catching the disk requires a stretched out dive to grab it just before it, and I, both hit the well-manicured turf.

"Nicely done!" John yells. "You're a lot faster than a short pudgy guy has any right to be."

"First, I keep my speed well cloaked until a need requires it, Mr. Driver. You know about manufacturing misconceptions, that sort of thing? And second, I'm not pudgy. I prefer words like solid or linebackeresque."

"You ever participated in a road rally, Farm Boy? Know what that is?"

"I appreciate the nifty right angle turn, Driver. Nicely done, yourself! And the answer is no, although I've a vague idea of what's involved in one. Why would you possibly ask?"

"Because for the next two weekends you and I are going to participate in road rallies over by the *steel gauze*. I am, of course, the Driver. So that makes you the Navigator."

"I'm unaware of that schedule. And what's with this navigator stuff? Thought I was Farm Boy."

"We are," says Lynx, "each of us, many different people. Names change as quickly as do schedules. Ain't no sense posting 'em."

"I'm going to Schwäbisch Gmünd on Monday. We'll practice your road rally skills on the drive. It'll make for a fun trip."

★★★

John's VW Beetle—he calls her Rosie for reasons only he, and maybe Marieka, know—is a sophisticated machine, well equipped for road rallies, but also for espionage. John's uncle Lech is a race circuit mechanic working for Team Lotus, a Formula-1 racing consortium based in England. And last winter Lech customized John's Rosie in the Team Lotus shop. He rebored the engine, added a supercharger, and installed race tempered struts and brackets, tires with steel belts, a hidden shortwave radio receiver, a spoiler arcing over the engine compartment, and several electronically locked compartments for hiding the contraband John might find himself, at times, carrying across international boundaries. It has twice the horsepower of showroom models and more gauges than an airliner. It's candy-apple red, makes real cool noises, and has a very small "Team Lotus Racing, London" painted on the left rear edge of the spoiler. John regularly flies it above 160 kph on some fairly rough terrain. His uncle also taught him how to drive the thing.

At this first rally, John instructs me, the navigator, to maneuver us into finishing between sixth and tenth. He knows he's got the talent and hidden mechanical power to win outright, but we're not going to do that. In order to prevent us from making too high a finish, we stop and pretend to adjust the tension on a strut or the gas flow through the carburetor. Such technical delays will save him the publicity of having our picture appear in a local paper holding a trophy.

★★★

John and I have just completed our second rally, laid out over country roads near the Iron Curtain northeast of Fulda, in the general area where some nuclear missile bunkers are supposedly being constructed. As we drive, John clears up the fog surrounding Fulda. I learn there is no town by the name of Fulda. It is short for the Fulda Gap, the valley where the Soviet invasion is expected to occur.

I get to showcase my talent for never getting lost. I manage to waste some time sneaking down back roads looking for extraneous construction equipment, albeit without actually managing to see any. And I'm still able to finish us nicely in seventh place.

To celebrate a successful contest, several participants retire to a local *gasthaus* to review the day's fun and compensate for the day's menu of granola bars and sausage sticks. After the meal, John makes sure I'm comfortable among the other celebrants, then whispers in my ear, "I've gotta change Rosie's oil. Then I gotta talk to a guy. Be back at 1904. Grab some sleep if you can. We'll leave immediately for Zurich."

Since I'm sitting at a long table in the midst of other sweaty rally contestants, I'm not in the right position to yell, "Zurich? You're crazy. I've got a Critical Path Network to massage tomorrow, and…"

I should have realized something strange was coming. John's got his full beard and a black watch cap covering his curls. He looks less like the front man for a rock band and more like a longshoreman or coal miner. I'm wondering if I should've grown my beard also, so as to respect his disguise. Then I remember what Lynx told me—I must be flexible. I must adapt to the situation. I've got my backpack, and it's well stocked. I'm prepared for whatever schedule exists in John's head. Wow! I'm gonna see Zurich! It's supposed to be a pleasant place.

★★★

John never uses even-hour and half-hour marks for scheduling his daily adventures. Lynx told me that's an IRA shorthand Sully taught them. If contact X tells you he'll meet you in Fulda at 1630, you immediately know it's a trap, because whenever contact X sets a time in Fulda it will end with a four. John told me he'd return at 1904. I understand if he's not in sight by 1914, I must leave immediately before something explodes.

I'm anxious but right on schedule at 1904. And well before any device is set to detonate, John walks in, slides over to the bar for a beer, then casually sits next to me.

"Hi, Wall! My rowdy friends treatin' you right?" He slaps me on the shoulder and instantly controls the conversation, like he's got all night to play.

"I didn't have time to take a nap," I say. "Your friends, being quite rowdy, kept me awake."

I am, however, quick enough to realize the language shift from German into Polish. Whatever's being discussed now's of interest only to John and his Polish buddies. What that means, I can only imagine.

"Okay, Wall." John returns to English. "Let's hit the road. Say goodbye to your new friends." We hug and backslap as if that confirms this farm boy from Iowa means something special to a group of possible Polish and East German road rally guys, or potential international spies, or ersatz church art connoisseurs who somehow found themselves partying together in a neighborhood *gasthaus* in a village northeast, I think, of Fulda.

As John and I exit the *gasthaus,* he bumps my shoulder to get my attention, then points to my left. I turn and see, out half a kilometer distant, a row of what look like streetlights spaced evenly along what I assume is a roadway.

"Streetlights, huh? I'm tellin' myself they're not normal streetlights, right?"

"No, they're not, Wall. Look carefully. There's shimmering on the ground between those lights where one should see vehicles if it were a road."

"Okay? I'm supposed to see nonexistent cars not driving on something not a road which is lit by non-streetlamps. That right?"

"Close! You're actually looking at the famous Iron Curtain. Beyond those lights is East Germany. How about that? You wanna crawl through the mine fields and touch it? Get close enough to breathe some communist air?"

"It looks as good as it'll ever look," I say. "It's as close as I'll ever get."

"Well, Farm Boy," he says as he removes his watch cap and shakes his curls free, "we'll see about that!"

★★★

Uncle Lech's improvements allow us to drive Rosie straight through the night. John and I share the driving to stay sharp, like drivers on twenty-four-hour endurance runs. As we enter the western Zurich suburbs, John says, "Okay, I'll navigate through the maze to get to Jacob's place. But you pay attention. Next time you'll do this by yourself."

John drives into the center city, through the *Hauptbahnhofplatz*, along the southern shore of the *Zurichzee*, then cuts sharply onto a side street headed away from the lake. He turns into a driveway, and the garage door rises exposing a huge, several-car garage. The door closes immediately, even before John quiets Rosie's engine. A distinguished looking man sporting a professionally-manicured, graying beard stands inside the door.

"Uncle Jacob!" says John. "It's great to see you!"

"Everything go smoothly?"

"No problems. Everything's good. Come here, Wall. This is my favorite uncle, Jacob Kritzner. Or, really, he's Marieka's favorite uncle."

"It's a pleasure to meet you, sir."

"Thank you, Wall, for helping us. Are you hungry?"

"We need sleep right now, Uncle Jacob. Give us three, four hours, and then we'll be ready for one of your exceptional breakfasts."

"Maybe fresh trout from my cousin in Zug. Pan fried in butter with garlic, a little cheese and tomato. Ach, you never tasted anything so good."

"You're in for a treat, Wall. Jacob's an expert with lake trout."

John and I head up a stairway. "There're things you need to know about Jacob."

"Lot's a stuff I need to know. And probably some it's best I don't know, huh?"

"Three decades ago, before even the idea of an Iron Curtain, Marieka's parents and several members of their extended families—teachers, scientists, musicians, and medical doctors—saw the danger signs looming and left Warsaw in the middle of the night, before the Germans invaded. Some, like Jacob's family, settled with relatives in Zurich and others, like Marieka's family, in southern France. Marieka's uncle Jacob is now head of Gastroenterology at Zurich Zentrale Hospital."

"All this chronology is nifty stuff, John. But what's it got to do with me?"

"Jacob also wears another hat. He's the link between the material repatriation organizations operating in the East Bloc countries and the organizations that return the recovered valuables to their rightful owners now living in western Europe, the United States, and Canada."

"And just so I know in case my mother asks me, where do I fit in with respect to those two organizations? And also, why shouldn't I immediately hitchhike myself to Greece? Maybe find myself a monastery?"

12 THE NECKARSTEINACH STORY

Lieutenant General Alvin W. Bekker is a generous and understanding superior officer. At least that's true for whoever's signing his papers. Typical of his largess is his attitude regarding approval of leave time. The official army leave form consists of five sheets: Clappsaddle's copy, the duty office, paymaster, leave clerk's copy, and the applicant's copy.

Brian Olsen, the Accountant, shows me how to fill the thing out for maximum efficiency. "Say you need fourteen days. You mark fourteen in the box on sheets one, two, and five. Then insert zero days on the paymaster's copies three and four. That way you can be gone as long as you want, although nobody in the records or personnel offices think you're gone, and they don't deduct leave time from your account."

"That's called cheating, right?"

"Oh, I don't think so. We're maximizing system flexibility so as to maximize output."

"Wow! Sounds impressive. Who wouldn't want that?"

"Exactly! Our ghost general must insist you do this because, as you might understand from your recent trip to Zurich, you'll be away from Heidelberg often for secondary and tertiary agenda work, for line-of-duty education, and for career advancement. Though understand, the career being advanced refers to your personal career."

"As I grow, so the army grows?"

"Well said! Lieutenant General Bekker has even authorized learning to ski seminars in Garmisch-Partinkirchen. And two guys spent two weeks at the Vienna Konzerthaus supposedly attending a correspondence course titled Designing a Cello Repertoire. That earned them a commendation for ingenuity from our ghost general."

"Devious and underhanded," I say, "but neat. Should I be worried why I'll need that much leave? The possibilities arouse my wanderlust. Makes me think I need a vacation before the tension of such necessary travel becomes unbearable."

"That seems a reasonable thought."

"I could run off to Paris. Lots of architecture to study there."

"Good choice. Your train will arrive at Gare du Oest. There's a great little *gasthaus* on the Rue de Ecole du Medicin near the Sorbonne. The owner's a friend of our ghost general. And Notre Dame's but a ten-minute walk."

One of the Lt. General Bekkers in the room says, "I'll complete your paperwork this afternoon."

The Paris trip changed my perception of the olive drab world into which this army's immersed me. It allowed me to switch my hat from army to artist. The train traveled through Karlsruhe and crossed into France near Strasbourg. Shortly thereafter I was startled by the sudden appearance of a spear of sunlight thrown across the little fold-down table on which I'd spread out my map of Paris. I'd forgotten about sunlight, hadn't seen it for a while. It may've been outlawed in Germany. By the time I disembarked at the Gare du Oest, only a few, little, fluffy white marshmallows remained floating in a limitless expanse of bright blue. Gone were dark gray things skimming over the hilltops, condensing the already heavy atmosphere beneath them. Gone was the sense of doom and dismemberment, of drab olives, and even of Vietnam. I walked along the Seine, eagerly breathing in this undemanding, uplifting, atmospheric bouquet. My mind throws me no images of nuclear weapon bunkers, road rallies, John's import-export business, and especially Vietnam.

★★★

The Saturday after I return from Paris I awake to an amazing sight, a beautiful clear sky above my lovely Neckar Valley. John and Lynx tell me it's against German regulations to waste a day like this indoors. Several residents of Sully's hotel organize a picnic and invite me along. By late morning our group's having a good time picnicking in a secluded grassy meadow on the northern bank of the Neckar, a dozen kilometers upstream from Sully's hotel, near the village of Neckarsteinach.

I'm prone on a flat, moss-covered rock on the north bank of this black river, playing scientist. I watch dozens of recently hatched minnows, or the German equivalent of minnows, buzz around in a tight clockwise swirl in a shallow pool of gurgling black water. I'm not doing this minnow watching alone.

"Wow, look at 'em go! You think baby fish get dizzy?" asks Truck Girrard. He's Lynx's four-year-old son, and he's prone on a second flat rock adjacent to mine. He sticks his chubby finger into the pool and stirs the blackish water counterclockwise in an attempt to get the swarming fry to change direction.

"I don't think that'll work, Truck. The fish aren't swimming. They're just being spun by the water. It's the water, powered by the river's current, that's doing the swirling, not the fishies."

"Okay! Just thought they might enjoy looking at life differently."

"Perhaps they might," I say. "That's not a bad thought. You're one conscientious guy." His father walks up and stands a few meters away on the bank and watches us two mismatched kids work our science project. I roll onto my side and look up at him.

"Why'd ya call him Truck? What's that story?"

"I suppose I overcompensated for my folks naming us kids after cats," Lynx says. "I've got two sisters, Puma and Tigre, and I didn't want my son stuck with a similar gender ambiguous name. We were living in California then, and Truck sounded pretty good to our friends at Berkeley. At least it sounded masculine. I'm having second thoughts. Should've called him Diesel, a masculine Germanic name, with a similar reference to machines. At least that's two syllables, so it has dimension! We're thinking of changing his name, though we haven't convinced him."

"I've gotten used to Truck, Dad. It's a good name. Think tough, dependable, hardworking."

"He's a born scientist, Lynx. And an artist!"

"Yeah! And a handful! I'm supposed to inform you nature lovers that the food's ready. Time to stop whatever research you're doing and come up to the blankets so we can eat."

I get up and help Truck hop over a few rocks to solid ground. Truck jumps into his father's arms, and the three of us head up the slight hill on a narrow path beaten into the low weeds, then across the grassed field toward the food.

Four blankets are spread out on a mown, grassy area ten meters above the river. In front of us, every so often, a small diesel barge chugs past bringing some bulk material to some port farther up or down the Neckar. Truck'll wave and shout and usually gets the boatman to wave back and his dog to bark. Across the river a wooded hill rises steeply, immediately from the water's edge up for a couple hundred meters. The steepness assures that most of the river surface on that side remains in shadow most of the day. It's an excellent fishing spot. And it is isolated.

Our isolation's also guaranteed by the electrified fence and the demonic power, or at least the misunderstood scientific power, inherent in the monstrous, white, brilliantly sunlit, concrete dome. It looms like St. Peter's in the Vatican, a hundred meters into the sky behind us on the other side of that electric fence.

Marieka, because of her association with the Max Planck Institute, has access to this picnic and fishing area adjacent to the Neckarsteinach atomic reactor site, because a portion of the equipment housed inside that electric fence belongs to Max Planck. This reactor has a degree of research function in addition to its power generating function.

Marieka knows where the concealed trail exits from the entry road and then weaves through the woods ending at this bucolic picnic and fishing area, and she knows the combination to the gate's lock. Matters being discussed today on these blankets in this meadow have nothing to do with any critical paths the US Army's constructing. Today we're supposed to enjoy a beautiful autumn afternoon amidst fluttering leaves and gurgling water.

After the food's consumed and the port distributed, John stands, claps his hands, and addresses the group. "I think now's a good time to confront Wall with teaching moment number six."

I notice he's morphed into his 'the Driver's' persona even though today he's clean shaven.

"I'm sorry, John," I say quickly. "No can do. I'm on a picnic, and it's the weekend. Someone, maybe it was Sully, told me there's no business talk allowed on the weekend. Also, I've been counting. It's teaching moment number eight."

"Stuff it, Wall," says the Accountant. "You've been invited here today to soften you up, make you pliable, ease your anxiety, and put you in a positive frame of mind. You telling me that hasn't worked yet? You need more port?"

"I'm relaxing with my friends on a picturesque piece of real estate, and I am not—"

"You're being a jerk, Wall," says Rhoda. "Although the work here's dangerous, it's not likely to be as fatal as Vietnam. Tense, confusing, and in some folk's distorted vision, vaguely illegal. But not life threatening, for you anyway, I should think."

"Words like 'vaguely-illegal,' and 'for you anyway' bother me. As opposed to who? You guys?"

"Exactly! You're a US born, US citizen traveling on a US Army passport. You are untouchable here. You can go almost anywhere in Europe legally and with nobody asking you questions, and that's especially important with regards to East Berlin, Norway, Austria, and Switzerland. And international protocols other than execution are in place if you're caught where you shouldn't be. Normal army personnel like you have certain privileges. Most of us…" she swirls around and points to her blanket mates, "aren't so lucky. Most of us have dual citizenship because our parents were born on the other side of the curtain and still have extended families living over there. Chances are, if we're stopped and questioned on that east side, despite the official protocols concerning such stoppages, you'll never hear from us again. No protocols, other than the knife, exist for us if they catch any of us wandering around over there."

"But not for guys like you," says Lynx. "There are protocols in place to protect you over there."

"Even our ghost general has no power east of the Iron Curtain," says the Driver.

"Be thankful you can do more to help your fellow humans by helping us here than you could ever do crawlin' through the Asian jungles," says Marieka.

A barge chugs into view, heading downriver toward Mannheim. As I'm concentrating on the barge, the Driver says, "I think it's time you met the boss."

I quickly consider two questions. First, I'd assumed Driver is the brains behind this rather unique group of freedom fighters. If it's not him, who? And second, did I just hear Marieka threaten me with Vietnam if I didn't answer her question with 'yes'? I watch the Driver's eyes. They're purposely intent on the barge. It's chugging along with nary a wake, while its German shepherd barks at us from its deck. Seems maybe the Driver's expecting 'the big boss' to step off that barge, walk across the water's surface, climb up the bank, and glide across the grass to our blanket.

"Wake up, Wall," says the Driver. "Concentrate. You've met Marta, your new friend Truck's mother. She's the glue that holds the whole informal organization together, and she provides the power source for our operation."

Marta, dressed as I'll forever picture her, wears an Amish style hippie dress and stands barefoot, holding Truck on her shoulder, gently rocking him toward sleep. His eyes are closed, and he's almost there. Her eyes also appear headed toward sleep. She's either very relaxed or in a hypnotic trance, like she's back at Berkeley grooving to the Grateful Dead.

"You've made quite an impression on my son, Wall. He tells me you know about fishies and other 'good stuff,' whatever that means."

"Truck's a sharp kid, Marta. We had a good time."

"I was still a child," she says as she looks down at him sleeping on her shoulder and pushes a curl out of his ear, "and as innocent as Truck, when they executed my father... a single bullet to his forehead, on the street in front of our house, as I watched from our dining room window." Marta reports this with no obvious emotion. She's swaying gently with her son.

This bucolic, almost religious, Madonna and Child figure standing barefoot in the grass beside a river, accompanied by soft prayer-like words, instantly burn into my brain. I doubt she'll ever fade away.

"My mother and two brothers remain in Poland. One's still in jail. I want them out, Wall. I want that Iron Curtain removed. Families must be made whole, our churches rebuilt, our people and property reunited. You must help me tear holes in that fence, Wall."

I see a mother, with her sleeping child on her shoulder, asking for my help. I can imagine but one answer to her plea. "I'm human, Marta. And although I know what 'human' technically means,

I think morally it means I must say 'yes, I will help.' I've no choice, do I?"

"I don't think you do," says John. "Though Marta will, single-handedly, tear that *metal gauze* down with or without your help, we'll be honored if you choose to help us. And you realize the pressure is increasing exponentially. Witness our discussion with our Czech friends the other day at the *gasthaus*."

"The Mongols have the tanks," says Lynx, "but we have Marta. I believe the advantage is ours."

"Tensions in the east are accelerating," says Marta. "We must increase our transportation capacity. How soon can you get yourself a car?"

13 The 360 on the Autobahn Story

I initiate discussions with the Fiat dealer in Heidelberg, eventually resulting in my purchase of a bright yellow, Fiat 850 Spider convertible. That's eight-hundred-fifty cubic centimeters! Not even one liter! Motorcycles and yard tractors have bigger engines. I'll have trouble besting old ladies in their Audis. But the top comes down, it handles beautifully, and it'll allow me to ease the tertiary agenda's burden. John convinced our ghost general to cosign a bridge loan for the down payment from the USAEUR credit union. Eventually, I'll refinance it with the local bank back in Iowa that held the paper on my Triumph. Because I plan to bring the thing home with me, it must be outfitted for the US market. Fiat does that outfitting in Stuttgart, so I traveled down there to accept delivery.

Propelled by my little Fiat, I'm now equipped to cruise western Europe running errands for the Driver and our ghost general. Now I can also start planning my grand tour to study historic and modern European architecture in preparation for an academic position after I'm released from the olive drab machine and allowed reentry into the real world. That I find myself actually planning my own future startles me. It means the specter of dying in Vietnam may be releasing its hold on me, allowing me to suspect there may actually be a future in my future.

★★★

In this expanded atmosphere of personalized empowerment, my ghost general allows me to eschew the house jet and drive my Spider to the next meeting in Brussels. And because the Cartoonist is running in deadline mode with his graphic novel, the Driver's my passenger today. He'll be running the projector.

It's a cold, bleak morning... overcast and spiced with a severe western wind. The gusty wind plays sneaky little games with my little car, especially in areas of open industrial and farm country. Somewhere near Köblenz, the landscape changes quickly when the Autobahn slices a long and fairly straight-line hole through a dense forest of tall, old-growth pine. In this green tunnel we're not pestered by that crosswind and are comfortably flying straight north on a relatively traffic-free Autobahn.

For a Fiat 850 loaded with two passengers and their gear, the word 'flying' is perhaps an exaggeration, but we're on schedule. A slight snow is swirling about. The air temperature hovers within a degree of freezing. The road surface is thinking about turning slick. After eight or nine kilometers of dense forest, I see a brightness a kilometer ahead, suggesting to me that this tree-formed tunnel might be ending. It's possible this claustrophobic forest landscape will soon open up. A large, yellow sign with flashing orange lights agrees. The squiggly-lined drawing on it suggests that heavy winds are probable as the road leaves the protection of the trees, and therefore we drivers should note this dangerous condition and slow down. I take my foot off the gas, but I do not fool with the brakes.

"Hey, John," I say. "I'm seeing super-bright lights behind me, and they're closing very fast. Could they be cops?"

John turns for a look. "It's a Porsche. That guy's no cop. He's an idiot! See the snow blowing across the road ahead? He should pass us before we leave the woods. We'll let the wind smash him first."

I've eased off the gas, but it's slippery so I don't risk my brakes. The red Porsche is half a car length in front of us when the tree cover abruptly ends. Being in the left lane, the Porsche gets the full blast of the west wind. For a second or so, the wind's full power is blocked from punching my Fiat. It does, however blast that red Porsche and causes the driver to lose purchase on the slippery pavement. He begins a very graceful spin on the powder-snow-covered road.

Instantly, the scene goes slow motion. The red Porsche—John tells me it's a brand new one—does a smooth, even beguiling, 180-degree spin as the wind blows him left to right, so that at one frantic point he's directly in front of me, in my lane, and both us drivers are looking hard at each other's eyeballs. The Porsche's spinning wheels are pushing him toward me! We're now partners in a high-speed polka. I've no choice. I must tap my brakes—once, twice, short quick stabs. I hope to prevent my own rotation but, pushed by the wind and with traction eased by my brake-work, the front of my Fiat begins its own slow, clockwise spin, just as the Porsche starts the completion of his 360 degree one. That powerful red Porsche and my dinky Fiat are waltzing on the Autobahn! As the Porsche completes its full circle, it regains purchase, and its driver somehow regains control, pulls out of his spin, and continues screaming down the highway, uncaring of the havoc he's left in his wake.

★★★

"It was a beautiful thing to watch," John says. It's the next afternoon, after the NATO presentation's completed, and we're having lunch with some of John's friends in the Brussels *gasthaus* where we've taken rooms for the night. "That Porsche completed his 360, somehow found purchase on the slick pavement, straightened himself out, and went screaming down the Autobahn like he'd practiced the maneuver. But, my man, Wall," he raises his stein in a toasting maneuver, "did an even better bit of driving!"

I sip some beer. "Nice you could enjoy it… I couldn't. I was busy keeping that Porsche off my front bumper. When I meet that idiot I'll smack him in the nose."

"Not likely you'll see him again."

"Wrong-o! I know exactly who that jerk is. His license—ROT GEIST—was maybe two meters from my eyeballs."

"A new red Porsche with RED GHOST tags?" says one of our new friends. "I've connections, Wall. An hour on the phone tomorrow, and I'll find the jerk."

"I gave his number to the polizei. They'll find him."

"I didn't notice his license," says John. "I was busy with some high-powered praying, and I'm convinced that made the difference."

A waitress comes over with more beer, then removes our dishes. John continues my story.

"Wall did a great piece of driving, and although our 360 spin was every bit a work of art as the Porsche's, we, unlike the Porsche, started our maneuver in the right-hand lane. We had no highway width to work with, and so, by the time we completed our 360-degree spin, the wind had pushed our right side tires off the pavement and onto the gravel shoulder, eventually digging into the grass."

I take over the narrative. "As my turning slowed, I managed to pull out of the spin just as the Porsche did, but by the time we stopped, all my tires except the driver-side front were on the grass and we're tilting backward, starting to slip down the berm."

"I open my window and lean out," John says. "It's too slippery to climb back up onto the road. Our only solution is to slide down. A grassy farm path runs parallel to the Autobahn's elevated berm. However, that farm lane's forty or fifty meters down, at the bottom of this forty-five-degree slope, covered in tall, icy, slippery grass. We're starting to slip down, so Wall puts it in first gear so he has some breaking against gravity, then beautifully power slides down this slippery slope in his toy car without flipping us over."

"Toy car?" I ask. "I believe your exact words at that time were, 'marvelous piece of machinery.' My Spider's rear engine weight kept that rear aimed downhill, and it's so low to the ground it couldn't flip. I'm glad we had my Spider and not your Rosie. She'd have rolled down that slope like a soccer ball and bounced like one when it hit the bottom."

"It took forever," says John, "slowly slip-sliding down that slope. But we did make it to that farm lane, then followed it back to a local farm. We really surprised that farmer. He watched us drive around cows, through his pasture, and into his yard."

"Great hospitality," I say. "Guy's wife filled us with pastries."

"A polizei patrol showed up in time for pastries too. They'd been in pursuit of that Porsche, saw the whole thing, and watched from the berm top as we smoothly exited at the bottom. Told me they were impressed. Many cars spin out at that point, but few survive undamaged. And they were thankful I got his plate number as they'd never been able to get close enough to read it."

Several days later, in a regrettable fit of candor, the Driver enthusiastically related this story to several of the officer corps after we'd returned to Heidelberg. Eventually this 360-degree story got to General Clappsaddle, who, in the only direct order anyone ever remembers him giving to any enlisted man at the headquarters building, forbade anyone from taking private transportation to those Brussels' meetings ever again. And he did that even though he admitted that this very entertaining story did not result in any physical or mechanical damage to either personnel or machinery. John suggested that unlike most Clappsaddle drivel, I'd best obey this order.

14 THE UNIVERSITY OF HEIDELBERG STORY

If I walk west through the Marktplatz from the front steps of the Heiliggeistkirche, then cross the street, I eventually approach an arched stone gateway, which allows me access into the ancient University of Heidelberg Commons. In the year 1386, a set of massive wooden doors was installed in this archway. They could be locked at appropriate times to protect students and faculty during episodes of civic unrest, or to shut out ideas which the local bishop or prince thought heretical or diabolic.

In the early 1960s, when parts of Germany were deliberately being walled off, the University of Heidelberg, seeking the opposite condition, opted for openness. That motive led to the removal of the badly deteriorated, heavy, wooden doors and the installation of a set of sliding glass doors. When closed, these frameless glass panels filled the entire opening and are only revealed by a slender vertical joint running top to bottom in the center. When opened, the glass leaves retreat into the stonework of the adjacent nine hundred-year-old stone wall such that no visual evidence of a barrier remains within the archway. It's a very neat visual trick.

Though used mostly by pedestrians, this archway is large enough to accommodate a delivery van or a small shuttle bus, yet small enough to prevent access to a post WWII model Soviet battle tank. Granted, even when closed, the glass door would offer little deterrence to a Soviet tank. If a Soviet tank positioned itself outside the commons gate, the battle for Europe would, by then, be over. The Iron Curtain would be toast and Heidelberg something similar. This glass gate forces me to realize that my job here in Heidelberg, in a nutshell, is to make sure no Soviet tank ever plants itself in front of this invisible door.

★★★

It's 1706 hours on the second Sunday in December 1967. It's cold and quite windy, and it's dark. These conditions have driven most patrons inside, though a few tables support hardy guys like us, huddled next to the gas-fired heating devices. Such conveniences make this roof garden at *Alte Brücke* the perfect place for a clandestine meeting. The Driver, the Accountant, the Innkeeper, and I have just completed such a meeting with one of The Driver's Polish associates, during which the word Berlin was often used. I said little. I mostly listened and did my job—I kept the beer mugs full. After our guest leaves, I signal the waitress for one more round for the four of us.

"Do I need to know any pieces of that conversation I didn't understand?" I ask. "My Polish is non-existent and my German minimal, and it's more suitable to non-technical conversation with my grandmother."

"It's not necessary you understand every word," says John. "You understand enough. And you'll pick it up quick. I wanted you here today to listen and learn so you will know we're deadly serious, and we're not alone."

"Should I be concerned that guys named O'Sullivan and Olson are speaking Polish and German out here? I should probably ask why you pseudo spies are sprachen zee Deutsch and Polski, rather than conversing in the native Anglaise? That wasn't to keep me in the dark, was it?"

"No! It's because Heidelberg's a tourist town. Visitors from the States and local army families," he nods at the table on the other side of the heating device, "hang around here. I can't have those people recognizing my English, asking me directions to the castle, or overhearing arguments about nuclear arsenal preparedness. They must see and hear us as natives. We don't bother them. We look strange and talk strange. They pay us no attention."

"Hey guys," says Brian, "we'd better get going. We've twenty minutes to get to the lecture."

"You've not been to one of her lectures before, have you, Wall?" asks Sully.

"I know nothing about what's happening. I go where John wants me to go. He makes sure I learn only important stuff."

"Every second Sunday she gives a lecture," says John. "They're very popular, so Marieka's saving us seats."

"Okay, I'll bite. Who's giving the lecture?"

They laugh. It's their little secret. They won't tell me.

We walk through the ancient stone gateway into the commons and approach a kiosk which will inform me of the reason I'm here. A metal holder offers a flier. John translates it for me: Marta Girrard, Visiting Lecturer on Medieval History from the University of California at Berkeley will lecture on "The Iron Curtain: The Certain Irony of a Medieval Device Dividing a Modern State."

"That's our Marta?" I ask. "No one told me she teaches here. How cool is that? Explains why little Truck has pretty much an adult vocabulary."

"It's not a big lecture hall," says John. "And it'll probably be filled."

The amphitheater dates from the fifteenth century. That's before slide projectors and microphones, though it's been updated with modern seating, sound, and lighting. We enter at the bottom, right of the stage, and I see seats rising at a sharp angle allowing the audience to feel intimate with the speaker. People seated in the audience can monitor the entry doors to watch for friends entering the room. And folks entering at the bottom easily spot friends already seated.

"There's Marieka," says John. He points where Snow White is sitting, a third of the way up the slope. I see her too. Everyone knows she's here. I could pick her out even without her dwarfs. I notice several admirers hovering, arguing their case, thinking they have a chance to make an impact. Lynx stands next to her, keeping the admirers at bay. He's transformed himself into a serious and quite formidable presence; the responsible husband of the speaker persona. He's wearing an expensive, dark gray business suit, and his white hair is tied in a neat braid banking down his back. His forehead is clear of medieval messages. He looks exactly what a doctoral candidate in Cosmic Mathematics should look like.

"You here to accept your Nobel Prize?" I ask.

"Not tonight. I'm practicing being serious. Thanks for coming. Marta appreciates your support. But you must be ready for her words, for the effect of the blast cloud she'll produce."

"You've let blast clouds infect your whole life, haven't you?" I ask. Distracted by my snippy remark, I don't notice this wizard wave his wand over the seats, though I do notice the atmosphere in the room suddenly change. The conversation din abates. Every eye focuses on the small figure in a black dress with a multicolored shawl covering her shoulders.

Marta's standing to the left side of the stage talking with another woman. Rather she's standing still as stone and watching the other woman's graphic arm movements trying to explain something. The other woman loses. The lights dim. The crowd settles into their upholstered chairs. Marta walks purposely to the center of the stage and stands transfixed, a prudent rational messenger from a saner and more reasonable world. She's illuminated by a small array of klieg lights. It appears there'll be no introduction.

"Guten abend!" She speaks softly in German, the official language of the school, though many in the audience are foreign—certainly many from places east of the *steel drapery*, places which are the subject of her talk.

"During the fifteenth century, scholars from this university transformed it into the strongest proponent in all of Europe of the Humanistic attitude toward learning, toward a physical understanding of our physical world. Strangely this humanistic path to the truth, what one now might consider a modern scientific attitude, was at that time called the Via Antique. The name was meant to force an opposition to the scholastic system used in most every university in Europe at the time, and which, for some interesting reason, had been known as the Via Modern.

"Indeed, Scholasticism was the modern way of learning ever since Thomas Aquinas, in the thirteenth century, more or less codified it as such. And Aquinas was right in that it was a modern path. It certainly was modern in respect to the ancient Greek and Roman learning methods used in the centuries long before him.

"Unfortunately, in our present time, far too many cultured and knowing people have returned to the late Middle Age, returned to modern learning and thrown away Humanism. They've reverted to intellectual scholasticism, toward a medieval mindset. They've returned to the ancient ways, the sarcastically named Via Modern.

"My friends, I'm convinced of the need to reinvigorate the Humanist effort on this campus. I believe this institution has the historical portfolio and the intellectual power to lead such a transition in Germany, in all of Europe, indeed, throughout the entire world. Though it is Humanism I am preaching, I will not call this new way Via Antique as they did in the fifteenth century. We are far past that. The appropriate word now is revolution. The old Via Antique is now the new Via Revolution!

"That is because no longer do bishops and kings have the power. Now people have the power! Therefore, I have power! And you have power! And you have the numbers. You, collectively are much more powerful than I am.

"I am urging both sides to throw away those ancient ways of the Via Modern. Embrace the concept of Humanism. Humanism means understanding that intelligent people, using their human brain, can build a society based on rational thought. We need armies of intellectuals on both sides of the divide working to subvert the intent of the Iron Curtain—non-military, liberal thinkers proposing humanistic even creative strategies that don't rely on, or perhaps even disdain, historical data, but which analyze the existing condition in the current operating political environment.

"The US Army and the NATO Army will resist this Humanist solution. They will not easily give up their weapons and armies. That unfortunately is going to take a long, long time. And our people will continue to suffer. It is too late for us. I'm convinced of that, but this must be a historical and generational struggle. And we must start the process now if we want our grandchildren to live as humans. We must start now!"

Perhaps the heating system has gone berserk. I wipe moisture from my forehead with my sleeve. I know Marta's right. As a divider between two countries or two cultures, any curtain, even an Iron Curtain, is in itself a feeble barrier. A curtain needs huge armies and concentrated weapons stationed along both sides to give something as flimsy as a curtain its strength as a barrier. This curtain needs NATO and USAEUR armies on the west, and Soviet and Warsaw Pact armies on the east, all composed of soldiers, officers, and civilian overlords who are governed by extremely conservative operating strategies. NATO's afraid Warsaw Pact armies will invade the west in a massive slogging ground war ordered along the lines of what Napoleon's army did centuries ago, though in the reverse direction of course, pushing from east into west.

On the opposite side, the Soviets fear the west will fire massive nuclear salvos from the new weapons they're amassing, then rush in and take control of the resulting nuclear wasteland. Both these fantasies are based on warring models from twenty-five or one hundred years ago; maybe even five hundred years ago when countries routinely sacrificed hundreds of thousands of men in mega battles like those depicted above the couch in the reception room of USAEUR headquarters. The historical fantasies were driven by nationalist and religious zealotry, which thought nothing of sacrificing millions of religious humans to the cause.

★★★

Our little group leaves the auditorium and begins the walk through the commons. Marieka grabs my left arm, and Marta takes my right. Marieka says, "We want you to see something, Wall. Walk with us." She points toward a low stone wall twenty meters into the dark.

"What can I see there?"

This wall encloses an area of hedging. Marta produces a tiny flashlight and trains it on two weathered bronze plates, each about ten centimeters square, inset flush with the wall top. Etched into the left-hand plate's surface are the words "Martin Knoll, 1416." And then, the right plate: "Anna Kirchner 1935."

Marieka explains. "These two plaques commemorate the two people murdered in this commons since the twelfth century." She reads from an information kiosk pamphlet: "In 1416 Mr. Knoll, a Hussite, was beaten to death by an angry mob following his lecture supporting Joseph Huss, the firebrand religious zealot burned by papal edict at the Council of Constance. Then in 1935, Mrs. Anna Kirchner, a twenty-three-year-old medical student, was shot to death by her uncle, Professor Dr. Herman Volmarr because she'd married Dr. Jacob Kirchner, a lecturer at the medical school. Dr. Kirchner was a Jew. And Dr. Volmarr, a Nazi with a leadership position, feared his advancement would be imperiled if he allowed his niece's marriage to continue. Jews were things to be detested, not to be married or be educated as doctors!"

I'm stunned. "That's your uncle Jacob Kirchner? Our Jacob?"

"Yes, Wall! This reprehensible deed inspires us all to help Jacob in his work. Hitler's savagery cemented expatriate Polish Catholics like John to expatriate Polish Jews like me. There is no curtain between us. We cry as one people!"

★★★

It's the next Sunday, and I'm bent over my drafting board in the Hotel Neckargamünd's library watching snow plopping heavy outside my window. Some Christmas freak decorated this room with hundreds of twinkly green and red things. They've forced me well into the spirit. Brandy's in my snifter, and church organ music's blasting on my radio. I'm trying to work. Now that I have my Spider I must use it for good purpose, so I'm organizing my travel schedule to support my Great Architectural History Tour. I've got maps and brochures spread out.

A knock on the door and John enters.

"Hey, Wall. I've been thinking about your 360-degree maneuver. I've got an idea."

"The 360's over, John. You should be thinking 'bout something else. My Christmas present, maybe."

"If you'd a hotter engine in that thing, it could've generated the power to pull you out of that 360 quicker, might have kept all four tires on the pavement, like that Porsche did. May have prevented us from needing to slip down that slope."

"A hotter engine? You think Santa Claus'll fit that down our chimney?" I take a peek over to the fireplace to make an assessment of the degree of Santa's difficulty.

"I'm thinking a different kind of magic. You know uncle Lech? He's a magician."

"I've never met him so I don't know him, and I don't think his doin' any wand waving around my car's gonna happen."

"Hey, give Lech a chance. He's a genius! Says he's got a line on a used Abarth supercharger. He could drop that baby into your car and boom! You got a rocket!"

"I don't want a rocket, John—"

"So I had this idea. Lech works for Team Lotus Racing in London. The German Grand Prix's in Hockenheim this year, April seventh. Team Lotus is sending several cars, and he's coming over too. Hockenheim's only twenty kilometers away on the Karlsruhe road. Lech says if you bring your Fiat, he'll look at it and see if he can fit that Abarth into it."

"I don't think so, John. I can't afford that."

"He's also sent us vouchers so we get into the track free, courtesy of Lotus Racing." John waves the vouchers in my face. "Merry Christmas, Wall!"

"I give up. Can't pass up a deal like that, can I? I'm working on my travel schedule for the next few months right now. I'll pencil in Hockenheim for April seventh."

15 THE 4TH HEIDELBERG STORY

It's three days before Christmas. I'm slumped in my usual position in an overstuffed chair in the hotel library, warmed by a halfway decent fire crackling in the stone fireplace. I'm reading a seasonally appropriate book, Dickens' *A Christmas Carol*. The three of them, John, Lynx, and Sully, burst through the door, stride across the room, and stand, straight line rigid, in front of me.

They make no impact at all! Nothing! I can't even see them.

"It's a snowy December evening," I pretend to read from my book. "So, a Polish guy, a Dutch guy and an Irish guy walk into this German bar. They're wearing long, gray mobster coats to hide their machine guns, and they're all chewing Juicy Fruit with an intensity that would terrify their own mothers—"

"I'll give you five bucks if you can come up with a punch line for that intro," says John.

"I don't need a punch line. You guys look pathetic. You gonna rob a bank?"

Sully holds up a shapeless gray vestment. "I've brought you a matching mobster coat. The Driver's taking us to a brothel for a *coterie du procurement*."

"Sexy sounding French words do nothing for me. And my machine gun's in the shop. I think I'll pass. You guys knock yourselves out."

"Short term, you'll be secure staying here and cuddling with Dickens," says Lynx. "But you gotta think long term. You gonna be safe several months from now? When those Mongols come rumbling across the *Alte Brücke*?"

"Oh, for God's sake, Lynx, that's pathetic! You're paying too much attention to Clappsaddle's reverse-Napoleonic fantasies."

"We don't think you want to stay in that chair." John's tone suggests he's thrown me an order and not a casual request. "It's snowing, cold, and dreary out there. Seems the ideal time to get you to a brothel. Especially since Sully's taking his old gray Citroën."

"So, if this *coterie du procurement* is such enchanting entertainment, why's Sully taking his rusty Citroën? Why not use your pretty Rosie? She's the ideal car for mobsters looking for a party in a brothel, for God's sake."

"We're headed into a working-class area of town unfrequented by Americans, or even modern thinking Germans. Any flashy car, such as my bright red Rosie, or Lynx's blue Volvo, even your colorful but underpowered Fiat, will draw unwanted attention. We've got to be stealthy tonight. You're gonna see nothin' but gray cars bringing gray guys to this gray party."

"Gray and party don't usually come in the same salad, guys, so I—"

Sully throws the standard issue, dark gray coat at me. "You can't wear your effervescent ski parka. You'll attract the wrong crowd. This coat will do the trick. It's the serious diplomat look."

"Flashy brothel girls don't party with guys wearin' gray coats. Even Dickens wouldn't write that."

"Next thing we'll work on, gettin' you a flashier reading list." They laugh as we stumble out into the snow, one gray blob after another.

After a half hour drive to western Heidelberg, Sully finds the neighborhood he's supposed to find and manufactures a parking space by bouncing the passenger side tires up onto the sidewalk and parking in the German manner, as the several other cars here have done. It's a narrow street, and two cars cannot pass if one side doesn't park on the sidewalk. The street's lined with four-story masonry blocks. Most of the grade-level businesses have closed, and the upper level residences have their shutters locked. A few flickering neon business signs add a pinch of pastel. A lonely lamp across the street at mid-block throws a circle of dirty yellow on the new snow. Everything else is gray. No Christmas cheer around; could be it's illegal here, or celebrated in May, or something.

We jaywalk across the cobbles toward that streetlamp. I turn and look at Sully's gray Citroën. It's almost vanished. It's blended itself into the background. Swirling snow enhances the camouflage, effectively forcing everything over a few meters distant into that background. Gray, furtive, and vaguely human forms, bundled, hooded, and scarf wrapped against the blowing snow, occasionally emerge from that background and brush past us on the narrow walk.

I turn as passersby pass and watch them to make sure they disappear as they're supposed to do.

"Seems to me, Wall, it's the ideal night for a *coterie du procurement* at a brothel. What do ya think?"

"You gonna tell me what story's being told here, Driver? Like other things I've witnessed in Heidelberg, seems neither the reason for this party nor the choice of the brothel as venue are important, though something quite important apparently will happen in this brothel during the time this party's happening. I sense red lights flashing, but they're not telling me beware of brothel, they're tellin' me beware of Mr. Driver. Makes me think some Dickens character might show up tonight."

"This story's more intriguing than your Dickens. It's almost about romance. It's about this German guy trying to get his daughter to Buffalo."

"What? Like Buffalo in New York? That's plain screwy, John. Whatever *coterie du procurement* means, it ain't nothin' 'bout romance, right?"

"Wrong, Wall. Let's take one Joseph Braun, a German engineer working in Clappsaddle's accounting office. His cubicle is back by the water cooler. You must have run across him... big German guy, small blond mustache. He's been trying to attach his daughter to an American soldier, trolling for a GI who'll take her back to the US and thus away from the turmoil and unrest here in Germany. The daughter, though not beautiful, is healthy, blond, and buxom in a beerhall-waitress way. And she loves to party. Braun's reeled in one Craig Bodine, a nerdy accountant toiling in Clappsaddle's accounting office, who's agreed to marry her, then hustle her back to the US. Braun wins. His grandkids will live in the promised land. The blessed wedding event's set for tomorrow."

"I can't imagine that event as being close to blessed."

"Your friend, Joseph—"

"He's your friend, John, not mine."

"Okay! Our friend, in his 'father of the bride' duty, convinced the unsophisticated nerd from Buffalo of the need to participate in a traditional, or maybe only local, German pre-nuptial ritual—that of the father of the bride taking his nerdy soon-to-be son-in-law out to get his equipment tuned up so he'll be ready and knowledgeable about what he might be doing to his daughter on her wedding night. Several of Craig and Joseph's buddies will then toast him on passing his test drive."

"Stop it!" I say. "None of this stuff has anything to do with me. Why'd you drag me out here to witness this erotic test drive?"

"I invited us," says John. "Since Joseph's technically one of Lieutenant General Bekker's subjects, you might be required to support him. Plus, I can't come out here by myself! Marieka doesn't allow me into brothels alone."

Apparently we haven't parked anywhere near the brothel, so we four guys are shuffling several blocks through this residential neighborhood in the snow. A church bell, muffled by the thick atmosphere, meekly tolls 1900 hours.

"We're not here to watch the test drive, Wall. We're here because the Wizard and I need cover for a discussion about a product distribution problem in need of a quick solution and perhaps one other thing appropriate for discussion in a brothel."

They all laugh. Then John stops us suddenly at an intersection. He points down the side street. "Lynx and I will go first, at 1906.

You and Sully walk around the block and at 1916 enter and join the party."

"Why don't we all go together?" I ask.

"Because, one of the things you gotta learn. Four guys can't enter a brothel in unison."

"Wow! Things I don't know."

"Normally it's ones and twos. We can't advertise we're having a *coterie du procurement*."

"Cut it out. Who'd possibly worry about the size of guy-groups entering a brothel in a snowstorm? Who'd even have a meeting in a brothel?"

"I've done that," says John.

"Me too," says Sully. "Happens all the time."

"Okay, Driver. I'm thinking this must be another teaching moment, right? Maybe seventeen or something?"

"Could be, Farm Boy. Keep your eyes open and your tape recorder spinning. You might learn something. See you inside at…" He checks his watch. "…1916." He and the Wizard walk down the side street and fade into the background.

"I suppose you know where this brothel is, huh?" I ask Sully. "I'm thinking that in this neighborhood there ain't gonna be rotating red lights and floozies posing on the windowsills."

"This is a respectable establishment, Farm Boy. No sordid, low-end stuff like in Amsterdam. We're talkin' a business class brothel."

Ten minutes later, at 1916, Sully and I climb the eight stone steps, enter the vestibule, then approach the reception podium. The place appears to be the lounge of a formerly-classy, nineteenth century hotel. There's a worn, leather-covered bar, a dozen stools, leather booths, lots of aged woodwork, copper pots stuffed with ferns, and on the ceiling the requisite eighteenth century painting of cherubs and floozies flitting through a filmy firmament.

"This seems a strange question to utter on entering a brothel, Sully, but why don't I see any girls? I may be a hick farm boy, but I do know girls are the basic commodity utilized in a brothel, right?"

Sully speaks to the ancient maître d', but in Czech. That's weird. Only word I understand is "Braun." Both the gentleman and his tuxedo seem as old as the building, though it could be the orange tinted, fake, gas-lit lighting fixtures aging everything in the room a couple hundred years.

The ancient one studies Sully's card. He speaks to Sully and me, but in English, and probably for my benefit. "May I take your coats?"

Czech and English spoken in a German brothel with no girls? My sensibility sensor arcs toward its redline. Sully tells him we'll keep our coats. I think that's code. It might mean we're not here for the girls, if even there are girls someplace.

"Follow me, gentlemen." The maître d' guy walks us past the bar, through the leather and greenery, and into a private room.

I recognize the tuxedoed Joseph Braun. He's talking with the Wizard and the Driver. Everyone but Braun is wearing Christmas sweaters or flannel shirts.

The tuxedoed Braun notices us enter. "Hey, guys!" His voice suggests he's already had too much to drink. "Thanksh for coming out on thish nasty night. Let me get you drinksh."

John, Lynx, Scotty, and I sit around a small table. Braun, rather perfunctorily, sets four smallish flutes of tap pilsners onto our table. I know something goofy's happening, but I've no clue what. I grab my glass and take a sip.

"Yuk! Oh for God's sake. This stuff's half water."

"Sorry, Wall," says John. "This is creepier than I imagined."

"So, we'll make your lesson quick," says Lynx. "You don't realize it yet, but of the four of us, you're in a spot of unique danger, and it's our duty to alert you to it."

I quickly scan the room. A dozen harmless American guys getting sloshed on cheap beer. Seems dumb, but not particularly dangerous. "Okay, give me the juicy part."

"Basically, we three're married and you're not. Also, we married guys are somewhat hardened to life on the street, and you are one naive farm boy."

Sully continues the thought. "A naive, unmarried, farm boy with a highly marketable profession is in grave danger in western Europe, especially here at USAEUR headquarters. You've a target on your back."

Sully actually leans his chair back and studies my dorsal area.

"Okay! You're frightening me. What's goin' on?"

"Unless you're aware of the danger you're in, your chances of ending up in this room again, but as the guest of honor, are very good. We can't have that happen."

"That's some intro! I'll need an upgrade to Guinness—"

"Focus!" says John. "In these treacherous times many highly motivated German girls—and Czech, French, sometimes even English girls—make their number one career priority to escape the dump that's Europe and enter the US where they can grow both careers and children in a secure environment. Their maternal instincts are running in overdrive. They must marry a GI—some smart nerdy guy who's been thinking of nothing but math, economics, or architecture for the past six years and has little experience with the serious mating game they're playing."

"You jerks are worrying about my marital status? Giving me dating tips? I've a yellow Spider. What more—?"

"Pay attention, Wall!" John says. "You're easy prey for a beguiling fräulein. Just ask our host, Joseph. He's already exported his eldest daughter. He knows USAEUR guys are like ducks in a shooting gallery. And every month several of those ducks get shot… inside our building."

"You can't be that next duck, Wall. For your own good and for our good, we gotta make you ambush proof."

"Poor Craig," says Sully. "For him, this party's more a wake than a wedding. His night in this brothel's worse than any night in a helicopter in Vietnam."

"Here's a list of things you gotta be aware of, Wall. Pay attention. You may want to take notes."

★★★

On the way back, Sully swings his Citroën around the traffic circle in front of the Hauptbahnhof then heads east on the Hauptstrasse into the business and tourist district. Sully's put me in the front passenger seat, so I get an unrestricted view.

"Look at this, Farm Boy," he says, "ain't this somethin' else? It's Christmas Friday, and even with the snow it's packed to the gills with shoppers, partygoers, gawkers, students, and military guys. Unlike our gray and discrete business meeting earlier tonight, there's nothing gray or discrete here."

"It's a cross between Mardi Gras and a demolition derby," says John. "It's also the place where every drunk with a flashy car needs to impress this raucous crowd with his ability to dodge the trollies, bicyclists, and pedestrians while maintaining a speed twice the posted limit."

"This seems too narrow a street for such raucous partying," I say.

It's a street designed for the fifteenth century, and it isn't working well in the twentieth. Two narrow sidewalks abut the building faces, and two streetcar tracks are set in the middle. Parking spaces line each curb, and one lane each way supports moving traffic. Cars must stop to allow people from the sidewalks to cross the slippery cobblestone roadway to access the streetcars in the middle.

A silver Audi, coming the opposite direction to our Citroën, crosses the tracks behind a trolley, jumps into our lane right in front of us, then flashes his headlights in my eyes to broadcast his dangerous maneuver. His maneuver isn't possible unless Sully pounds his brakes. I'm thrown against the dashboard and know I'm gonna die. However, the jerk jumps back across the tracks in front of the stopped trolley, narrowly missing clipping Sully's front bumper. It's not a maneuver attempted by a sober driver.

"Okay." I pick my heart and other stuff off the floor. "Can I return to the monastery now? Farm Boy doesn't need such excitement."

Soon traffic grinds to a crawl, then to a stop. The Driver opens the back door and steps out for a look. "I see blue flashing lights ahead. I'm gonna take a look. Stay here."

We're going to stay whether John wants us to or not. The street's in phase-ten gridlock.

Ten minutes later he's back. "It's as I feared. Some drunk lost control and hit several drunk pedestrians. Everyone's still alive, but several need an ambulance. Unfortunately, everyone involved is American. That's common. It's the Vietnam thing again. Army guys get drunk, their goblins emerge, and people get hurt. It's a big problem, Wall. Here's your teaching moment number nineteen. This is the reason Lieutenant General Bekker insists on providing a safe bus whenever executives in your Critical Path office go into town to party. We've enough PR problems without army drunks killing other army drunks. Like at the brothel, we thought you had to see this circus to believe it. This kind of thing causes tension between natives and occupiers."

"I'm cutting through this alley," says Sully. "Gotta get us home before midnight."

"Before you quit teaching moment number nineteen, tell me what the hell actually happened back at that brothel."

"What?" asks Lynx. "Must I explain the 'birds and bees' to you? Thought even naive Iowa farm boys knew the basics of the brothel business."

"You know damn well that's not what I mean. I saw evidence of a highly intricate maneuver, orchestrated in very slow motion just so's I'd notice it, and produced with more mirrors and chaff than I am used to, even in this strange land. I know the maneuver had something to do with the Czechs. I recognized one of the guys at the bar—the Crawler. Met him at Jerry Black's separation party. After we two purposely don't recognize each other, you come over and just like you did in Fulda tell me, 'I'll be right back, Farm Boy, gotta change Rosie's oil.' We both know we took the Citroën. So I know something else is happening. Then I notice, all of a sudden, the Crawler's missing at the bar, and I think maybe he's helping you change that oil. You gonna fill me in, John?"

"Doesn't appear you're confused, Farm Boy. I'm thinking we won't need any more teaching moments."

"Driver's right," says Sully. "Farm Boy's learned more in that brothel than the groom did."

They all laugh, though I'm hearing nothing funny.

The snow's falling heavier. There's half a dozen centimeters piled on the street. Sully obeys a stop sign at the intersection to the Neckargamünd road. A streetlight illuminates the pristine, smooth, white surface. Not a single vehicle track spoils it. Sully guns the engine, swings out into the intersection, and performs a beautiful donut, looking geometrically perfect in the middle of the intersection.

"Couldn't resist that unspoiled snow, guys. See that, Farm Boy. I got me a fancy car too. She ain't a looker like the Driver's Rosie, or your toy car. She gets no style points. But she's just as talented, and the best thing—no one remembers that old lady parked in front of a brothel."

Sully spins the car around another ninety degrees, then heads up-river.

"The fun's over guys," he says. "We're going home."

16 THE 1ST LaNAPOULE STORY

Once or twice a month I make the run to Zurich. I carry a reinforced canvas bag secured with a lock and stuffed with a packing material that gives no clue as to the nature of the contents, if there are contents. They might be plumbing supplies. And sometimes I drive John's Rosie because its secret compartments might hold additional stuff. I follow the route John and I took on our first Zurich trip—the path ending in Uncle Jacob's garage several blocks uphill from the south shore of the Zurichzee.

While in Zurich, I take advantage of being isolated in the mountains with no interruptions from Lt. General Bekker's minions. I've my drafting board and so spend a few days working uninterrupted on my design competition. Jacob arranged a room at Frau Sitzmann's Zimmerhaus, a six room pension located several blocks west of his house. Frau Sitzmann almost adopts me. She allows me use of her enclosed sun porch, feeds me split pea soup, and as a bonus allows me access to her collection of Spanish guitar music including three recordings of Rodrigo's *Concierto de Aranjuez*, in my opinion the absolute best accompaniment for creative design work.

★★★

And I also spend some time at the ski resort the US Army operates near Garmisch-Partinkirchen, a village on the German-Austrian border where a friend, Todd Werner, heads the ski patrol. Todd worked for Lt. Gen. Bekker in Heidelberg when I first arrived, but Bekker sent him to Garmisch because he was uniquely qualified to help our tertiary agenda. Todd's a mechanical engineer, so talks like an engineer. He tells friends he's working for the army's Critical Path office performing torque and stress tests on his appendages at the Garmisch-Partinkirchen White Inclined Plane Facility.

Though Garmisch-Partinkirchen is in Germany, the US Army ski resort is not. It's located across the border in Austria and accessed only by a spectacular aerial tramway that leaves from Garmisch and swoops south over a lake to the top of the mountain. The ski slope, unseen from Garmisch, is on the south side of that mountain. This ski area and its secure tramway was built by Hitler in the 1930s as an exclusive playground for top-level Nazi bigwigs. Todd's able to secure complimentary lift tickets and meal passes for me because we both work for Lt. General Alvin W. Bekker's Critical Path office. At times, Todd will give me packages to return to our ghost general. Transporting Todd's parcels does not require me to travel under Bekker's orders, because I cross no borders monitored by either the Austrian or Swiss border patrol, who sometimes require such things.

And therein lies the interest Lt. General Bekker has in Garmisch-Partinkirchen. The ski facility is on the southern slope in Austria. But entry to the ski facility is on the northern side, accessed via the aerial tramway from Garmisch, Germany. Since only US Army personnel traveling on US Army passports can use the tramway, there's no need for the Austrian Border Control office to monitor this particular crossing into Austria.

However, the ski facility is serviced via an access road from the Austrian side, and that pries open a small crevice in the overall border security system. That crevice allows the limited-access tramway to play a vital part in the Prague to Vienna to Heidelberg pipeline for Polish and Czech heirlooms. It allows me to carry my drawing board, and often other parcels, across the border unsupervised.

★★★

I occasionally visit another exotic venue on the French Riviera. My alma mater, The University of Illinois School of Architecture, recently established its European Studies Program at a facility in the fishing village of LaNapoule, a few kilometers west of Cannes. One of my professors at the U of I, Christian Harrsh, heads the program there. Chris taught my undergraduate class in Critical Path Analysis so, in a way, may be responsible for me being sent to Europe rather than Vietnam. Harrsh continuously needs additional design staff at his LaNapoule facility, and when I informed him I was stationed only a day's drive away, he asked me if I would, once or twice a semester, come down and teach a two-day, sketch problem segment.

My first step was to submit the required leave request to my ghost general requesting four days professional training leave in March to teach Harrsh's class in LaNapoule. I wasn't prepared for the intensity of my ghost general's response. I received a rather curt summons to report to the Accountant's office. I was unaware the Accountant ever summoned anyone to his office. A summons seems almost as harsh as a direct order, and that sort of thing only occurs in the real army.

I knock on the open doorjamb and walk in. The Driver's behind the desk, and the Accountant stands at its side. They've serious looks on their normally jolly faces.

"Sit down, Wall," says the Driver.

The Accountant, using an unusual and rather serious mood-setting maneuver, walks over and closes the door. "What's going on in LaNapoule?" he asks me. "What's your interest there?"

"Nothing sinister guys, I'm teaching a sketch problem at the architecture school."

"That seems a fairly lame rationale, Wall," says the Accountant. "What's really happening?"

"Nothing's goofy here guys. It's where my University of Illinois Architectural School recently started its foreign study program. I can show you the proposal, job description, and the contract form I received from Christian Harrsh, the director of the school. It's at my desk. I've gotta sign the contract and return it as confirmation. It seems fairly harmless. On the other hand, working with you goons, I can't take anything at face value. What'd I step into?"

"You really set off an alarm, Wall. Remember, I told you Marieka's parents relocated to France."

"Oh, for God's sake, John! No way that's the same town!"

"We were married in LaNapoule," John says. "Marieka's mother still lives there. The Nazi SS had little interest in the coastal south during the war, which allowed refugees a haven."

"And it's on the open water, with many commercial fishing boats," I say. "So less rigorous customs attention than in neighboring Cannes, huh?"

"You see why you spooked us? Just be vigilant down there. Keep your eyes and ears open, and let me know if anything weird occurs."

"If I did that, we'd be talking for months. Weird occurs every day in this army, right?"

"Lieutenant General Bekker will approve your leave as professional enrichment," says the Accountant. "Though you realize that since the purpose of the trip is legit, the thing will earn zero points in our ghost general's contest for creative excess. Truth's an automatic disqualifier. I'm keeping the cello repertoire scam first on my list."

"Oh, Wall," John says, "check in with me a few days before you leave. Since you're going there, you might do me a favor."

"Okay. Should I worry about that? Might I step into something messy down there?"

"Shoo, Mr. Architect. Go back to your drawing board!"

17 THE 2ND ZURICH STORY

Architectural historians consider the Swiss-born French architect Le Corbusier to be, with Mies van der Rohe and Walter Gropius, one of the primary drivers of the modern architecture movement. Le Corbusier's buildings are located from Chandigarh, India to Harvard University, but he lived in southern France and built many of his most beloved works there. I'm fascinated by Le Corbusier's work, and given that he'd recently died in 1965 and that the University of Illinois' European school is located in southern France, I thought it reasonable that the sketch problem I'm preparing for my students have a Le Corbusier theme. I'll have them design a freestanding piece of civic sculpture, a monument to commemorate Le Corbusier's life and work.

I set only one design restriction—the designs must represent Le Corbusier's spirit or character without using any raw undecorated concrete, the one building material associated with him. I hope the strangeness of the presented problem will result in my students not simply grabbing a historical template as a base for the design. I'm hoping the unusual design requirements will push them to find new tools for their design methodology toolbox and give them a proper challenge.

★★★

Such a monument already exists and is the inspiration for my sketch problem topic. It's located in Zurich so I'm sure none of my American students will know this. Neither the existence of this monument nor its thematic connection to Le Corbusier is much known, at least outside the Zurich arts community. However, it is this existing sculpture that gave me the idea for my sketch problem. This sculpture is a non-Le Corbusean thing, a very strange construction of painted and weathered steel that from one angle looks like a giant farm tractor.

★★★

I'm in Zurich now and, although still March, little green buds are popping from the brown twigs. The beautiful warm day forces me to leave Frau Sitzmann's porch and take my drawing board to the lakeside park. I'm hoping the venue change will allow me to discover new tools for my own design methodology toolbox.

I sit on a folded blanket, lean against a tree, prop my drafting board against my knees, and concentrate on my design for the Prix de Roma, an international competition for recently graduated architects. The prize for winning the competition is, as noted in its title, a year of study in Rome. As I work, I periodically glance over my drafting board and notice that strange Monument to Le Corbusier pushing itself out of the grass twenty meters in front of me. Today is the second day I've taken advantage of this beautiful spring weather by placing myself against this tree facing this enigmatic monument while working on my design. That monument gives me great pleasure, encouragement, and certainly inspiration. Architects, like other artists, are both trained and naturally conditioned to be visually aware, so as to notice things and then wonder about the things noticed.

While I work in the park, thousands of people pass on the crushed stone walk ten meters behind me. Of those thousands, maybe ten individuals have been inquisitive enough to leave the walk, wander across the lawn, and look at my work. And of those ten, only one is inquisitive enough to interrupt me with a question. It doesn't surprise me that the one observer asking that one question is another architect. He's only doing what architects are trained to do—to question the odd occurrence in any situation and ask the question that presents itself.

This particular inquisitive guy seems about forty years old, with longish blond hair brushing his shoulders. His clothes are casual and seem appropriate for this Alpine spring day; cream-colored dress shorts, a light blue knit shirt, and a white linen jacket over his left shoulder. From his right shoulder hangs a blond, calf-leather case on a wide strap. He stands close and studies my work, looks toward the Corbusier monument, and then back at my drawing.

"Was ist das?"

I look up at him, and say, "Guten Morgen."

"Morgen!" The stranger points to my board. Then he says something in German I don't understand, although I understand the word 'Corbusier.'

That means he knows the philosophy or history of my monument. I maybe should be civil to him. "Sprichst du Englisch, bitte?"

"Ahh, you're an American?"

"That I am. I'm a visitor to your pleasant park on this pleasant day. It's a wonderful park."

"It certainly is. I thought you might be sketching our Iron Tractor. That seems strange because, though I am daily on this walk, I've seen no artist ever do that before. Apparently you aren't doing that either or, if you are, you're being very creative."

"You're correct. The drawing on my board is not connected with the Corbusier monument. I'm an architect and working on a design not even remotely connected with it. I only find this a comfortable and inspirational place to work."

"I also am an architect," he says. He slips the case from his shoulder and extends his hand. "Gerhardt Stopak."

From my sitting position, I extend my hand to meet his. "Wall Kneuble, Gerhardt. Nice to meet you. I appreciate you taking an interest in my strange work."

"So, Mr. Kneuble, why do you travel from America to sit on the ground in my park?"

"I'm occasionally in Zurich for other business and use my time to work on my submittal for the Prix de Roma competition. I'm behind schedule."

"You come? All the way from the States? To work here?"

"No, no. I'm living in Heidelberg."

"You should not have to sit on the ground with that board on your knees. My office is right up the hill. Only a few blocks. Come. I'll give you a desk and tracing paper, and you can do some proper work." He pulls the drafting board off my knees. "Come! You must have a proper desk. Grab your blanket and bag. Please."

"That's very kind of you, Mr. Stopak."

"It is not a kindness to you, but a pleasure for me. Come! And tell me about your competition entry for the Prix de Roma."

As we walk through the park and turn away from the water, I brief him on the competition. Then he tells me his story. Gerhardt has dual US and Swiss citizenship and has studied, taught, and worked in both countries. His mother, a second generation Polish American, and his father, a Swiss resident, but born in Poland, now both live in his mother's home town of Austin, Texas.

We two architects leave the park. We cross the highway at the traffic light. Soon Stopak turns us into the Albisstrasse, a narrow, steeply sloped, one way, one lane street with parking on the left side only.

I stop short. "Your office is here? On the Albisstrasse?"

"Yes? Why? Is there some problem?"

"My business in Zurich is with a gentleman who lives up there." I point. "Just off this street. It's another odd coincidence, that's all. My recent life is filled with odd coincidences."

"Many Jews evacuated Warsaw in the late 1930s before Hitler's Storm Troopers attacked. Some came to this area of Zurich. I'll wager your friend has a Polish surname. Am I correct?"

I'm not sure I should answer his question.

"You're very kind, but I don't want you to interrupt—"

"Nonsense, Mr. Kneubel, I insist. Here we are." He turns sharply and motions for me to open the green wooden door at 147 Albisstrasse. "My office is here on the first floor, and my apartment's on level six." He introduces me to the other two people in his office then gets me settled at a work station. "I have errands to run, Wall. I'll be back in an hour. If you need anything ask Tomas or Elsa. When I get back we'll all go into the park for lunch. There are several wonderful cafes."

18 THE ORANGE STORY

It's a week past the equinox and so spring should, at this time, be evident. However, I'm not sure the sun's gotten the memo yet. It's dark, it's bleak, and it's raining hard in the valley of the Rhine. I'd left the Hotel Neckargamünd at 0600, and now, half an hour later, it's still dark, so I'm thinking my calendar must be wrong. I plod through rush hour traffic in Karlsruhe, then across the Rhine into France.

I drive south through the eastern French countryside, aiming for the architectural school in LaNapoule where I must teach my sketch problem tomorrow. The slower travel in the rain crushes my time schedule. Worse, if the rain continues it may also ruin some photography I'm hoping to fit in. Around 1100 I leave the main motorway for a paved local road which takes me through pastures and farmland. The rain lessens to a drizzle. Then, soon thereafter, a small wooden sign—"Ronchamp - 3km"—instructs me to leave the paved surface and continue on a narrow gravel road. I do what the sign tells me, and I'm instantly rewarded. The rain stops.

I've never given credence to theories that have metaphysical creatures controlling physical events in order to advance personal agendas, but the cessation of the rain did make me briefly reconsider the question. I might be enticed into thinking that such intervention caused the rain to cease at this appropriate moment. Or maybe it was some other guy, the one who'd been fiddling with my personal Critical Path Diagram. Perhaps that AESD office in Brussels has power down here in France.

Whatever the reason, in the several minutes it takes to drive the few kilometers up the road and into the small parking area in front of the Chapelle Notre Dame du Haut de Ronchamp, the clouds retreat. The sky opens to the brilliant blue I'd ordered as a backdrop for my photographs of this exquisite white concrete chapel Le Corbusier completed in 1954. This small chapel is revered as perhaps the most significant icon of twentieth century modern architecture. It is to modern architecture what Picasso's *Guernica* is to modern painting.

After photographing Notre Dame du Haut, I drive south to Lyon, then to the village of Eveux sur Arbresle. Here awaits the second Le Corbusier building on my schedule, the convent of Sainte Marie de LaTourette. As I command, the sky remains blue until I complete my work and no longer have need of it. Then clouds quickly return, and the spigot reopens. I must assume those AESD regulators allotted my photographing of Corbu's work a deed of higher moral importance than me maintaining my schedule.

Traffic on the two-lane road south of Lyon is heavy with trucks and slowed by fog, rain, and tire spray. It's still raining at 1900, but now it's dark. I've no chance to reach LaNapoule tonight. I leave the highway at the small town of Orange and find a pension, near the center of town, where I purchase a meal, a beer, and a room for the night. I call Christian Harrsh and tell him I'll start early the next morning and anticipate arrival in LaNapoule in time for the scheduled 1000 breakfast with my sketch problem class.

★★★

The next morning I'm awake before 0600, anticipating a quick start toward LaNapoule. I stumble to the window, throw back the curtains, and open the sash. The rain's passed, and the red-orange sun seems on schedule this morning, about to peek its nose above the horizon. My room's on the fifth floor, and thus my window's elevated enough to allow me to look over the heavy masonry walls and directly into the center of the single best preserved ancient Roman amphitheater in all of Western Europe. It is right there! It's so close a baseball tossed through my open window into that amphitheater would surely bounce down those stone steps and onto the stage.

This unexpected view of this ancient Roman construction startles me. I should've been aware of these ruins. I'd studied this important amphitheater in my architectural history courses. However, when I'd checked in last night I'd been thinking of nothing but alerting LaNapoule of my delayed arrival and going to sleep.

The impressive blood-orange glow is spreading its soft warmth over the ruddy stonework of the amphitheater, and I see the chance for a great photo. I cannot let this pass me by. I throw on some clothes, grab my camera bag and tripod, and hustle myself down the stairs, around the block, and into the amphitheater in the hope of using that early reddish light to bring new life into those old dead stones.

Even at this hour, two other visitors are enjoying the light show in this ancient amphitheater. A young couple about my age, probably Americans from their dress and mannerisms, are carefully climbing up the seating tiers, yelling to each other, playing, and laughing. They act like college kids or newlyweds, and I pay them little attention. My time schedule is tight. The sun's disk is beginning its entry dance, and its orange light will soon evaporate.

The young couple approaches my position and, taking me to be a native, the man asks me in reasonable French if I might take a photograph of them with their camera. "You'll have to wait till I finish my shot." I'm curt with them, but I have to be. "The sun's moving quickly. The color won't last."

"You're an American!" she says. "Where're ya from?"

"I need quiet!"

They watch me work in silence. I get my shot, then I take their silly picture. They yak at me while I stow my camera stuff. Seems they're on a honeymoon from a town in Iowa, only twelve miles south of my home. Neither of us, however, recognize each other's names. They laugh at the coincidence, but I can't dawdle. I cut off the interview quickly. Even so, I must redline my Fiat all the way to LaNapoule.

★★★

I think little of that brief encounter in the amphitheater again until Tuesday afternoon. John and I, and several of the guys from the Critical Path office, leave our desks and, as we often do, reconvene around the corner table at our usual conference venue, Der Blaue Schwein. John's brought the conversation around to the topic he's called this meeting to discuss. This season's road rally schedule's been released, and our various side trips must be planned around that schedule. They've scheduled five rallies on weekends from July through September. The start locations are in various areas in the eastern regions of West Germany. We Critical Path guys must schedule inspection trips to the construction sites around these rally events, the NATO briefing events, my trips to Zurich, and most importantly, my teaching gigs at LaNapoule and my extensive investigations of European architecture.

"And I haven't been to London yet," I say. "I've also got to see the Acropolis in Athens, and there is Florence and Rome. I don't think I can waste five weekends bouncing around back roads."

"Relax," says John. "Just settle down. That's why we're meeting here, to fit our trivial work around your important historical investigation schedule. There'll be enough time to climb Greek and Roman ruins."

"Oh, John, that word 'ruins' reminds me. You asked me to tell you when I find weird things. A weird thing happened while I was en route to LaNapoule last Saturday."

"You found weirdness? Why's that not surprising?"

"It's about six in the morning, and I'm photographing Orange's famous ancient amphitheater over which the early sunrise is spreading an intriguing orange light. Two American tourists, the only other visitors on the site, seeing I'm a photographer, thus familiar with how cameras work, accost me, point to their camera, to themselves, then to me. The man, in reasonable tourist French, asks, 'Would you take our picture?' I considered swearing in German, but I complied. They're about my age and, turns out, on honeymoon from an Iowa farming town only twelve miles from my home. We knew many people in common, but didn't know each other. You think that encounter might be classified as weird?"

"That's weird. Though it seems innocent enough. That kind'a stuff happens all the time."

"I've got them in my memory now. If I see those faces again, I'll know I'm being watched, huh? I'll be suitably alarmed, take some swift evasive action."

"I don't think you have to panic yet. Official watchers are much subtler. You'd never notice them. But there's a lesson here. Always understand the possibility someone could be watching. If you're paying attention, you'll be able to see incongruities in the background. If something as flagrant as meeting another Iowa resident in another ruin occurs in the next few months, I'd scram as quickly as I could. I'd think a second coincidence, unlike your single meeting in Orange, is probably not a coincidence."

19 The Hockenheimer Ring Story

John's driving me crazy. He's pressuring me to stuff a supercharged engine into my weak little Fiat. The pressure's affecting my real work, whatever that is.

"If Lech can fit that supercharger in, you'll need a set of stronger tie rods and a reconfigured rear deck cover." He plops some glossy papers on my desk. "Here's a list of some upgrades you also may be interested in. If you order them through Team Lotus Racing, Inc., Lech will get you the company discount."

"Will you cool it John?" I stomp a foot and flail an arm for a bit of dramatic effect. "You've got me a date with this girl, and though I've yet to meet her, you're already pushing me to build our kids a swing set. Cool down, will ya? You're way ahead of the curve here. You've more important stuff to worry about, like building nuclear missile sites, or containing International Communism, or running contraband across the border."

"It's not contraband. And don't worry about financing, Wall. I've talked to Lieutenant General Bekker, and he'll approve a bridge loan to finance that supercharger if you can work a deal with uncle Lech at Hockenheim."

I find it easier to acquiesce than argue. "I'm glad you're having fun, John, though you realize this thing doesn't have me bouncing off the ceiling with you yet. Such silliness ain't happening. I'm not buyin' an Abarth, and I'm hoping after Hockenheim life's gonna proceed normally again."

"Not as long as you're in Germany, Wall. Ain't nothin' normal happening here."

★★★

Race day for the German Grand Prix emerges as a typical April day in the Rhine Valley. It's overcast and cool, with handfuls of drizzle being tossed around. I'm driving John to the Hockenheimer Ring in my yellow Fiat. He's hoping that mingling among the high-powered exotic metal assembled there will embarrass both me and my toy machine and might lead to my agreeing to let his uncle work magic on my car.

"Great day for a race, huh?" says John. "There's the turnoff up ahead, on the right."

John tells the guy directing traffic an almost lie, that we've business with Team Lotus and are expected. He shows the guy the admission vouchers with the Team Lotus Racing letterhead, and for some reason the guy believes him and points us down a side road that tunnels under the racetrack, eventually accessing the garages and caravan parking area. Guys always believe whatever garbage John gives them. He could talk his way into saying Mass at the Vatican. We both look respectable today. Most of John's beard and curls are gone, and we're both wearing the official Team Lotus sweatshirts Lech sent him.

We arrive a couple hours early but find Lech busy with preparatory things in the garage. We should've assumed he'd be unavailable; one doesn't interrupt a doctor prepping for heart surgery. However, there's other interesting stuff around, so we investigate it. Lech's given us passes enabling us to wander through garages, watch mechanics frantically working, and listen to many passion-powered words in several languages. We hear pneumatic things pounding and engines revving.

Tension is building for the headline event—the 1968 German Grand Prix. They're running several shorter preliminary races on the infield dirt track to warm the crowd. We lean on the fence and watch a race featuring a class composed of 850cc Fiat sedans that have been seriously customized with Abarth modified engines, suspensions, and other equipment. The little sedans skid around the turns, and their supercharged Abarth engines blast their distinctive high-pitched screams.

"Aren't you excited? Lech will drop one of those babies into your Fiat, no trouble. Boom! You'll halve your time to Zurich."

"Not after I'm stopped for speeding and spend the night in a Bavarian jail."

"I read somewhere that since those Abarth engines are so respected as professional equipment their drivers are immune to speeding citations. The polizei are mesmerized by the sound screaming at 9500 RPM and are unable to make arrests."

"That engine's so far out of my financial situation. But I'll tell you what, John. I'll agree to supercharge my Spider if you'll talk your Lieutenant General Bekker into paying for it. I'll be using it for his work, right? And don't those things run on rocket fuel? Don't think I can afford that either."

"You think only about problems, Wall."

"I'll give you problems! I won't be allowed to slip it back into the States because it'll fail dozens of environmental tests."

"Ya got to think 'bout solutions and advantages. Just like our other stuff, it'll be shipped on an army freighter where nobody does customs inspections. Even if the thing's illegal, who will know once it hits the Interstate? Or care? Also, the sweet sound of that Abarth will be of great chick magnet potential. You think about that?"

"I've enough magnetism, thank you. And it's only fifteen minutes till start time. We'd best start working our way to the grandstand."

The drizzling rain has stopped, and though the track's moist it's not wet enough to be hazardous. "It should burn off quickly," says John. "Ideal racing conditions!"

"Does seem a great day for race watching." I point upward. "Clouds reduce my sunburn potential."

One lap at this Hockenheimer Ring track is about four and a half kilometers, of which only one kilometer, I'll guess, is visible from the grandstands. The remainder is hidden in the dense woods. It's an asphalt and concrete ribbon carved through a mature forest.

Jim Clark, the current Formula 1 points leader places his Lotus on the pole in the front row, and he leads the pack out of the woods and past the grandstand on the first two laps. On the third lap Jim Clark's car does not emerge from the woods!

The crowd, in absolute shock, watches the remaining cars slow and eventually stop dead in the center of the track in a disorderly, haphazard configuration in front of the grandstand where John and I are sitting. Uncle Lech has secured primo seats for us right behind the pits, so we're now watching and hearing all the yelling and confusion. Drivers leap from their cars and run across the patch of grass right in front of us and into the pit area. Howling sirens and flashing red lights disappear into the woods. Then everything quiets. The crowd is eerily still, a confused and anxious still. It's so hushed, John and I hear nothing but the sound of our own breathing. And now I hear a few isolated raindrops crashing onto the concrete steps of our grandstand.

Most spectators would not have noticed if one of the forty or so cars did not show up as they zipped past pit row in a rather compact bunch on the third lap of the race. But when it's Jim Clark's car that's missing, everyone in the stands recognizes that. It's like if Mickey Mantle or Willie Mays went over the wall into the stands after a fly ball and didn't come out. Clark's the premier Grand Prix driver in the world, the reigning world champion, and all of a sudden his car's not on the track where it's supposed to be.

Eventually a somber voice on the speaker system tells us Clark's car left the track as he apparently accelerated out of a chicane and hurled itself into the thick forest without leaving any skid mark from a braking effort. He left no evidence of the crash on the track. Clark's Lotus apparently exploded into shrapnel as it bounced off several mature pine trees well into the forest.

And Jim Clark has died!

And no one saw it happen.

We soon learn that Clark was already well ahead of the pack so other drivers didn't realize the problem till they got through the chicane onto the straight track and didn't see Clark's car ahead of them, like he'd been before the turns. His car had just vanished. First came confusion, then the realization hit, and by the time they got to the pit area in front of our seats, their tears poured out and forced them to stop.

In all likelihood his death was instantaneous. The cause of the crash remains a mystery. No compelling reason for the crash has been proven. The crash scene was described as a real mess. John and I can see the other drivers are a mess. The entire grandstand crowd's a mess. Everyone's standing in reverent silence. A light, tentative rain fills the air with tears. A somber voice tells us the race is canceled—tells us to go home and cry.

Track officials lock the place down quickly. The garage and the caravan areas are sealed off. Things are so tightly controlled John has difficulty getting a message to his Uncle Lech. Not even John! He also has a difficult time talking us into the secure compound area to collect my Spider. No one, including his uncle Lech, cares a fig anymore that my seriously underpowered Fiat needs an Abarth.

The great Jim Clark just died! Right out there! In those pristine pine woods!

I'm overpowered by thoughts of death. Dr. King's death, only three days ago, has left its open wound. I think a lot about my New Jersey friend James Fisk. His sister worked with King; she could've been holding his hand as he died. Then there's Marta's father killed on the cobbles in Warsaw. There's Jacob's wife in the commons in Heidelberg. There's Vietnam with dead bodies thrown from helicopters and landing in rice paddies. I imagine seven thousand nuclear warheads arcing over the *steel fence*. Imagine the death that will cause. I think of Jim Clark's mom—any soldier's mom, my own mom—opening that black-edged telegram.

John looks over, sees me fighting tears. "You thinking about the 360, Wall?"

"I'm thinking about my mom, John. And black-rimmed telegrams. But yeah! That 360 as well. Almost a telegram to our moms there, huh?"

"Could've been us, Wall. Just like Clark, we shoot off the road into the woods, wrap ourselves around our own black pine?"

"Would've been a shame, John. I go through all this trouble to avoid dying in the rice paddies, and then, boom! Some meatball in a red Porsche! No sense in that, huh?"

"Damn! You gonna be okay to drive back?"

"I'll be fine. But I think we better leave soon. Let's get ourselves back to Neckargamünd before it all seeps deep into my brain, and I gotta cry."

20 THE FORK IN THE CRITICAL PATH STORY

The primary reason for describing any path as critical concerns the potential for a situation to become worrisome, even to the point of crisis, if an event referenced to a particular node does not occur on time. If an event fails to happen at its scheduled time, the diagram assumes the condition of being worthless as a controller of future events. And that failure has a potential for shutting down the project. Such a critical situation came to light at 1113 on the second Wednesday morning in May. That's when node 672 on the master Critical Path Diagram turned not green.

Node 672 refers to a specific piece of information regarding bunker forty-six, which is located at... well, its exact location on a topographic type map isn't a real concern for either my Critical Path Diagram or the staff working in my Critical Path office. That's because, for security reasons, my Critical Path office staff does not know, or at least is supposed to not know, the actual physical locations of the bunkers referred to by the construction projects numbered one through seventy-four.

It is also possible, or almost certainly the true situation, that many of the numbered sites contain no construction at all, though their scheduled construction is being monitored on the master Critical Path Diagram laid out on the wall in room number... well that particular room, for security purposes, has not been given a number.

Some CIA or Defense Department muckety-muck thought that if the room doesn't have a number then no one will be able to tell a spy which room he must break into in order to pilfer Critical Path information. I know that sounds stupid, but it's the story I've been told.

The routine phone call has been placed by one of our engineers, an American civilian named Helen. She placed the call on the appropriate Critical Path office telephone to the number listed in the big book at the front of the room as the appropriate construction site phone for bunker forty-six. Like she's done many times before, Helen asked her question to the voice on the other end. "I am checking on the current color of node 672. According to my schedule it's supposed to have been colored green by yesterday. Can you confirm its color as green?"

The answer returning through the phone was not comforting. "No, ma'am, its color is still not green."

That response set off several alarm bells in my Critical Path office because, according to the rules driving any Critical Path, when the time-line passes the location of any node, that node must be colored either green, indicating the task has been completed, or red, indicating it's not been completed. However, by international consensus, the color 'red' carries a degree of panic in its soul, and we know panic acts to lessen the efficiency and morale of any office. Therefore, our Lt. General Bekker has ordered that the word 'red' must never be used in our Critical Path office. But on occasion, nodes are noted as being colored 'not green' because that sends the same information up the chain without the sense of negative condition or even abject failure connoted by the word 'red.'

There's also a possibility that the construction at bunker forty-six, the project responsible for producing this 'not-green' node, does not actually exist. And that means its current color status is, in some sense, meaningless. It could be true that the voice Helen spoke with over the phone has no idea if the project exists either. It's probably impossible for me to tell exactly what condition occurred to produce this currently 'not-green' colored node.

Lt. General Bekker's minions might hope that bunker site forty-six is one of the imaginary or faux sites set into the system to confuse the spies working for the Warsaw Pact as to the exact parameters of our nuclear weapons capability. If that's the case, then Helen needn't worry about the lack of the green colored node. But neither Helen nor I know if bunker forty-six is a faux site. If we did know that, it would make our present conversation a waste of our time. So, to preserve the possible fantasy, I must have Helen make a number of inquiries regarding the several preceding nodes in order to ascertain just why the node 672 is colored 'not green.'

Two days of phone calls by Helen allow her to illuminate the problem. It seems the role set for node 672 is to record that "confirmation that the bolt location templates, detailing the exact size and location of all hinge and locking hardware for the automated steel doors, have been received at the construction site."

The 'not green' status therefore tells her those templates have not been delivered to the construction site. And that means the steel reinforcement around the opening cannot be fabricated... which means the concrete cannot be poured in time for the wall to be ready to accept the monster door when it's delivered two months from now and set on those hinges. That door, an exotic, fifteen-ton, steel behemoth, must be set into place before the remainder of the bunker can be constructed so when the new Pershings arrive they can be immediately slipped inside their cozy cave.

It appears the designer of the hinges, a firm in Birmingham, Alabama, for good structural reasons changed from four separate hinges per door to one continuous hinge. But that piece of changed information was never received by the Berlin engineering firm that has the responsibility for constructing the reinforcement cages for the bunker walls.

Helen, one of the more conscientious civilian engineering drones in our Critical Path office, is distressed and troubled. She's almost in tears. "Wall, it doesn't look like that node's going to be colored green for some time. It's going to screw up the entire project! What are we going to do?"

"It'll be all right, Helen," I say. "I'll make the problem go away. I'll fiddle with the Critical Path Diagram, and that will slip the problem past Clappsaddle and his NATO buddies. It's not like we'll need that door to protect a real nuclear bomb. We all know it's only the idea of new Pershing rockets that's important and not the shiny disgusting pieces of hardware themselves."

"You're not supposed to talk like that, Mr. Kneuble!"

I know immediately that I've done some supervisor-drone damage here. I should have realized poor Helen does not have a sense of humor. I'd better think of something supportive to say to her. I take a sip of my Earl Gray to calm myself down and slip into a more serious, responsible persona.

"The bad news, Helen, is that if there is a problem at this node, it will probably show up again as a problem on every bunker on our diagram, so we gotta solve it quickly. However, the first thing I gotta do is reconfigure the Critical Path Diagram so that the problem's not obvious to the NATO generals. Can't have those guys going bonkers. They expect their shiny new Pershing rockets to be slipped into those bunkers starting next February. After I fix the diagram, the two of us must fix this glitch fast. Any clue as to how we're gonna do that?"

Helen has quit crying, but that's replaced by quivering from the load of responsibility I just dumped on her with the word 'we.' She says, "I have to make sure those templates get to the job site. But I don't know if those templates are designed yet. The CP Diagram doesn't tell me that. That might take weeks!"

I must step up here and ease her pulsing anxiety. "Hmmm," I say. "The bunker's general contractor is in Berlin, right?"

"Yes, but they can't know where to place the reinforcing without first seeing the template."

"I know, I know. But I have an idea. I've not been to Berlin yet. There are some great new church buildings up there I need to study. I'm thinking I could travel up there on my own time so Clappsaddle will never know there's a problem needing to be fixed. Then, as long as I'm in Berlin, I can discretely sneak over and talk to the guys at that German structural design firm. They surely know the door's weight and its size. Those things haven't changed. So I'll just talk with those guys and configure a flexible solution to the hinge anchorage problem. After I do that, I can authorize the coloring of that node to green and save everyone a bunch of headaches. And nobody but you and I and a couple engineers in Berlin will even know there's been a problem. I think I can easily sell Lieutenant General Bekker on that idea."

★★★

I walk over to Lt. General Bekker's office. I tell Driver I can maybe fix the 'not green' node by slipping myself into Berlin and talking to the contractor.

"I've been wanting to get to Berlin, Driver. Several new churches and that Philharmonic Hall? Is that a neat piece of design? Then there's the housing blocks built for the World Exposition, and—"

"Just settle down, Wall. I keep tellin' you, you're in the army, or some similar organization. You should be concentrating on doing army things, or at least pretending that the army things are as important as your personal things. You've fabricated a very weak excuse just to get you to Berlin to look at its architecture, especially since I think bunker forty-six is probably a faux site anyway, and so it doesn't matter where that damn door reinforcement's located."

"But, John, it's a system-wide problem. If it showed up here, soon it will show up on an actual site with an actual door and real hinges, and—"

"Cool it, Wall. I didn't say Lieutenant General Bekker would not sign off on it, I only said you were making a weak case for going to Berlin. Let's see if we can strengthen it, maybe by doing something of interest... to my work."

We look at each other. We both know we're playing a piffling game.

"You can fly up to Berlin to look at buildings on your own time, but as long as you are going to be there..." The Driver pauses to allow the concept of heavy responsibility to crash onto the tabletop between us. "I've become concerned that the Critical Path Schedule we monitor, the one that traces the construction progress of NATO's infrastructure changes to support their new Pershing rockets, might have unintended consequences."

"Like what?" I ask. "I can't imagine any unintended consequences of us hiding seven thousand nuclear warheads around western Europe."

"Behave yourself, Wall. I'm seeing evidence that our schedule might also be driving the Soviet's schedule for lowering the hammer on Prague and Warsaw."

"Anybody can see that," I say. "Those Mongols gotta make their sneaky move now, before NATO's improved hammer is operational. Everybody knows that. But what's that got to do with me lookin' at buildings in Berlin?"

"Well, while you are in East Berlin I'll have you talk to some people. See if what I just said is true, or maybe I'm just havin' a bad dream."

"I think I specifically told you Berlin, Mr. Driver. I definitely did not say anything about going to East Berlin. I could get shot in East Berlin." We look at each other. We both know we're both still playing a piffling game.

21 The Berlin Story

Part 1 - East Berlin, May 19, 1968

My meetings in East Berlin with the Driver's contacts will take advantage of the fact that I am a 'born in America' army guy and have no apparent family ties to Eastern Bloc countries. For some reason, we normal-type army guys—as long as we're wearing our uniform, have a valid army visa, and carry orders from our commanding officer noting the reason for the incursion into East Berlin—seem to present little concern for caution to the American border guards manning the humongous liftgates at the Brandenburg Crossing into East Berlin. For instance, I met one American diplomat who visits the Berliner Opera Haus over there every week.

This situation is but an extreme example of an often-confirmed historical truth—that of a soldier on one side respecting the basic humanity of a comrade soldier from the opposite side. I've heard East German enlisted grunts are more afraid of their own officer corp, top heavy with Russians, than they are of us fellow grunts in the US Army. And that results in acts of reciprocity, including gifts of cigarettes and chocolate, given to the East German guards by US border guys. The system has been arranged so that US guards check only US citizens going through their checkpoint into East Germany, and East German, or sometimes Soviet, guards check only East German citizens, or sometimes West German citizens, going into the west.

This strangeness seems to me to suggest that a rather large hole may exist in the tight security one usually associates with phrases like the Iron Curtain or the Berlin Wall, but I put this information in the same closet where I'm now storing the many other pieces of weird information I've collected during my short time in Germany. That closet's almost full, yet I've a year remaining before I must leave Germany.

★★★

All American military personnel must enter East Berlin through the infamous Checkpoint Charlie inserted into the Brandenburg Gate entrance set up on Friedrichstrasse. I simply present my army passport and my leave papers to the guard at Checkpoint Charlie. Those papers note that I'm cleared by my commanding officer, a certain Lt. General Alvin W. Bekker from the headquarters of the US Army in Heidelberg, to be a tourist in East Berlin on this date for the purpose of studying recent East Berlin church architecture. After a rather perfunctory look at my papers, I am allowed through.

I walk a hundred meters down the Friedrichstrasse to the East Berlin checkpoint where I'm waved through without a word. I've been told no civilians are allowed through this checkpoint. Nevertheless, several gray-suited workers of either East or West Berlin origin seem to be doing just that. The origin of these drones is hard to discern because they're plodding the cobbles cowled and cowed, like hunchback robot workers in old Flash Gordon movies. A small, gray, unmarked bus, carrying a few gray passengers, passes me, as does a dirty delivery truck taking bread or plumbing supplies through this no-man's land between the two checkpoints. I wasn't expecting quite so much activity.

Once through both checkpoints I must, for a few grimy blocks, continue walking down Friedrichstrasse. It's been almost a quarter century since the Great War ended, and yet the Soviets still preserve this dreary street as almost a museum installation, perhaps for some propaganda reason or to keep the memory of that war alive so their East German puppets can wallow in it. Two idling Soviet tanks chortle rancid diesel vapors into the mist. They seem to be supervising a group of grimy workers removing—or they might actually be installing, as in an art project—pieces of broken buildings and left-over wartime rubble. I pass unoccupied, boarded-up windows, unrepentant bullet-riddled stonework, and piles of uncollected trash. A sense of dark opera pervades the place. It seems they haven't cleaned this street since the war ended. I don't understand the purpose of this black propaganda effort.

After several bleak blocks, I intersect Unter den Linden, the once beautiful tree-lined parkway much romanticized in nineteenth century German prose and song. Some effort has been made to clean the rubble and rebuild the broken structures along this parkway, though it's still dreary, gray, and infected by military symbolica and clumsy, bold-fonted signage. Unter den Linden, athough not suitable for civilized use by urbane humans, still seems targeted for more development than the rest of this city, at least the parts I'm allowed to see. A few pieces of new construction are evident along Unter den Linden and continue into the Alexanderplatz. It's impossible to miss the ugly, silver-ball-topped TV tower which claims to be the tallest manmade structure in Europe. It's supposed to make me gaze upward in wonder and, by so doing, fail to notice the rubble still strewn about at ground level.

As an architect, I'm interested in Berlin's post-war churches, many of which were the first structures to be rebuilt, even before housing, hotels, and offices, to replace those bombed during the war. Some incorporated portions of the old bombed-out churches in their reconstruction. I've come to Alexanderplatz hoping to find a small, new church that I've been told reacts against the heavy brutalism of many West German churches, of which the Kaiser Wilhelm Memorial Church in West Berlin is a good example. The Kaiser Wilhelm's new carillon tower is separated from its new nave by a bombed-out remnant of the original medieval structure that has been left in its charred, bombed-out intactness between them. The metaphor there is powerful, though confusing, and therefore controversial.

The US border guards prohibited me from bringing my cameras into East Berlin, but they allowed my sketchpad. It's my sketching tools that validate my excuse for being in East Berlin. I'm but an architect studying church architecture, so I'm not seen as a military or propaganda risk. I've been instructed to keep myself to the main avenues and squares and sketch only religious buildings. I promised them that's all I'd do. The MP guys gave me a four-hour time window. I must return though the same checkpoint by 1547. I try hard not to irritate the American MP guys, so I stick to sketching churches and record nothing about the dreary background landscape, the scenes of social and structural rubble and despair that East German officials would rather not want me bringing into West Berlin.

I'm interested in the new architecture and not interested in watching people, though many of them are quite watchable as they shuffle about looking like automatons. Some of those people will be watching me. I cannot tell which might be official watchers, though the guard told me, "You will be watched." So I move about deliberately. I act in ways to put watchers to sleep. I sit quietly and sketch in my sketchbook.

I'm sitting on a bench in a small plaza and working on a pencil drawing. A few passersby stop and take interest in my work. One or two engage me in short bits of conversation as, I would assume, one human being reacts to another in every other place on the planet. I realize there's a human component to a bombed out and depressing, dreary, gray city peopled by dreary, gray, almost-dead inhabitants.

This area near Alexanderplatz seems to have more new construction than other sectors. Many new buildings use raw concrete and large expanses of glass but pay little attention to detail. There's nothing extraneous—no curved lines, no ornament. Some might consider this work brutalist, or insensitive, perhaps designed without any sense of humor.

I'm intrigued by the combining of concrete and glass. I'm thinking of my students in LaNapoule. I may be able to develop a sketch problem for them based on what I am seeing here, sitting on this stone bench in this small garden off the busy Alexanderplatz. I'm examining the concrete and glass of the new Gesukirche, which I understand is built over the rubble of the original fifteenth century church shoehorned into this awkward site. Though a small church, it's hard to capture in a pencil sketch. In the right light, the angled glass walls allow a view into the sparkling interior, but that same glass also reflects the charred and broken remnants of the surrounding buildings. I find it difficult to mesh both concepts. I don't know who designed this church, but its concrete roof structure is similar to another icon of post-war, German church architecture I'd studied a few weeks ago at the Mariendomkirche in Neviges, designed by Gottfried Bohm.

Glass by itself cannot support heavy structural loads, yet the glass walls in this church appear to support the concrete roof structure piled above it. The architect is playing a visual trick on the viewer. Portions of the concrete upper structure, visually unattached to the ground, seem to defy gravity. The impression this imparts, it seems to me, is that it's impossible to force this church to crumble into the ground by any bomb thrown by any human. This structure's bulk is not something attached to the ground but yearning for the heavens. When next bombed, the resulting rubble of this church may very well project itself upward toward heaven. This is a difficult concept to capture in a pencil sketch, and I'm struggling with it.

I notice a woman, dressed like other women in the square, deliberately remove herself from the main stream of pedestrian traffic and walk across the dozen or so meters in a direct line to my bench. She sits down abruptly on the cold stone quite close to me, then deliberately does not watch me work. Eventually I look over at her. She looks straight ahead, avoiding my eyes. She seems several years older than I am, maybe thirty-five, it's hard to tell.

Her silence forces me to make the first move. I say, "*Tag.*"

"Good afternoon, Mr. American soldier." She twists her head. A slight smile appears on her face. Her eyes light up. Ten years of her apparent age immediately evaporate. I'm unprepared for this. It's obvious who I am. I'm wearing my US Army uniform, for God's sake. I'm a soldier in the foreign army technically at war with her country. I am, theoretically, her enemy. I'm unsure how to react. The first step, I'd guess, is to return the smile.

"It is not right that you make such a simple, gentle sketch of our complex brutal monstrosity of a church. What makes you want to do that?"

It seems obvious to me now who this girl might be. She's either a Stasi agent watching me, or one of the Driver's spies checking me out, or a naive art historian wanting to set me straight, or a mendicant looking for food money. Or, maybe a prostitute! I am unsure how to play this. So I stick with what I know best, sarcasm.

"It's a gentle sketch because I'm using a fine pointed pencil." It's the ugly side of my nature. I'm often flippant and disrespectful of other people's serious concerns. I raise my mechanical pencil so she can see the thinness of its lead. "This is a delicate tool. No crayon chunks or charcoal slabs for me."

Her smile breaks into a laugh.

That encourages me. "And you are wrong, young lady. That building is not a monstrosity but an extraordinary piece of symbolism."

"Says you!"

I feel blunt irreverence in her response. It may mean I'm talking with that naive art historian person. My natural reaction is to counterattack.

"Yes, I most certainly do say!" I watch her face. She's still smiling at me. "And I might ask you why such a wonderful smile is jumping out to me from under that dark cowl you've wrapped around your face. Shouldn't such a weapon be more obviously displayed?" I point across this little park. "You remind me of that church there, huh? Heavy dark things hovering over the light poetic parts. Some symbolism there too, I imagine."

She laughs again. "Tell me, Mr. Soldier Man, why are you here sketching our church?"

"Despite this nice green uniform," I say, "I'm an architectural student. And I'm interested in Berlin's recently built churches."

She says nothing, just studies my drawing. So, I press on.

"I notice you seem knowledgeable in both art and English. And I should like to know why."

"You say you're an architect? If that's so, then you must be familiar with the name, Hans Scharoun?"

"He's the architect of the new Berliner Philharmonie, right?"

"Yes, he is. You've studied that building?"

"I've yet to look at it. Today's my first day in Berlin."

She digs into her cowled wrapping, then extracts a card and a pencil stub. She makes a few pencil strokes on the card.

"Come to the main lobby of the Philharmonie tomorrow afternoon, at 1736." She smiles at me again. "We can continue our discussion of German Brutalism. Then, if you like, we can listen to some Beethoven."

"You have access to the west? How's that possible?"

"I live in the west, as you call it. I'm in East Berlin on a limited permit to see my sick mother." She looks at her watch. "I gotta go." She jumps to her feet, thrusts the card at me and turns and hurries down the narrow street, headed for Alexanderplatz.

I look at her card. It tells me only the address and telephone number for "Office of the Curator, Gallery 65er @ Der Berliner Philharmonie."

I lose sight of her gray tunic as it's absorbed into a sea of other tunics bobbing toward Alexanderplatz. I turn the card over. She'd printed "1-7-3-6" on the back.

★★★

I've more work to do here, so I rise, cross the garden, and enter this strange church through a glass door in a glass wall. I walk slowly down the aisle toward the altar. I sit in an ancient pew which could have been salvaged from the rubble of the previously bombed medieval church. I place my lunch bag on the pew and remove my drawing materials from my shoulder bag, which I place on the pew on my other side. Mesmerized by the remarkable medieval altar, apparently rebuilt using remnants salvaged from the original, I open my sketchbook to record this wondrous, gravity-defying visual achievement.

I believe I'm the only person in this strange church. After working on my sketch for some time, I hear a noise; someone's knocked over a waste basket or candle stand. An old man materializes from behind a concrete wall at the front. He carries a push broom, which he uses upside down as a cane to help him shuffle down the aisle. With some purpose he stumbles into my pew. He sits down, deliberately leaving a meter of pew length as a sort of no-man's-space vacant between us. I hear him breathe heavily. He smells awful. Among other odors I discern tobacco, alcohol, and something oily, maybe exhaust fumes from a tank.

"*Tag.*" He says this more softly than he looks capable of. He studies my uniform with suspicion.

"*Tag,*" I say back.

"You?" he points at me, then points to my sketch. "You? You the architect?"

"Ja. I am the Architect. And you, sir?"

"Ja, und also nein! Once I was architect. Once I work on this church." He points a grubby finger to my sketch pad, open to the drawing I'd just made of the concrete structure hovering above the altar. "So I tell you," he jabs his crooked finger, "your sketch is wrong!"

I stare at him. "How am I wrong?"

He tells me he designed that altarpiece to symbolize not the uplifting stuff I'd drawn of concrete hovering and yearning for heaven, but to represent the concrete power of the concrete Soviet regime which could, at any time, crash down and crush the spirit of this fragile East German Catholic community.

"Concrete might come crashing down any minute," he says. "You, however, are a romantic, so can't see that. You look at a rose and are taken by beauty of its flower. But me? I see its thorns as they press themselves into the forehead of our Savior. That is the rose I know. I understand the thorns! People in the church are crushed with a concrete crown of thorns." His voice gets softer and softer. He wanders through his dream.

"I'm no longer architect," he says. "I am now, the Janitor."

I look at him closely, and I smile.

"I think of my sister in Prague," he says. "Her rose blossom is about to be crushed and its thorns pressed into her flesh by the Mongols. They did it to us here in East Berlin. Just when people… they start to dream… they build a church… they are mesmerized by the blossom… then comes that damn concrete. It's… it's pushing down. Then comes the thorns crushing into our foreheads… now, now comes the blood…"

The man says nothing more. We take several minutes of silent rest. He could've been praying, dozing, perhaps even dying in place, it's impossible for me to know. When he thinks it's proper to continue, he says, "They took my license then, to embarrass me. Make me janitor. They make big mistake." He smiles. "This only place in whole wicked city I find peace."

"Maybe, with time, things will get—"

"Ach, they'll never get better. Tell the Driver the big trucks started last week. They load tanks on trucks. Now trucks heading toward Prague. Tell him he's got three months, maybe four."

I say nothing. I watch him intently.

"And soldiers also, I'm told. They're preparing to move a battalion. Also, I believe, into Prague."

"Should I worry about you, Mr. Janitor?"

"Ach, nein! Do not worry for me, Mr. Architect. I'm already dead. You must, however, worry about my sister in Prague. She has no time... no time left to dream... time... no time even to live."

He picks up his dirty lunch bag and rises slowly from the bench. "Three months, maybe four. But no more. Soon it'll be over. I don't think The Driver can do anything now but pray. But, please... please... tell him he must pray for me, and pray for my sister... and pray for Prague."

He grasps his broom and hobbles toward the altar. He bows low at the rail before the altar, genuflects with some apparent pain, and disappears behind a section of concrete wall.

I open the crumbled paper bag remaining on the seat and peek into it. I see my apple, an orange, a wrapped sandwich, and one cookie. I look at my watch. I don't have time to eat. I close the bag. I must go back to work with my sketching. I wander around inside and study everything differently, as the old man said I should. When it's time, I exit this place of interesting symbolism and begin the return to Unter den Linden, then the checkpoint. I anticipate no problem bringing my sketchpad and my uneaten lunch in the crumbled bag back through the gate. I am this dreary afternoon, simply, der Architekt.

All I've done, as any watcher would certainly confirm, is sketch churches and details of churches and make several stabs at talking to passersby who take time to talk with me. Seems nothing at all interesting or unusual has occurred on this first excursion into East Berlin. Nothing much interesting at all.

I do, however, find myself pressured by the Janitor to say a prayer for his sister. But that I cannot do. I've neither the standing, the tools, nor the belief it would make any difference. Though I do hope she survives the confrontation with her personal apocalypse when the tanks eventually clatter into Prague. Hope is the only weapon I have. It's as far as it's possible for me to go. Indeed, it's the only weapon anyone has. And though it may be of comfort to me, it will never be of help to the Janitor, nor certainly to his sister. And we all know that.

Part #2 - West Berlin

The next day I do some shopping. I'd brought only grungy clothes to Berlin, since I only own grungy clothes. I buy a cream-colored sports jacket, perhaps appropriate for someone acting as the Architect. It's similar to the one my Zurich friend, Gerhardt Stopak, wears. However, he's six foot two and slender, while I am five foot eight and built like a linebacker, so I'm not sure the effect will be at all similar. It should, however, be appropriate for Beethoven, for the magnificent Der Berliner Philharmonie, and for my date, or whatever it is, with the Curator.

The clothes are also appropriate for me to wear while talking with the engineering firm about bunker forty-six. That, theoretically, is why I'm in Berlin. Our files tell me I'm looking for a Berlin firm called HDC, GmbH, supposedly a subsidiary of a Houston-based oil field development firm. The Driver bet me lunch at Der Blaue Schwein that I'd find HDC was nothing but smoke. He was right. I did spend several hours looking and confirmed only that it was an illusion, a mirage, another sign of obfuscation. If the projects aren't real, why would their engineers need to be real?

★★★

I understand exactly what the Curator's cryptic time requirement code—the numbers she wrote on her card—mean. And so, wearing my stylish new jacket, I step through the Berliner Philharmonie's main entry doors at exactly 1736. As I expect, I see her as soon as I enter the lobby. And I'm certain she sees me. I notice the professionally administered instant scan of disinterested eye contact with no facial giveaway. She knows what she's doing. She doesn't wait for me to cross the room toward her, but turns quickly and walks into the cavernous hall and back toward the coffee shop. She's thirty meters ahead of me, and I watch her walk. I enjoy watching her walk because she's ditched the gray amorphous body cloak, and now, in a blue sweater and swirling skirt, she looks like an art curator should look. She walks confidently with the hint of arrogance art curators should project. She's definitely not a spy now. This is her show, and I'm not going to spoil it. I give her time. I casually walk into the cafe. I see her in a small booth on the far side, and I slowly walk over.

"Hello, Miss Curator," I say. I sit down opposite her. I still do not know her name, though we must make like we've known each other for years, a couple of properly dressed business acquaintances about to finalize a purchase agreement on a painting. "I'm happy to see you made it off the reservation before your time expired yesterday."

"Yes, I did. The Stasi permit me into East Berlin to see my dying mother twice every week for three hours. I must play by their rules. There'll come a time when I'll need the good will."

A waiter stops by. I order us cokes and some cheese and sausage to snack on.

"So, hello there, Farm Boy. Welcome to free Berlin. I usually meet with the Driver. Is he okay? No serious reason I'm not talking with him today?"

"No, there's just so much he can do. He's very busy. Since I had to be in Berlin for other business, I'm doing his work. He told me I'd talk to you. Told me I'm to ask about your mother."

"My trip to see mother was uneventful."

"How is your mother? What kind of sick is she?"

"It's a common disease, a broken heart in a broken body. She lives only to die because there's no reason left to live. She's probably right. She's only a few months left. She's breaking my heart."

"I understand what you mean. Thank you for asking me to the symphony."

"It's my pleasure. Good music, like good architecture, is necessary for a good life. Since I work here in the Philharmonie building, I can get complimentary tickets for unsold or no-show seats. Every seat in the concert hall is a good seat, acoustically speaking. It makes little difference where we do our listening."

We eventually do our listening in fairly uncomfortable seats. Or maybe they're fairly awkward seats, or fairly electric seats. I smell her perfume. I feel her arm occasionally brush my arm. We both listen actively, sometimes acknowledging a tense passage with a tense look or a tense hand touching an arm. It's like driving through the mountains in my Spider with one foot on the brake and the other on the gas. There are times the exterior sensation overpowers me. I could be in control, but I know the danger if I let my mind get too taken with the scenery.

And, of course, I am taken by the scenery. I've heard this music before; Beethoven is familiar. But I've not heard it bounce off these walls before, so I am studying the location and cant of those walls and other features of the architecture. This building's shape is based on pentagons, a geometric tribute similar to the Kaiserwilhelmkirche's octagons and hexagons. I cannot imagine a reason why both buildings would be so strictly geometrical in their organization. Perhaps it's to do with focusing the sound. Perhaps it's only German! I spend some time worrying about acoustical aspects of pentagons versus hexagons and lose track of the music and also, I'm embarrassed to admit, the fact that this girl next to me has placed her hand on my arm. I'm fairly certain I've screwed something up. I'll have to pay more attention.

After the concert we walk to a cafe on Kurfürstendamm. We sit in the pleasant garden and start with a bottle of wine. "I know this is all business, dear Curator, but it would make it much more pleasurable if I could call you something other than the Curator. What if I made up a name for you? How about Anna? It's my German grandmother's name."

"Thank you, Wall," she says. She watches me intently as I react to the fact that she already knows my name. She smiles. "The Driver told me all about you. Said I should know you really are a naive farm boy and should ease you into Berlin party life. I think you ought to know that I don't make a habit of picking up American soldiers in the Alexanderplatz. I was working under orders."

"So you know my non-code name, but I still don't know yours."

"You were correct." She smiles, blushes a bit, then gives me the lie. "My name really is Anna. Not sure how you knew that."

"Sure," I say. "I understand. And, just so you know, my real name's not Wall. It's Bekker, Alvin W. Bekker."

"I'd rather call you Wall." She knows I'm messin' with her, so she reaches over and gives my hand a quick little pat. "Okay, okay. I give up. I am Ruta."

So Ruta and I spend a long time discussing her mother and other East European political problems with veal and wine. It's the ideal time for enjoying a garden in Berlin. The strong summer heat's not yet arrived, and the lilacs or similar bushes perfume the air. Blinking lights and joyous conversations bounce around us. I shiver, thinking that less than a mile east of here my second new friend, the Janitor, is probably passed out in a dirty alley, smelling of urine and sweat and separated from a high intensity incandescent streetlamp by the hard-edged shadow cast by his Stasi watcher leaning over his inert body.

"I know Germans treated the Russians like dirt during the war," she says. "That certainly would be a reason for them to treat us the same now. Swallow some of our own medicine. I understand that. Foreign policy based on revenge. Tit for tat. Have you read much European history?"

"Enough to know that book is full of tits for tats."

She laughs. "But Poland, Hungary, and Czechoslovakia, they did nothing to deserve such dehumanizing treatment from the Soviets. At least you and your western allies treat us West Germans and West Berliners like humans. The Soviets are not doing the same on the other side. They're acting like barbarians."

"Though I agree with you, I can offer you nothing to ease your pain. I'm but an entry-level army guy, and not even a good one of those. I'm neither a general nor an ambassador. I've no power."

"Oh yes you do." A different Ruta is suddenly talking. I can tell from the radiating steam. "We people have the power, therefore I have power, and if I have power then you have power. And I know you. You're a much more powerful person than I am."

"You didn't, by any chance, earn your degree in Heidelberg, did you?"

"Why, yes I did. But, why would you ask me that?"

"Those words you just said—'The people have the power, blah, blah, blah.' If I'm not mistaken, I've heard similar words straight from Professor Marta Girrard's lips. She speaks those words to her audiences in Heidelberg."

"You know our Marta?"

"Well, yes I do, and I know her well enough to know what you mean when you say, 'our Marta.'"

"Then you also know that since you're in the army, you too have the power. As I've been telling the Driver, you've got to act fast, Farm Boy. I've heard the Mongols started moving tanks and troops from East Germany. And you know where they're going, don't you? Get ready to dive into your bunker, Wall. The great attack we've all been preparing for is, I'm afraid, about to happen."

"Yeah, others've told me the same thing, though so far we don't see aerial photographs picking up any of that activity."

"Mongols aren't stupid!" Another steam powered ejection. "Look harder! They do their crawling around at night so your spy cameras can't see them. Student groups here in Berlin, SDS for instance, the *Sozialistischer Deutscher Studentenbund,* argue that your US

Army must strike them right now. Take those tanks out while they are still on their trucks, before they reach Prague. I know it's possible. I know all about your Pershing missiles and your fighter jets with the bombs under their wings. Use your weapons! Use them now! You must do that for us. For Prague!"

"Ruta, I—"

"You drop thousands of bombs every day in Vietnam. The Soviets have thousands of tanks grinding toward Warsaw. Seems things are matching up nicely there, huh? All we need is but one day's worth of your Vietnam bombs."

"I cannot—"

"Doesn't have to be nukes. Just make a few those tanks go boom in the night. That's all we'd need. Force those Mongols to sprint toward the Urals. It's not so hard to understand."

I don't think patting her hand and offering her soothing, little-sister-who-just-broke-her-doll type words are appropriate here, but that's about all I can find in my arsenal. "I've been studying interesting stuff for twenty years, dear Ruta, but I know nothing about initiating nuclear conflagration. I don't think—"

"Then start thinking! Think of my dying mother as Warsaw. Both of them are sick with the same disease. I've watchers on the other side of the fence. They see things, and now I know things, and now I am telling these things to a representative of what I've been told is the most powerful force for good on this earth. My question to you, Farm Boy is, what are you going to do with this information?"

"I do know people who're anxious to get your information, and perhaps they know what to do with it. I promise you I'll share it with them. But I cannot say I've any influence with, or even an ability to talk directly to, army guys who push nuclear buttons."

I'm so far out of my comfort zone I cannot even remember normality. I haven't the foggiest idea of how to navigate out of here. Though I don't know why, I reach over and take both her hands in mine. I'm assuming verbal contact alone is somehow inadequate for this message. "Ruta, there is one thing you must understand. I'm promising you that none of those super-bombs hidden around western Europe will ever be fired. Ever Ruta! Ever!"

"You cannot talk—"

"Ever, dear Ruta! Ever!"

"Then tell the Driver that once Prague's brought to heel, Warsaw is next. The tanks and crews are already being assembled. While everyone's watching Prague smolder, they blitzkrieg Warsaw. Tell him that I, just like him, have family in Warsaw. Tell him he must use his Pershings now. If he doesn't, everything's gone. Neither the Driver nor I will see our grandmothers again."

"Ever, dear Ruta! I know you're distraught, but those Pershing things will not ever be fired. That'll never happen."

"Don't say never to me! You're in Heidelberg. You know the name of the general whose finger's on the red button. And you're gonna convince him to push *that* button. You're a tough guy. You can be forceful. Or you tell our Marta where the button is. She'll push it."

"I do know what button you're talking about. And I'd guess Marta even knows where it is, though I do not. And I assure you, dear Ruta, that button will never be pushed. Especially Marta will never push that button. It's an evil button, and pushing it'll only result in such unbelievable destruction it'll make the impending crushing of Prague seem like a snowball fight. I can assure you, nobody's gonna push that button."

"Then use your tanks and the thousands of soldiers you've kept huddled in tents in the mud along the *metal fence*. That's why they're camped out there! Isn't it? Forget about Vietnam. Concentrate on our brothers in Prague and Warsaw. You certainly can push that button. Push those Soviet pigs out of my country, out of the Driver's country, and out of the Bassist's country. If your soldiers must die, have them die in eastern Europe rather than in Asia. If nothing else, do it for me, Wall."

I don't know what to tell her. Maybe I should bring her to our NATO briefing in Brussels, have her to talk directly to NATO generals. Wouldn't that be a circus?

"There's nothing I can do, Ruta. Nothing except weep for your situation. I see only one intermediate path between, on the one hand, doing nothing but watching the Soviet tanks crush Prague, and on the other, pushing the button that promises end-of-the-world, nuclear devastation. That intermediate path is called time. Over time, say another twenty or maybe forty years, the thousands of baby steps taken by you and me and the good people of eastern and western Europe will gradually lead to a situation which may be reasonably comfortable for both sides. That is long range and uncertain, but it may bring the day when there is no Iron Curtain. But that way's not going to happen any time soon."

"We've been on your middle path for over twenty years already. Did you see anything green poking out of the gray rubble when you were sketching in the Alexanderplatz yesterday? I don't think another twenty years is going to make any difference either. And I'm afraid that I, as a human being, cannot sit here talking to you while the Soviets crush my cousins in Warsaw, can I? I cannot sit here and watch my poor mother die of a broken heart, can I?"

"Time, dear Curator! Time is the only answer, the only weapon able to solve your problem. Time! And what you must do is to keep the pressure on the clock to make sure that time is advancing forward all the time."

"That'll take too long. I'm not going to wait, Farm Boy. Neither Marta nor I, nor any of us in the free west, will sit quietly next to our mother's bedside and cry. Instead, I'm gonna find us a few tanks and a few bombs."

There is nothing more I can say to her. We seem to have no common ground. I'm exhausted, and I need sleep. I hear the beautiful bells of the Kaiser Wilhelm Memorial Church carillon telling us it's 2330. There's no 2300 curfew in Berlin, so here the night activity is just beginning. I now also hear something else. It sounds like a parade—drums and singing, loudspeakers shouting.

"What's that noise, Ruta?"

She laughs, pushes back her chair, then jumps to her feet. "Demonstrations are a constant here, and the night's still young." Miss Hyde has left the table and Miss Jekyll slips right in. "You're the architect, you'll appreciate this. Come! Come on, come on!" She reaches out for my hand.

I stick some Deutschmarks under the ashtray, then allow her to pull me out to the sidewalk. A demonstration of a few hundred students, complete with bullhorns and banners, is entering Kurfürstendamm from a side street.

"See that sign, Mr. Architect? Those marchers are engineering and architecture students from the Berlin Technology Institute. They're marching against the evil Emergency Acts. Those fascists in Bonn are forcing all us students into slavery. Listen, they're singing 'We Shall Overcome.'"

"German architects listen to Pete Seeger? Or Joan Baez? That doesn't sound right."

"I think it's not their words, but your Reverend King's. And you Americans shot him last month for preaching non-violence. Please explain that. And yet you refuse to be violent with Moscow?"

"What's Reverend King's connection with German students?"

"He was in East Berlin four years ago. He told my mother and me to be patient. 'We shall overcome,' he said. And 'Voices of freedom will overpower the oppressors.' He was wrong. Dead wrong, as it turns out! We're not overcoming anything."

"Did Dr. King mention time? Did he tell you it'll take time?"

"Your President Kennedy also spoke in Berlin. Then you Americans shot him too! What's the lesson here, Farm Boy? Talk nice to us Berliners and somebody shoots you? Only proves words don't work. Maybe it's time we do some shooting."

"I cannot even begin—"

"It's midnight!" she says abruptly. "I've got a meeting. Our group's planning things. And we don't have time!" With both hands she grabs my new jacket, pulls herself up, and kisses me.

"There," she says. "That's got to last till the next time. You hurry back, Wall. You find me bombs. Then you hurry back. We both have to make decisions. We must take responsibility and perform appropriate actions!"

None of my senses are operating. I'm thinking a fuse someplace overheated. I'm not hearing that 'we shall overcome' stuff anymore.

I watch her run down Kurfürstendamm. She's angry with me. Or maybe I am just in the wrong place. She's angry with the whole world. Perhaps she's not angry with me, specifically. Part of me even hopes she'll find some button to push. I cross Kurfürstendamm and head toward the Tiergarten and my *gasthaus* over near the US Embassy. The noise from cafes and clubs and sounds of partying accosts me as I walk. I hear the bells of the Kaiserwilhelmkirche chime 0030. How'd it get this late? I hear the demonstrating architects in the street behind me. Almost seems my senses have returned to normal.

The walk should take thirty minutes, but it's taking forever. I hear Ruta. I hear her crying for her mother. I cannot let her sorrow be the thing about her I remember. I want to remember her smile, her smell, the music, and her touch on my arm. And I'm positive that kiss is stored someplace safe. That thing put quite a dent in my armor. She's maybe dented it, but I'm confident she'll never break through it.

Part #3 - Heidelberg

The next morning I'm on the 1000 flight from Tempelhof to Mannheim. I retrieve my Spider, grab a quick lunch, rush back to Heidelberg, and around 1400 stride into the Critical Path office with what I believe is the usual bravado for a reporting spy. John and Lynx are in Lt. General Bekker's office eating the last of Clappsaddle's donuts. Apparently we won the alert lottery while I was busy with Ruta. I go right to it and jump on John.

"Thanks a lot for setting that Curator person on me, Driver. I'm lucky I got out of Berlin alive."

"I kinda thought you two might hit it off. Ruta's big into art and architecture, smart as a whip, and can turn some heads if she wants to. That's all good stuff, huh Wall? What possibly could have gone wrong?"

"She may be all those positive things, John. But she's also a caged tiger. She sees armed Mongols creeping into Warsaw and East Berlin. She's cornered and has nowhere to go. She thinks I personally can throw what she calls 'my Pershings' over the *iron fence*. I think I'm glad she's on our side, if indeed she is. Could be she's only on her side. She's marching against the nukes, yet fixated on pushing the red button and won't be happy till either Warsaw is an Eden or Europe's sloshing in radioactive cinders."

"She's worried about her mother. It's only natural."

"She's crazy! Everyone in Berlin's crazy. You General Bekkers have gotta help me understand this nuclear missile thing. The more nukes everybody's got, the less the chance anybody's gonna use 'em, right? Therefore, we stuff our bunkers full of 'em. Soldiers too. The more each side's got patrolling the *steel fence* the higher the odds nothing's gonna happen? Is that bizarre? The world's gone mad, right? Everything ends up looking like East Berlin no matter who wins. I could be safer in 'Nam!"

"You're wrong," says the Wizard. "It really matters. It'll take a whole year of conventional all-out warfare to approximate the same damage a couple nukes will do in a few minutes. Those Pershings are extremely efficient at instant mass destruction."

"Of course I see the benefit in that," I say. "Who doesn't? And it sure makes tons of sense for me to waste a couple billion dollars to install more powerful, or more efficient, Pershings. Tell me, what's the point of my job here? Why must I install updated nukes in brand new concrete bunkers? Even with the pitiful outdated nuclear arsenal we have now, we can do instant, Europe-wide, nuclear conflagration. Even with outdated nukes, it'll take the same four or five decades for the ground surface to cool down to where the Janitor might even start thinking about slogging through the radioactive waste and pouring some new concrete."

"You're the one needs cooling down, Wall. You saw the mess in East Berlin. It's been almost a quarter century, yet they still haven't cleared out their debris, and that stuff's not even radioactive."

"So our best path," says the Wizard, "is to make sure it's the third option that gets implemented. We first make certain the nukes will never be usable, and then we encourage every student, politician, and intellectual on both sides of the Berlin Wall to keep the pressure on their respective governments to liberalize living conditions and think about flower gardens instead of tanks. That's the path Marta's pushing. It's going to take a long time, but it can be done without the mass destruction promised by the other two methods. It's essentially the same peaceful protest dream Dr. King pitched to the East Berliners four years ago."

"Look where nonviolence got him. The world's gone nuts!"

"His nonviolent path," says John, "will take the same half century as will Ruta nuking the bastards now!"

"You set me up, Driver. You've made it so I've gotta go back into Berlin. I'm now the guy who has to convince Ruta she's nuts, that us jerks in Heidelberg ain't gonna help her and her friends start World War III. She's not gonna be happy with that news. She's not going to be happy with the messenger either, especially when I tell her the only weapon she can use is Dr. King's soft, non-violent words. She knows what soft words did for him! She wants somebody's blood. She'll not be able to watch her mother die or prevent Prague and Warsaw from dying either. There's no way I can ease her pain, is there?"

"No, Wall. I don't think so," says the Driver.

"There is one way," says Lynx. "You must be aware that Ruta does have one other option—one having the certainty of making sure her children, at least, can be raised safe and happy. She can marry that farm boy who'll bring her back to the States and, at least for her little isolated portion of the world, make sure—"

"You're out of your mind. That's one nuclear option I'm not taking. You're the one who told me to beware of kissing German girls. I'm heeding your advice, Lynx. I'm not yet strong or crazy enough not to. Plus, our ghost general hasn't inserted that marriage node into my Critical Path yet. At least I'm not aware of it."

"Might be a good idea if Marta talked with her," says Lynx. "Point out that the Curator has a serious job keeping pressure on the Soviets, so that after twenty or forty years it may be possible she'll be able to find a path for her kids, or most likely her grandkids, to live free, productive lives. Maybe Marta will be able to comfort her."

"I see absolutely no chance of that," I say. "Neither me, nor Marta, nor the Bassist. And not you either, John. I don't believe anyone can comfort her."

"You just said the magic words, Wall."

"Magic words? What the hell, John? What magic words?"

"The words 'I don't believe!' I'd think those words will put you close to hell."

"Don't get me started on your religious fantasies—"

"Like I've told you before, Wall, your problem is that you do not believe. I'll have you talk with my friend Father Lev. He'll council you on the positive aspects of believing."

"First Ruta, now you! Stuff's either true or not true. I don't believe untrue things. I don't believe Clappsaddle's fantasies, I don't believe your guy Bekker exists, I don't believe seven thousand nuclear warheads are waiting for their buttons to be pushed, and I don't believe Father Lev's archangels can swoop down here and push that button any more than Ruta can push it. Believing metaphysical stuff is ignorant. I'm not doin' it!"

"To be honest, I can't believe Ruta would push the button," says John. "But I gotta believe Lev's archangels will find a way to do it. I've no choice. I gotta believe that. It's my only option also."

"You believing archangels can stop Soviet tanks is only one step dumber than the Bassist believing his strange Czech rock music can stop 'em. Prayers are a bit like music, huh? Neither can explode and kill people. On the other hand, neither can make Ruta happy, or even safe. She's no option but to cry."

I've had enough for one day.

My mind races through that choreographed tango she led me through in Berlin, ending with that kiss. I think I might be lost. "Lynx is right about one thing. I will acknowledge that Ruta has one other option—me!"

Just saying those words stuns me.

"Fortunately," says John, "we three guys also have another option. We have tickets out of this mess. Next spring we'll chicken out… go back to the US and start our real life and leave the Curator and the Bassist with the rest of these true believers in the east bearing the entire burden of this strife by themselves."

"So you believe you can get off that easy? Just bail out and believe Father Lev's archangels will fix stuff. That, certainly, is not believable!"

"I think it is about all we can do, Wall. In twenty or thirty years maybe, we come back and see if things are better. If they are, maybe our friends and relatives will take me back. Maybe they won't. Lots of maybes with no good answers. It means we three have to get used to hearing the world cry. I know the listening's getting harder. But I'm satisfied I've done what I can do. I gave it the good try. However, I must also accept I have my own life to live."

I've already moved on. "I think I'm gonna run down to Zurich and hide in Stopak's design studio till my army time is up. You jerks play your cold war games up here without me. I can't wrestle with saving western humanity or even saving one pretty girl. I can't sacrifice my life for either Ruta or Prague. I just won't do it. I'm leaving and heading down to Der Blaue Schwein. I'll drink beer and work on my resumé. In several months my bad dream will be over, I'll be back into the real world, and I'll need a great resumé. And I'll need to quickly forget about all this nonsense. I'm hoping beer will help."

22 The Paris Story

After the May 20 riots, student protest movements start splintering. In addition to anti-Vietnam and pro-German student issues, there are anti-government, anti-Shah of Iran, anti-nuclear proliferation, and pro-NTMs (Nuke-The-Mongols) demonstrations. Protest is becoming broader and less specific. The whole world's a mess. Everything needs redoing. As a result more things get thrown, windows get broken, people get punched, and fires get lit. The invasion of Prague is inevitable, and Warsaw's not far behind. The idea of the US hiding seven thousand nuclear bombs in western Europe seems stupid on the one hand and, on the other, seems a blessing.

Groups release tension by throwing verbal artillery at the US and NATO. The US and NATO respond by increasing readiness exercises along the *steel fence* and even patrolling in downtown Heidelberg. Many previously hidden NATO weapons are elevated to CRS (combat ready status.) In response, Soviet generals amass additional troops on their side of the *steel fence*. Scared and clueless soldiers scurry about like rabbits. The 68er Bewegung (students on the move for social change in 1968) and half the SDS think they can intimidate the US into attacking the Mongol horde with a nuclear fusillade, while the other half of SDS are violently anti-nuclear and want to chain their bodies to the damn warheads if they could find them. Everything's in chaos.

★★★

And things aren't looking any brighter in gloomy Heidelberg either. Even my view out the window to the castle is depressing. Everything is depressing. John and Lynx walk by my cubicle. They're both stuffing their faces with donuts.

"You look out of it this morning, Wall, so we brought you a donut. These things are proven depression antidotes."

"Thanks, guys. But I'm okay. I'm not hungry, just tired and confused."

"Confused? What possibly is there to be confused about?"

"I find myself in a strange and uncomfortable situation. I had a long talk with Ruta last night. Could be I'm afraid, and perhaps I am lost."

"How's Ruta holding up?"

"Not well, John. Her mother wants to die. The Stasi have cut her mother-visits to one per week and probably will cut her off completely soon. Any visit may be the last time she'll see her mother alive. It's very sad."

"Certainly that's sad, but there's nothing you can do about it, Wall."

"I know. I'll never be able to solve her problem. But it's hard watching her suffer. Her world's falling apart."

"You must stay focused on your future. You can't get lost in her maze. You can't solve her problems."

"Yeah, that's what she says too. But then in the next sentence she's pushing me to push the button and throw one of 'my Pershings' over the fence."

"Now you know how I feel," says John. "I got the Bassist calling me two, three times a day. He sees Soviet tanks hiding everywhere. He sees smoke in the air and piles of bloody bodies on the ground, like the painting above the couch in USAEUR's main entry. The Bassist's a romantic, though lately he's mostly a drunk romantic."

"He's a frightened romantic," says Lynx. "We've got our hands full keeping him from self-destructing. He told me yesterday I had to push just one button. 'One or two! That should do the trick. Those Mongols would run for the Urals.' Supposedly that'll leave Czechs and Poles free to reconstitute their own nations."

"I don't know about you guys," I say, "but I'm uncomfortable standing in the middle of these pro and anti-nuclear-proliferation zealots, and the flinging-atomic-things-at-Moscow crazies. I understand we're responsible for knowing the readiness status of NATO's nuclear arsenal, even though none of us know, as a fact, a single thing about that arsenal. I don't know how many weapons we have, where they are located, if any of them are operational, or where that button that the Bassist or the Curator want us to push is located."

"We're just college guys building nuclear weapons," the Comptroller says. "We don't push buttons."

"Technically, only Lynx is still a college guy," I say. "And the rest of us don't build weapons—we only monitor their construction, and we don't do that well. We only throw chaff and adjust mirrors. We might be able to alter the Critical Path, to make that path something other than to nuclear conflagration, but I doubt it. Designing a path to peace is impossible. However, I'm thinking maybe there's a way we can confuse things, install doubt in the system."

"I've been working on a mathematical algorithm to do that," the Wizard says. "Thank God for computers."

We look at each other. We understand what Lynx just said.

I try working my way through Lynx's proposal. "So, we three guys control the computers that control the Critical Path. And that Critical Path, in a sense, controls the implementation of new nukes. If the new nukes happen to get lost in our complex critical pathways, who will be able to find them? Could Clappsaddle ever be sure they are actually where they are supposed to be and ready to have their buttons pushed?"

"All we need to do is alter a few pathways on the current network," says John. "First the Wizard does the magic with the math, then Wall strategically inserts several red or even not-green nodes onto the big board. Those nodes would, like a stick stuck into a bicycle's spokes, immediately stop forward progress."

"And if we do it right, no one will know where we've inserted them. That's maybe not a real roadblock," I say, "but certainly it's a perceived roadblock the NATO brass has come to understand as real because no one, even including us three, will know where those not-green nodes are located. And it's probably also true that forward progress disruption may occur even if the spoke our stick strikes is a faux spoke, built of illusion rather than steel."

"You've got to do it guys," says the Comptroller. "Like Lynx just said, 'Thank God for computers.'"

"We can't tell either Ruta or the Bassist this bad news," I say. "I think I've convinced her I cannot push that button. But she's still under the impression that one of my stronger or better connected friends will find a way to push it." I look at John.

"Thanks a lot, Wall!" John throws a paper wad at me.

I easily evade it. "And she is crying a lot. I'm still working on that."

The phone on my desk rings.

"Hi Ruta! Driver and I were just talking about you." She's screaming at me, gasping and hyperventilating. I can't make out her words. "Just slow down, Ruta."

"The world is falling apart, Wall! I hate you Yanks!"

"Take a deep breath. What's going on? I can't understand—"

"You just shot Bobby Kennedy! What're you gonna do about that? You better push that button now. You gotta do something! Do it now!"

But before I can even compose an answer, the line goes dead. I look up, and here comes Rhoda.

"Oh my God!"

My personal eye-in-the-sky is running full speed across the room toward us, and she's screaming out "Oh, my God" over and over.

I cradle the dead phone.

"Oh my God!"

"Oh my God!"

"Bobby Kennedy's just been killed. Can't you do something?"

"Can't I do something?" John is stunned. We all are stunned.

"Do something?" I suppose I could grab her a Kleenex? That might help. Or maybe, I should push that button and bomb Moscow. That might help her too! I have no idea!

★★★

The world's falling apart. I can't have Ruta staying in Berlin. Things are exploding there. Kennedy's shooting struck a match, and its gonna hit a gas tank soon. That's because of what Kennedy's brother told Berlin five years ago—"Ich bin ein Berliner!" In Berlin, the attack against Kennedy is understood as an attack against Berlin because many Germans hoped brother Bobby would exit Vietnam like he said, then refocus munitions on the Warsaw Pact. The SDS are mad, marching, and threatening to set the city afire. Chances for real violence are sky-high. I also know a lot of demonstrators are drunk in Berlin. A lot of police are very brutal in Berlin. Chances of Ruta getting caught up in the turmoil are almost certain.

I've gotta get Ruta out of Berlin. Kennedy's death does not infuse students in Paris with the same passion as it does in Berlin. So I talk her into meeting me in Paris. We'll take a few days and let the temperature in Berlin cool down. She promises me she'll take the early flight into Paris tomorrow morning. I'll take the morning train and meet her at the hotel on Rue Ecole du Medicin where I've stayed before.

What the hell have I just done? Have I jumped off a cliff? Maybe out of a helicopter? I have no idea where I am going to land, and I am scared out of my wits. All of a sudden this situation is much more dangerous than Vietnam.

★★★

We walk down Rue St. Michel and stop at a cafe set under the trees in the Parc du Luxembourg. We have cheese and wine. We watch student groups chase each other around the fountain throwing slogans at each other. Thank God we're in Paris. They're only throwing words around here. In Berlin they're throwing Molotov cocktails. Ruta and I behave like civilized folks, drinking merlot and discussing killing—killing Bobby Kennedy, killing nuclear proliferation, and in a sense, killing religion.

We get to Notre Dame late in the afternoon. It's dark inside, though outside the sky is cloudless. For a Gothic structure the nave windows are relatively small, dark, and now certainly dirty, and it's not light and airy as Gothic should be. A choir's practicing somewhere. Acoustics are terrible. Sound slips off this stonework rather than jumps off it. This structure's a horrible music venue. We sit in a pew west of the crossing, and I listen to Ruta talk about her quite bleak future. We talk about being a Catholic, about suffering, about believing, about forgiveness, about the persistence of evil. Good things to talk about in a church. We talk way too much about me, though I'm pretty much black and white. She's the color model and, I find, much harder to reconcile nuance and distortion.

"So you're telling me there's no hope. No chance of you throwing bombs or troops at the Soviets. No chance for my mother. No chance I'll ever be happy here. Then you tell me no chance you're even gonna try believing in God."

"One can't try to believe," I argue. "One either jumps off the belief cliff or stays atop the rational mountain."

"Rational mountains are overrated," she says. "You're sayin' you're not even going to try? You're willing to make both of us miserable for the rest of our lives. How can you live with that?"

"I don't choose to not believe. I just can't accept made-up stuff. Fairies and purple cows don't exist."

"I'm not talking about fairies. I'm talking about God."

"They're the same thing, Ruta. I've always assumed educated people who know how nature's constructed don't require fairies or gods. There's no evidence supernatural entities do anything. Or, if they are doin' stuff, there's no way we humans know what they're doing. So why fight over whose god is right. Please, accept only physical evidence. Accept that supernatural is only another word for I'm afraid or I don't know."

"That a simplistic view, Wall. Not worthy of the kind of marvelous power that must move the planets around or allow butterflies to flitter."

"I'm sorry, Ruta. We cannot make this work. And it's not because of anything we have control over. You gotta listen to your God. Seems He is telling you I'm a jerk, and you shouldn't waste any time on me. He's doing that for a purpose. And I'm assuming it's a good one, and you should listen to Him. He's probably looking out for you."

"God doesn't think such convoluted thoughts."

"How do you know? Or, maybe the problem's me. You want me to lie to you and pretend that I believe just so we'll be together. If I did that, both you and I would have to know each of us were lying. So I can't see that working long term, can you?"

"After several years I could wear you down. I could eventually convince you, don't you think?"

I just look at her and shake my head.

"So that's the way it is, huh? All muddled up and convoluted. Be assured I am gonna find me that watertight argument, Wall. But I'd better think about it some first, huh?"

"I think so. How about we make the best of being here, and we walk over to Sainte Chapelle. I think I saw an ad posted over there. It's Vivaldi night. Let's see if tickets are still available."

"Deal!" she says. She puts her arm through mine, and we head across the plaza toward Ste. Chapelle. "You understand Vivaldi's a stop-gap measure, you jerk. That tomorrow I'll mount another charge. I might catch you at a bad time or with the right wine and drive a successful argument right into your heart."

"I wouldn't hold your breath, Ruta. And it's not my heart you have to worry about. That's the wrong target! It's science that you've got to overpower, so you gotta aim your weapon higher, toward my simple brain!"

23 THE 1ST PRAGUE STORY

The bomb explodes at ten o'clock on the evening of August 20, 1968. Thank God it's not the nuclear one! It's only four hundred thousand barbarian boots and five thousand Mongol tanks that smash into central Prague. Boot and tank vibrations break windows and rattle china cabinets, bookshelves, and residents. They loosen the street bricks, crunch through street lamps, bollards, vendor stands, and trees. They topple statuary, and they quickly crush the rather meek Czech independence movement—that brief bittersweet period of mildly liberalized communism many called the Prague Spring.

Czechoslovakian patriots protest the invasion with public demonstrations and a bit of brick throwing, but most use Reverend King's non-violent dissent methods like prayer, poetry, and music because they're the only weapons available. But these soft methods require a long time line for success and cannot resist the rather immediate violence of Soviet tanks and Warsaw Pact boots. The excitement's over in two hours. Before the churches toll midnight, the invaders remove First Secretary Alexander Dubcek, repeal his liberalizing reforms, and instigate a normalization procedure under a new government more in line with the thinking of the Soviet minders.

★★★

Eight months before the Soviets smash Prague, back in December of 1967, I'd helped Sully move several boxes of electrical equipment into the attic rooms of his rather strange hotel-rooming house. It's his parents' equipment, and they are both IRA liberation consultants who've moved to Prague as tactical advisors to the underground dissident community there. It's their shortwave equipment we'd moved into his attic. I also helped move in suitcases, clothes, and other stuff for the Bassist and the Poet, the two Czech University of Heidelberg music students whose job will be to operate this information link to Prague whenever the expected invasion happens.

Sully considers housing these Czech students an absurdist metaphor for hostage taking. He'll hide the non-hostage Czechs in his hotel to balance the potential injustice of his non-hostage parents being hidden—and now in danger of being arrested and imprisoned—in Prague. I personally don't see how anything's being balanced here. But then, I'm neither Irish nor Czech. I'm an outsider.

Both Sully and his Czech expatriate boarders have long expected this Soviet invasion. They have prepared for it, and they receive the sad news directly from Prague via their secret radio even before the tanks come to rest in front of the city hall. The shortwave signal blasts the sad news from a secret and probably movable transmitter in Prague. The sad news flies through the Fulda Gap and reaches the almost invisible antenna balanced atop the small spire capping the observation deck of the southernmost tower of Sully's picturesque little hotel in Neckargamünd. The message explodes once it's received, and the shock wave wakes every member of the Critical Path office team living in the hotel. The Poet stays with the radio to monitor reports, but the Bassist, the Driver, and the Painter are quickly on their feet, down the stairs, out the door, and across the gravel to the Driver's red VW.

"Where the hell they off to?" I ask Sully.

"They're headed for the Heiliggeistkirche."

"In Heidelberg? Why?"

"The Heiliggeistkirche was not targeted by the Allies during The Big War, and so it's still standing in all its medieval majesty as a proud symbol of good in a world gone crazy. During the Big War, that tower was a strong presence, poking itself through the heavy fog of evil and touching the goodness of the light above."

"That seems a rather strained metaphor," I say. "What are you trying to tell me here?"

"The Heiliggeistkirche is a vital piece of the underground's information gathering and distribution system. The Bassist is required to broadcast the truth regarding the Soviet's rape of Prague to the whole world. And he needs to get to the Heiliggeistkirche to do it."

It was because I was trying to understand this rather bizarre reaction to the news of the Prague invasion that I came to understand why the Painter takes an academic interest in church bells.

"The church bells are but a diversion. It is not the bells in the Heiliggeistkirche, but the steeple itself that's the important thing." He points in the general direction of his own little south tower. "Our tiny steeple works just like that of the Heiliggeistkirche, and Domkirche St. Petrus in Köln, and several other of the very few city churches preserved from destruction during the Big War.

"The underground took advantage of the vertical height offered by the preserved church steeples and concealed their shortwave antennae in them. The Heiliggeistkirche is located within walking distance of both the University of Heidelberg and the headquarters of the US Army in Europe. Unlike the low-power equipment tacked to my roof, that Heiliggeistkirche station can broadcast a strong signal over all of Europe."

I watch the Bassist climb into the passenger seat. Like a young mother with a newborn, he is tenderly clutching a tape reel of a concert given last week by the Czech underground rock band, The Plastic People of the Universe. It's not a high-quality recording because he pulled it off the radio himself, and his equipment's elementary. For this emergency, the Bassist doesn't care about tone quality. Sully tells me the Bassist plans to continuously play his tape during the next weeks, interspaced with any new news seeping out of Prague. He will play the music as a symbol of the new resistance, as a rebuke to the Soviet's barbaric actions, and as a threat to any non-democratic sympathizers that the proud and formidable Czech spirit will not be crushed by five thousand filthy, ugly, Russian tanks.

Sully and I watch the Driver spin his VW through the gravel in the entry court and disappear under the *porte cochère*.

"Of course," says Sully, "we all know that the Bassist's broadcast is an entirely symbolic exercise. Such symbolic actions may vent anger but can, at least in the short term, provide but an illusory or perhaps chimerical response to five thousand Soviet tanks. However, he hopes his act will allow new Czech music to be heard on both the east and west sides of the Iron Curtain over the next few months. That's essential, because without the Bassist's broadcasts, no new music—except the sound of tanks rumbling through the rubble and the bricks bouncing off them—will be heard east of the *metal drapery*. Like the Bassist has often said, 'Music from The Plastic People of the Universe will bring that *steel blanket* crashing down.'"

"Seems to me," I say, "our Bassist has stepped off the belief cliff."

"He's content he is doing the best he can for his people. But he wants more. He wants to turn Moscow to rubble. He wants one of us to push the red button. He speculates that American bombs will work better than the musical artillery thrown by The Plastic People of the Universe. I think he's probably right there. Bombs will be more effective than rock music. But then, almost anything hurled at a tank will make a bigger dent than will rock music—even the Bassist's classical-based rock music."

Though dramatic and frightening, the Warsaw Pact invasion of Prague was not unexpected, so most Czech students in Heidelberg were prepared for the explosion. Even so, the blast cloud propagated by the event swept into the University of Heidelberg community, empowering many loosely organized groups to react with ad hoc protest actions. An ordered, rational response to a Mongol tank invasion is an inane concept and one impossible to implement. As might be predicted, demonstrations by groups like the SDS and the 68er Bewegung turned violent, and reasonable chunks of that violence were focused on the US military, on West German political leaders, and on entrenched university faculty, many of whom maintained ties with pre-war ideologies of the National Socialist Party.

Repercussions from the invasion of Prague immediately affect the set of activities being conducted under the auspices of Lt. General Alvin W. Bekker and on those of his boss, General Clappsaddle. Clappsaddle's response is powered by the realization that he must spend more time in Brussels with NATO generals, thus reducing his golfing time in Heidelberg. His army is stressed, because in addition to increased patrol and practice operations in the tense areas along the Iron Curtain, it must now assist the understaffed German police to combat the almost continuous student—and now even non-student—demonstrations. Olive drab men and equipment patrol campus courtyards and *gasthaus* patios. Though they're armed with military weapons, the students have them scared silly. They're throwing food, poetry, and music at Clappsaddle's army guys who, unlike the Mongol horde, will not throw stuff back at them. Clappsaddle either does not know where the red button is or has been ordered not to push it. Maybe he wants to wait for the new Pershings with the advanced warheads I am scheduling to go online next February. Clappsaddle seems unsure of generating a reaction.

Therefore, in a typically simplistic bureaucratic move, Clappsaddle does perhaps the only thing he can do; he doubles the number of alert exercises every month thinking such action makes him twice as prepared for the impending Soviet non-attack. He'd much rather pretend to fight, or perhaps think about preparing to fight, Warsaw Pact tanks and infantry than to actually confront unorganized street gangs, organized student groups, and professors like Marta Girrard who are stirring emotions and confusing military mentalities.

The heightened tension pries open fissures in Lt. Gen. Bekker's shadow military operation, and his authority and stature begin to seep out through them. Clappsaddle's new military paradigm requires a less ethereal presence than the one our imaginary ghost general has used to his advantage over the years. His intricate network, delicately woven into sources of underground information, has within hours been blown away by the firestorms generated by the bomb blast in Prague.

Multilevel links between east and west, pathways painstakingly constructed over the last ten years, now lie twisted and broken. Watchers who've been watching their fence for years and who've developed rituals of observing and of not observing certain blind spots in their radars, have been replaced with new eyes and new inspection regimens with more powerful sensors and sharper knives. Many of the Critical Path office's friends in the Czech underground, including dozens of expatriates left stranded in Heidelberg, quickly turn surly, even vicious.

A dense somber cloud settles in—the uncomfortable heavy realization that the very existence of our Critical Path office is tied firmly to the nuclear mass-destruction principle that every one of us in General Bekker's crew personally abhors. That dismal cloud is particularly dense and particularly somber this evening inside Der Blaue Schwein. And the associated rain is so heavy I can hardly see the storefronts across the street.

"What's our path now?" asks the Painter. "Till now we've not known, or even cared much, if any of this nuclear junk we're tracking is real. It's all about vectors and nodes on a chart. Do we now have to concern ourselves with what's true? Do you think we should stop playing in our sandbox and make some waves? Find out what the hell is really going on out there?"

"We can't have some Vietnam-diseased general assuming our Pershings are real, can we? Ya think there's a chance one of 'em will stumble around, looking for a button to push?"

"You really suppose any of the things are real?" I ask. "I understand it's not our job to know, but is there any way we *can* know?"

"What happens if we just refuse to give any information about the nukes to NATO?" asks Lynx.

"I don't think it matters," John says. "Giving NATO no reports is little different than giving them the worthless reports we've been giving them for years. Either way they learn nothing. No change there, right? Second, if we stop doing our Critical Path work, I'll be unable to continue my recovery work for Uncle Jacob, the very existence of which depends on that construction program to provide us with operational cover."

"It would be fun to watch though," I say. "If we don't monitor the construction, they'd have to start doin' it themselves. And the only way Clappsaddle can be sure the bombs are available is to physically drive his own jeep past every bunker, hangar, and runway extension, and inspect each one himself!"

"And even that ridiculous idea has a huge loophole," says John. "Who's gonna tell Clappsaddle where to drive to find those forty-one or sixty-seven construction sites. And how does he tell when he's looking at a faux site?"

"I wish Clappsaddle luck. We've not found one construction site, except for Schwäbisch Gmünd, Fulda, and Wackernheim, even though the Driver and I've driven road rallies through the supposed construction areas looking for them."

"Do you think," asks Joseph, "that one strange and unexpected result of the Prague invasion might be the possibility that the nuke program will be exposed as the big scam we think it is?"

"Could be," says the Wizard. "And what would the repercussions of that be? Would the Soviets move to quickly attack us or fall down laughing? Would President Johnson lock himself in the bathroom to avoid answering embarrassing questions? And how will Frank Zappa react?"

"The Bassist might never talk to us again. He may take his anger out on me personally."

"You guys are dwelling on the down side. You've skipped the good parts."

"Are you seeing any good parts here, Wall? Mutually assured destruction doesn't have good parts. Least not that I can see."

"You don't know where to look," I say. "I'm thinking about Clappsaddle doubling alerts. Means the congratulatory donut rewards program will deliver twice every month. That's a big win for our side, don't ya think? We rake in twice the donuts!"

24 THE 2ND PRAGUE STORY

Two weeks later I'm in Lt. General Bekker's office. We various General Bekkers are working on long-term scheduling.

"Oh, no!" says the Driver. He waves a sheet of paper he's just pulled out of an envelope. "More horrible news!" He reads to us, "Due to increased security and tension, the last two road rallies for this season have been canceled."

"I thought we might be able to win one of those," I say. "I've already cleared a spot on my desk for the trophy."

"That ain't gonna happen, Wall. We'll be having no more fun in the mud near Fulda. It's the Mongol's fault. Them and their tanks. Damn them."

This cancellation illuminates the fact that Lt. General Bekker has two separate problems. The first concerns opening communications between Prague and the Czech expatriate community in Heidelberg so that intellectual, political, and musical information can once again travel unencumbered across, through, or under, the Iron Curtain. The second concerns reinvigorating Uncle Jacob Kirchner's Polish heirloom and art smuggling operation.

"It's gonna take years to reopen or reconfigure the paths required to transfer information, material, and people to Heidelberg from Warsaw and Prague," says John. "Access is not possible now. We'll need years."

Progress is also crawling because a new wall of distrust is manifest between Lt. General Bekker's operatives and the expatriate underground community who suspect Bekker is too closely connected to the US Army of Occupation. All this depression, radicalization, and forced acquiescence crushes Lt. General Bekker's morale and infects his rational thought processes.

"Our problem is not just with the Iron Curtain," I say. "The rules have changed with respect to Berlin's *concrete wall* too. The Stasi won't allow the Curator to visit her mother, or me to visit the Janitor. That strange relaxed protocol regimen at Checkpoint Charlie is no longer relaxed, though it does remain strange."

"Any idea when they'll open the gates again?"

"Impossible to tell, John. Nobody'll even talk to me now. It's gonna take a while. The Stasi guards are having too much fun being the bad guys. The US guards are under constant attack from the Curator. She bangs on their windows every day and threatens them with attacks from student mobs and our Pershing missiles. She tells them she knows guys who can push buttons. The guards don't believe her, not yet."

"But she may be right," says Lynx. "Her pounding daily on their window may be more effective than you threatening to push red buttons."

Our scheduling meeting eventually dissolves as there's nothing we can see that needs scheduling.

So with nothing much to do at this time of introspection, except to creatively obfuscate the data on the official Critical Path Diagram and hope it delays the completion of those imaginary nuclear construction projects, we Critical Path guys turn our minds to civilian interests. We do things that can actually be done. The Painter paints, the Cartoonist cartoons, I'm designing a mountain cabin for Gerhardt Stopak's office, and I hear the Bassist pounding his piano in the adjacent room; he's doing a bit of composing.

Technically, the Bassist is not a Critical Path guy, but a homeless Czech composer. However, the Driver took pity on him and, in a symbolic attempt at solidarity with the Czech underground, provided him a vacant office in the Critical Path suite and 'borrowed' an unused spinet from a storage room of the NATO briefing theater on the first floor. It presents a bizarre image, an expatriate Czech composer, pounding on a NATO piano in a room provided by a Polish-American ex-soldier working under a ghost general in the US Army Headquarters building in a German university town. It's absurd! It's hard for me to imagine anything worthwhile being produced in such a strange environment.

Also, the Comptroller is running on short-timer status. He's focused on returning stateside. Two other civilian guys leave. The plumbing supplies courier delivers us no replacements. Gradually, our Critical Path office is fading away. By February, when those Pershing-1As are snug in their bunkers, the office will vanish—poof! Our compatriot, Todd Werner, the ski patrol guy from Garmisch-Partinkirchen stopped in yesterday to check in whatever keys he'd previously checked out from Lt. Gen. Bekker. With only four months left on his clock, and with the ski season about to start, the army yanked him from Austria and is flinging him to Saigon. Since there are no ski mountains in Saigon, he's frightened silly. I'm in shock. I'm also an army guy with four months left and a disappearing army job. I also see my Vietnam specter rising from the swamp I've been storing it in.

"Damn," I say, "my helicopter dream's gonna visit me tonight."

"Let's not worry about dreams, Wall. We gotta concentrate on reality."

"I see no reality here, Driver. Therefore, I'm gonna supply my own. Stopak needs me in Zurich. If the army calls, tell them I'm working on a secret project in a foreign country. There's a precedent. The army trained me to be creative. In New Jersey I worked off grid because the army couldn't find me army work there either."

"But you gotta stay flexible, Wall. General Bekker will need you periodically."

"No problem. I'm a resilient guy. I can do flexible."

"You're gonna have to. I'm stuck at the Iron Curtain, punching holes and digging tunnels. You may be floating without purpose, but our jobs," he motions toward Lynx and then to himself with a forkful of sausage, "have become much more difficult."

"Oh, and a third thing," I say. "I just scheduled another sketch problem in LaNapoule for the second weekend in November. That's not a lot of lead time, but it should work."

"Confirm that with the Comptroller. I think he's leaving in September. Gonna work on Wall Street. He'll make gazillions, though there's a downside... he's gotta wear a suit."

"Damn! Everyone's going home! You're leaving too, Lynx. When's that?"

"That just changed, Wall. The university asked Marta to stay on for the spring. They're having personnel problems. Incoming visiting professors are canceling their commitments because of student unrest. Some professors don't realize a passionate student body's a positive thing."

"Neat! Marta must be ecstatic."

"And me too," says John. "Without her connections to east block underground and intellectual sources, I can't tear many holes in the Iron Curtain."

25 The Concert at the Castle Story

It's been a month since the Mongols smashed Prague and extinguished the Prague Spring. The atmosphere in Heidelberg has turned pungent and dour. A new and brutal season, the Heidelberg Autumn is pounding my beautiful city. Old men are drinking and yelling. Students and professors are burning theses and hurling bricks. Mothers keep their children inside, so the bricks do little harm.

Mother Nature, joining with the students, is throwing temper tantrums. Last night, in a fit of anger, she sent in a much too early killing frost that turned wet green leaves to solids. Then this morning she hurled an evil wind which dropped the leaf-stones to the ground. Frozen fog and freezing drizzle pasted the leaf debris to the cobblestones. The slippery surfaces ruin the cadence of marching soldiers and spin the tires on the trucks that carry them into the Marktplatz and to the University Commons to confront yet another, or perhaps it's the same, continuous student demonstration.

Many in the Critical Path office cry in sympathy with the Czech students and Mother Nature. Around midday, dozens of us, including John, Lynx, Josef, and Sully, bundle ourselves up and walk, along with several hundred protesters, the kilometer and a half to the castle for a protest rally. As we approach the castle grounds we're struck by the devastation our Mother has wrought.

The normally exuberant castle gardens have been beaten down by the continuous frozen drizzle and the violent hard frost that last night smashed the blooms. Thousands of roses lie limp, defeated, and bent in submission. Perhaps they also mourn for friends living under siege in Prague. It's only September twentieth, one month since Prague's invasion. It's several weeks too early for a killing frost. Seems time's also broken.

"Look at these poor roses, Lynx!" I reach down and force one of the deceased stems back to the vertical. "The poor things have given up." The yellow rose is coated in frozen drizzle and flash frozen. It's brittle as a wine goblet and explodes into powder when I fondle it. I release the stem, and it plummets itself down into the frozen mulch. "Seems they're compost already," I say.

"It's not their fault," says John. "Damn sun won't shine. Won't bring them light or heat. You've driven your frosty tank through my garden, Mother."

"You've smashed my people!" Sully yells this up into the sky which produced the frozen drizzle. He stretches both his arms up into the dank fog. "No more o' your killing, Mum! Do your job! Bring light to my people huddling in the shadows, here in this garden and certainly in Prague!"

Almost immediately a small break appears in the clouds, and a ray of sun slips through.

"Nicely done, Sully," I say.

"Forecast says the sun will pop out this afternoon," Sully says. "Supposed to dry out and warm up. Temperature's supposed to jump into the mid-teens in a few hours for the concert."

"Your parents still in Prague?" I ask him. "Heard anything since the tanks rolled in?"

"No, mate! Not a word. I don't worry m'self with 'em, though. They're professionals, me mum 'n dad. They be knowin' what they be doin'."

"You don't fool me. You're worried about them."

"Well, maybe a wee bit. I shoulda heard from 'em. It's prob'ly 'cause the 'wave is down. The Bassist's receivin' only sporadic messages. They must be movin' their transmitters around. Hidin' 'em from the Mongols. Me dad'll figure it out soon. He's a cleva' bastard."

★★★

The Heidelberg castle has been a mostly unusable structure for hundreds of years. It's actually a former castle. Like many similar Rhineland Palatinate castles, its undergone several cycles of alternating construction and demolition over two millennia. Essentially, it's the bombed-out shell of several former attempts at castle building, alternately built and bombed since the first structure was erected, before the Romans got here.

Most all the roofs are gone, leaving pieces of wall with sections missing and craggy tops sticking into the sky. One irregularly shaped interior courtyard has somehow escaped the cannon, allowing its enclosure walls to maintain their original three story height. This seventeenth century courtyard is almost intact, with crenellations and gargoyles and several of the requisite statues watching over the activities in the yard from niches set into these four surrounding walls. This courtyard is now used as an outdoor musical venue because its non-parallel walls bounce sounds around in unique ways. The acoustics are wonderful, especially for small orchestral works.

This venue will host a strange and different sort of violence later in this soon to be warm afternoon—a performance of musical warfare organized by The Critical Path office's resident Czech composer, the Bassist. He's molded a group of fellow expatriate musicians into an informal group he's named The Mothers Hurling Bricks. The name of his musical ensemble represents the people of Prague who actually threw bricks and other things at the Soviet tanks in Wenceslaus Square a month ago today. The Mothers Hurling Bricks honors the well-established but currently silenced Prague musical ensemble called The Plastic People of the Universe, whose members have been arrested and their music crushed by the new

Prague government.

The members of TPPU are still jailed. The Bassist believes his new group is a holy instrument, assembled to continue The Plastic People's work. They'll record and play TPPU's music in the west, even broadcast it back into Czechoslovakia in an attempt to keep The Plastic People's music alive. The Bassist means to mock the authorities who've jailed the Plastic People, and who're outlawing their performances in Prague. As a symbol of his solidarity with Prague, Lt. General Bekker supplied the piano and the studio for the composer, allowed TMHB to rehearse in the NATO auditorium, and magnanimously agreed to underwrite the production of this concert.

We're anticipating a tremendously emotional show because tonight The Mothers Hurling Bricks will debut the Bassist's exciting new work of political rock music, *Requiem for Prague in A, a composition for Tanks, Machine Guns, and a Flute*. His orchestration is for a chamber group including strings, horns, and tympani. The Painter will play an electric harpsicord, and the Driver will play the featured flute part on his violin. John can handle that, having years ago performed with the Chicago Youth Symphony.

This joint, east-west musical event represents a powerful yet delicate bit of international fence-mending. The Driver, joining with the Bassist in playing his *Requiem for Prague in A*, is making an act of philosophical solidarity between the American civilian people and the Czech expatriate people. Any goodwill achieved by this joint venture is limited and will not impact the US Army or the US Government who are still preoccupied with Vietnam and nuclear proliferation, and who will pay no attention to either The Plastic People of the Universe or The Mothers Hurling Bricks, what with people and mothers currently being crushed by the Soviets over on the other side of the *steel drapery*.

It's no surprise to anyone that a certain amount of frustrative violence may accompany, or result from, playing music arranged for military weapons. It's also no surprise that such music, born of violence and oppression, will never replace the fluffy pink music of the Beatles, who sit atop the international pop charts. The Bassist and his Czech friends, however, do not read the situation in that way. They believe their classically based, emotional laden, serious rock music will quite easily overpower the fluffy stuff currently infecting the western world. They believe this New Czech Music will encourage the student population in Heidelberg and other European, and even American populations, to think more about ugly gray tanks than pretty yellow submarines.

★★★

It seems obvious to me, as it certainly must to the Bassist, that his new composition, *Requiem for Prague in A, a Composition for Tanks, Machine Guns, and a Flute* cannot be performed with actual tanks and real machine guns, at least until after the Mongols and their tanks are physically removed from Prague. So an approximation of the sounds of the listed instruments is necessary. The Bassist has his bass mimic the tank, has a snare drum parody the machine guns, and a flute, or in this case John's violin, plays the flute part. The piece runs nineteen minutes and thirty-two seconds, intending to document the time that first Soviet tank took to crawl the length of Prague's Wenceslas Square pushing through the fervid crowd filled with mothers hurling their bricks and several other things at that tank as it imperially crawled itself to a stop at the far end of the square in front of the Prague City Hall.

    The bass plays a twenty-two note continuo, representing the slowly moving Russian tanks. It's a low rumbling, repeated at constant tempo for the entire nineteen plus minutes. The snare drum throws sporadic machine gun fire. The flute cries the voice of Prague's citizens. It cries softly and sometimes yelps with pain in response to the actions of the machine guns. The flute attempts to humanize the violence depicted by the military instruments. It's a difficult piece to listen to. Harmony is abandoned and much discordance introduced. It must not be performed in venues where those hearing it have easy access to real military weapons.

26 The Richard Nixon Story

Though I've been spared the sump of Vietnam, I'm periodically visited by its specter, a single-scene nightmare, a snapshot in fantasy-time, a truncated dance with neither prologue nor climax. Once again I'm in the helicopter with Marley's ghost. I see Davie Groetken in there too, firing his red-hot machine gun out the open door. I hear Marley's chains rattling. I see sweat and smoke swirling. Much inside the open door is black, and various things on the outside flicker red and orange. In front of me, an impossibly thin soldier with oversized red eyes fires his machine gun, nonstop, into that red-orange opening—thut thut thut thut... thut thut thut thut... thut thut thut thut.

The sound is deafening. A continuo of helicopter blades adds a bass line—thwop thwop thwop thwop... thwop thwop thwop thwop.

"Rap rap rap rap!"

Immediately the dream is shattered. I recognize that last noise, and it's not part of my ghost's usual script!

"Hey, Wall!" The smash on the door jamb again. Rap rap rap rap!

I'm a soldier, right? I'm instantly alert. My eyes open, my head pivots, and I see my door opening, a head sticking through the opening. Instinctively, I reach out for my rifle. Damn, I don't have a rifle. I've never had a rifle.

I recognize the head popping into the opening.

"John? What—"

"It's time to go, sleepyhead. Get a move on!"

I glance at my clock—0230.

"It's two-thirty in the stupid morning, John. What's the problem?"

"No problem, Wall. Opportunity is knocking." He raps again, a dum-da-da-dum-dum thing on the door. "Civics lesson time."

"Civics lesson? It's the middle of the night, you jerk. Nothing civic happening this time of night."

"Okay, I'm wrong. Maybe it's not the middle of the night!"

"What? You drunk?"

"Get up. You remember what day this was?"

"What day this was? You're talkin' code again."

"Over in the States, it's now 2030 hours yesterday evening, and that yesterday was, or now still is, election day. Since it's our job to know such things, a bunch of us are headed for the office to watch election returns on Lieutenant General Bekker's new Motorola."

"What?" I look at my alarm. "John, it's 0230 here where my body is, and that's all that counts. I'm sorry, John, but I was in the middle of this great dream. A blond German girl and I—"

"Stuff it!" he says. "Be downstairs in six minutes." I see his head retreat. I see my door close. I hear him rap rap rap rap once again on that door.

"Shit!" I tell my body.

There's gonna be payback for this! my body tells me back.

★★★

The party's already in full swing when we enter our office in the headquarters building. I see folks yakking and drinking coffee. Lt. General Bekker's big TV is blasting too loud for me. I huddle in a back corner, hoping I can catch a few winks, knowing I'll learn stuff as soon as anyone else learns stuff. There's no gaiety in this room even to start with. After they shot Kennedy, the obvious good choice was Mondale, but he was smashed back at the convention, so everyone's hoping now for Humphrey. And they're doing their hoping full well knowing that's not happening either. That evil warmonger Nixon's gonna win it. And so it is, or was. By 0416 the excitement dies down, replaced by a dark blue funk.

"Damn," I say. "Those jerks actually picked Nixon!" The TV screen shows excited people back in DC jumping and screaming. No screaming or jumping is happening in this room. Folks are so angry they can't finish their donuts. A few even cry.

John sits on a layout table next to the Painter. "Shit!" he says as I approach. "What the hell do I do now, Wall? Nixon'll keep dumping bombs on Vietnam, while Prague and Warsaw slowly burn. Europe's getting screwed again."

"They're leaving it up to us," says the Painter. "I, for one, think we gotta step up, do foreign policy over here ourselves."

"I believe we can do that," I say. "We control Nixon's Pershing rockets. We use that as leverage. Send Nixon an ultimatum. Tell him if he steps down now, turns the reins over to Mondale, we'll allow the construction to continue. If he doesn't, we trash the Critical Path Diagram, and all his secret new Pershing rockets disappear into the bureaucratic vapor from whence they came."

"And then they court-martial you," says John. "They can do that."

"It's Farm Boy what would do it," I say. "Guy's not a real person. He's harder to track down than I am."

Sully joins us. "Damn you Yanks. Christ sake! What're you guys thinking? Ya can't do anything right. My parents will never be gettin' outta Prague now!"

"The American electorate has just told us to screw ourselves," says the Painter. "And I for one am not going to stand around moaning and crying and waiting for that to happen."

"I just talked to the Bassist," says John. "He's really ticked off. Says his shortwave link to Prague's gone down. He lost connection about the time the TV called it for Nixon. He blames his transmission problems on Nixon. Bad vibrations are causin' havoc."

The Comptroller stays on task and returns the discussion to nuclear warheads. "When you thinking your nukes goin' to be coming on line?"

"Not so's you'll be able to use 'em any time soon," I say. "I ain't even gonna think 'bout that. Don't even ask."

"Here's the solution," he says. "Every system's gotta be tested, right? So you guys insert a systems test node into your Critical Diagram. Since it's all symbolism, we don't need the warhead in it. Now, since the node says you gotta do a test, somebody's gotta run the test. We tell the Mongols not to worry, it's only just an empty rocket with no warhead. Systems tests can be helpful even when there's no nuke in the nosecone. Know what I mean?"

"Wouldn't that make some impression?" asks someone.

"I like that," the Painter says. "Virtual war with virtual weapons. We could tell them we fired it even though we didn't. They'll panic when it doesn't show up on their radar."

"You guys badly need sleep," I say. "We only monitor construction progress. We don't push buttons. Never even seen buttons. Only Clappsaddle knows about buttons."

"He'll be drinkin' in the officers' club tonight," the Driver says. "Celebrating Nixon's victory. We'll ambush him, late, say about eleven. He'll be stable as Jell-O by then. Maybe persuade him, or coerce him, into makin' that test."

Lynx walks over with a new donut. "Seems one of your friends is happy, Wall. Marta was just on the phone with your Berlin buddy, Ruta. Seems she's glad Nixon won. Thinks he'll listen to her. Thinks she'll be able persuade him to use your new Pershings on Moscow. She thought Humphrey a wimp because he'd never use your pretty new nukes."

"They're not my nukes, Lynx. And you're wrong. That's not good news. Ruta knows no matter who is president, he's never gonna be pushing any buttons. She's using irony on Marta. Never mind what she tells Marta… she's not happy. As long as the Soviets are dancin' in Prague, she can't visit her mother. Then Warsaw's gonna be hammered next. She's not close to happy. Her SDS group's splintering and losing influence. Her mother's dying without her. She's got no path to happiness. She must be crying. Hell, I'm almost crying just thinking about her."

★★★

Later, near the end of the morning, after the donuts are gone, the party mess is cleaned up, and I've had a long nap, I catch the Painter walking slowly across the room in my direction. He approaches my desk cautiously; one artist not wanting to interrupt another's work. I sense him standing a few meters away. I look up. "Oh, hello, Joseph," I say. "You need something?"

"Well, yes I do. I need a favor, and I'm wondering, might you help?"

"Sure. What's up?"

"I think it classifies as business. Lieutenant General Bekker should sign off on it. It falls under the broad tent of transportation support."

"So ya need a ride? Where to?"

"I must do some work in Köln," he says. "And the sooner I do it, the better. Maybe like even drive up there this afternoon? Is that possible?"

"I haven't been there, yet. But that Köln Cathedral's on my must-see list. I'll check with the Driver. See if I'm free. If he okays the timing, we've got a deal. How long will we be gone? I've got a teaching gig in France on Saturday, so I gotta be back here by Thursday night. That fit your schedule?"

"Sure!"

"Great! I'll run this past the Driver."

I hop down from my stool and start toward our ghost general's office.

"We can stay at my grandma's house," he says.

"Your grandma lives in Köln?"

"Then tomorrow morning, I'll give you a tour of that Domkirche. I played hide 'n seek in there as a kid."

"You grew up in Köln?"

"As the war ended, the entire central city, except for the Domkirche, had been bombed flat. Several years later, Mom and I moved back into the neighborhood and lived with my grandmother. Her building was one of the first to be rebuilt. I spent a lot of time playing inside the Domkirche. I know every nook and corner of it. About the time I turned ten dad moved us back to the States."

27 The Köln Story

We're runnin' up the Autobahn in my Fiat Spider in this dreadful November rain. That means the top's up. I'm okay with that, being an average sized guy, but my passenger, Joseph Brunelli, he's a bulky guy, six foot three and about 250 pounds, and so he feels cramped in my little convertible. And, as usual, the tight accommodations are pushing his mood deterioration. He's not a cheerful guy to start with; he's lived too much of his time under clouds. We're both used to that; we've almost adjusted to the situation by now.

We leave Heidelberg, cross the Rhine on that new stayed-cable bridge at Ludwigshafen, then head up the A61 through Koblenz. Joseph wants to get to Köln immediately so he can check out the bells in the steeple of the Domkirche. At least that's the story he's giving me. I tell him I think he's full of shit and I know our speeding toward Köln is somehow connected with those tanks crashing into Prague.

I'm thinking there's more to his story than he's telling. First, there's the 'immediately' part. Those bells aren't going anywhere soon. They've been hanging in that steeple for six hundred years, and the whole world knows how they look and sound by now. Second there's the 'check out' part. They've only just finished repairing the war damage on that steeple so all the bolts and anchors shouldn't need checking for another six hundred years. I'm thinking Joseph's doing something else. And I'm betting it's connected with those five thousand Soviet tanks that crashed into Prague August twentieth.

MOTHERS HURLING BRICKS

Five thousand Soviet tanks! Two hundred thousand troops! Seems too many Mongols to squeeze into Prague. They've smacked Prague into the stone age. The army guys in my office—hell, army guys all across Europe—are still walkin' on the edge. That many tanks rumbling around make army guys in West Germany do weird things—things like my friend Joseph and I are doing on this rainy afternoon.

"Let me worry about my job, Wall. Your job is to drive. Just do that. And do it faster, please."

Joseph is correct. I'm not driving aggressively. I allow two big black Audis to scream past me doing at least 140 clicks, and in this rain! Then we're attacked by one of those articulated behemoths the Europeans call juggernauts. It throws more spray than my wipers can handle. I'm driving blind for a while hoping I don't run out of roadway before my vision clears.

"Faster is not an option," I tell him. "Why is it when we gotta go someplace, you always schedule rain? Rain slows things down. And you know that. And you know that makes me grumpy 'cause I can't put my top down. Then you feel cramped, so you're grumpy too. Can't put up with this shit much longer, especially since I'm a happy kind of guy. You might start looking for another chauffeur with a bigger car. Maybe even a truck."

"Neither weather nor cabin size got anything to do with my discomfort. And I'm not grumpy, just introspective."

This is why Joseph and I don't talk much on these trips. But silence is not my style. I keep trying.

"Didn't realize your grandma actually lives in Köln, Joseph. You never told me Brunelli's a German name. Always assumed it's Italian."

"I'm not Italian either. Dad's from Knoxville. Mom told me she met dad in Zurich during the war. Dad was deep into Secret Service stuff and wasn't thinking about starting a family. I may have been a mistake, or maybe a sly calculation on my mom's part. Mom and I were forced back to her mother in Köln. When I was old enough to run, my parents found each other again and found the crack in Grandma's prison wall, which Mom and I quickly ran through."

"Didn't realize you've had such an interesting journey. How'd your grandma take your running to America?"

"Grandma disinherited mom first thing. Cut her off hard. She hates the idea of Americans, so couldn't have her daughter attached to one. Grandma's got only Aunt Greta, whose husband died on the Russian front, and me. Somehow she's emotionally separated me from my evil parents."

"Sounds like a novel… maybe a movie."

Twenty kilometers south of Köln I switch to the A555 heading north into the city. Soon Joseph points to the northwest and, amazingly, initiates some conversation all by himself.

"See there, Wall. Your clouds are leaving so you can watch your sunset. Make you feel better?"

About two inches of sky has opened up, and the low sun is splashing the remaining cloud undersides with reds and oranges. He points again. "And, there's your church!"

Silhouetted in front of that two inches of bright colorful sky I see the iconic twin towers of 'my' church, the Domkirche St. Petrus. I'm tempted to stop the car and set up my camera. I would've done that if one, I wasn't in heavy traffic in the rain on the Autobahn, and two, I'd been alone. But I know Joseph would not allow me such frivolity. He's an impatient type guy. And, strange for an artist, he's not a guy given to spontaneity.

The orange sky behind the black towers is a neat visual, but I can't get intoxicated by that yet. We're getting closer to the city, and traffic's getting crazier. Joseph tells me to aim for the church towers, so I exit onto local Highway 51 which follows the west bank of the Rhine into the heart of the city. I aim directly toward the Domkirche's towers. His grandma's house is several blocks southeast of the Domkirche in the Rheingarten district. I exit 51 just north of the

Deutzerbrücke and enter his grandma's small residential neighborhood overlooking the Rhine.

"Grandma's house is right up ahead," he says. "Aunt Greta told me to watch for a granite obelisk guarding the drive."

"You've been here before then?"

"Not since I was ten, when Köln was still black rubble. Since I've been stationed in Heidelberg, Aunt Greta's driven down to see me twice. She's a neat lady. We get along nicely, but Grandma, she's still a Nazi."

"But she agreed to put us up for the night. That's a positive sign, right?"

"It was Aunt Greta's idea. She runs the house now. She keeps an eye on grandma. Told me it's my turn to visit her. There's the obelisk, on the right."

I turn into the drive, park on the cobblestones, and we hike through the hedges and flowerbeds toward the front door. Joseph stops dead and looks over his shoulder. I look too. The Domkirche's dark brown towers hover threateningly far above this neighborhood's trees and houses. I can feel their pressure way down here.

"Those towers are something else, Joseph. They're overpowering."

"The tallest manmade structures in the world until Eiffel built his tower."

It's another photo opportunity, but this one ain't gonna happen either. "It's a classy neighborhood, Joseph. Your grandfather must have been close to the top of some food chain, huh?"

"Grandfather's factories built tanks and trucks for Hitler, like his father built stuff for the first war. He'd plenty of money and clout. But when the Americans bombed Köln to rubble, that rubble included all of Grandpa's factories and all of Grandpa's city, except for the Domkirche. Mom told me Grandfather's body was never found. That's one reason my grandma hates Yanks—they bombed her life to smithereens."

"Since I'm one of those evil Yanks, should I be concerned she's gonna shoot me as I walk through her door? Should I stay at a *gasthaus* tonight?"

"It'll be okay. Grandma's quite feeble now. She needs Aunt Greta and a slew of servants to make her house work. Grandma's eighty-five, fragile, and quite dotty. She still thinks she's a Nazi, though she's forgotten what the word Nazi means. She's got herself turned around so she doesn't understand the concept of the US Army occupying her Germany or the idea that I'm an occupier. Thinks if I'm a soldier living in Germany, I must be a German soldier."

"You think you're gonna be able to manage that situation… maybe end up inheriting this pile all by yourself? It'd be a great place for parties. If you want, I can draw up the plans to turn it into a small hotel. What would your Aunt Greta say about that?"

"I'm not a German anymore, Wall. I'm an American peace-keeper now, and I'm concerned only with stopping Soviet tanks from rumbling indiscriminately through Warsaw and, perhaps later, through Köln."

★★★

Like Joseph says, Aunt Greta's a peach. She shows us our rooms, serves us tea in the drawing room, and tells us Grandma's not well and will stay upstairs. It seems reasonable to expect she will be unaware an American soldier is sleeping in one of her beds, sitting on one of her dining room chairs, eating her food, or relaxing with a bit of her port in her conservatory, overlooking her smooth-flowing, chocolate-brown Rhine, and listening to her own daughter play Liszt on her treasured Bösendorfer grand piano.

And that Bösendorfer is one impressive piano! Greta told me it was, at one time, Franz Liszt's piano. Liszt played this instrument at an 1857 concert to raise money to complete construction of the Domkirche's towers. He then donated the instrument to the auction, and one of Greta's ancestors put in the winning bid. Her father moved the Bösendorfer out of the city during the war to protect it. He moved much of the artwork and other furniture to the family's country estate as well. And he sent his two daughters to live with friends in Zurich.

"After the war, Grandmother rebuilt the mansion, brick for brick, to its prewar splendor, then returned the furniture, the artwork, the Bösendorfer, and after some forceful persuasion, her two daughters, and in the bargain, me," Joseph explained.

He goes to the window to watch birds in the garden and barges on the Rhine beyond get swallowed by the dusk. I'm attracted by the Bösendorfer and move my fingers respectfully over the keyboard.

I look at his Aunt Greta. "May I? Just a few bars? I'd love to hear the sound."

Greta nods her approval, and I sit on the bench, in awe of this beautiful machine. I gather some courage and tentatively play the first several bars of Mendelssohn's *Andante Maestoso in E minor*. I'd played that well recognized funeral march for a high school recital because, well, it's andante and relatively easy to play. It's the only recital piece I still remember parts of. Also, it's got some neat heavy chords, a wonderful test for judging the sound quality of an instrument.

I'd only just gotten into it when Aunt Greta slices her arms horizontally through the air. "Nein, nein!" she screams. "Mother forbids Mendelssohn! Not on her Bösendorfer."

I stop immediately. "What's the problem?"

"He was a Jew," Greta says. "Mother does not allow Jewish music to be played on her piano!"

That outburst breaks Joseph's concentration. He rushes over from the windows to the piano. "Get off that bench, Wall!" he orders me. He roughly pushes me off the far side. He's bigger than I am. He can do that. He places himself on the bench. "I will punish Grandmother with Jewish music till she gets sick of it." He pounds out that *Andante Maestoso* loud enough to wake the dead, certainly loud enough to wake his grandmother. Aunt Greta stands stunned. She must steady herself with one hand on the piano. Slowly though, a smile emerges, and she seems to enjoy the promise of the confrontation she will have to have with her mother.

Grandma's nurse bursts into the room. "Quiet please! No loud piano! Frau Schturner must rest. The noise is causing her pain, is causing headache."

"Tell Grandmother I do not wish to give her a headache. But I need to give her a piano lesson. I will play quietly on her piano. But tell her also, I will play Mendelssohn on her piano. This piano is designed with Mendelssohn in mind. Liszt was Mendelssohn's friend, so I'm thinking Liszt must've played his Jewish friend's music on this very piano. So, if Liszt played it, I must also play it."

Both Aunt Greta and I are startled by Joseph's outburst, as well as his now delicate touch on Liszt's piano. "Grandmother remembers this!" he says. "She's heard me play it before. It's standard teaching repertoire, and I played it on this very instrument when I was nine or ten. She'll understand my message."

★★★

The next morning, Joseph and I leave at 0706. Aunt Greta said the church would open for 0730 Mass. It's not yet dawn, though smidgens of pink brighten the eastern sky. It takes us twelve minutes to walk the side street, cut through an alleyway, and emerge in a small cobblestone courtyard on the north of the church. Two dim lamps throw splotches of dirty light and illuminate two elderly women moving through the courtyard. They walk slowly, mutually supporting each other, their four legs doing better than two independent pairs might do separately.

Joseph grips my shoulder. "Wait," he whispers. "We'll let them pass."

They turn onto a narrow walk guarded by a low hedge, climb the seven stone steps to a platform, then vanish, right through the stonework. Only after they disappear do I see the doorway hidden in the black shadows just before the transept crashes into the nave.

"This door's open," Joseph explains. "But the front doors don't open for tourists until 0930. By then we'll have morphed into tourists."

We climb the stairs and note the heavy door is held open with a metal hook so old women need not strain to pull it open themselves. We step into the vestibule. Its dark space is difficult to comprehend. The transept chapel is lit softly by four, low-wattage fixtures swinging gently from the ceiling on invisible chains. A slight wind through the open door sways those fixtures, setting faint shadows dancing on the walls. I discern the two women kneeling in one of the dozen pews fit into this small, north transept chapel. A single candle flickers on the otherwise bare altar. Several vigil lights whimper in their stand. Nothing else moves.

I follow Joseph. We enter the nave, and as he starts walking horizontally up the side aisle, I look vertically into the ceiling vault. I sense I'm in an enclosure, but the ceiling and the walls are too far away and shrouded in too much darkness to confirm that. This space is unbound; it doesn't register as an enclosed room. It's a hundred and fifty meters to that ceiling, more than enough to accommodate a vertically oriented football field. I'm inside a cavern. I hear several slapping noises, then things with wings brush past my ear and disappear into that vastness. More evidence of a cavern. I stumble and smash my toe against a chair. It hits another chair. That small noise is amplified by the concentrated stonework to sound like a dozen guys tromping down the aisle on their horses. I look hard, but I can't see *them* either.

"Those were bats, Joseph! Inside this church!"

Joseph grabs my arm, pulls me upright, and yells a whisper into my ear. "Pay attention. You can study architecture and wildlife later.

We must go quickly, and silently, up this side aisle, then across the back to the south tower. Stay close so you don't lose me."

"You said you'd show me the church. You didn't say you'd show it to me in the dark with horses stomping and bats swooping about. You're givin' me one cheap tour."

"Be patient," he says. "You Americans expect things to happen instantly. Sometimes you must wait for the daylight to come to you."

My eyes eventually accustom to the dark. A faint light forces itself through the massive high windows on the south side. Joseph leads me west, down the north aisle, until we intersect the north tower.

"The north tower's empty. Nothin' up there but spider webs and bats. It's the south tower that's important." We turn left, walk past the doors leading from the main entry, and cross to the south tower. We take a right then two lefts, go through an arched opening, then up fifteen steps. We bang our noses into a metal gate which prevents access to the continuing set of stairs spiraling up into the tower. Joseph tries the handle.

"It's locked," he says. "Thought it might be. I'm thinking they still hide the key where they did when I was a kid. I'll be right back. Stay here!"

I've no choice. It's so dark I can hardly see the metal grillework my fingers are now curled around. I'm thinking that's Joseph's fantasy. No way the key is on the same hook of twenty years ago.

"Okay, I got the key," Joseph says. "Still on the same peg. Some key's probably hung on that peg for five hundred years." He ignites a flashlight, inserts the key, opens the grillework, pushes me through it, then extinguishes the light.

"Keep the gate open. I'll put the key back. I don't need it to get out, and I might forget to rehang it later."

He's back in a jiffy. "Okay, ready for a climb? I think it's about five hundred steps. After about three hundred we'll find openings in the masonry designed to let sound out, and they'll let some daylight in. And it should be daylight soon."

"I'm ready, Joseph. You're my leader. So lead on."

"We'll go slowly. Feel the wall with your hands and test every step before you take it. Climbing winding stone spirals in the dark's tricky. We'll maintain a slow deliberate cadence. I'm not gonna' race to the top to impress you with my conditioning. We don't have to hurry… there's nothing to see yet. But once we reach the bell chamber, there'll be plenty to see."

We climb deliberately, as Joseph wants. I place one foot after another, one hand over the other hand. I feel the stone wall. It's cold, moist, and sometimes slimy. After a hundred steps, the strange motion of almost slithering up the wall becomes somewhat comfortable.

"Hey, Joseph," I say. "We've turned ourselves into bugs. I feel I'm a spider climbing this wall, not some guy stepping steps. It's weird."

"You're the one who's weird, Wall."

"No, really. Look at me. I'm like Gregor Samsa! Blunky, blunky, blunky. I'm climbing up this damp stone wall!"

"Don't you go weird on me, Wall. Concentrate on the steps, and keep your feelers on the wall."

"Ah, so you have read Kafka? Ya know what I'm sayin', huh?"

We eventually reach the bell chamber. It's a huge room looking, on the inside, much too big to fit into that narrow spire one sees when standing on the cobblestones outside. I see eight bells, set in three ranks, separated vertically from each other by three meters. The lower rank consists of only the Great Bell. It's the biggest bell I've ever seen. It's close to eight meters across! The next rank carries two bells and the highest has five smaller ones.

"Just a few more steps, Wall. There's an observation platform above the bells which'll give you great views of the city. You must stay there. I'm going up higher."

"If something interesting's up there, shouldn't I look at it too?"

"It's too dark and too dangerous."

"Since I'm the svelte coordinated guy, shouldn't I be the one goin' up?"

"You're not allowed! Stay here!"

He vanishes up a twisting set of smaller stone stairs into the darkness. His footfalls echo about, but eventually dissipate. Theoretically, since he's a corporal and outranks me, I should respect a direct order. On the other hand, neither of us are uniform-wearing army guys so neither of us pays attention to stuff other army guys tell us to do. So maybe I should go up? He might need protection from bats, spiders, or other creatures that occupy medieval church steeples.

I get over it. Let that goofball do his work. Daylight's pouring through the openings now. I'll watch the city come alive as morning sunlight creeps slowly toward the western horizon. A few office towers and apartment blocks attempt to emphasize the vertical, but continuous red tile roofs of mostly low-rise buildings are overpoweringly horizontal. It's another great photograph I'm not going to shoot.

The sun slices through the thin broken clouds and splatters ochre-colored shadows over red-tiled roofs. To the south, I see the Rhine, a black snake slithering through the city. It'll stay black for some time since the sun won't be high enough to bounce any reflections off it for hours. In the west, two long, dark-blue shadows cast from the Domkirche's twin towers slide out over the rooftops. I try to place where my position might be with respect to the tower's shadow. Perhaps it's half a kilometer away. I try to imagine the effect produced if I had the power to accelerate time, like in time-lapse photography. I force those shadows to scuttle quickly across the landscape as the sun races toward noon. I lose track of real time.

After some time, the light show settles down, and I return to the floor of the bell chamber. I transfer my attention to the ancient mechanics of the bell suspension system. It's a bizarre and ingenious construction. I try to understand how they raised the bigger bells up here in a time in the fifteenth century without truck, cranes, or helicopters. I lose track of historical time.

I forget Joseph's still above me. Eventually, I'm aware of a rhythmic pounding sound. It frightens me at first, but soon I understand. Joseph is descending stone steps above. Soon he emerges from the shadows. I watch him slither carefully down the remaining steps. He walks toward me. He's got that 'I know something you don't' look. I cut him off at the knees.

"It's 533."

"What?"

"You were off by 33 steps. There're 533 to the observation platform."

"You actually counted them?"

"Well, yeah! Someone has to make sure the world's pivotal pieces of information are correct. That's one of my jobs. Somebody says there're sixty-three missile bunkers spread along the Iron Curtain. Somebody's gotta go count 'em. Essentially, that's what the army's payin' me to do. I count stuff. And also, I ask questions. Like what did you find up the steeple, and how many more steps did you climb?"

"I don't count steps. That's not my job."

"So! Does that mean you'll tell me what, exactly, is your job?"

"My job is keeping my driver entertained." He points westward. "See those exotic shadows out there?"

"Nice topic-change, Joseph. I'm not biting."

"Though it's a fascinating view, Wall, I've no memory of it. When I last stood here twenty years ago as a ten-year-old, I was confused and alone, and I saw nothin' but desolate rubble and gray fog. I don't think I knew the word desolate then, but that's how I felt, desolate and alone. I was anxious about looking out here today. Didn't know how I'd react seein' new modern rooftops rather than twisted rubble piles."

"And how're you taking it?"

"It's strange, but I feel nothing. No tears, no shame, nothing wrenching in my gut or tugging on my heart. It's empty in here." He thumps a fist on his breast.

"It's maybe empty in that cavity, but I doubt the cavity above us is empty. What exactly is up there? Need I count those steps, also?"

"Will you stop with the counting? I'm working on a project for our Prague friends. All I'll tell you is, it concerns information distribution."

Those two interesting words, information distribution, are the last words our two brains will recognize for a long time. Several of the higher-register bells we are sharing this room with start to ring.

The strength of the noise bouncing around in that small stone enclosure instantly deafens us. My head throbs as sound waves rattle my skull. Sound waves paralyze me with pain, overpower my sensory system, and shudder vibrations through my body. Joseph and I react instantly. We stumble down the steps as fast as we dare.

After several dozen steps, the sounds become muffled by the heavy stonework piled above us. Or maybe I've become deaf. Soon I realize that great bell's tolling, one deep-throated bong every ten seconds or so. We're lucky that great bell didn't ring as we stood directly beneath it and reached up to touch it. I would now be severely injured rather than severely discomforted.

We escape, hoping our pain will dissipate with altitude or time. We're super careful, because if we stumble and tumble down any reasonable chunk of those 533 stairs, we'll be dead. On the good side, we'll be released from the excruciating pain generated by those bells.

By the time we reach the bottom, the tolling has ceased. At least we cannot hear it any more. It's almost 1000 hours now, and it's obvious this great nave has been transformed since we last walked down here. Daylight pours through the stained glass windows. Tourists surge through the doors, and conversational din bounces off the stonework. There are no bats and no silence. Joseph, it seems to me, is also transformed.

"This isn't the church I remember," he says. "I remember the darker one, the debris, and the sadness. I don't remember these windows. Perhaps they'd been covered with protective blankets. I remember no light, no crowds, no music. It's so different now. I feel nothing. I can't persuade myself to cry."

I hear a hint of music slipping under the still vibrating bell residue. I see a string quartet assembled under the central crossing, and they're providing background music for the gawkers. I think it's Vivaldi's *Four Seasons*.

"Don't worry, Joseph," I say. "Nobody can cry when Vivaldi's in the room."

★★★

Joseph's Aunt Greta isn't crying either. I hear her playing Liszt on her Bösendorfer as we return through the garden door. It's not easy to overpower the dissident bell noises still pounding, but they ease their grip when soothing Liszt is applied. Greta quickly talks us into staying over another night to make sure our ears, our balance, and our cranial pressure return to normal. She knows of a clinic if it's needed.

After lunch, Joseph spends some time talking with his grandmother while I take a nap. Then we sit in the garden and let Aunt Greta serve us lemonade.

"Could Grandmother've suffered a small stroke, Aunt Greta?" asks Joseph. "Perhaps the excitement of my visit overwhelmed her? Or Jews banging on her piano, or the Soviets doin' Blitzkrieg on Prague? That's many military metaphors for an old Nazi in one day. She could've broken a wire or blown a fuse someplace. She told me, in a detached dreamy voice, that she enjoyed listening to little Greta and Verna doing their lessons on the Bösendorfer yesterday."

"I noticed the same thing, Joseph," says Greta. "She seemed not to know who I was this morning and asked me 'where are my girls, and what are they doing?' Grandma's living in a strange dream. She's been very angry for a long time… angry at Americans, angry at your mom and dad, angry at student protesters, and angry at Jews. Anger's consumed her."

"Maybe it broke her," I say. "I don't think it's that uncommon."

"There's a sad part to this," says Joseph. "Yesterday, she may've not loved me, but she at least knew I was her grandson. In this afternoon's dream world, I'm not yet born. My mother's still a little girl practicing her piano lessons, and that's way before I show up. She's not talking to me, but to a vision who won't show up for another twenty years."

"Now, that's weird, Joseph."

★★★

By Thursday morning our ears have stopped ringing, so we head back to Heidelberg. The temperature's way up, the top's down, and the wind's brisk and behind us. Joseph holds a folded newspaper rigid, but he's not reading it.

"I can't forget about those bells, Wall. Damn! I'm sorry. I didn't expect them to ring."

"You're the expert. Bells only do one thing. They ring!"

"Don't be a smartass. I mean they don't ring to mark the hours. Greta swore they rang only to announce Sunday Masses."

"You think maybe it was a test, like tornado sirens back in Iowa?"

"No, you jerk! Greta found out they scheduled a private Mass yesterday for a former resident who, like my mom, fled Köln during the war, and who, for some reason, wanted to be interred in the family tomb."

"Would your mom do that? Return herself to Köln to sleep with your grandmother?"

"Not in a hundred years. Seems to me, once that chord gets severed, it's severed."

"Yeah, and the same is true for our Czech friends. Those Mongols' tanks surely severed mother Prague from her children living in the west."

"I'm afraid so. I'll bet neither you nor I will ever be allowed into Prague in our lifetimes."

Joseph returns to his newspaper. I concentrate on the road. Time slips by. We cross the Rhine at Ludwigshafen again, this time going east. That knocks me out of my funk and brings me back to real time. I don't feel my ears ringing anymore.

"I think my hearing's almost back to normal, Joseph. I was in no shape to drive yesterday. Aunt Greta was kind to let us stay another day."

Joseph stays silent so I pull another string.

"Joseph, can I ask one more stupid question?"

"What's that?"

"You're the church bell expert guy, right?"

"Ja! So?"

"I'm back to wondering what happened in the tower? How's it that, although the Domkirche houses several of Europe's most historic bells, you ignored them and climbed up into the steeple where there are no bells?"

I see Joseph considering this question. I sense gears meshing at high speed. I try again.

"I'm not an ignorant guy, Joseph. I've talked with John and your Czech friend. I think maybe a shortwave antenna and some transmission equipment are hidden up there. I assume our Czech friends are using that transmitter to send messages and music back into Prague. I'm thinkin' maybe some bat gnawed through a wire? Maybe you fixed that, am I right?"

"I better not answer your questions, Wall. All I'll say is Lieutenant General Bekker will be greatly pleased you drove me to Köln to survey the bells."

"But you scarcely looked at them!"

"That's all I can tell you. Everything else must come from the Driver or Lieutenant General Bekker. However, as you said, I am a bell expert. So, I'll tell you one of those bells, that big one we stood under, is named Pretiosa and was cast in 1448. It weighs over 23,000 pounds!"

"So, in your parallel universe you think Lieutenant General Bekker can sleep easier if I learn a few interesting bits of bell history?"

"And, at the time of its installation, Pretiosa was the heaviest bell cast in Western Europe."

"Okay, Mr. Expert. I get it. You know lots of physical stuff about church bells, but what about the metaphysical stuff?"

"Bells aren't metaphysical things. They're inert hunks of cast metal."

"You ever wonder why medieval bishops needed bigger and bigger bells in their taller and taller church steeples?"

"I'd guess so they could notify more people of any upcoming Mass."

"Wrong-o, Mr. Bell Guy! Their primary purpose, at least when the 'I need a bigger bell in my tower' nonsense started, was to scare devils away from church gatherings. The heavier the bell the more powerful the devil it repelled."

"That didn't work very well," says Joseph, "did it? People still enjoy sinning, and those devils are still drivin' their tanks around Prague."

"Seems to me that bishops needing bigger bells in their steeples is similar to generals needing bigger Pershing missiles along their *steel curtain*. Also seems such bombast and noise has the same effect on the Mongols as bell noise has on devils—absolutely nothing! Devils pay no attention to bells! Soviets pay no attention to Pershings! That's what devils do. It's what Mongols do. Big bells or big missiles? Don't make a diddlypuck worth of difference."

Joseph's not seeming to care about metaphysics. He goes back to physical stuff. "The biggest bell in that church, it's called St. Petersglocke, is the largest free-swinging bell in the world and was installed around 1923 much lower in the tower. We did not see that one."

"That's the same time your mom and your Aunt Greta were doin' their Liszt exercises on their Bösendorfer. Would've thought those pretty Liszt songs might have kept those mean Nazi devils at bay. But I don't recall that working either, huh?"

"But—"

"Forget about bells, Joseph. Read your paper. I've gotta concentrate on my driving. This traffic's absurd. Too many trucks on this highway, and I've not enough road."

28 THE 2ND LANAPOULE STORY

I understand words like 'the appropriate time' can be ambiguous and that sometimes ambiguity is necessary. But sometimes, like now, ambiguity is just ridiculous. I'm parked in a rather informal asphalted area adjacent to the dock in LaNapoule, and I'm waiting with the blue Mediterranean lapping at the ancient granite seawall several meters in front of me for 'the appropriate time' to arrive.

Being November, few tourist type people are wandering about, but it's a pleasant day, so I might as well enjoy the full benefit of sitting on the dock next to the Mediterranean, an enjoyment that includes the seagulls screaming and doing diving exercises. I am, after all, parked adjacent to a fish pier. I put my top down, admonish the seagulls regarding unsuitable sanitary behavior, and wait for the appropriate time.

When I'd told the Driver I was heading for LaNapoule, he'd given me a parcel—the normal, locked diplomatic pouch like I've delivered to many places. He told me I should, first thing Saturday morning—first thing is another rather ambiguous instruction—drive my yellow Spider onto the fishing pier in LaNapoule. He told me, "Sit in the car and wait for the appropriate time to deliver the bag."

Ten or fifteen minutes drag by with nothing happening, appropriate or not. Just my seagull friends and I having a pleasant time. Eventually I notice the fisherman. He's walking slowly and with a slight limp. And he's wearing the internationally certified, traditional, yellow anorak. He shuffles past my position, then suddenly stops, turns, and looks with some interest at my yellow Spider.

The man goes to the front, studies the car, then looks up at me. He shakes the hem of his sleeve and puts a twinkle in his eye. "Nice color for a car," he says in pretty good English. "Matches my anorak."

I'm thinking 'the appropriate time' may have walked over with this fisherman. So I laugh. I point up to the sky. "Seagulls giving me enough shit." I think I can also be flippant. "Don't need fishermen dishing it out too."

The man laughs. "You sound like an American." He points at my Spider's license. "Army guy, huh?"

I nod.

"You the Driver?" he asks.

"No," I say. "But I know him."

"Hmm, you might be a Farm Boy?"

I nod again.

"I'm the Welder. Driver tells me you have a package for me. Is that so?"

"It is, sir. I'll get it for you."

I get out, go to the front of the car, open the trunk, and retrieve the Driver's pouch. I extend the pouch to this Welder guy who for some reason is dressed as a fisherman.

"Merci," says the Welder.

I don't release it yet. "Do you have a receipt for the Farm Boy?" I ask.

The man takes a paper from his pocket, unfolds it, smooths it some, and gives it to me.

"Merci."

The man takes the package and starts to walk away. Then he turns back and smiles. "Say 'thanks' to Johnnie for me, will you?"

"I will, Monsieur. I'll tell him 'merci' from the Welder who's wearing fisherman gear."

I fire up my Fiat. Now that the appropriate time has passed, the rest of the day is mine, so I head up the hill toward the University of Illinois' Architectural School. I look at my watch—it's 0806. My students aren't expecting me till 1000, so I've plenty of time to set up my bit of architectural theater.

★★★

There are times when an architect must first solve a particular structural problem because, as the design evolves, the solution found for the aesthetic problem may be suggested by a clever solution of the underlying structural problem. With the bells of the Kölner Domkirche St. Petrus still faintly dancing in my head, I've decided to give my design class a sketch problem about design process rather than design composition. Make my students do their bit of creative thinking in a situation where they'd certainly have no preconceived notions. Get down to the basics of raw design power.

I start with the dozen Polaroid photographs I'd taken of the Kölner Domkirche St. Petrus, and some historical brochures I picked up at the church's information kiosk. My fourteen students—most from the upper midwest, a few from New England, and one from Thailand—gather around while I explain the various design features of this huge church.

"Now imagine," I tell them, "that you, the best young architects in western Europe in 1448, are summoned by the archbishop of Köln. Next, imagine I'm the chief legate representing Pope Nicholas V, who is providing the major chunk of financing. The pope has sent me to articulate the importance of this design problem to you and that he is very interested in your solutions."

I switch to the somber voice such a papal legate may have cultivated. "Gentlemen, my name is Bishop Nicholas of Cusa. My pope is providing funds for this project and has ordered me to choose an architect. You'll be given a test, the winner of which will be awarded the commission. But this commission is only a preliminary test. If the project is constructed on time and on budget, Pope Nicholas V will bring the successful architect to Rome to work with Leon Batiste Alberti on the schematic design work for the other Domkirche St. Petrus, the new one my pope is building in Rome."

I leave de Cusa, walk to the opposite side of the room, and reenter my lecturer persona. "You architects have the advantage of knowing that Pope Nicholas' new cathedral in Rome will, after centuries of construction be the greatest architectural monument in the history of the world. That should pile some bit of incentive on you.

"So, here's the problem you must solve. The king of Castile's donated the heaviest bell ever cast in Europe to the Kölner Domkirche. His daughter must marry a German prince in that church in six months, and by that time that super-heavy bell must be up in that tower ringing out news of his little princess' wedding. But the bell weighs 23,000 pounds. And the existing bell chamber is 533 steps up into the south tower. There's a small derrick perched on the north tower, but worthless for this project. Your sketch problem is to design the system that will get that heavy bell into the existing bell chamber, way up there." I point up toward the ceiling to see if any of my students are so intrigued they follow my point.

"I can almost see the archbishop pointing up to the place, halfway to heaven. The cost will be a consideration, and the bell must not be harmed. And it must be done quickly. The wedding is exactly six months from tomorrow.

"But there is also a downside. Unless the princess gets her bell, the wedding will be canceled, the treaty with the Germans scrapped, and most likely several dozen people, including the architect, put to death. Maybe a war will be necessary retaliation. The failed architect might be liable for the deaths of thousands of German and Spanish army guys and most likely his own also. How about that for incentive?"

My students make sounds like they are suitably impressed with my presentation.

"Okay guys, it's now 1015 Saturday morning. Archbishop de Cusa will start judging your design work at 1600 tomorrow. Show him you perform well under pressure and have the ability to jump-start the Renaissance pretty much all by yourself. Using fifteenth century equipment, design a way to raise that big bell into that lofty tower."

★★★

It's now Monday morning, and echoes from yesterday's design presentation party still bounce around in my head. I've started later than I planned, but by 0900 I'm on the road back to Heidelberg. I'll go up through Switzerland into Germany, follow the Rhine up to Karlsruhe, then hop east to Heidelberg. It's early in November, and a brilliant blue sky is driving the bright sun's warmth deep into the rocky landscape, causing the white limestone outcroppings to glisten. I can't resist. Even though it's November, I stop on the side of the deserted road and put the top down.

I'm winding through the rolling foothills of the Alps, aiming toward Grenoble, and it's so beautiful it makes my knees weak. Brilliant white limestone outcrops contrast with the bright green grass. Goats, colored to match that limestone, wander the green pastures like movable rocks. At times I catch a glimpse of the distant southern Alps poking into the sky. A hawk swoops overhead. I power through the curves, running through the gears and brushing past the limestone. Portions of that vertical rock face are so close that at places they extend into the asphalt pavement surface. The road is narrow but vacant, so I can utilize the entire lane-and-a-half width, and drive as fast as I dare. It's the most fun this Iowa farm boy has ever had in a car.

I downshift and power around a sharp curve. I come out of it too fast and am startled by the mirage! I'm assaulted by an apparition gyrating in the middle of the road! My autopilot takes over, I quickly downshift, slam the brakes, and skid to a stop. When real time returns, I've but ten meters to spare.

An elderly peasant couple stands in the middle of the road blocking my path. He's a wizened old man and looks to be about ninety. She appears ageless, perhaps not even human. They're flapping arms as birds do wings. And they're screeching like owls. I can't believe they'll ever get off the ground. At least she won't because she's almost two meters high and must weigh half a ton, though her husband, like something popped from a cartoon strip, is a meter and a half tall and pushing eighty pounds.

"Merci, monsieur." They aim French gibberish at me, ending with, "Merci, merci, monsieur."

The two advance and push against my Spider, one positioned in front of each headlamp. She's at the passenger side, and he's on the driver's. They start again with jumping and wing flapping, she less so than he. They yell French words at me. I understand nothing.

"You speak English?" I ask foolishly.

"Merci," she says. Looking like she's won, she waddles around and opens the passenger door. She's babbling in French, thinking she's telling me something I can understand. She points at my passenger seat, then starts to wedge her bulk through the door.

"No! No!" I say. I wave my arms to reinforce my position in a vocabulary I think she may understand. I'm thinking this is one weird carjacking. "No! No!" I lean over and push against her bulk. I try to keep her out of my car. Seems I've confused her. She steps back.

But she keeps talking, emitting a constant stream of excited, even desperate-sounding words. Her companion, I'm thinking he's her husband, knows words are useless and so, instead, waves his arms, points to himself and then his wife, and then to my car. He does this again and again, like a dance step.

I try to explain my position. I point to his huge wife, then to my little passenger seat. I use the international symbol for there's no way that huge fat lady will fit into that tiny seat. I make obvious, probably unsympathetic, half-circular motions with my hands indicating *Lady, you are way big*. I point to my Spider's passenger seat and form a tight small circle with my thumbs and forefingers. "The car is very small," I say with very small, high pitched words.

She nods in agreement, smiles, points to the seat and then to herself. She nods with purpose. "Oui, oui!" That look says I may weigh a ton, but I am going to squeeze myself into that seat, and you're not going to stop me.

Her husband continues bouncing next to my driver's window. He points to his watch, then looks to the blue sky, or maybe the sun. "*Temps, temps.*" He screams something I somehow translate as *You moron! Time is of the essence. We need help.*

He points down the road in the direction the car is headed, then points to his watch. He flashes both hands, ten gnarly fingers extended into my face, then points down the road. "*Dix kilometer, dix kilometer.*"

I hold up my ten fingers and ask, "Ten Kilometers?" And I point. "That way?"

"Oui, merci. Oui."

While I'm distracted with him, the car lurches violently. The landscape tilts ten degrees. I jerk around to assess the damage. The wife's urged her bulk thru the passenger door and plopped herself, sort of, into the passenger seat and its environs.

"Merci, merci, merci."

"No!" I yell, "*Pas possible! Pas possible.*" The little car lists so much I hear the corner of the open door scraping on the asphalt. I'm afraid it will twist under the load.

She smiles like a two-year-old with ice cream and waves for her husband to come around to her side. I, instead, direct the old man to climb into the rear of the car behind me to lessen the pressure on the passenger side door. Understandably, he waddles around to her side. They've forced the door open as wide as the hinge permits. Its edge scrapes across the pavement again. They yell "Merci!" again.

From my driver's seat and with one foot depressing the clutch and the other on the brake, I grab the man's shirt with both hands and physically drag him off his wife's lap, then arc him with both his feet kicking over into the back between me and the mountainous lady and work him into position sitting behind me on the driver's side with his skinny legs dangling over the left side. That counterbalances his wife's bulk and frees up the passenger side door so it no longer scrapes on the pavement. It's not close to closing, but it's not scraping.

The lady points up the road. The man holds all his fingers in front of my face and once more yells, "*Dix kilometer.*" He points to his watch, then to the road ahead.

They both scream, "Merci, merci!"

Apparently, I've no choice. I slowly let out the clutch. The car starts to move!

The two of them start with nonstop signs of the cross. "Merci, merci!"

I get up to about ten kilometers per hour, my tachometer is well into the red, and I need to shift into second gear.

I can't find the shift lever! It's buried beneath several hundred pounds of fleshy thighs… or something. I poke the husband to get his attention, make intricate motions with my right hand while steering with the left. I point to the fleshy problem. "I can't shift this thing, and I can't get us there in first gear." I stop the car on a slight downward slope. I have to keep my foot on the clutch, because I can't find the shift knob to put it in neutral.

Somehow I get across my problem to him. He jumps down and goes around and helps to lever his wife's bulk up just enough to uncover the shift knob. In the split second between his jerking her body up and gravity pulling her back down, I quickly slip the car into third gear and remove my hand. He relaxes his hold. She sits again and reburies the shift knob. With my help, he assumes his former position, and we all start off again slowly down the hill.

"Merci," I tell them.

We lurch along at perhaps fifteen kilometers per hour, max. The sky still miraculously stays blue. The wind is nonexistent. My Spider is whining in third gear, climbing over the redline on the downhill segments, and straining to stay alive on the uphill ones. The noise from my passengers continues nonstop. They argue and scold and laugh and interject a "Merci" and a sign of the cross whenever I look at either of them.

In half an hour—or maybe it is several days—we round a curve and enter a broad valley still somehow very green though it's early November. I notice goats on the grass close to the road and think about panicking. The goats stay put, the road straightens, and my car eases down the gentle hill toward a village. The view of the town causes both my passengers to renew their jumping and screaming.

"Merci, monsieur."

The underside of my right fender scrapes the tires with each jump. I can smell the resistance. "Sit down!" I yell with appropriate hand gestures. I point to the front of the car where the scraping is now continuous.

The old man points ahead. "L'Arenas, L'Arenas." He cries big juicy tears and points to his watch. I can't keep them quiet. They're jumping and yelling, the car lurching and the tires scraping. "*Avante*," they yell, assuming aggressive words, like a jockey yells to his horse, will make my Fiat go faster.

We approach the village on a long downslope. I can see the entire place, and it can't house more than three thousand people. I see a picture-book village with a church and a town square at the center. As we enter the built-up area, several villagers sprint out and run alongside my Fiat. "Hero, hero!" they chant. I recognize other words, some very suggestive words I translate as 'parade,' 'marshal,' and 'armistice.'

A rather substantial girl with long braids jumps onto the left rear of my Fiat next to the old man. She helps balance the fat lady in the passenger seat, but the extra weight pushes metal hard onto a tire.

"No, no," I yell. "Get off!" It does no good. A young man hops on the front driver's side. I yell, "Off! Please! My poor little Fiat!"

"Merci, merci," all the passengers yell in unison.

Since the gear shift knob is unavailable, I cannot downshift, and the engine struggles to pull us forward in third gear at such a slow speed. My poor car jerks and coughs. I finally push the clutch in. The car slows. Several young men from the crowd sense the problem, run around behind the car and start to push me toward the finish line—the old Roman fountain in front of the church in the town's central plaza.

My Fiat, exhausted, finally stops. A boisterous crowd surrounds us. Several guys, assisted by the girl with the braids, pull the old man off and hoist him up onto the shoulders of two younger men, one guy holding each leg. "Hero, hero," the crowd shouts. I think they mean him, not me.

Another group of men push fat and pull extremities and somehow ease the woman out of the constriction of the passenger seat and onto her feet on the cobblestones.

The Fiat lurches with relief, and a woman dressed in a traditional peasant gown pulls my head toward her ample bosom and kisses the top of my head. "Hero, hero." She, I think, means me.

A young man shoves a stein of beer at me.

"Does anyone speak English?" I ask him.

"I know English," says that rather substantial girl who jumped onto my car first. She runs over to me, throws her arms around my neck, and gives me a tight squeeze. "Thank you for bringing us our George," she says. Her English is very good, almost without a French accent, like she'd learned it in the US. And though she jumped up onto my car easily, she does not look either athletic or lithe enough to be able to do that.

She's younger than I am, early twenties maybe, with long, black braids festooned with huge, purple bows. She's wearing jeans and, like many in the crowd, a purple sweatshirt with "11 - 11 - 11" stenciled in white letters across the front and the years "1918-1968" set beneath it.

"I'm Georgette," she says. "The gentleman who came in with you is my grandfather, George Dumont. I am named for him. It is my honor to tell you why you are a hero today." She performs a curtsy motion, like Maria must have, except the maneuver isn't as effective in jeans and a floppy sweatshirt as it was in the movie with a lithe peasant girl in a billow-skirted peasant dress.

★★★

Over the course of the next several hours, which are filled with good cheer, food, and beer, Georgette tells me what has caused all the excitement. I'd delivered my hitchhikers into the town square just before the eleventh hour, on the eleventh day, of the eleventh month of November, the very hour that the armistice ending World War I had been signed exactly fifty years ago today. The old gentleman I'd driven into town is George Dumont, the local hero from that First World War, who had, for many years, acted as grand marshall of this village's Armistice Day parade. Today marks the fiftieth anniversary, and so today the parade could not have been held without him. Apparently the couple's old truck wouldn't start, and without me happening along to remedy the situation the town would have had no reason for a parade, and most likely the beer would have gone to waste.

Georgette introduces me to many of the town's residents, dozens of whom are relatives. She insists I walk in the parade behind George and his wife, who is balancing herself on a bench fixed to a small cart pulled by a lawn tractor. Georgette introduces me to familiar folks along the parade route. I shake hundreds of hands. I'm back-slapped by hundreds of guys and kissed by hundreds of ladies and girls.

The parade route isn't long, perhaps half a kilometer, from the central church to the cemetery on the edge of town. At the cemetery, hundreds of white crosses set too close together in perfect rows are today decorated with flowers to honor First World War soldiers. Georgette tells me this is an honorary cemetery, a sort of monument. The actual remains of these men lie in Verdun where most died in a two-day span in August 1916. In a separate plot, a dozen crosses mark the actual graves of underground operatives L'Arenas lost during the Second Great War. Georgette shows me two graves of particular interest. The crosses mark grandfather George's son, her uncle, and his daughter, her mother. They are also being celebrated as heroes today.

Georgette was but a couple weeks old when her mother stood atop a cut, carved for the railroad track through the mountainside near the Swiss border, and heaved grenades down onto a passing German troop train. She'd hurled several of them right into the ventilation opening on the top of the cars, so the explosion happened inside the car with maximum casualties. Eventually, German sharpshooters riding with the train put her in their sights, and one of them did the deed, but not before several hundred German soldiers were killed or maimed.

The Armistice Day parade here in L'Arenas celebrated not only the end of the Great War in 1918, but also the heroic slaughter of a hundred German occupation soldiers in November 1944.

Georgette makes sure I am having a good time, however something about this party doesn't seem right to me. We are celebrating the brave wartime deeds of her grandfather and her mother. But I'm not at all sure I understand what dancing, eating, and drinking beer have in common with a million French soldiers dying at Verdun, or one's own mother getting killed while assassinating dozens of Germans.

I'm wondering if I came back fifty years from today if folks in Fulda or Schwäbisch Gmünd would also be dancing, drinking beer, and celebrating the hurling of seven thousand nuclear warheads over the *steel fence*. In fifty years, Moscow and Prague might still be piles of radioactive debris. All this celebration over guys dying en masse fifty years earlier obliterates any thought of what I am supposed to be doing today. Even so, I eat, dance, listen to music, and thanks to Georgette, have an extraordinarily good time.

It's not till late in the afternoon that I realize I'll never get back to Heidelberg. I broach the topic with Georgette.

"Don't you worry," she says. "My brother says you can stay with him. He's got plenty of room, and there's enough food and drink in the church basement to last till morning."

She is surprised to learn I live in Heidelberg. "I am a student there also," she says to me. "Only not this semester. I'm staying home to help my father on the farm and earn some tuition money. But I'm going back for spring semester."

"What are you studying?" I ask.

"I've almost finished premed studies. I plan to start medical school next fall."

"Do you know Marta Girrard? She lectures in history."

"Everybody knows Professor Girrard." She says this as lights flash in her eyes. "I took history from her in my third year. Professor Girrard's the most electric person in the whole world. How can you know her?"

"We maybe are good friends. I work with her husband and have played with their little boy, Truck."

"Oh, wow! She's so smart and so courageous. Such an inspiration! I've got an idea. Will you speak with several of my friends? You must tell them about Marta. She once spoke at the University of Grenoble where many of my friends go. Please come talk with us."

"I'd like that," I say. "But first, I haven't seen your grandfather, George, since the mob took him off my car. I must talk with him to learn his story, one soldier talking to another. Could you translate?" Maybe if I talk with him I can understand how I'm supposed to feel about splattering seven thousand nuclear warheads around Western Europe. Should I feel honorable? Will someone be placing flowers at my little white cross, or doing whatever the opposite of that is?"

★★★

The next day, the local garage pronounces my car road-worthy, and I continue toward Heidelberg, accompanied by a vicious headache and many wonderful memories. And Georgette's in my car too. She tells me she must make arrangements for her enrollment in the spring and tells me she'll accompany me to Heidelberg in exchange for my talking with her friends last night. I figured that since her grandparents had already hitchhiked with me, I couldn't turn her request down. She's now almost family. She also says she knows the shortest path through the mountains and guarantees it will save us half an hour.

I watch the little town of L'Arenas disappear from my mirrors. I concentrate on the narrow road as it parallels a small stream. Together we curve around the side of a gentle mountain.

"Merci, L'Arenas!" I yell. The sound bounces back at me from the cut face of rock I'm whizzing past at the time.

"Merci!" Georgette yells. Her sound bounces off the rock face also. Her braids, still festooned with the purple bows, flounce about in the breeze. I see the snowcapped Alps poking into the sky in the distance ahead. A hawk swoops over our heads, urging us to follow him up the river. It's gonna' be another beautiful day.

However, every so often a thought forces itself into my brain, obscuring those impressive snowcapped Alps. I think of the black devastation that may result from Lt. General Bekker either causing the entire NATO stockpile of seven thousand nuclear warheads to quietly disappear into the web of Critical Path diagrams, thus initiating that decades long, millions casualty, slogging ground war of World War III, or pushing the button and quietly slipping seven thousand state-of-the-art nuclear warheads into the communist airspace on the other side of the *steel fence*. If I return to Heidelberg fifty years from now, will I be kissed as I was kissed yesterday and paraded through the Marktplatz, or will I be hanged there, facing the bombed-out shell of the Heiliggeistkirche?

29 The Last Berlin Story

It's warm for a Berlin December. The sun is strong, the wind is nonexistent, and the air is clearer than I can remember it ever being. We hear Mass at a chapel at a small Jesuit school, after which Ruta and I walk into the Tiergarten and sit on a bench in the sun. A few small chirpy birds hop over to see how we're doing. Ruta's still seething. She's boiling mad at God, first for permitting the Stasi to close their door in the *concrete wall,* and second for not directing me to throw Pershings over the *steel fence.*

"Why would God do that to me, Wall? Why? He's had four months to work on it." She pounds on my chest with her fists. "He's trying to coerce you into pushing that button. I'm trying to coerce you to push that button. Why won't you push that button and nuke those Mongols?"

The fantasy of her god wanting me to push the nuclear button acts to short circuit a few pathways in my brain. I think about Georgette. If her god killed a million guys at Verdun, would he even flinch at me killing a million more by having me push a button? I don't understand god stuff, but I really can't understand gods doing that sort of killing on such a Noahic scale. I don't have metaphysical arguments or emotional salves. I can't negotiate for her with this god guy she thinks is punishing her. I'm quite sure I'm lost.

She looks up at me with tears bubbling over her lower lashes. "You have a kind and sympathetic heart, but you're unwilling to believe."

"That's the problem, dear Ruta. Willing has nothing to do with it. It's only a matter of whether he physically exists, and it is obvious that he doesn't."

"But you first have to believe. Only then you can see Him. I can see Him! And you must believe in order to help me. You must believe with me! As it is now, you are a stranger, one who cannot possibly understand what it means to be Catholic in Warsaw, or in Prague, or even in East Berlin. If you cannot understand that, you cannot help stop my tears! I don't think you can help Berlin, or Germany, or even your United States."

Words are useless things. They cannot work here. So I hold her tightly to me and feel her cry. She may be right. I doubt I've the power to do anything for her. But certainly that's her problem rather than mine. I simplistically think beliefs can be changed relatively easily when confronted with facts. I decide to take a chance.

"Say you believe pigs fly," I tell her, "so I throw several dozen out the hayloft door. They dive into the ground. Seems obvious then. *Pigs don't fly.* If you still believe pigs fly, then my ability to help you is zero."

"I don't believe pigs fly, you jerk. But I do believe God will kill Mongols if we pray hard enough."

"You're coming close to those flying pigs," I say. I could tell her that I don't think there are any nukes, so her god can't make me toss them. I'll bet most, if not all those seven thousand warheads, must be faux warheads. I'd like to be able to tell her that, but even though no one has specifically told me, I'm pretty sure that information is one giant military super-secret that I'm not supposed to reveal.

Eventually, she lifts her head. "Okay, Wall." She wipes her fingers across her wet eyes. "Enough of this! I'm not supposed to let you see me cry."

"It's my job to comfort you. As you can see, I'm doing one rotten job of that. Sorry."

"You're doing all you can, and please realize I know you're trying hard. Thank you." She pushes me away, jumps up, and claps her hands. "But, I have the solution. The symphony's playing Mozart this afternoon. I'll finagle us tickets. We'll let Mozart work on my tears. Could be he's better at that than you are. Then we'll have a nice meal and a stroll down Kurfurstendamm. I'll promise not to cry when you hold me. And maybe I'll let you return to Heidelberg tomorrow morning with your spirits elevated. And, for a while at least, I'll have a smile on my mug."

★★★

That next Sunday afternoon I'm reclining on soft pillows in the projecting bay window in the library at Sully's Neckargamünd Hotel. This window seat juts out from the stone walls and hovers over the black water of the Neckar. Mid-December is an ideal time for contemplation and dreaming, so I've church organ music blasting on the radio. The door's closed to keep the sound in the room. A fire's blazing in the hearth. I'm attempting some serious daydreaming.

That's what I'd planned on doing, but it's hard staying focused. I've got a lot on my mind. I've got a collection of Kafka's short stories open on my stomach. I've got a Bach fugue stomping around the room. I'm watching huge snowflakes dive into the Neckar beyond my bay window. And I'm trying to figure out what I'm doin' with Ruta. Where might she fit into that tangle of vectors and nodes existing in my personal Critical Path Diagram?

"Wake up, Wall!"

I'm confused. My senses hadn't registered another person enter the room. "Hey, John. Where'd you come from? It's okay, I'm not napping."

"Right! How'd you like to listen to some real live organ music? Powerful noise you won't be tempted to sleep through."

"I wasn't sleeping! But real organ music? Who wouldn't want that?"

"There's a recital at the Heiliggeistkirche, starting in an hour. The organist is a student from Warsaw, a colleague of my friend, Father Lev."

"That would be neat," I say. "Ahh, but knowing you're a devious guy, I sense there's a catch."

"Not to worry. The concert's free."

"Nothing's free, John! I know there's a catch. I'm guessing your buddy, Father Lev, put you up to this. You guys think maybe after the pipe organ softens me up, you two will try again to talk me into dreaming Catholic dreams, right? Maybe over beers at Der Blaue Schwein? Am I right?"

"I—"

"Just so you guys know, I'm on top of my game. I've recent experience fighting off Catholic dreams. Last week in Berlin I was ambushed into a similar discussion with your buddy, Ruta. She also thinks talking ecclesiastic words will get her, or maybe me, or even us, saved or something. And, to tell you the truth, I would much rather discuss fantasy dreams with her than with you two carnivores. I know for a fact she wields persuasive weapons you guys only dream about."

"Oh, I don't know. I think my Bach's more persuasive than her Mozart."

I'm thinking there's only one way he could make that Mozart crack. He's talked to Ruta. That means the devious bastard's helping her push her 'god agenda.' But Bach is Bach, especially on a church organ, so even after his taunting remark I agree to accompany him to the concert. But I must pay attention. John's right about one thing—Bach is more persuasive than Mozart. More logic, less frivolity. That lowers my odds.

★★★

After the concert, Father Lev's friend, Henryk the organist, accompanies the three of us to Der Blaue Schwein. I'd love to dissect the structure of Bach's fugues with Henryk, but I know that's not on this afternoon's agenda. I'm outnumbered, three religious zealots to one non-zealot. That may be staggering odds for a philosophical discussion. However, I'm intent on a scientific discussion. Having facts on my side overpowers multitudes of keen opponents. I can talk about physical things, and their medieval philosophical drivel won't touch me. It'll be a piece of cake.

I begin my statement before they've touched their beer, operating under the concept that a quick offense bests a conservative defense. "In an attempt to focus the area available for today's discussion, I'll concede and maybe even applaud the positive social attributes of a belief-based theology. Unfortunately, it's the theological parts that are problematic. Those parts are illogical—simplistic Dark Age mysticism. I'm a humanist, a scientist, and an artist. I, unlike you, live in the present. I pay no attention to Dark Age dicta, and you shouldn't either. All this mushy stuff about good and evil super-entities swooping around my ears is but unscientific make-believe."

I feel I have 'em on the ropes already. I tell them they'd better sharpen their knives because I have a long experience repelling metaphysical nonsense. Back in the fifth grade, I confronted the nuns regarding the physical impossibility of The Assumption of Blessed Mary—the live body floating up into heaven story. "Your story doesn't consider gravity," I'd told Sister Somebody. "Mary can't 'float.' She must 'accelerate to escape velocity.' And she won't be able to travel faster than the speed of light and so, though she began two thousand years ago, she's not close to even leaving our galaxy yet!" That confrontation was the last of many straws for my poor mom who ordered me to close both my ears and my mouth when in religion class. "Not a single peep! You hear me?"

Though I never came any closer to accepting Catholic cosmology, I did, however, obey my mom and bought into the 'be a good boy and love your neighbor' part of the deal. The fact that those moral tenets remain powerful in my life is a blow against my three inquisitors. If I were a bad guy they'd have a better argument. I, however, treat most everyone with civility. I'm honest, hardworking, and respectful of others, my body, and my mind. I've never stolen stuff, punched people, smoked, did drugs, or had illicit sex. Part of the reason is that I'm normally oblivious to the fact that other people are active in the same environment I inhabit, and so I never feel the need to impress them or interact with them. I pay little attention to people. I concentrate on sports, music, astronomy, and architecture.

"Even today," I argue, "most normal despots, dictators, kings, and even presidents, base their major decisions—like which princess to marry, or what country to invade, or the nature of the contraband John's smuggling under the Iron Curtain, or even how many nuclear warheads to hide in Fulda—on imaginary metaphysical data four or five centuries out of date."

"You can't blame nuclear proliferation on God, Wall." Father Lev weakly confronts my most outrageous accusation.

"I'm not throwing blame, Lev. I'm only assessing attitude. Nuclear proliferation's only the last in a long line of Christian warfare stratagems."

Lev regains his authoritative voice. "There're no such things as Christian warfare stratagems."

"Certainly there are. Crusades, Hussite stake burnings, Portuguese decapitating Moors in Africa and India, Spanish Conquistador's shooting Aztecs, even the USA marching Florida Indians to death camps in New Mexico or somewhere."

"You don't know what you're talking about."

"Sure I do! Look it up! Every one of those military actions was authorized, directly or indirectly, by papal edict. I've been studying war and killing since living here in Europe—it's hard not to. I've discovered theology and metaphysics are driving most all the hostilities bubbling up around here. And things aren't going to change until we forget about spirits in the sky and start thinking about people on the ground."

"What about the Bible? The Ten Commandments? Thou shalt not kill?"

"That's still metaphysics, Lev. You think an old bearded guy lounging on a cloud in his pajamas can carve words into a stone with his fingernails? Not possible in a physical world. It takes human guys with chisels to carve words into rock. We live in a twentieth-century scientific world, yet we all know its ancient metaphysical arguments are still prompting humans to fire seven thousand nuclear warheads, or charge five thousand tanks, or repatriate several hundred Catholic and Jewish artifacts, or whatever I'm helping you guys repatriate."

"You haven't touched your beer yet, Wall." Lev is frustrated. "Have a drink, take a breath, and settle down. Allow your brain to relax so it can function naturally."

I pay him no attention. "I'll show you what I mean. Last week I was in Berlin talking with our mutual friend, Ruta." I motioned to make sure the clergy at this table understood the 'our' means John and me. "She wanted to visit her mother in East Berlin and hear Mass at that small concrete and glass church just off Alexanderplatz. She wanted me to go with her. Sadly, the checkpoint's still closed. The Stasi don't care about Ruta's mother! They're not going to allow either of us into East Berlin. Ruta had some sharp words with the guard. I pulled her away before they jailed her, and after a bit of stomping and crying we made do with Mass at a small chapel near the Philharmonie.

"She was angry with me because I would not admit I saw Archangel Gabriel swoop in, tap me on the shoulder, and order me to personally start World War III as a first step in reinstating her 'visiting her mother' ritual. After Mass, as we passed the Jesuit standing at the rear of the chapel, she asked him about the possibility of God using nukes. Unfortunately for Ruta, the priest agreed with me. He'd not noticed God's messenger fluttering around the nave with a nuclear nosecone. Though she'd made a serious point, that Jesuit, a bit too quickly I thought, dismissed her profound query with less sincerity than he should have. Ruta lunged at him, and I had to struggle her outside into the fresh air before he could either call the police or summon that other guy, Gabriel, to help him defend himself."

30 The Zug Story

I'm scheduled to separate myself from the US Army two weeks from now, on February 24th. Other than the army giving me a piece of legal paper—the Document of Separation—not much in my life will change. My room at Sully's Neckargamünd Hotel will be there for me when I'm in town. My desk at USAEUR's Critical Path office will be available for me to use for my monthly updates on the diagrams—I've made a financial arrangement with the Defense Department to continue monitoring the monthly Critical Path Diagrams until the few remaining construction projects fill in their green nodes. And in Zurich, I've arranged a deal with Frau Sitzmann for more permanent accommodations, because I've contracted with Gerhardt Stopak to finish a couple small projects for him.

My work for the army is screeching to a halt. Very few nodes on the Critical Path Diagram remain not-green. I'm sure several of them will never turn green, though I've made sure the NATO generals will never see that. The new bunkers should be ready to accept the new Pershing missiles, or so the Critical Path ensures me. If they are real, we're ready to slip those suckers into their new concrete envelopes. No more need of Fridays in Fulda, Saturdays in Schwäbisch Gmünd, or breakfasts in Brussels.

On other fronts, Prague and East Berlin are still unavailable. The SDS and the 68er Bewegung have lost both their power and their direction. And a final nail... The Mothers Hurling Bricks have canceled this month's commemorative playing of the *Requiem for Prague in A* because The Mothers Hurling Bricks has disintegrated as a group. It's the middle of winter. Most everything is bleak. Little stimulates or inspires. Much is dead.

Since not much is changing, no celebration has been planned by my comrades at the Critical Path office to mark the occasion of my separation, though I personally think a bit of partying might be a positive thing for my office's morale. Few of us remain. I'm thinking I might plan my own party, like my predecessor Jerry Black did, just to insert a bit of frivolity into this dour and fast-vanishing Critical Path group.

In order for me to remain in Europe after I leave the army, I have completed paperwork to prove full-time employment and an itinerary with proof of financial capacity. I submitted a veritable stew of separate elements that Lt. General Alvin Bekker eventually approved, but which were much scrutinized by the civilian folks in the appropriate US Army office in New York that, apparently, had the ultimate approval authority for these things.

My plan includes working for the Critical Path office as a consultant, for the University of Illinois in LaNapoule as a visiting lecturer, and for Gerhardt Stopak in Zurich as an architect. I also submitted a travel itinerary to take up the slack periods in between the working gigs, such travel being done to study various aspects of medieval European architectural history in preparation for my eventual graduate study work when I do return to the States. Lt. General Bekker invented the prestigious Ingenious Planning for Separation Award especially for me, and that event did require a bit of a celebration at Der Blaue Schwein.

That party, it turned out, was a less than joyful affair. My plans began to unravel almost as fast as I made them. I had to color several nodes on my self-constructed Critical Path as not-green. That means my future is not now predictable. It's difficult to have a casual beer with a couple friends to celebrate my future when several nodes on the path to that future refuse to turn green.

★★★

I've driven by myself, overnight, from dreary Fulda to now sunny Zurich with my last delivery for the Driver. He told me the pouch is empty except for some paperwork. I don't believe him. He told me it will be my last trip. I might believe that. He tells me nothing will be coming across, or under, the *steel fence* for the foreseeable future. That part is certainly true. That border's now solid as steel. The Driver is pessimistic the operation can ever be reactivated. There's just too much military activity happening too close to the *metal curtain* by parties on both sides.

My trip into Zurich ends as usual by entering Jacob's garage. I arrive at the normal time, 0756, and Jacob is waiting with the same smile and greeting. But I notice that the garage door does not quickly close behind me, as it's always done before. I'm trained by now to notice the danger in any break with the established routine. I put myself on alert.

"Guten Morgen, Jacob. A fine day, ja?"

"Guten Morgen, Wall. I have for you a little surprise!"

"Always ready for a surprise, Jacob. Does it have anything to do with not closing the door?"

He smiles. "Yes, it does. I want to take you for a drive. Show you something special you need to see. You can leave your stuff here. We'll be back this afternoon."

"You think I should take my camera along, or maybe my machine gun will be needed?"

"You army guys!" He smiles at me. "Always with the machine guns. This is Zurich. No need for guns here. But do bring your camera."

"Where're you taking me?"

"I'm thinking this may be your last trip to Zurich for me, and I don't want you to return to your flat American prairie without visiting a special place. Come, we'll take my car."

We walk across the garage to Jacob's silver Audi with the four-wheel drive and the spiked mountain tires. "Gerhardt tells me you've been to Zug before, but you've never seen it with snow."

"That's right. I'm designing a house for Gerhardt in the mountains above Zug. I visited the site in early October, before the snow."

"Zug's magical with snow. Absolutely magical!"

Zug is a fairy-tale town half an hour south of Zurich, on Lake Zug. The lake is mostly ice-free and brilliantly blue to match, or reflect, the sky. It's a mystery to me how Zug gets any snow since its sky is always devoid of clouds. It is seriously blue today. Luscious piles of snowy mountains jump for the sky behind the town. Jacob drives through Zug, turns onto a blacktopped canyon road, and drives back into the mountains for a few kilometers. He turns into a hundred-meter-long drive carved out of a two-meter-high snow drift by a serious snow blower. A garage door set into a masonry rock wall opens as we approach. This time, as is normal, the door closes behind us.

We grab our bags and exit through a door in the front of the garage onto a walkway carved into the rock face. We climb seven flights of eleven steps, each under a partially Plexiglas-covered walkway that curls around the canyon wall allowing continuous views of mountaintops and sky until, at the top, our path dead-ends at a square, black, polished metal wall—nine, one-meter-square black panels wide by nine, one-meter-square black panels high. I look a question mark to Jacob. He smiles a sly smile back at me. He clicks an opener, and two of those meter-square panels pivot out, providing us with a portal through the wall. I see no hinges, knobs, or handles.

"Very clever, Jacob," I say. "Pretty slick. This is Gerhardt's work, ja?"

He smiles at me and nods.

Once inside, I say, "I recognize this now, from photos Gerhardt has on his office wall. Nobody told me it's your house. This is something else!"

Jacob's cabin is essentially one big room. It's a perfect, nine meter per side, glass cube—except for that entry wall of polished black metal, which in the right light deceptively reflects the sky and snow almost like the glass does. A wall of meter-square, black marble tiles encloses the bath, heating, storage functions, and in the upper levels, the sleeping areas. An elevator goes straight from the floor up through the glass ceiling to a deck on the top. The same one-meter-square, black marble tiles pave the floor and act as a sink for the solar heat now flooding into the space. The one meter square marking the exact center of the nine-by-nine-meter floorspace is not opaque marble but a single sheet of thick tempered glass. Jacob reverently points to it.

"My Anna is here," he says. "This is her house. She is safe here. No one will harm her here."

His few words change the essential quality of this bright, sun-filled room. I look through the glass to a reliquary holding an urn, an eternal flame, colored glass flowers, and a scroll containing a calligraphic text. I'm unable to say anything. This cabin is transfigured into an anteroom, a foyer of sorts, or perhaps a tramline terminus for whatever transportive device is accessing the pearly gates some folks are convinced exist above these mountains and beyond that bright blue sky.

Jacob explains the history. "You've probably heard the story from John. In 1935, I was a lecturer at the University of Heidelberg Medical School. I was twenty-seven, and Anna was but twenty-three. She was killed because she'd had the temerity and the impertinence to marry me, a Jew. And an even worse sin, a Polish Jew. Her rabid uncle, the head of the Medical School, believing his status was in peril if stained with the blemish of a niece who'd married a Jew, and infected by the disease Hitler was spraying over the country, shot

Anna point blank with a pistol in broad daylight on the university commons. He claimed he must do it to protect his family's ethnic purity. His despicable act, assassinating his own niece, was a warning to everyone at Heidelberg—Jews must not be linked to him personally or be associated with the university professionally. The campus and the city erupted violently, and though several colleagues defended me heroically, many more could not make that sacrifice. The message to me was clear. I could not stay in Heidelberg. I fled to Zurich."

It is difficult to react to such a statement with words. And I, being unprepared for the shock, find it impossible. I walk over to the great windows and stare out at the white-draped mountains and the cobalt blue sky.

"What I do, Wall, to release my pain and assuage my grief, to make myself feel better, is to do a bit of hiking. Come, I have snowshoes, and the trail is comfortable and well-trod."

★★★

As we walk up the mountain, we talk about people killing people. We talk about Mongols in Prague and the damage seven thousand atomic warheads will do to Eastern Europe. We talk about angry gray tanks and mothers hurling bricks. We talk about my friend Ruta who's not being allowed to watch her mother die. We talk of the specter of dying in Vietnam's jungle.

We agree that the Iron Curtain is keeping one group of people from living in communion with one other group. However, it's also true that that *steel fence* is keeping those two sides from killing each other.

"The evil persists," he says. "It'll take time, maybe several generations."

"I'd like to think I can do something for Ruta," I say. "But I'm unable to make the sacrifices needed to help her. Is that wrong, Jacob?"

"We can only do what we can do. It's easy to see why she's troubled. She must worry about her future. But I'm afraid the only weapon she has left in her arsenal is time. Unfortunately, any healing time, like John and Marieka's time and their friend Marta's time, and sadly even at my age, my time, has not yet arrived. I'm still waiting."

After an hour we find ourselves several hundred feet higher in the canyon. Jacob stops in front of a bench carved from a single bolder. "I rest here a while before I return. This view's amazing!"

"It's going to be tough going home. There's no vertical emphasis in Iowa. The abject horizontal normalcy of the place is gonna drive me nuts."

"I understand transition will be difficult, Wall. But you must be satisfied that you have done good work here. I'm grateful. We're all grateful for your help."

"It's been exciting, Jacob. But strange. Nothing here is stable. I've seen the landscape change with a word or a gesture. New things pop up every day and from all directions, like a graduate level course in how to operate as a human."

"I want to thank you for the work you've done. Alas, the entire system's now shut down. Nothing's gonna happen for at least a year. We have to reconstruct our system infrastructure. And I'm doubtful that'll happen. Nixon has neither the time nor incentive to care about us. He's focused on his own big picture. Desperate individuals, like me and your Ruta, are too small to be seen. We're just going to have to suffer for some while."

"I'm glad I could help. And you're losing John too. He and Marieka are headed back to the States, even before I go."

"John promises to return to Europe after things get better, though I'm positive that won't happen. Would you want your children to grow up over here? But we'll find a way through the rubble, Wall. We must be patient. Eventually things will work out. It is hard to get that message across to the younger students. It will all take time. The path to human dignity is several generations long. We're better off now than we were two hundred years ago. We all have to do our part, and maybe in another hundred years it will be better yet."

We stare at the scenery for a while.

"I lost my Anna to an act of violence driven by a lunatic. One might consider that you lost your Ruta to an act of non-violence driven by a passionate man."

"I'm fairly sure you're talking nonsense, Jacob. Though it's a mildly comforting even self-serving thought, I'm still voting for nonsense."

Jacob rises from the bench. "I guess I'm not making a lot of sense." He checks his boots and snowshoes. "Most times I'm sure there's no overall plan, just us humans bouncing around like pool balls on a tabletop."

"Once we start walking, you gonna stop with the metaphors?"

"Let's get back to the cabin, Wall. Once the sun slips behind that mountain it gets dark and cold quickly."

★★★

When we get back to the cabin and open the door, the smell hits me. Hot mulled wine and other unfamiliar smells fill the cabin. My danger sensors kick in.

"Ahh!" says Jacob. "Doesn't that soup smell fantastic?"

"Okay, Jacob! You gonna tell me what's going on?"

"*Guten Nachmittag!*" yells a chorus from the kitchen.

"John? Marieka? What are you two doing here? You're supposed to be in Heidelberg."

"We are, Wall. You see before you an illusion."

I can believe that. Once again John's metamorphosed. He's shed the Frank Zappa shell. He's clean shaven. His hair is still curly but shorter than I've seen it before and nicely trimmed. He's wearing a suit. He's a corporate boardroom guy, maybe a Chicago Symphony fundraiser guy.

"I've seen plenty of those illusions this past year. They're hard to tell from reality any more. And Gerhardt is with you? Are you also an illusion?"

"Jacob and I thought it proper," Gerhardt says, "to have a going home party for you three. We're all going to miss you. You've helped us tremendously. And we want to thank you. Come, let me pour you a wine."

This glass room is placed perfectly such that the low winter sun can slip its rays between two mountain peaks and thus illuminate and warm it in mid-day.

Gerhardt Stopak stands between me and that sun so his head is lost in the glare. "I've a piece of not-so-good news, Wall," he says. "And also a piece of extremely good news. I shall do the not-so-good item first. It's the harder thing to do."

"You pour me mulled wine to give me bad news? Isn't that a fairly sneaky thing to do?"

"As you know, I'll be teaching the fall semester at the University of Texas. And I looked forward to having you in my office in Zurich until August. But I'm afraid that's not now possible. I'm closing my office here within the next few weeks. I must go back to my mother. She's been diagnosed with cancer and has been given only a short time. I knew she was sick, just not how serious it was. I'm sorry, Wall, but I cannot stay. I have to be with my mother."

"It's the right and wonderful thing for you to do, Gerhardt. It's what you must do. I'll be fine. It'll work out."

"I can help you," John says. "I'll see to it that Lieutenant General Bekker approves, as an emergency measure, any adjustment of your return you need in order to accommodate the changes in your schedule."

"Thank you, John. The big problem I see is scheduling my car's return so that it'll be in New York before my plane arrives. I haven't started that ritual yet."

"We'll make it work," John says. "At least you still separate from the army over here, which means I can still use your two thousand-pound allowance to ship Jacob's heirlooms back. But that's my worry. We'll do scheduling on Monday, when we're back in Heidelberg."

"Do you technocrats want to hear the extremely good news now?" asks Stopak. "Or you gonna keep jabbering about schedules and weight limits?"

"Okay, okay. What's your good news?"

Stopak takes an envelope from his jacket pocket, takes a piece of paper from it, and holds it up. "This letter, from the Graduate School of Design at Harvard, states they'll be pleased to accept you as a Master Degree candidate in Architectural History."

"Wow! Thank you, Gerhardt. That's great news. You were more confident of that happening than I was. Thanks for presenting my case to the GSD in such a marvelous way. Wow. You're right. That's great news."

"You deserve it, Wall. You've convinced me you think as an architect should. The GSD had no choice but to accept you."

"See, Wall," says John, "what Gerhardt just revealed is that you finally know who's designing your personal Critical Path. That's a huge weight removed. You know it's your friend Gerhardt pushing buttons and not our ghost General Bekker or some other ghost general in the Pentagon."

"You have a point, John. I can be thankful for that."

"I've no idea what you army guys are talking about," says Gerhardt. "But getting released from the army's tether must be a relief."

"The bigger relief, Gerhardt, is that I'm finally released from the threat of Vietnam. The army does weird things, and any day they could've thrown me on a plane and dumped me into the jungle. I am free of that terror now. Hopefully the helicopter dreams will go away too. And I'm thankful my mom will finally be able to relax. That's the big gift. But there's one other loose end—Ruta! How'm I gonna figure that out? I've got no good options there. And I've only a couple months now to find one before that whole thing goes up in smoke."

31 THE LAST HEIDELBERG STORY

It's April third, the one-year anniversary of Reverend King's death. There's a demonstration at the university commemorating his death and by association hundreds of other deaths in Prague, Warsaw, Germany, and even in Vietnam. I could not amass the energy to join in. I stayed in my room and packed my duffel. It's my last day in Germany. I fly out of Frankfurt in the morning. And except for a few loose ends, this is the last day of my life operating under some other guy's Critical Path design. I'll be back in the States tomorrow as a free man, a man free to plot my own, hopefully not critical, path.

As far as I know, some army guys are slipping the last Pershing 1A rockets into their impressive new bunkers exactly as my Critical Path foretold. I'm not sure that means I've done a good job or failed miserably. Nobody's told me what difference either my failure or success will have on my future, or for that matter, the future of Europe.

As far as I know, some guys in Greece and Norway are now practicing takeoffs and landings on my brand new concrete runways with their old B-52s with the up-to-date atomic warheads snug in their bellies. As far as I know, The Plastic People of the Universe have not yet pushed the Beatles off the charts, or the Mongols out of Prague. As far as I know, no road rallies are being scheduled near Fulda this coming year. As far as I know, Nixon's not planning to stop pushing army guys out of flaming helicopters. As far as I know, mothers in Prague have stopped hurling bricks, and other folks in Prague have pretty much stopped being human.

But there are a few things I know for certain. I know the rats are deserting the ship. John and Marieka left for Chicago last month. Gerhardt has left for Texas. I know the Bassist has stopped pushing his music into Prague; he's afraid nobody's listening to it; afraid his music's dead too. I know the Curator is still unable to see her mother, unable to know if she's dead or not dead. And I know the flower gardens at the castle grounds are, after this very brutal winter with no maintenance or attention, very dead indeed!

And I know the flowers are dead because I am sitting on a stone bench with a huge granite Bacchus statue cavorting behind me, and I'm looking at weeds where, in a normal April, roses would be blooming. An intermittent rain bothers us, but it's not the cause of the gloom. It's the lack of roses causing that. The roses are not here because they were not pampered as they've been for hundreds, maybe thousands, of winterings before. They spent the harsh winter untrimmed, uninsulated, and unbagged. Hundreds of thousands of bulbs were not moved to winter storage and were frozen in place. Fertilizing and pruning and other preparatory work was not done during the fall of violence or this winter of discontent. Post Prague demonstrators trampled on them, the harsh weather blasted them, city resources were redirected to urban damage control, and now everyone's crying because the flowers are gone. It's the kind of collateral damage that accompanies even a cold war. It begins to rain; a light, misty, almost-drizzle. It's a cold war type rain. Nevertheless, it's still wet. I feel a bit of water cross my forehead, run down my nose, and spend a couple seconds on the edge before jumping off.

I'm sitting here looking at wet weeds and puddles in the dirt. I'm talking with Václav, the Bassist, who's locked out of Prague, and Ruta, the Curator, who's locked out of East Berlin. We do have some nice wine, and we are trying hard to be cheerful. It's a damned tough job. We're all close to tears. We are talking about the death of Reverend King, the death of Bobby Kennedy, the death of Prague, and the soon to be death of Ruta's mother. Death hangs flaccid all about us.

"The past is over," I tell them. "It's gone, and it cannot be revived." I say those philosophical words but none of us, including me, believe me.

"You are maybe right," Václav says, though he doesn't seem convinced. "Yesterday was my last transmission into Prague, and after that, who knows? Tonight I leave for Berlin to start my future. Prague must somehow learn to play their music without me."

"Václav will be teaching bass and composition at the conservatory at the Berliner Philharmonie," says Ruta. "He's a talented musician and a great teacher. Everyone there is excited he's coming."

"They'll not allow me into the orchestra yet. I'll substitute, but teaching and composing should keep me busy."

"And I also have news," says Ruta. The drizzly rain is mostly stopped now. It's replaced by a faint smile that manages to sneak across her face. "In a couple months I'm being promoted to Assistant to the Curator. It's a salaried position with a great future, but I must work hard. And that means my past also is mostly over. I'll not have time for SDS and the demonstrations and the screaming and the throwing. I'll have to behave myself."

"I'm thinking," I say, "once the Stasi understand you're more curator than brick hurler, they may make it easier to see your mother."

"I hope you're right, Wall. They might allow an assistant curator easier access than a political bully."

Someone takes exception to that lie; it begins, again, to rain.

We leave the dead gardens and take the funicular down the hill into Heidelberg. Though our heads are bursting with future dreams, there seems little to say about present conditions and the past nightmares that have by now been buried in social debris.

I can't remember intermediate time passing, but I find myself, suddenly, at the Hauptbahnhof. The rain's let up, and the overnight train to Berlin is waiting. I give Ruta a last hug, knowing it must compensate for a lifetime of hugs, hugs I'll never be able to give her. I don't know any words for a time or a feeling like this. Crying, she pulls away. I give Václav a quick hug. I've talked to him before about keeping an eye on Ruta. I can find no words to say now to him either. The conductor blows his whistle in my ear. I think that's a message.

Despite the whistle in my ear, I grab Ruta before she steps up into the carriage. I give her one last hug. I don't want my last memory of her to be of her crying. I'm fairly numb, but even I sense a different genus of sadness now looking at me. Seems her entire body's doing the sobbing, though somehow not her eyes. I've absolutely no idea what to do. Václav pulls her away, almost carries her up the steps. The two of them vanish into the third coach. I stand rigid. The conductor pulls up the stairs, gives me one more evil look, then closes the door. Immediately the carriage moves away. I watch as her car, in slow motion, slides around the curve behind that awful gray housing block. Only when I'm certain the carriage is vanished, do I find the courage to whisper… "Goodbye." Perhaps she heard that. Probably not.

It begins to rain, again. This time it's the serious stuff, accompanied by a bit of thunder.

"Damn." I say the word with some force, though I'm almost positive she will not be able to hear it. And even if she did…

32 The Vietnam to Iowa Story

The first army box, labeled **TSN9-16215**, and accompanied by a young lieutenant and an elderly sergeant, arrived at the loading dock of the Ludwig-Bosch Funeral Home in Larson, Iowa at 9:47 on Wednesday morning. This box, **TSN9-16215**, contains the remains of army paratrooper Davie Groetken. Davie died in Vietnam some time ago, though his remains only recently made this trip home. The lieutenant presents this first army box to Davie's mother, Doris, who's left shoulder is supported by her remaining son, Jim, and her right one by Father Amos Strelling, her pastor from St. Joseph's Catholic Church. The word 'supported' is but a weak metaphor. She's beyond requiring support. No one supported her when she stood knee deep in the rice paddy and watched Davie fall from the tumbling helicopter, and no one felt the splash when he buried himself in the muck. She remembered every minute of the several days of screaming and pointing at the ripples until the searchers finally found Davie's body. She needed support then. But now? She's too numb to even understand 'support.'

But she's one of the lucky mothers who actually received her son's box, so she might accept the arrival of this first army box as a blessing; as 'closure' rather than 'the end of the world.' She and Father Strelling found the strength to schedule the requisite wake, a closed casket ceremony of course, for the next day at one o'clock in the afternoon. And then, on the day after that, on Friday, June twenty-third, Father Strelling would celebrate, as if that's anywhere near the correct word, Davie's Funeral Mass as St. Joseph's regular eight o'clock morning service.

★★★

At approximately the same time as Doris Groetken and Father Strelling were accepting delivery of the first box, Susan Kneubel, working in her kitchen eight blocks east of the Ludwig-Bosch Funeral Home in Larson, Iowa, answered her telephone. She heard another lieutenant, another smooth, non-threatening voice, tell her a crew from the Army Depot in Sioux City had scheduled the delivery of a box for her son, Walter, for the next day, Thursday, June twenty-second, at 10:54 in the morning. Susan told the lieutenant on the phone that it was critical they deliver it on time because she had other army business she must attend to—the wake for a friend's son killed in Vietnam. The lieutenant assured her the box would be delivered at exactly 10:54 and take but a few minutes to offload.

That second army box, one labeled **BHD6-2727L**, was delivered at exactly 10:54 on Thursday morning. The delivery of this second army box or, most likely, the very concept of there even being such a thing as a second army box, hit Susan Kneubel hard. She cried steadily for over an hour. She took another shower, reapplied her makeup, sipped a bit of tomato soup, and only then drove to the Ludwig-Bosch Funeral Home for Davie Groetken's wake. The delivery of the second army box made attending Davie's wake a much more difficult thing to do. It made the hug she gave her friend Doris much fiercer. It made the sad afternoon at Davie's wake almost unbearable.

★★★

I'd returned from Germany a couple months ago and found an opportunity to work for an architect in Sioux City while waiting for my box of army stuff from Germany to be delivered. I'm working long hours on deadline, so I don't get home until 8:52. Mom runs from the sink where she's working and attacks me with a hug so fierce it scares me. Running and hugging are not things done cavalierly in the Kneuble household, especially by Mom, so I'm immediately aware of the grave disturbing vapor pressurizing the room.

"Mom! What's wrong?"

"Nothing's wrong, Son. I need to hug you while I still have you here to hug."

I'm shaken by the dark subtext. "What's that mean?"

Slowly my mom releases her grip. She allows me to stagger back from the hug.

"You're frightening me, Mom. What's wrong?"

She leads me over to the kitchen table. "Sit down, Son. I'll pour coffee."

After a couple sips, she reaches across the table, clasps both my hands, and squeezes them hard.

"I was afraid to tell you yesterday, but I must tell you some very sad, sad news. Doris Groetken's son Davie was killed in Vietnam. It happened some time ago, but only yesterday the army delivered Davie's body in a box. Then, this morning, the very next day, the army delivers your box into my garage. Yesterday his box. Today your box." She blows her nose with a tissue. "The timing just got to me. I was at Davie's wake all afternoon, and all I could think about was the army delivering boxes to mothers, and the sadness of it all crushed me. Then, coming home, I drove into my garage and saw your huge, ugly, army box again."

"I'm sorry, Mom. I remember Davie. I took the bus with him to basic. I tried to talk him out of paratrooper school. Told him to think of his mother. He said he wanted to jump out of helicopters and shoot Viet Cong. I blasted him, called him an unsympathetic slob. We never talked after that. Davie, however, did show up in my technicolor nightmares. He always died in my dream. I'm not at all surprised he's died now for real."

"So I've got to ask, Wall—what's with your huge green box? I was expecting a cardboard mover's-type box, not such a monstrosity! All those locks and metal straps made me think of Davie Groetken's box. What on earth have you shipped home from Germany?"

"I don't know what's in the box. It's my friend John's stuff, so if I were to guess, I'd say maybe paintings and other religious artifacts from Polish and Czech churches, stuff buried in Poland and Eastern Europe before WWII to keep them safe from the Nazis."

"What?" I can tell Mom didn't expect that. Even I'm startled by those strange words.

"They're not stolen?"

"I don't think stolen is the correct word, Mom. According to John, they originally belonged to churches destroyed by Hitler and were hidden or buried so the Nazis couldn't steal them or melt them down. After the war, life under Communist persecution was no better than life under the Nazis, and many Polish Catholics fled to the west. My friend John's parents ended up in Chicago. These artifacts belong to his parents and other Polish immigrants who are now in Chicago. That's my guess, Mom. That's the best I can do."

"I don't want that army box in my garage. Get it out of there."

"I understand, Mom. I'll call John now. I know him. He'll be on the road at daybreak tomorrow."

"He'd better be," Mom says.

Mom's frightening me, so I call John in Chicago. I reach him at 10:06 p.m. and tell him he's gotta pick up his stuff immediately.

John says, "Great, I'll pick it up tomorrow."

"Great," I say. "Mom wants that box gone quickly."

Only after the brief conversation's over do I realize John didn't mention an arrival time. I look at the atlas. I know how fast John will drive those 525 miles, and I assume he'll leave Chicago at sunup, so I expect an early to mid-afternoon arrival. Larson's not close to any interstate, so he must use two-lane roads across northern Iowa and bisect many small towns. That will slow him down. That means I can sleep in and be ready for his arrival at, say, 2:16 in the afternoon. John never did anything on the even hour, and this time, I'm sure, it'll be no different.

★★★

There's a huge box elder tree in our front yard, and the morning sun's high enough for sunlight to filter through its leaves and bounce globules of light onto the bright yellow sheet metal of my Fiat Spider, which I've parked beneath the tree on the concrete driveway in front of the left-hand garage door. That Spider left Germany by freighter a month before I flew over, and it was ready for me to pick up when I arrived in New York. It's now parked with its nose but an inch from the locked garage door, and it's standing its guard duty stoically, like any army-trained soldier might stand.

Army box number two rests on the concrete garage floor on the inside of that locked overhead door. It's four feet high by six feet wide by ten feet long, and with its seals and locks intact. Mom tells me two guys in an olive drab truck with the number **IA63** stenciled above the front wheel well delivered this box set on a wheeled dolly that enabled them to push it into the garage. My mom watched them wrestle with it and treated them to lemonade for their effort.

Stenciled on the top and on two sides is the code **BHD4-2727L**. I don't know about the "L" or the numbers, but I'm quite sure the first three letters mean Bremerhaven, Deutschland. It's the same code typed on the receipt I had given my mom and that she, in turn, gave the delivery guys. That receipt asserted the contents of that box belong to me. That is most certainly not the truth. I have neither the key to the locks, nor a clue as to the contents. This box, though it has my name on its paperwork, is stuffed with John's junk.

And there's a reason for that. Army stuff isn't considered imported; therefore, it doesn't go through customs. The army will ship one, five-hundred-pound box of uninspected stuff back to the States for Wall, the private, free of charge. My commander, Lieutenant General Alvin Bekker knows how to manipulate the system, so he suggested that I discharge from the army in Europe, thereby achieving a civilian status. The army will now ship two thousand pounds of stuff back for Wall, the civilian, which in my case means John can slip two thousand pounds of repatriated Polish religious artifacts past the customs inspectors. At least that's what I'm assuming John's doing. If not manipulated by a highly moral operation such as the one our Lt. General Bekker is running, there's the possibility some might assert such a maneuver is illegal.

I'm staying home waiting for John today, so I'm sleeping in. My mom, on the other hand, is a creature of habit. I can alter my schedule and sleep in when I want to. Mom's mornings are regulated by an unchanging clock. She'll be in the kitchen, in her summer dressing gown, fixing her breakfast, no matter what else is happening. She'll bring the *Des Moines Register* in from the hook under the mailbox on the front porch where it's always placed so she'll not have to actually step on the cold or wet porch to retrieve it. She'll pour her coffee, take her paper, sit at the kitchen table with her toast, and start her day reading the editorial page. It's the same every morning.

But this morning, the earth's axis has shifted. Things start differently. First, my mom dresses before she comes down because she plans to attend that Funeral Mass for Davie Groetken. Second, she no sooner opens the paper when the front doorbell rings.

She looks at the clock above the sink. It's 6:43 a.m. A doorbell ring is a truly unusual event so early in the morning in this small rural village. So it's not unreasonable that her first thought is panic. Her husband's away on business, her aged mother and eleven-year-old daughter are asleep upstairs. Effectively, she's alone. It's not until she opens the door and sees the well-groomed, nicely dressed, young couple standing on her porch on the other side of the screen door that she remembers that her son, recently home from the army, is also upstairs. She'd forgotten he's sleeping in this morning because he's expecting visitors from Chicago.

She stares at the two of them through the locked screen door.

"Mrs. Kneuble?"

That relaxes her a bit. These people actually know who she is. "Yes?"

"Good morning, ma'am. I am John, Walter's friend from Chicago. I talked with him last night. He told me the army box arrived yesterday. We are here to retrieve our material from that container. Oh, excuse me, Mrs. Kneuble, this is my wife, Marieka."

"Well, he is expecting you, but he thought maybe you'd get here after lunch. This is a bit of a surprise! You made good time."

The young man swings a bouquet of flowers from where he'd been concealing them behind his back. "For you, Mrs. Kneuble. For your trouble. And, ma'am, I've a rather unusual request. I must change the oil in my car. Is there a place where I can pull off the road and do that?"

"Walter's upstairs, still sleeping. I'll wake him. He might know a place. I have my car serviced at Tom Baack's Sinclair, just down the hill on Plymouth Street. But I don't think his garage is open—"

"Don't worry Mrs. Kneuble, I'll find a place. I'll be back…" he looks at his watch, "at 7:01." He gives the bouquet to his wife.

"Marieka will stay here, explain what's happening, and keep you company until I return." John turns quickly and walks to his car.

Marieka, stranded on the porch outside the door says quietly, "If I can beg a cup of coffee, Mrs. Kneuble? I'd be much obliged."

For some reason my mom does not later remember, she unlocks the screen door and invites this young woman into her kitchen to wait for her husband to return from his oil changing ritual. After coffee is poured and the flowers put in a vase, my mom says, "If you'll excuse me for a minute, I'll run upstairs and waken Walter.

He should know you're here." She runs up the stairs thinking the less time she's out of the kitchen the less time that woman has to clean out her silverware drawer. She's back quickly from her errand and finds Marieka reading the sports section of the *Des Moines Register*. She feels relieved.

"Sorry, Mrs. Kneubel, you were reading the first section, so I didn't think you'd mind if I took the sports. I must see how my Cubbies did last night. They were playing the Dodgers out in California. When we left it was the top of the seventh, and we were behind four to two."

"You'll be happy to know that they tied it and got two runs in the eleventh to pull it out," my mom says. "It's so wonderful to talk to another Cubs fan. Not many of them out here. I grew up in Chicago, and my father took me to many a Cubs game. It's my only connection with the Windy City still alive. I listen to almost every game."

"I've only been in Chicago for a few months, Mrs. Kneuble, but already John's mother has turned me into a Cubbie. She's taken me to Wrigley Field and explained the game. It's quite complicated."

★★★

I'm downstairs in a flash. I cannot imagine Mom being comfortable alone with Marieka. But when I pop into the kitchen, the two of them are giggling like schoolgirls. I go right at Marieka.

"You could have warned me you guys would show up at the crack of dawn and frighten my mom. Why didn't you tell me?"

"Good morning to you too, Wall," Marieka says sweetly. "I assumed you understood how he operates. We were on the road fifteen minutes after you called. Seemed the normal thing to do." She gets up and gives me a quick obligatory hug. "Like he told you to do, we keep our backpacks packed and ready to go on a moment's notice."

"Where's John?"

"He's changing Rosie's oil."

"That's weird, Marieka. Even for John."

"He said he'll be back at 7:01," says my mom. "I remember he said 7:01. Isn't that odd?"

"John's an odd guy, Mom. His leaving fifteen minutes after I call him is odd. His bringing you flowers is odd." I take the keys from the hook next to the refrigerator. "While he's messin' with his silly oil-change ritual, I'll move your car out of the garage so there's room for us to work on the box."

When John returns, he backs the trailer into the garage where my mom's car had been, so the load transfer from the army box to John's trailer will be easy. John then pops the locks, and we unbolt the straps and remove the lid. I see the interior of my box for the first time.

But it's still a puzzle. I see boxes! The crate's completely filled with modular cardboard boxes. Many are eighteen inch cubes or six inch by forty-eight by forty-eight-inch flats and several six-foot-long cardboard tubes. Each box is labeled with a four-digit number. It's the most well-ordered packing job I've ever seen; nothing out of place, nothing shifted during the trip across the Atlantic. I suppose I should've expected nothing less from him.

"What the hell's goin' on here, John? I wait all this time hoping to see something like Blackbeard's treasure when I open this box. But I see nothing but more boxes."

"So, what's your problem, Walter?"

"I need enlightenment! What'm I seeing?"

"You're seein' cardboard boxes. Thought that might be fairly self-evident."

"You saying I gotta guess? Okay, here's my guess. The big square flat ones look like paintings, 'bout the size of many I watched Joe Brunelli work on. Bigger canvases are in the tubes, right? And the small cubes, maybe your baseball hat collection. Am I right?"

"They're not baseball hats. They're toasters."

"I tend not to believe you, John. Legally the stuff's in my box in my garage. I'm gonna open one, peek into it, and if I see Braun toasters, I'm not letting you take the stuff out of my garage. I'll call the cops."

"I don't have a problem with you looking since you pretty much know what the stuff is anyway. The boxes contain church artifacts like vestments, chalices, and candlesticks... things removed from various Warsaw parish churches before the Nazis crashed in, trashed, and burned 'em."

"That's what I'm expecting, but I gotta be sure, don't ya think? Open that one!" At random, I point to 4228.

John opens it, and it reveals four pair of rather beat up pewter candlesticks embellished with dark carvings. He holds one up and squints at the inscription. "These seem ordinary things, however they are four hundred years old and were a gift from the archbishop of Prague. They're representative of artifacts here. Many have personal connections to the Polish community at St. Agnes, in Chicago."

"You took all this trouble, did all those faux road rallies, all the trips to Zurich, all that sneaky stuff for a few tinny looking candlesticks? I wasted a year helping you collect trash when I could have spent my time in Greece studying temples?"

"These are precious religious heirlooms, Wall. These precious things anchor my mother and our family to our past and connect us with God because we consider them God's tools. They're tools required for our life."

"Not for me, John. It's stuff like this, and even more, the belief that stuff like this is important, that forces people to hurl Pershing missiles over the *steel fence* at one another. It's also the reason the Bassist was hurling his music over that same *steel fence*. It's the reason guys jump from helicopters in Vietnam."

Neither of us wants to talk about this, so we ratchet up the work pace. I am assuming Mom and Marieka remain in the kitchen discussing the Cubs, other Chicago things, and perhaps some other things as well. Marieka could be telling my mom things I either did or didn't do while in the army in Germany. That wouldn't have been hard. I understood medieval church architecture and concrete rocket bunkers, but don't remember 'girl stuff' like food or people or parties. I'm apt to trash that kind of info. I wonder if Marieka is telling Mom about Ruta.

I can imagine how Mom would react if I'd sent her a letter: Hi, Mom. I'm gonna marry this German dissident, and I've found a way to bring her back home. Or, perhaps a worse scenario: Mom, I've met a Polish girl in East Berlin, so I think I'll stay over here. Oh, and by the way, I may not be able to get back across the wall, or maybe I might get shot trying. There's a good chance you'll not see me, ever again. That'd be as jolting to her as a telegram from Vietnam was for her friend Doris.

John wakes me from my hallucinations. "Hey, Wall, what's the situation with you and Ruta?"

"Ain't no situation there. Ruta's in Berlin. I'm here."

"That all you're gonna tell me? She's in Berlin, and—?"

"And nothing. I cannot make the decision to change the entire vision of my future, to tell us both lies about metaphysics, to struggle with her every day for the next thirty years until she's allowed into Warsaw or East Berlin again. I just can't do it, John. And she wouldn't want me to do it either. It wouldn't work. But thanks for asking. I'm going to miss the Mozart loving, Assistant to the Curator version of Ruta. But I cannot say the same for the religious zealot, bull horn shouting, hurling Pershing missiles over the Berlin Wall version."

We finish securing the ties and locks on John's trailer. Mom and Marieka walk into the garage. How they knew we'd just now finished our work is a mystery. Anyway, Marieka gives my mom a goodbye hug and pats me on the shoulder as she walks out to the front by the red VW.

"Thank you, Mrs. Kneuble, for all your trouble," says John. He does a respectful little head nod. "If we leave now," he looks at his watch, "we'll get back around 4:55, maybe miss rush hour traffic around Chicago. We're a few minutes ahead of schedule. Thanks for your help, Wall. And St. Agnes' Parish thanks you too."

I go so far as giving both of them a hug, and I pat Rosie on that custom spoiler cousin Lech installed over her engine compartment. John then fires her up, waves meekly for a guy like John, and pulls out of the drive at 7:35. Mom and I stand next to my Fiat and watch John turn at the corner and head downhill toward the highway.

My mother puts a soft hand on my shoulder and gently squeezes it. "Under no circumstances will either you or I ever utter one word about what just happened here this morning. Not a single peep, Walter! You understand me?

"And also, under no circumstances will you mention any part of this German story to your father. As far as your father's concerned, these last two years have been permanently erased from any record he might ever happen to gain access to. Am I clear, Walter?"

"Yes, ma'am." I nod reverently. I think I'm clear about this. Still, I feel another squeeze. I feel a need to respond. "Not a single peep, Mom."

I'm not clear on much else though. I note she used formal, even legalistic language and called me by my given name, Walter. That means something solemn has been spoken. One thing my army training did not teach me, but is nevertheless imprinted on my mind, is that when my mother looks at me like that and uses my formal name, my only response is, "Yes, ma'am."

Since our house is built on one of the higher points of land in town, our side yard yields some long views over the rural countryside. I walk out the drive into the middle of 8th Avenue and look north between the box elder trees, across the fields my high school football team used for practice, beyond that over the western extension of Calvary cemetery, then beyond that over a mile of waving, green corn fields. There's a short segment, perhaps a quarter mile, where the Illinois Central railroad tracks and State Highway 3 run parallel on the far side of that cornfield as they both cross a set of culverts, then aim themselves east toward Chicago.

I stare at that short segment of Highway 3. I know those culverts well. It's where I, as a six-year-old, crossed under the highway and the tracks following the stream to its confluence with the Floyd River several miles beyond. Soon I'm rewarded with a view of that little red VW pulling the little white trailer crossing over those two oval aluminum culverts, then moving east toward Chicago.

"Goodbye, John," I say softly. It crashes down on me that everything of my recent past has just crossed over those culverts. It's all gone now—John, Gerhardt, Ruta, and Lieutenant General Alvin Bekker. Though to be honest, Bekker's been pretty much missing since I've first known him. "Good bye, Mr. Driver," I whisper. I'm certain I'll never see any of them ever again. But that's not necessarily a bad thing! They are all part of my army nightmare. And now the whole thing's gone. Good riddance, I'm thinking.

The Iowa landscape beyond is not, as many foreign folks assume, dead flat, but is composed of endless, monotonous, rolling, corn-covered hills. I watch the next hill crest eastward. It's about three or four miles distant. I watch until I see it reappear... that small white trailer. I follow it as it slowly climbs that distant rolling hill and then as it even more slowly slips down behind it. Finally, it's all gone, gone over that hill, swallowed up by that vast green sea of corn.

The End

ACKNOWLEDGEMENTS

Many talented people helped me transform my story into this wonderful book. Ian Graham Leask lived in Germany a few years after I left, and helped me develop the right voice for this novel. Thanks to Gary Lindberg who designed the book and Rick Polad who edited it. Lee Orcutt encouraged me to remove unnecessary content. Wendy Henry, Jacquie Trudeau, and Al Rieper gave constant editorial support. And I must acknowledge my 98-year-old mother who, in the rather limited way our discussions must now take place, released me from my promise (reported in Chapter 32) to never mention this story ever again.

ABOUT THE AUTHOR

Bill Nemmers spent eighteen months from 1967 to1969 in the U.S. Army in Heidelberg, West Germany, analyzing the progress of construction projects undertaken to upgrade certain structures related to the Army's nuclear missile defense system. After discharge, he spent several years as an architect in Boston before opening his own practice in Maine. For the last decade, he has been writing in St. Paul. His novel *Crude*, set in North Dakota, was published in March 2016. He is currently working on a sequel to *Crude*, and a nonfiction work examining Portugal's Prince Henry the Navigator's influence on 15th and 16th century Cosmology and Architecture.

CPSIA information can be obtained
at www.ICGtesting.com
Printed in the USA
BVHW070505060223
657828BV00002B/276